RAVISHED BY DESIRE

NEW YORK TIMES BESTSELLING AUTHOR

BRENDA
JACKSON

RAVISHED BY DESIRE

ARABESQUE®

ISBN-13: 978-0-373-83179-1

RAVISHED BY DESIRE
© 2010 by Harlequin Enterprises S.A.

The publisher acknowledges the copyright holder
of the individual works as follows:

A LITTLE DARE
© 2003 by Brenda Streater Jackson

THORN'S CHALLENGE
© 2003 by Brenda Streater Jackson

www.kimanipress.com

Printed in U.S.A.

CONTENTS

Dear Reader,

When I first introduced the Westmoreland family, little did I know that they would become hugely popular with readers. Originally, the Westmoreland Family series was intended to be just six books—Delaney and her five brothers, Dare, Thorn, Stone, Storm and Chase. Later, I was dying for my readers to meet their cousins—Jared, Spencer, Durango, Ian, Quade and Reggie. And finally, there were Uncle Corey's triplets—Clint, Cole and Casey.

What started out as a six-book series blossomed into fifteen books featuring the Atlanta-based Westmorelands. I was very happy when Kimani responded to my readers, who asked that the books be reprinted, and decided to reissue two books from the series, *A Little Dare* and *Thorn's Challenge*. I'm even happier that the reissues are nicely packaged in a two-in-one book format.

Ravished by Desire contains the first two brothers' stories. Dare Westmoreland and Shelly Brockman's story is a special one of lost love rekindled. Tara Matthews and Thorn Westmoreland's story is my take on the fairy-tale classic *Beauty and the Beast*. Indeed, both stories are classics in their own right.

I hope you enjoy these special romances as much as I enjoyed writing them.

Happy Reading!

Brenda Jackson

THE WESTMORELAND FAMILY

Scott and Delane Westmoreland

John (Evelyn)

- ② Dare (Shelly) — AJ, Allison
- ③ Thorn (Tara) — Trace
- ④ Stone (Madison) — Rock
- ⑤ Storm (Jayla) — Shanna, Johanna
- ⑥ Jared (Dana) — Jaren
- ⑪ Spencer (Chardonnay) — Russell
- ⑧ Durango (Savannah) — Sarah
- ⑨ Ian (Brooke) — Pierce, Price
- ⑩ Casey (McKinnon) — Corey Martin
- ⑫ Clint (Alyssa) — Cain
- ⑬ Cole (Patrina) — Emilie, Emery

James (Sarah)

- ⑦ Chase (Jessica) — Carlton Scott
- ① Delaney (Jamal) — Ari, Arielle
- ⑭ Quade (Cheyenne) — Venus, Athena, Troy
- ⑮ Reggie (Olivia)

Corey (Abbie)

Madison

---

① Delaney's Desert Sheikh
② A Little Dare
③ Thorn's Challenge
④ Stone Cold Surrender
⑤ Riding the Storm
⑥ Jared's Counterfeit Fiancée
⑦ The Chase is On
⑧ The Durango Affair
⑨ Ian's Ultimate Gamble
⑩ Seduction, Westmoreland Style
⑪ Spencer's Forbidden Passion
⑫ Taming Clint Westmoreland
⑬ Cole's Red-Hot Pursuit
⑭ Quade's Babies
⑮ Tall, Dark...Westmoreland!

Ponder the path of thy feet,
and let all thy ways be established.
—*Proverbs* 4:26

To my husband, the love of my life and my best
friend, Gerald Jackson, Sr.

And to everyone who asked for Dare's and
Thorn's stories, this book is for you!

A LITTLE DARE

Prologue

The son Dare Westmoreland didn't know he had needed him.

Shelly Brockman knew that admission was long overdue as she stood in the living room of the house that had been her childhood home. The last box had been carried in and now the task of unpacking awaited her. Even with everything she faced, she felt good about being back in a place that filled her with many fond memories. Her thoughts were cut short with the slamming of the front door. She turned and met her son's angry expression.

"I'm going to hate it here!" He all but screamed at the top of his lungs. "I want to go back to Los Angeles! No matter what you say, this will never be my home!"

Shelly winced at his words and watched as he threw down the last bag filled with his belongings before racing up the stairs. Instead of calling after him, she closed her eyes, remembering why she had made the move from California to Georgia, and knew that no matter how AJ felt, the **move** was the best thing for him. For the past year he had been failing in school and hanging out with the wrong crowd. Because of his height, he looked older than a ten-year-old and had begun associating with an older group of boys at school, those known to be troublemakers.

Her parents, who had retired and moved to Florida years ago, had offered her the use of her childhood home rent-free. As a result, she had made three of the hardest decisions of her life. First, deciding to move back to College Park, Georgia, second, switching from being a nurse who worked inside the hospital to a home healthcare nurse, and finally letting Dare Westmoreland know he had a son.

More than anything she hoped Dare would understand that she had loved him too much to stand between him and his dream of becoming an FBI agent all those years ago. Her decision, unselfish as it had been, had cost AJ the chance to know his father and Dare the chance to know his son.

Crossing the room she picked up AJ's bag. He was upset about leaving his friends and moving to a place he considered Hicksville, USA. However, his attitude was the least of her worries.

She sighed deeply and rubbed her forehead, knowing she couldn't put off telling Dare much longer since chances were he would hear she'd return to town. Besides, if he took a good hard look at AJ, he would know the truth, and the secret she had harbored for ten years would finally be out.

Deep within her heart she knew that it was time.

Chapter 1

Two weeks later—early September

Sheriff Dare Westmoreland leaned forward in the chair behind his desk. From the defiant look on the face of the boy standing in front of him he could tell it would be one of those days. "Look, kid, I'm only going to ask you one more time. What is your name?"

The boy crossed his arms over his chest and had the nerve to glare at him and say, "And I've told you that I don't like cops and have no intention of giving you my name or anything else. And if you don't like it, arrest me."

Dare stood to his full height of six-feet-four, feeling every bit of his thirty-six years as he came from behind his desk to stare at the boy. He estimated the kid, who he'd caught throwing rocks at passing cars on the highway, to be around twelve or thirteen. It had been a long time since any kid living in his jurisdiction had outright sassed him. None of them would have dared, so it stood to reason that the kid was probably new in town.

"You will get your wish. Since you won't cooperate and tell me who you are, I'm officially holding you in police custody until someone comes to claim you. And while you're waiting you may as well make yourself useful. You'll start by mopping out the bathroom on the first floor, so follow me."

Dare shook his head, thinking he didn't envy this kid's parents one bit.

Shelly had barely brought her car to a complete stop in front of the sheriff's office before she was out of it. It had taken her a good two hours in Atlanta's heavy traffic to make it home after receiving word that AJ had not shown up at school, only to discover he wasn't at home. When it had started getting late she had gotten worried and called the police. After giving the dispatcher a description of AJ, the woman assured her that he was safe in their custody and that the reason she had not been contacted was because AJ had refused to give anyone his name. Without asking for any further details Shelly had jumped into her car and headed for the police station.

She let out a deep sigh. If AJ hadn't given anyone his name that meant the sheriff was not aware she was AJ's mother and for the moment that was a comforting thought. As she pushed open the door, she knew all her excuses for not yet meeting with Dare and telling him the truth had run out, and fate had decided to force her hand.

She was about to come face-to-face with Sheriff Dare Westmoreland.

* * *

"Sheriff, the parent of John Doe has arrived."

Dare looked up from the papers he was reading and met his secretary's gaze. "Only one parent showed up, Holly?"

"Yes, just the mother. She's not wearing a wedding ring so I can only assume there isn't a father. At least not one that's around."

Dare nodded. "What's the kid doing now?" he asked, pushing the papers he'd been reading aside.

"He's out back watching Deputy McKade clean up his police motorcycle"

Dare nodded. "Send the woman in, Holly. I need to have a long talk with her. Her son needs a lot more discipline than he's evidently getting at home."

Dare moved away from his desk to stand at the window where he could observe the boy as he watched McKade polish his motorcycle. He inhaled deeply. There was something about the boy that he found oddly familiar. Maybe he reminded him of himself and his four brothers when they'd been younger. Although they had been quite a handful for their parents, headstrong and in some ways stubborn, they had known just how far to take it and just how much they could get away with. And they'd been smart enough to know when to keep their mouths closed. This kid had a lot to learn.

"Sheriff Westmoreland, this is Ms. Rochelle Brockman."

Dare swung his head around and his gaze collided with the woman he'd once loved to distraction. Suddenly his breath caught, his mouth went dry and every muscle in his body froze as memories rushed through his spiraling mind.

He could vividly recall the first time they'd met, their first kiss and the first time they had made love. The last time stood out in his mind now. He dragged his gaze from her face to do a total sweep of her body before returning to her face again. A shiver of desire tore through him, and he was glad that his position, standing behind his desk, blocked a view of his body from the waist down. Otherwise both women would have seen the arousal pressing against the zipper of his pants.

His gaze moved to her dark brown hair, and he noted that it was shorter and cut in one of those trendy styles that accented the creamy chocolate coloring of her face as well as the warm brandy shade of her eyes.

The casual outfit she wore, a printed skirt and a matching blouse, made her look stylish, comfortable and ultrafeminine. Then there were the legs he still considered the most gorgeous pair he'd ever seen. Legs he knew could wrap around his waist while their bodies meshed in pleasure.

A deep sigh escaped his closed lips as he concluded that at thirty-three she was even more beautiful than he remembered and still epitomized everything feminine. They'd first met when she was sixteen and a sophomore in high school. He'd been nineteen, a few weeks shy of twenty and a sophomore in college, and had come home for a visit to find her working on a school project with his brother Stone. He had walked into the house at the exact moment she'd been leaning over Stone, explaining some scientific formula and wearing the sexiest pair of shorts he had ever seen on a female. He had thought she had a pair of legs that were simply a complete turn-on. When she had glanced up, noticed him staring and smiled, he'd been a goner. Never before had he been so aware of a woman. An immediate attraction had flared between them, holding him hostage to desires he'd never felt before.

After making sure Stone didn't have designs on her himself, he had made his move. And it was a move he'd never regretted making. They began seriously dating a few months later and had continued to do so for six long years, until he had made the mistake of ending things between them. Now it seemed the day of reckoning had arrived.

"Shelly."

"Dare."

It was as if the years had not passed between them, Dare suddenly thought. That same electrical charge the two of them always generated ignited full force, sending a high voltage searing through the room.

He cleared his throat. "Holly, you can leave me and Ms. Brockman alone now," he thought it best to say.

His secretary looked at Shelly then back at him. "Sure, Sheriff," she murmured, and walked out of the office, pulling the door shut behind her.

Once the door closed, Dare turned his full attention back to Shelly. His gaze went immediately to her lips; lips he used to enjoy tasting time and time again; lips that were hot, sweet and ultraresponsive. One night he had thrust her into an orgasm just from gnawing on her lips and caressing them with the tip of his tongue.

He swallowed to get his bearings when he felt his body begin responding to just being in the same room with her. He then admitted what he'd known for years. Shelly Brockman would always be the beginning and the end of his most blatant desires and a part of him could not believe she was back in College Park after being gone for so long.

Shelly felt the intensity of Dare's gaze and struggled to keep her emotions in check, but he was so disturbingly gorgeous that she found it hard to do so. Wearing his blue uniform, he still had that look that left a woman's mind whirling and her body overheated.

He had changed a lot from the young man she had fallen in love with years ago. He was taller, bigger and more muscular. The few lines he had developed in the corners of his eyes, and the firmness of his jaw made his face more angular, his coffee-colored features stark and disturbingly handsome and still a pleasure to look at.

She noted there were certain things about him that had remained the same. The shape of his mouth was still a total turn-on, and he still had those sexy dimples he used to flash at her so often. Then there were those dark eyes—deep, penetrating—that at one time had had the ability to read her mind by just looking at her. How else had he known when she'd wanted him to make love to her without her having to utter a single word?

Suddenly Shelly felt nervous, panicky when she remembered the reason she had moved back to town. But there was no way she could tell Dare that he was AJ's father—at least not today. She needed time to pull herself together. Seeing him again had derailed her senses, making it impossible for her to think straight. The only thing she wanted was to get AJ and leave.

"I came for my son, Dare," she finally found her voice to say, and even to her own ears it sounded wispy.

Dare let out a deep breath. It seemed she wanted to get right down to business and not dwell on the past. He had no intention of letting her do that, mainly because of what they had once meant to each other. "It's been a long time, Shelly. How have you been?" he asked raspily, failing to keep his own voice casual. He found the scent of her perfume just as sexy and enticing as the rest of her.

"I've been fine, Dare. How about you?"

"Same here."

She nodded. "Now may I see my son?"

Her insistence on keeping things nonpersonal was beginning to annoy the hell out of him. His eyes narrowed and his gaze zeroed in on her mouth; bad timing on his part. She nervously swiped her bottom lip with her tongue, causing his body to react immediately. He remembered that tongue and some of the things he had taught her to do with it. He dragged air into his lungs when he felt his muscles tense. "Aren't you going to ask why he's here?" he asked, his voice sounding tight, just as tight as his entire body felt.

She shrugged. "I assumed that since the school called and said he didn't show up today, one of your officers had picked him up for playing hooky."

"No, that's not it," he said, thinking that was a reasonable assumption to make. "I'm the one who picked him up, but he was doing something a bit more serious than playing hooky."

Shelly's eyes widened in alarm. "What?"

"I caught him throwing rocks at passing motorists on Old National Highway. Do you know what could have happened had a driver swerved to avoid getting hit?"

Shelly swallowed as she nodded. "Yes." The first thought that came to her mind was that AJ was in need of serious punishment, but she'd tried punishing him in the past and it hadn't seemed to work.

"I'm sorry about this, Dare," she apologized, not knowing what else to say. "We moved to town a few weeks ago and it hasn't been easy for him. He needs time to adjust."

Dare snorted. "From the way he acted in my office earlier today, I think what he needs is an attitude adjustment as well as a lesson in respect and manners. Whose kid is he anyway?"

Shelly straightened her spine. The mother in her took offense at his words. She admitted she had spoiled AJ somewhat, but still, considering the fact that she was a single parent doing the best she could, she didn't need Dare of all people being so critical. "He's my child."

Dare stared at her wondering if she really expected him to believe that. There was no way the kid could be hers, since in his estimation of the kid's age, she was a student in college and his steady girl about the same time the boy was born. "I mean who does he really belong to since I know you didn't have a baby twelve or thirteen years ago, Shelly."

Her gaze turned glacial. "He *is* mine, Dare. I gave birth to him *ten* years ago. He just looks older than he really is because of his height." Shelly watched Dare's gaze sharpen and darken, then his brows pulled together in a deep, furious frown.

"What the hell do you mean *you* gave birth to him?" he asked, a shocked look on his face and a tone of voice that bordered on anger and total disbelief.

She met his glare with one of her own. "I meant just what I said. Now may I see him?" She made a move to leave Dare's office but he caught her arm.

"Are you saying that he was born after you left here?"

"Yes."

Dare released her. His features had suddenly turned to stone, and the gaze that focused on hers was filled with hurt and pain. "It didn't take you long to find someone in California to take my place after we broke up, did it?"

His words were like a sharp, painful slap to Shelly's face. He thought that she had given birth to someone else's child! How could he think that when she had loved him so much? She was suddenly filled with extreme anger. "Why does it matter to you what I did after I left here, Dare, when you decided after six long years that you wanted a career with the FBI more than you wanted me?"

Dare closed his eyes, remembering that night and what he had said to her, words he had later come to regret. He slowly reopened his eyes and looked at her. She appeared just as stricken now as she had then. He doubted he would ever forget the deep look of hurt on her face that night he had told her that he wanted to break up with her to pursue a career with the FBI.

"Shelly, I…"

"No, Dare. I think we've said enough, too much in fact. Just let me get my son and go home."

Dare inhaled deeply. It was too late for whatever he wanted to say to her. Whatever had once been between them was over and done with. Turning, he slowly walked back over to his desk. "There's some paperwork that needs to be completed before you can take him with you. Since he refused to provide us with any information, we couldn't do it earlier."

He read the question that suddenly flashed in her gaze and said, "And no, this will not be a part of any permanent record, although I think it won't be such a bad idea for him to come back every day this week after school for an hour to do additional chores, especially since he mentioned he's not into any after-school activity. The light tasks I'll be assigning to him will work off some of that rebellious energy he has."

He met her gaze. "However, if this happens again, Shelly, he'll be faced with having to perform hours of community service as well as getting slapped with a juvenile delinquent record. Is that understood?"

She nodded, feeling much appreciative. Had he wanted to, Dare could have handled things a lot more severely. What AJ had done was a serious offense. "Yes, I understand, and I want to thank you."

She sighed deeply. It seemed fate would not be forcing her

hand today after all. She had a little more time before having to tell Dare the truth.

Dare sat down at his desk with a form in front of him and a pen in his hand. "Now then, what's his name?"

Shelly swallowed deeply. "AJ Brockman."

"I need his real name."

She couldn't open her mouth to get the words out. It seemed fate wouldn't be as gracious as she'd thought after all.

Dare was looking down at the papers in front of him, however, the pause went on so long he glanced up and looked at her. He had known Shelly long enough to know when she was nervous about something. His eyes narrowed as he wondered what her problem was.

"What's his real name, Shelly?" he repeated.

He watched as she looked away briefly. Returning her gaze she stared straight into his eyes and without blinking said, "Alisdare Julian Brockman."

Chapter 2

Air suddenly washed from Dare's lungs as if someone had cut off the oxygen supply in the room and he couldn't breathe. Everything started spinning around him and he held on to his desk with a tight grip. However, that didn't work since his hands were shaking worse than a volcano about to explode. In fact his entire body shook with the force of the one question that immediately torpedoed through his brain. Why would she name her son after him? Unless...

He met her gaze and saw the look of guilt in her eyes and knew. Yet he had to have it confirmed. He stood on non-steady legs and crossed the room to stand in front of Shelly. He grasped her elbow and brought her closer to him, so close he could see the dark irises of her eyes.

"When is his birth date?" he growled, quickly finding his equilibrium.

Shelly swallowed so deeply she knew for certain Dare could see her throat tighten, but she refused to let his reaction unsettle her any more than it had. She lifted her chin. "November twenty-fifth."

He flinched, startled. "Two months?" he asked in a pained whisper yet with intense force. "You were two months pregnant when we broke up?"

She snatched her arm from his hold. "Yes."

Anger darkened the depths of his eyes then flared through his entire body at the thought of what she had kept from him. "I have a son?"

Though clearly upset, he had asked the question so quietly that Shelly could only look at him. For a long moment she didn't answer, but then she knew that in spite of everything between them, there was never a time she had not been proud that AJ was Dare's son. That was the reason she had returned to College Park, because she felt it was time he was included in AJ's life. "Yes, you have a son."

"But—but I didn't know about him!"

His words were filled with trembling fury and she knew she had to make him understand. "I found out I was pregnant the day before my graduation party and had planned to tell you that night. But before I got the chance you told me about the phone call you'd received that day, offering you a job with the Bureau and how much you wanted to take it. I loved you too much to stand in your way, Dare. I knew that telling you I was pregnant would have changed everything, and I couldn't do that to you."

Dare's face etched into tight lines as he stared at her. "And you made that decision on your own?"

She nodded. "Yes."

"How dare you! Who in the hell gave you the right to do that, Shelly?"

She felt her own anger rise. "It's not who but what. My love for you gave me the right, Dare," she said and without giving him a chance to say another word, she angrily walked out of his office.

Fury consumed Dare at a degree he had never known before and all he could do was stand there, rooted in place, shell-shocked at what he had just discovered.

He had a son.

He crossed the room and slammed his fist hard on the desk. Ten years! For ten years she had kept it from him. Ten solid years.

Ignoring the pain he felt in his hand, he breathed in deeply when it hit him that he was the father of John Doe. No, she'd called him AJ but she had named him Alisdare Julian. He took a deep, calming breath. For some reason she had at least done that. His son did have his name—at least part of it anyway. Had he known, his son would also be wearing the name Westmoreland, which was rightfully his.

Dare slowly walked over to the window and looked out, suddenly seeing the kid through different eyes—a father's eyes, and his heart and soul yearned for a place in his son's life; a place he rightly deserved. And from the way the kid had behaved earlier it was a place Dare felt he needed to be. It seemed that Alisdare Julian Brockman was a typical Westmoreland male—headstrong and stubborn as hell. As Dare studied him through the windowpane, he could see Westmoreland written all over him and was surprised he hadn't seen it earlier.

He turned when the buzzer sounded on his desk. He took the few steps to answer it. "Yes, Holly?"

"Ms. Brockman is ready to leave, sir. Have you completed the paperwork?"

Dare frowned as he glanced down at the half-completed form on his desk. "No, I haven't."

"What do you want me to tell her, Sheriff?"

Dare sighed. If Shelly for one minute thought she could just walk out of here and take their son, she had another thought coming. There was definitely unfinished business between them. "Tell Ms. Brockman there're a few things I need to take care of. After which, I'll speak with her again in my office. In the meantime, she's not to see her son."

There was a slight pause before Holly replied. "Yes, sir."

After hanging up the phone Dare picked up the form that contained all the standard questions, however, he didn't know any answers about his son. He wondered if he could ever forgive Shelly for doing that to him. No matter what she said, she had no right to have kept him in the dark about his son for ten years.

After the elder Brockmans had retired and moved away, there had been no way to stay in touch except for Ms. Kate, the owner of Kate's Diner who'd been close friends with Shelly's mother. But no matter how many times he had asked Kate about the Brockmans, specifically Shelly, she had kept a stiff lip and a closed mouth.

A number of the older residents in town who had kept an eye on his and Shelly's budding romance during those six years had been pretty damn disappointed with the way he had ended things between them. Even his family, who'd thought the world of Shelly, had decided he'd had a few screws loose for breaking up with her.

He sighed deeply. As sheriff, he of all people should have known she had returned to College Park; he made it his business to keep up with all the happenings around town. She must have come back during the time he had been busy apprehending those two fugitives who'd been hiding out in the area.

With the form in one hand he picked up the phone with the other. His cousin, Jared Westmoreland, was the attorney in the family and Dare felt the need for legal advice.

"The sheriff needs to take care of a few things and would like to see you again in his office when he's finished."

Shelly nodded but none too happily. "Is there anyway I can see my son?"

The older woman shook her head. "I'm sorry but you can't see or talk to him until the sheriff completes the paperwork."

When the woman walked off Shelly shook her head. What had taken place in Dare's office had certainly not been the way she'd envisioned telling him about AJ. She walked over to a chair and sat down, wondering how long would it be before she could get AJ and leave. Dare was calling the shots and there wasn't anything she could do about it but wait. She knew him well enough to know that anger was driving him to strike back at her for what she'd done, what she'd kept from him. A part of her wondered if he would ever forgive her for doing what she'd done, although at the time she'd thought it was for the best.

"Ms. Brockman?"

Shelly shifted her gaze to look into the face of a uniformed man who appeared to be in his late twenties. "Yes?"

"I'm Deputy Rick McKade, and the sheriff wants to see you now."

Shelly stood. She wasn't ready for another encounter with Dare, but evidently he was ready for another one with her.

"All right."

This time when she entered Dare's office he was sitting behind his desk with his head lowered while writing something. She hoped it was the paperwork she needed to get AJ and go home, but a part of her knew the moment Dare lifted his head and looked up at her, that he would not make things easy on her. He was still angry and very much upset.

"Shelly?"

She blinked when she realized Dare had been talking. She also realized Deputy McKade had left and closed the door behind him. "I'm sorry, what did you say?"

He gazed at her for a long moment. "I said you could have a seat."

She shook her head. "I don't want to sit down, Dare. All I want is to get AJ and take him home."

"Not until we talk."

She took a deep breath and felt a tightness in her throat. She also felt tired and emotionally drained. "Can we make arrangements to talk some other time, Dare?"

Shelly regretted making the request as soon as the words had left her mouth. They had pushed him, not over the edge but just about. He stood and covered the distance separating them. The degree of anger on his face actually had her taking a step back. She didn't ever recall seeing him so furious.

"Talk some other time? You have some nerve even to suggest something like that. I just found out that I have a son, a ten-year-old son, and you think you can just waltz back into town with my child and expect me to turn my head and look away and not claim what's mine?"

Shelly released the breath she'd been holding, hearing the sound of hurt and pain in Dare's voice. "No, I never thought any of those things, Dare," she said softly. "In fact, I thought just the opposite, which is why I moved back. I knew once I told you about AJ that you would claim him as yours. And I also knew you would help me save him."

Eyes narrowed and jaw tight, Dare stared at her. She watched as immediate concern—a father's concern—appeared in his gaze. "Save him from what?"

"Himself."

She paused, then answered the question she saw flaring in his eyes. "You've met him, and I'm sure you saw how angry he is. I can only imagine what sort of an impression he made on you today, but deep down he's really a good kid, Dare. I began putting in extra hours at the hospital, which resulted in him spending more time with sitters and finding ways to get into trouble, especially at school when he got mixed up with the wrong crowd. That's the reason I moved back here, to give him a fresh start—with your help."

Anger, blatant and intense, flashed in Dare's eyes. "Are you saying that the only reason you decided to tell me about him and seek my help was because he'd started giving you trouble? What about those years when he was a *good* kid? Did you not think I had a right to know about his existence then?"

Shelly held his gaze. "I thought I was doing the right thing by not telling you about him, Dare."

A muscle worked in his jaw. "Well, you were wrong. You didn't do the right thing. Nothing would have been more important to me than being a father to my son, Shelly."

A twinge of regret, a fleeting moment of sadness for the ten years of fatherhood she had taken away from him touched Shelly. She had to make him understand why she had made the decision she had that night. "That night you stood before me and said that becoming a FBI agent was all you had ever wanted, Dare, all you had ever dreamed about, and that the reason we couldn't be together any longer was because of the nature of the work. You felt it was best that as an agent, you shouldn't have a wife or family." She blinked back tears when she added, "You even said you were glad I hadn't gotten pregnant any of those times we had made love."

She wiped at her eyes. "How do you think I felt hearing you say that, two months pregnant and knowing that our baby and I stood in the way of you having what you desired most?"

When AJ's laughter floated in from the outside, Shelly slowly walked over to the window and looked into the yard below. The boy was watching a uniformed officer give a police dog a bath. This was the first time she had heard AJ laugh in months, and the sheer look of enjoyment on his face at that moment was priceless. She turned back around to face Dare, knowing she had to let him know how she felt.

"When I found out I was pregnant there was no question in my mind that I wouldn't tell you, Dare. In fact, I had been anxiously waiting all that night for the perfect time to do so. And then as soon as we were alone, you dropped the bomb on me."

She inhaled deeply before continuing. "For six long years I assumed that I had a definite place in your heart. I had actually thought that I was the most important thing to you, but in less than five minutes you proved I was wrong. Five minutes was all it took for you to wash six years down the drain when you told me you wanted your freedom."

She stared down at the hardwood floor for a moment before meeting his gaze again. "Although you didn't love me anymore, I still wanted our child. I knew that telling you about my pregnancy would cause you to forfeit your dream and do what you felt was the honorable thing—spend the rest of your life in a marriage you didn't want."

She quickly averted her face so he wouldn't see her tears. She didn't want him to know how much he had hurt her ten years ago. She didn't want him to see that the scars hadn't healed; she doubted they ever would.

"Shelly?"

The tone that called her name was soft, gentle and tender. So tender that she glanced up at him, finding it difficult to meet his dark, piercing gaze, though she met it anyway. She fought the tremble in her voice when she said, "What?"

"That night, I never said I didn't love you," he said, his voice low, a near-whisper. "How could you have possibly thought that?"

She shook her head sadly and turned more fully toward him, not believing he had asked the question. "How could I not think it, Dare?"

Her response made him raise a thick eyebrow. Yes, how could she not think it? He had broken off with her that night, never thinking she would assume that he had never loved her or that she hadn't meant everything to him. Now he could see how she could have felt that way.

He inhaled deeply and rubbed a hand over his face, wondering how he could explain things to her when he really didn't understand himself. He knew he had to try anyway. "It seems I handled things very poorly that night," he said.

Shelly chuckled softly and shrugged her shoulders. "It depends on what you mean by poorly. I think that you accomplished what you set out to do, Dare. You got rid of a girlfriend who stood between you and your career plans."

"That wasn't it, Shelly."

"Then tell me what was *it*," she said, trying to hold on to the anger she was beginning to feel all over again.

For a few moments he didn't say anything, then he spoke. "I loved you, Shelly, and the magnitude of what I felt for you began to frighten me because I knew what you and everyone else expected of me. But a part of me knew that although I loved you, I wasn't ready to take the big step and settle down with the responsibility of a wife. I also knew there was no way I could ask you to wait for me any longer. We had already dated six years and everyone—my family, your family and this whole damn town—expected us to get married. It was time. We had both finished college and I had served a sufficient amount of time in the marines, and you were about to embark on a career in nursing. There was no way I could ask you to wait around and twiddle your thumbs while I worked as an agent. It wouldn't have been fair. You deserved more. You deserved better. So I thought the best thing to do was to give you your freedom."

Shelly dipped her chin, no longer able to look into his eyes. Moments later she lifted her gaze to meet his. "So, I'm not the only one who made a decision about us that night."

Dare inhaled deeply, realizing she was right. Just as she'd done, he had made a decision about them. A few moments later he said, "I wish I had handled things differently, Shelly. Although I loved you, I wasn't ready to become the husband I knew you wanted."

"Yet you want me to believe you would have been ready to become a father?" she asked softly, trying to make him see reason. "All I knew after that night was that the man I loved no longer wanted me, and that his dream wasn't a future with me but one in law enforcement. And I loved him enough to step aside to let him fulfill that dream. That's the reason I left without telling you about the baby, Dare. That's the only reason."

He nodded. "Had I known you were pregnant, my dreams would not have mattered at that point."

"Yes, I knew that better than anyone."

Dare finally understood the point she'd been trying to make and sighed at how things had turned out for them. Ten years ago he'd thought that becoming an FBI agent was the ultimate. It had taken seven years of moving from place to place, getting burnt-out from undercover operations, waking each morning cloaked in danger and not knowing if his next assignment would be his last, to finally make him realize the career that had once been his dream had turned into a living nightmare. Resigning from the Bureau, he had returned home to open up a security firm about the same time Sheriff Dean Whitlow, who'd been in office since Dare was in his early teens, had decided to retire. It was Sheriff Whitlow who had talked him into running for the position he was about to vacate, saying that with Dare's experience, he was the best man for the job. Now, after three years at it, Dare had forged a special bond with the town he'd always loved and the people he'd known all of his life. And compared to what he had done as an FBI agent, being sheriff was a gravy train.

He glanced out of the window and didn't say anything for the longest time as he watched AJ. Then he spoke. "I take it that he doesn't know anything about me."

Shelly shook her head. "No. Years ago I told him that his father was a guy I had loved and thought I would marry, but that things didn't work out and we broke up. I told him I moved away before I had a chance to tell him I was pregnant."

Dare stared at her. "That's it?"

"Yes, that's it. He was fairly young at the time, but occasionally as he got older, he would ask if I knew how to reach you if I ever wanted to, and I told him yes and that if he ever wanted me to contact you I would. All he had to do was ask, but he never has."

Dare nodded. "I want him to know I'm his father, Shelly."

"I want him to know you're his father, too, Dare, but we need to approach this lightly with him," she whispered softly. "He's going through enough changes right now, and I don't want to get him any more upset than he already is. I have an idea as to how and when we can tell him, and I hope after hearing me out that you'll agree."

Dare went back to his desk. "All right, so what do you suggest?"

Shelly nodded and took a seat across from his desk. She held her breath, suddenly feeling uncomfortable telling him what she thought was the best way to handle AJ. She knew her son's emotional state better than anyone. Right now he was mad at the world in general and her in particular, because she had taken him out of an environment he'd grown comfortable with, although that environment as far as she was concerned, had not been a healthy one for a ten-year-old. His failing grades and the trouble he'd gotten into had proven that.

"What do you suggest, Shelly?" Dare asked again, sitting down and breaking into her thoughts.

Shelly cleared her throat. "I know how anxious you are to have AJ meet you, but I think it would be best, considering everything, if he were to get to know you as a friend before knowing you as his father."

Dare frowned, not liking the way her suggestion sounded. "But I am his father, Shelly, not his friend."

"Yes, and that's the point. More than anything, AJ needs a friend right now, Dare, someone he can trust and connect with.

He has a hard time making friends, which is why he began hanging out with the wrong type of kids at the school he attended in California. They readily accepted him for all the wrong reasons. I've talked to a few of his teachers since moving here and he's having the same problems. He's just not outgoing."

Dare nodded. Of the five Westmoreland brothers, he was the least outgoing, if you didn't count Thorn who was known to be a pain in the butt at times. Growing up, Dare had felt that his brothers were all the playmates he had needed, and because of that, he never worried about making friends or being accepted. His brothers were his friends—his best friends—and as far as he'd been concerned they were enough. It was only after he got older and his brothers began seeking other interests that he began getting out more, playing sports, meeting people and making new friends.

So if AJ wasn't as outgoing as most ten-year-old kids, he had definitely inherited that characteristic from him. "So how do you think I should handle it?"

"I suggest that we don't tell him the truth about you just yet, and that you take the initiative to form a bond with him, share his life and get to know him."

Dare raised a dark brow. "And just how am I supposed to do that? Our first meeting didn't exactly get off to a great start, Shelly. Technically, I arrested him, for heaven's sake. My own son! A kid who didn't bat an eye when he informed me he hated cops—which is what I definitely am. Then there's this little attitude problem of his that I feel needs adjusting. So come on, let's be real here. How am I supposed to develop a relationship with *my kid* when he dislikes everything I stand for?"

Shelly shook her head. "He doesn't really hate cops, Dare,

he just thinks he does because of what happened as we were driving from California to here."

Dare lifted a brow. "What happened?"

"I got pulled over in some small Texas town and the officer was extremely rude. Needless to say he didn't make a good impression on AJ."

She sighed deeply. "But you can change that, Dare. That's why I think the two of you getting together and developing a relationship as friends first would be the ideal thing. Ms. Kate told me that you work with the youth in the community and about the Little League baseball team that you coach. I want to do whatever it takes to get AJ involved in something like that."

"And he can become involved as my son."

"I think we should go the friendship route first, Dare."

Dare shook his head. "Shelly, you haven't thought this through. I understand what you're saying because I know how it was for me as a kid growing up. At least I had my brothers who were my constant companions. But I think you've forgotten one very important thing here."

Shelly raised her brow. "What?"

"Most of the people in College Park know you, and most of them have long memories. Once they hear that you have a ten-year-old son, they'll start counting months, and once they see him they'll definitely know the truth. They will see just how much of a Westmoreland he is. He favors my brothers and me. The reason I didn't see it before was because I wasn't looking for it. But you better believe the good people of this town will be. Once you're seen with AJ they'll be looking for anything to link me to him, and it will be easy for them to put two and two together. And don't let them find out that he was named after me. That will be the icing on the cake."

Dare gave her time to think about what he'd said before

continuing. "What's going to happen if AJ learns that I'm his father from someone other than us? He'll resent us for keeping the truth from him."

Shelly sighed deeply, knowing Dare was right. It would be hard to keep the truth hidden in a close-knit town like College Park.

"But there is another solution that will accomplish the same purpose, Shelly," he said softly.

She met his gaze. "What?"

Dare didn't say anything at first, then he said. "I'm asking that you hear me out before jumping to conclusions and totally dishing the idea."

She stared at him before nodding her head. "All right."

Dare continued. "You said you told AJ that you and his father had planned to marry but that we broke up and you moved away before telling him you were pregnant, right?"

Shelly nodded. "Yes."

"And he knows this is the town you grew up in, right?"

"Yes, although I doubt he's made the connection."

"What if you take him into your confidence and let him know that his father lives here in College Park, then go a step further and tell him who I am, but convince him that you haven't told me yet and get his opinion on what you should do?"

Since Dare and AJ had already butted heads, Shelly had a pretty good idea of what he would want her to do—keep the news about him from Dare. He would be dead set against developing any sort of personal relationship with Dare, and she told Dare so.

"Yes, but what if he's placed in a position where he has to accept me, or has to come in constant contact with me?" Dare asked.

"How?"

"If you and I were to rekindle our relationship, at least pretend to do so."

Shelly frowned, clearly not following Dare. "And just how will that help the situation? Word will still get out that you're his father."

"Yes, but he'll already know the truth and he'll think I'm the one in the dark. He'll either want me to find out the truth or he'll hope that I don't. In the meantime I'll do my damnedest to win him over."

"And what if you can't?"

"I will. AJ needs to feel that he belongs, Shelly, and he does belong. Not only does he belong to you and to me, but he also belongs to my brothers, my parents and the rest of the Westmorelands. Once we start seeing each other again, he'll be exposed to my family, and I believe when that happens and I start developing a bond with him, he'll eventually want to acknowledge me as his father."

Dare shifted in his chair. "Besides," he added smiling. "If he really doesn't want us to get together, he'll be so busy thinking of ways to keep us apart that he won't have time to get into trouble."

Shelly lifted a brow, knowing Dare did have a point. However, she wasn't crazy about his plan, especially not the part she would play. The last thing she needed was to pretend they were falling in love all over again. Already, being around him was beginning to feel too comfortably familiar.

She sighed deeply. In order for Dare's plan to work, they would have to start spending time together. She couldn't help wondering how her emotions would be able to handle that. And she didn't even want to consider what his nearness might do to her hormones, since it had been a long time since she had spent any time with a man. A very long time.

She cleared her throat when she noticed Dare watching her intently and wondered if he knew what his gaze was doing to her. Biting her lower lip and shifting in her seat, she asked, "How do you think he's going to feel when he finds out that we aren't really serious about each other, and it was just a game we played to bring him around?"

"I think he'll accept the fact that although we aren't married, we're friends who like and respect each other. Most boys from broken relationships I come in contact with have parents who dislike each other. I think it's important that a child sees that although they aren't married, his parents are still friends who make his well-being their top priority."

Shelly shook her head. "I don't know, Dare. A lot can go wrong with what you're proposing."

"True, but on the other hand, a lot can go right. This way we're letting AJ call the shots, or at least we're letting him think that he is. This will give him what he'll feel is a certain degree of leverage, power and control over the situation. From working closely with kids, I've discovered that if you try forcing them to do something they will rebel. But if you sit tight and be patient, they'll eventually come around on their own. That's what I'm hoping will happen in this case. Chances are he'll resent me at first, but that's the chance I have to take. Winning him over will be my mission, Shelly, one I plan to accomplish. And trust me, it will be the most important mission of my life."

He studied her features, and when she didn't say anything for the longest time he said, "I have a lot more to lose than you, but I'm willing to risk it. I don't want to spend too much longer with my son not knowing who I am. At least this way he'll know that I'm his father, and it will be up to me to do everything possible to make sure that he wants to accept me in his life."

He inhaled deeply. "So will you at least think about what I've proposed?"

Shelly met his gaze. "Yes, Dare, I'll need time," she said quietly.

"Overnight. That's all the time I can give you, Shelly."

"But, I need more time."

Dare stood. "I can't give you any more time than that. I've lost ten years already and can't afford to lose any more. And just so you'll know, I've made plans to meet with Jared for lunch tomorrow. I'll ask him to act as my attorney so that I'll know my rights as AJ's father."

Shelly shook her head sadly. "There's no need for you to do that, Dare. I don't intend to keep you and AJ apart. As I said, you're the reason I returned."

Dare nodded. "Will you meet me for breakfast at Kate's Diner in the morning so we can decide what we're going to do?"

Shelly felt she needed more time but knew there was no way Dare would give it to her. "All right. I'll meet you in the morning."

Chapter 3

Dare reached across his desk and hit the buzzer.

"Yes, Sheriff?"

"McKade, please bring in John Doe."

Shelly frowned when she glanced over at Dare. "John Doe?"

Dare shrugged. "That's the usual name for any unidentified person we get in here, and since he refused to give us his name, we had no choice."

She nodded. "Oh."

Before Dare could say anything else, McKade walked in with AJ. The boy frowned when he saw his mother. "I wondered if you were ever going to come, Mom."

Shelly smiled wryly. "Of course I was going to come. Had you given them your name they would have called me sooner. You have a lot of explaining to do as to why you weren't in school today. It's a good thing Sheriff Westmoreland stopped you before you could cause harm to anyone."

AJ turned and glared at Dare. "Yeah, but I still don't like cops."

Dare crossed his arms on his chest. "And I don't like boys with bad attitudes. To be frank, it doesn't matter whether or not you like cops, but you'd sure better learn to respect them and what they stand for." This might be his son, Dare thought, but he intended to teach him a lesson in respect, starting now.

AJ turned to his mother. "I'm ready to go."

Shelly nodded. "All right."

"Not yet," Dare said, not liking the tone AJ had used with Shelly, or how easily she had given in to him. "What you did today was a serious matter, and as part of your punishment, I expect you to come back every day this week after school to do certain chores I'll have lined up for you."

"And if I don't show up?"

"AJ!"

Dare held up his hand, cutting off anything Shelly was about to say. This was between him and his son. "And if you don't show up, I'll know where to find you and when I do it will only make things a lot worse for you. Trust me."

Dare's gaze shifted to Shelly. This was not the way he wanted to start things off with his son, but he'd been left with little choice. AJ had to respect him as the sheriff as well as accept him as his father. From the look on Shelly's face he knew she understood that as well.

"Sheriff Westmoreland is right," she said firmly, giving Dare her support. "And you *will* show up after school to do whatever he has for you to do. Is that understood?"

"Yeah, yeah, I understand," the boy all but snapped. "Can we go now?"

Dare nodded and handed her the completed form. "I'll walk the two of you out to the car since I was about to leave anyway."

Once Shelly and AJ were in the car and had buckled up their seat belts, Dare glanced into the car and said to the boy, "I'll see you tomorrow when you get out of school."

Ignoring AJ's glare, he then turned and the look he gave Shelly said that he expected to see her tomorrow as well, at Kate's Diner in the morning. "Good night and drive safely."

He then walked away.

An hour later, Dare walked into a room where four men sat at a table engaged in a card game. The four looked up and his brother Stone spoke. "You're late."

"I had important business to take care of," Dare said grabbing a bottle of beer and leaning against the refrigerator in Stone's kitchen. "I'll wait this round out and just watch."

His brothers nodded as they continued with the game. Moments later, Chase Westmoreland let out a curse. Evidently he was losing as usual, Dare thought smiling. He then thought about how the four men at the table were more than just brothers to him; they were also his very best friends, although Thorn, the one known for his moodiness, could test that friendship and brotherly love to the limit at times. At thirty-five, Thorn was only eleven months younger than him, and built and raced motorcycles for a living. Last year he'd been the only African-American on the circuit.

His brother Stone, known for his wild imagination, had recently celebrated his thirty-third birthday and wrote action-thriller novels under the pen name, Rock Mason. Then there were the fraternal thirty-two-year-old twins, Chase and Storm. Chase was the oldest by seven minutes and owned a soul-food restaurant in downtown Atlanta, and Storm was the fireman in the family. According to their mother, she had gone into delivery unexpectedly while riding in the car with their dad. When a bad storm had come up, he chased time and outran the storm to get her to the hospital. Thus she had named her last two sons Chase and Storm.

"You're quiet, Dare."

Dare looked up from studying his beer bottle and brought his thoughts back to the present. He met Stone's curious stare. "Is that a crime?"

Stone grinned. "No, but if it was a crime I'm sure you'd arrest yourself since you're such a dedicated lawman."

Chase chuckled. "Leave Dare alone. Nothing's wrong with him other than he's keeping Thorn company with this celibacy thing," he said jokingly.

"Shut up, Chase, before I hurt you," Thorn Westmoreland said, without cracking a smile.

Everyone knew Thorn refrained from having sex while preparing for a race, which accounted for his prickly mood most of the time. But since Thorn had been in the same mood for over ten months now they couldn't help but wonder what his problem was. Dare had a clue but decided not to say. He sighed and crossed the room and sat down at the table. "Guess who's back in town."

Storm looked up from studying his hand and grinned. "Okay, I'll play your silly guessing game. Who's back in town, Dare?"

"Shelly."

Everyone at the table got quiet as they looked up at him. Then Stone spoke. "*Our* Shelly?"

Dare looked at his brother and frowned. "No, not *our* Shelly, *my* Shelly."

Stone glared at him. "*Your* Shelly? You could have fooled us, the way you dumped her."

Dare leaned back in his chair. He'd known it was coming. His brothers had actually stopped speaking to him for weeks after he'd broken off with Shelly. "I did not dump her. I merely made the decision that I wasn't ready for marriage and wanted a career with the Bureau instead."

"That sounds pretty much like you dumped her to me," Stone said angrily. "You knew she was the marrying kind. And you led her to believe, like you did the rest of us, that the two of you would eventually marry when she finished college. In my book you played her for a fool, and I've always felt bad about it because I'm the one who introduced the two of you," he added, glaring at his brother.

Dare stood. "I did not play her for a fool. Why is it so hard to believe that I really loved her all those years?" he asked, clearly frustrated. He'd had this same conversation with Shelly earlier.

"Because," Thorn said slowly and in a menacing tone as he threw out a card, "I would think most men don't walk away from the woman they claim to love for no damn reason, especially not some lame excuse about not being ready to settle down. The way I see it, Dare, you wanted to have your cake and eat it too." He took a swig of his beer. "Let's change the subject before I get mad all over again and knock the hell out of you for hurting her the way you did."

Chase narrowed his eyes at Dare. "Yeah, and I hope she's happily married with a bunch of kids. It would serve you right for letting the best thing that ever happened to you get away."

Dare raised his eyes to the ceiling, wondering if there was such a thing as family loyalty when it came to Shelly Brockman. He decided to sit back down when a new card game began. "She isn't happily married with a bunch of kids, Chase, but she does have a son. He's ten."

Stone smiled happily. "Good for her. I bet it ate up your guts to know she got involved with someone else and had his baby after she left here."

Dare leaned back in his chair. "Yeah, I went through some pretty hard stomach pains until I found out the truth."

Storm raised a brow. "The truth about what?"

Dare smirked at each one of his brothers before answering. "Shelly's son is mine."

Early the next morning Dare walked into Kate's Diner.

"Good morning, Sheriff."

"Good morning, Boris. How's that sore arm doing?"

"Fine. I'll be ready to play you in another game of basketball real soon."

"I'm counting on it."

"Good morning, Sheriff."

"Good morning, Ms. Mamie. How's your arthritis?"

"A pain as usual," was the old woman's reply.

"Good morning, Sheriff Westmoreland."

"Good morning, Lizzie," Dare greeted the young waitress as he slid into the stool at the counter. She was old man Barton's granddaughter and was working at the diner part-time while taking classes at the college in town.

He smiled when Lizzie automatically poured his coffee. She knew just how he liked it. Black. "Where's Ms. Kate this morning?" he asked after taking a sip.

"She hasn't come in yet."

He raised a dark brow. For as long as he'd known Ms. Kate—and that had been all of his thirty-six years—he'd never known her to be late to work at the diner. "Is everything all right?"

"Yes, I guess so," Lizzie said, not looking the least bit worried. "She called and said Mr. Granger was stopping by her house this morning to take a look at her hot-water heater. She thinks it's broken and wanted to be there when he arrived."

Dare nodded. It had been rumored around town for years that old man Granger and Ms. Kate were sweet on each other.

"Would you like for me to go ahead and order your usual, Sheriff?"

He rolled his shoulders as if to ease sore muscles as he smiled up at her and said. "No, not yet. I'm waiting on someone." He glanced at his watch. "She should be here any minute."

Lizzie nodded. "All right then. I'll be back when your guest arrives."

Dare was just about to check his watch again when he heard the diner's door open behind him, followed by Boris's loud exclamation. "Well, my word, if it isn't Shelly Brockman! What on earth are you doing back here in College Park?"

Dare turned around on his stool as other patrons who'd known Shelly when she lived in town hollered out similar greetings. He had forgotten just how popular she'd been with everyone, both young and old. That was one of the reasons the entire town had all but skinned him alive when he'd broken off with her.

A muscle in his jaw twitched when he noticed that a few of the guys she'd gone to school with—Boris Jones, David Wright and Wayland Miller—who'd known years ago that she was off-limits because of him, were checking her out now. And he could understand why. She looked pretty damn good, and she still had that natural ability to turn men on without even trying. Blue was a color she wore well and nothing about that had changed, he thought, as his gaze roamed over the blue sundress she was wearing. With thin straps tied at the shoulders, it was a decent length that stopped right above her knees and showed off long beautiful bare legs and feet encased in a pair of black sandals. When he felt his erection straining against the crotch of his pants, he knew he was in big trouble. He was beginning to feel a powerful and compelling need that he hadn't felt in a long time; at least ten years.

"Is that her, Sheriff? The woman you've been waiting on?"

Lizzie's question interrupted Dare's musings. "Yes, that's her."

"Will the two of you be sitting at the counter or will you be using a table or a booth?"

Now that's a loaded question, Dare thought. He wished—doubly so—that he could take Shelly and use a table or a booth. He could just imagine her spread out on either. He shook his head. Although he'd always been sexually attracted to Shelly, he'd never thought of her with so much lust before, and he couldn't help wondering why. Maybe it was because in the past she'd always been his. Now things were different, she was no longer his and he was lusting hard—and he meant hard!—for something he had lost.

"Sheriff?"

Knowing Lizzie was waiting for his decision, he glanced toward the back of the diner and made a quick decision. "We'll be sitting at a booth in the back." Once he was confident he had his body back under control, he stood and walked over to where Shelly was surrounded by a number of people, mostly men.

Breaking into their conversation he said, "Good morning, Shelly. Are you ready for breakfast?"

It seemed the entire diner got quiet and all eyes turned to him. The majority of those present remembered that he had been the one to break Shelly's heart, which ultimately had resulted in her leaving town, and from the way everyone was looking at him, the last thing they wanted was for her to become involved with him again.

In fact, old Mr. Sylvester turned to him and said, "I'm surprised Shelly is willing to give you the time of day, Sheriff, after what you did to her ten years ago."

"You got that right," eighty-year-old Mamie Potter agreed.

Dare rolled his eyes. That was all he needed, the entire town bringing up the past and ganging up on him. "Shelly and I have business to discuss, if none of you mind."

Allen Davis, who had worked with Dare's grandfather years ago, crossed his arms over his chest. "Considering what you did to her, yes, we do mind. So you better behave yourself where she is concerned, Dare Westmoreland. Don't forget there's an election next year."

Dare had just about had it, and was about to tell Mr. Davis a thing or two when Shelly piped in, laughing, "I can't believe all of you still remember what happened ten years ago. I'd almost forgotten about that," she lied. "And to this day I still consider Dare my good friend," she lied again, and tried tactfully to change the subject. "Ms. Mamie, how is Mr. Fred?"

"He still can't hear worth a dime, but other than that he's fine. Thanks for asking. Now to get back to the subject of Dare here, from the way he used to sniff behind you and kept all the other boys away from you, we all thought he was going to be your husband," Mamie mumbled, glaring at Dare.

Shelly shook her head, seeing that the older woman was

determined to have her say. She placed a hand on Ms. Mamie's arm in a warm display of affection. "Yes, I know you all did and that was sweet. But things didn't work out that way and we can't worry about spilled milk now, can we?"

Ms. Mamie smiled up at Shelly and patted her hand. "I guess not, dear, but watch yourself around him. I know how crazy you were about him before. There's no need for a woman to let the same man break her heart twice."

Dare frowned, not appreciating Mamie Potter talking about him as if he wasn't there. Nor did it help matters that Shelly was looking at him as though she'd just been given good sound advice. He cleared his throat, thinking that it was time he broke up the little gathering. He placed his hand on Shelly's arm and said, "This way, Shelly. We need to discuss our business so I can get to the office. We can talk now or you can join Jared and I for lunch."

From the look on her face he could tell his words had reminded her of why he was meeting Jared for lunch. After telling everyone goodbye and giving out a few more hugs, she turned and followed Dare to a booth, the farthest one in the back.

He stood aside while she slipped into a soft padded seat and then he slid into the one across from her. Nervously she traced the floral designs on the place mat. Dare's nearness was getting to her. She had experienced the same thing in his office last night, and it aggravated the heck out of her that all that anger she'd felt for him had not been able to defuse her desire for him; especially after ten years.

Desire.

That had to be what it was since she knew she was no longer in love with him. He had effectively put an end to those feelings years ago. Yet, for some reason she was feeling the same turbulent yearnings she'd always felt for him. And last night in her bed, the memories had been at their worse…or their best, depending on how you looked at it.

She had awakened in the middle of the night with her breath coming in deep, ragged gasps, and her sheets damp with perspiration after a hot, steamy dream about him.

Getting up and drinking a glass of ice water, she had made a decision not to beat herself up over her dreams of Dare. She'd decided that the reason for them was understandable. Her body knew Dare as it knew no other man, and it had reminded her of that fact in a not-too-subtle way. It didn't help that for the past ten years she hadn't dated much; raising AJ and working at the hospital kept her busy, and the few occasions she had dated had been a complete waste of her time since she'd never experienced the sparks with any of them that she'd grown accustomed to with Dare.

"Would you like some more coffee, Sheriff?"

Shelly snatched her head up when she heard the sultry, feminine voice and was just in time to see the slow smile that spread across the young woman's lips, as well as the look of wanton hunger in her eyes as she looked at Dare. Either he didn't notice or he was doing a pretty good job of pretending not to.

"Yes, Lizzie, I'd like another cup."

"And what would you like?" Lizzie asked her, and Shelly couldn't help but notice the cold, unfriendly eyes that were staring at her.

Evidently the same thing you would like, Shelly thought, trying to downplay the envy she suddenly felt, although she knew there was no legitimate reason to feel that way. What was once between her and Dare had ended years ago and she didn't intend to go back there, no matter how much he could still arouse her. Sighing, she was about to give the woman her order when Dare spoke. "She would like a cup of coffee with cream and one sugar."

The waitress lifted her brow as if wondering how Dare knew what Shelly wanted. "Okay, Sheriff." Lizzie placed menus in front of them, saying, "I'll bring your coffee while you take a look at these."

When Lizzie had left, Shelly leaned in closer to the center of the booth and whispered, "I don't appreciate the daggered looks coming from one of your girlfriends." She decided not to tell him that she'd felt like throwing a few daggered looks of her own.

Lifting his head from the menu, Dare frowned. "What are you talking about? I've never dated Lizzie. She's just a kid."

Shelly shrugged as she straightened in her seat and glanced over to where Lizzie was now taking another order. Her short uniform showed off quite nicely the curves of her body and her long legs. Dare was wrong. Lizzie was no kid. Her body attested to that.

"Well, kid or no kid, she definitely has the hots for you, Dare Westmoreland."

He shrugged. "You're imagining things."

"No, trust me. I know."

He rubbed his chin as his mouth tipped up crookedly into a smile. Settling back in his seat, he asked, "And how would you know?"

She met his gaze. "Because I'm a woman." And I know all about having the hots for you, she decided not to add.

Dare nodded. He definitely couldn't deny that she was a woman. He glanced over at Lizzie and caught her at the exact moment she was looking at him with a flirty smile. He remembered the other times she'd given him that smile, and now it all made sense. He quickly averted his eyes. Clearing his throat, he met Shelly's gaze. "I've never noticed before."

Typical man, Shelly thought, but before she could say anything else, Lizzie had returned with their coffee. After taking their order she left, and Shelly smiled and said, "I can't believe you remembered how I like my coffee after all this time."

Dare looked at her. His gaze remained steady when he said, "There are some things a man can't forget about a woman he considered as his, Shelly."

"Oh." Her voice was slightly shaky, and she decided not to touch that one; mainly because what he said was true. He had considered her as his; she had been his in every way a woman could belong to a man.

She took a deep breath before taking a sip of coffee. Emotions she didn't want to feel were churning inside her. Dare had hurt her once and she refused to let him do so again. She would definitely take Ms. Mamie's advice and watch herself around him. She glanced up and noticed Dare watching her. The heat from his gaze made her feel a connection to him, one she didn't want to feel, but she realized they did have a connection.

Their son.

She cleared her throat, deciding they needed to engage in conversation, something she considered a safe topic. "How is your family doing?"

A warm smile appeared on Dare's face. "Mom and Dad and all the rest of the Westmoreland clan are fine."

Shelly took another sip of her coffee. "Is it true what I've heard about Delaney? Did she actually finish medical school and marry a sheikh?" she asked. She wondered how that had happened when everyone knew how overprotective the Westmoreland brothers had been of their baby sister.

Dare smiled and the heat in his gaze eased somewhat. "Yeah, it's true. The one and only time we took our eyes off Laney, she slipped away and hid out in a cabin in the mountains for a little rest and relaxation. While there she met this sheikh from the Middle East. Their marriage took some getting used to, since she up and moved to his country. They have a five-month-old son named Ari."

"Have you seen him yet?"

Dare's smile widened. "Yes, the entire family was there for his birth and it was some sort of experience." A frown appeared on his face when he suddenly thought about what he'd missed out on by not being there when AJ had come into the world. "Tell me about AJ, Shelly. Tell me how things were when he was born."

Shelly swallowed thickly. So much for thinking she had moved to a safe topic of conversation. She sighed, knowing Dare had a right to what he was asking for. "He was born in the hospital where I worked. My parents were there with me. I didn't gain much weight while pregnant and that helped make the delivery easier. He wasn't a big baby, only a little over six pounds, but he was extremely long which accounts for his height. As soon as I saw him I immediately thought he looked like you. And I knew at that moment no matter how we had separated, that my baby was a part of you."

Shelly hesitated for a few moments and added. "That's why I gave him your name, Dare. In my mind he didn't look like a Marcus, which was the name I had intended to give him. To me he looked like an Alisdare Julian. A little Dare."

Dare didn't say anything for the longest time, then he said, "Thank you for doing that."

"You're welcome."

Moments later, Dare cleared his throat and asked, "Does he know he was named after his father?"

"Yes. You don't know how worried I was before arriving at the police station yesterday. I was afraid that you had found out his name, or that he had found out yours. Luckily for me, most people at the station call you Sheriff, and everyone in town still calls you Dare."

Dare nodded. "Except for my family, few people probably remember my real name is Alisdare since it's seldom used. I've always gone by Dare. If AJ had given me his full name I would have figured things out."

After a few brief quiet moments, Dare said, "I told my parents and my brothers about him last night, Shelly."

She nervously bit into her bottom lip. "And what were their reactions?"

Dare leaned back against his seat and met her gaze. "They were as shocked as I was, and of course they're anxious to meet him."

Shelly nodded slowly. She'd figured they would be. The Westmorelands were a big family and a rather close-knit group. "Dare, about your suggestion on how we should handle things."

"Yes?"

She didn't say anything for the longest time, then she said, "I'll go along with your plan as long as you and I understand something."

"What?"

"That it will be strictly for show. There's no way the two of us could ever get back together for any reason. The only thing between us is AJ."

Dare raised a brow and gave her a deliberate look. He

wondered why she was so damn sure of that, but decided to let it go for now. He wanted to start building a relationship with his son immediately, and he refused to let Shelly put stumbling blocks in his way. "That's fine with me."

He leaned back in his chair. "So how soon will you tell AJ about me?"

"I plan to tell him tonight."

Dare nodded, satisfied with her answer. That meant they could put their plans into action as early as tomorrow. "I think we're doing the right thing, Shelly."

She felt the intensity of his gaze, and the force of it touched her in a way she didn't want. "I hope so, Dare. I truly hope so," she said quietly.

Chapter 4

Dare glanced at the clock again and sighed deeply. Where was AJ? School had let out over an hour ago and he still hadn't arrived. According to what Shelly had told him that morning at breakfast, AJ had ridden his bike to school and been told to report to the sheriff's office as soon as school was out. Dare wondered if AJ had blatantly disobeyed his mother.

Although Shelly had given him her cell-phone number—as a home healthcare nurse she would be making various house calls today—he didn't want to call and get her worried or upset. If he had to, he would go looking for their son himself and when he found him, he intended to—

The sound of the buzzer interrupted his thoughts. "Yes, McKade, what is it?"

"That Brockman kid is here."

Dare nodded and sighed with relief. Then he recalled what

McKade had said—*that Brockman kid.* He frowned. The first thing he planned to do when everything settled was to give his son his last name. *That Westmoreland kid* sounded more to his liking. "Okay, I'll be right out."

Leaving his office, Dare walked down the hall toward the front of the building and stopped dead in his tracks when he saw AJ. His frown deepened. The kid looked as though he'd had a day with a tiger. "What happened to you?" he asked him, his gaze roaming over AJ's torn shirt and soiled jeans, not to mention his bruised lip and bloodied nose.

"Nothing happened. I fell off my bike," AJ snapped.

Dare glanced over at McKade. They both recognized a lie when they heard one. Dare crossed his arms over his chest. "You never came across to me as the outright clumsy type."

That got the response Dare was hoping for. The anger flaring in AJ's eyes deepened. "I am not the clumsy type. Anyone can fall off a bike," he said, again snapping out his answer.

"Yes, but in this case that's not what happened and you know it," Dare said, wanting to snap back but didn't. It was apparent that AJ had been in a fight, and Dare decided to cut the crap. "Tell me what really happened."

"I'm not telling you anything."

Wrong answer, Dare thought taking a step forward to stand in front of AJ. "Look, kid, we can stand here all day until you decide to talk, but you *will* tell me what happened."

AJ stuck his hands in the pockets of his jeans and glanced down as if to study the expensive pair of Air Jordans on his feet. When seconds ticked into minutes and he saw that Dare would not move an inch, he finally raised his head, met Dare's gaze, squared his shoulders and said, "Caleb Martin doesn't like me and today after school he decided to take his dislike to another level."

Dare leaned against the counter and raised a brow. "And?"

AJ paused, squared his shoulders again and said, "And I decided to oblige him. He pushed me down and when I got up I made sure he found out the hard way that I'm not some-one to mess with."

Dare inwardly smiled. He hated admitting it but what his son had said had been spoken like a true Westmoreland. He didn't want to remember the number of times one of the Westmoreland boys came home with something bloodied or broken. Word had soon gotten around school that those West-morelands weren't anyone to tangle with. They never went looking for trouble, but they knew how to handle it when it came their way.

"Fighting doesn't accomplish anything."

His son shrugged. "Maybe not, but I bet Caleb Martin won't be calling me bad names and pushing me around again. I had put up with it long enough."

Dare placed his hand on his hips. "If this has been going on for a while, why didn't you say something about it to your mother or to some adult at school?"

AJ's glare deepened even more. "I'm not a baby. I don't need my mother or some teacher fighting my battles for me."

Dare met his son's glare with one of his own. "Maybe not, but in the future I expect you not to take matters into your own hands. If I hear about it, I will haul both you and that Martin kid in here and the two of you will be sorry. Not only will I assign after-school duties but I'll give weekend work duties as well. I won't tolerate that kind of foolishness." Especially when it involved his son, Dare decided not to add. "Now go into that bathroom and get cleaned up then meet me out back."

AJ shifted his book bag to his other shoulder. "What am I supposed to do today?"

"My police car needs washing and I can use the help."

AJ nodded and rushed off toward the bathroom. Dare couldn't hide the smile that lit his face. Although AJ had grumbled last night about having to show up at the police station after school, Dare could tell from his expression that he enjoyed having something to do.

"Sheriff?"

Dare glanced up and met McKade's gaze. "Yes?"

"There's something about that kid that's oddly familiar."

Dare knew what McKade was getting at. His deputy had seen the paperwork he'd completed last night and had probably put two and two together; especially since Rick McKade knew his first and middle names. The two of them were good friends and had been since joining the FBI at the same time years back. When Dare had decided to leave the Bureau, so had McKade. Rick had followed Dare to Atlanta, where he'd met and fallen in love with a schoolteacher who lived in the area.

"The reason he seems oddly familiar, McKade, is because you just saw him yesterday," Dare said, hoping that was the end of it.

He found out it wasn't when McKade chuckled and said, "That's not what I mean and you know it, Dare. There's something else."

"What?"

McKade paused a moment before answering. "He looks a lot like you and your brothers, but *especially* like you." He again paused a few moments then asked, "Is there anything you want to tell me?"

Dare's lips curved into a smile. He didn't have to tell

McKade anything since it was obvious he had figured things out for himself. "No, there's nothing I want to tell you."

McKade chuckled again. "Then maybe I better tell you, or rather I should remind you that the people in this town don't know how to keep a secret if that's what you plan to do. It won't be long before everyone figures things out, and when they do, someone will tell the kid."

Dare's smile widened when he thought of that happening. "Yes, and that's what his mother and I are counting on." Knowing what he'd said had probably confused the hell out of McKade, Dare turned and walked through the door that led out back.

The kid was a hard worker and a darn good one at that, Dare decided as he watched AJ dry off the police cruiser. He had only intended the job to last an hour, but he could tell that AJ was actually enjoying having something to do. He made a mental note to ask Shelly if AJ did any chores at home, and if not, maybe it wouldn't be a bad idea for her to assign him a few. That would be another way to keep him out of trouble.

"Is this it for the day?"

AJ's statement jerked Dare from his thoughts. AJ had placed the cloth he'd used to dry off the car back in the bucket. "Yes, that's it, but make sure you come back tomorrow—and I expect you to be on time."

A scowl appeared on AJ's face but he didn't say anything as he picked up his book bag and placed it on his shoulder. "I don't like coming here after school."

Dare shook his head and inwardly smiled, wondering who the kid was trying to convince. "Well, you should have thought of that before you got into trouble."

Their gazes locked for a brief moment and Dare detected

a storm of defiance brewing within his son. "How much longer do I have to come here?" AJ asked in an agitated voice.

"Until I think you've learned your lesson."

AJ's glare deepened. "Well, I don't like it."

Dare raised his gaze upward to the sky then looked back to AJ. "You've said that already, kid, but in this case what you like doesn't really matter. When you break the law you have to be punished. That's something I suggest you remember. I also suggest that you get home before your mother starts worrying about you," he said, following AJ inside the building.

"She's going to do that anyway."

Dare smiled. "Yeah, I wouldn't put it past her, since mothers are that way. I'm sure my four brothers and I worried my mother a lot when we were growing up."

AJ raised a brow. "You have four brothers?"

Dare's smile widened. "Yes, I have four brothers and one sister. I'm the oldest of the group."

AJ nodded. "It's just me and my mom."

Dare nodded as well. He then stood in front of the door with A. J. "To answer your question of how long you'll have to come here after school, I think a full week of this should make you think twice about throwing rocks at passing cars the next time." Dare rubbed his chin thoughtfully then added, "Unless I hear about you getting involved in a fight again. Like I said, that's something I won't tolerate."

AJ glared at him. "Then I'll make sure you don't hear about it."

Not giving Dare a chance to respond, AJ raced out of the door, got his bike and took off.

"Ouch, that hurts!"

"Well, this should teach you a lesson," Shelly said angrily, leaning over AJ as she applied antiseptic to his bruised lip. "And if I hear of you fighting again, I will put you on a punishment like you wouldn't believe."

"He started it!"

Shelly straightened and met her son's dark scowl. "Then next time walk away," she said firmly.

"People are going to think I'm a coward if I do that. I told you I was going to hate it here. Nobody likes me. At least I had friends in L.A."

"I don't consider those guys you hung around with back in L.A. your friends. A true friend wouldn't talk you into doing bad things, AJ, and as far as anyone thinking you're a coward, then let them. I know for a fact that you're one of the bravest persons I know. Look how long you've had to be the man of the house for me."

AJ shrugged and glanced up at his mother. "But it's different with you, Mom. I don't want any of the guys at school thinking I'm a pushover."

"Trust me, you're not a pushover. You're too much like your father." She then turned to walk toward the kitchen.

Shelly knew she had thrown out the hook and it wouldn't take long for AJ to take the bait. She heard him draw in a long breath behind her and knew he was right on her heels.

"Why did you mention him?"

She looked back over her shoulder at AJ when she reached the kitchen. "Why did I mention who?"

"My father."

She leaned against the kitchen cabinet and raised a curious brow. "I'm not supposed to mention him?"

"You haven't in a long time."

Shelly nodded. "Only because you haven't asked about him in a long time. Tonight when you said something about being a pushover, I immediately thought of him because you're so much like him and he's one of the bravest men I know."

AJ smiled. He was glad to know his father was brave. "What does he do, fly planes or something?"

Shelly smiled knowing of her son's fixation with airplanes and spaceships. "No." She inhaled deeply. "I think it's time we had a talk about your father. I've been doing a lot of thinking since moving back and I need you to help me make a decision about something."

AJ lifted a brow. "A decision about what?"

"About whether to tell your father about you."

Surprise widened AJ's eyes. "You know where he is?"

Shelly shook her head. "AJ, I've always known where he is. I've always told you that. And I've always told you if you ever wanted me to contact him to just say the word."

Uncertainty narrowed his eyes, then he glanced down as if to study his sneakers. "Yeah, but I wasn't sure if you really meant it or not," he said quietly.

Shelly smiled weakly and reached out and gently gripped his chin to bring his gaze back to hers. "Is that why you stopped asking me about him? You thought I was lying to you about him?"

He shrugged. "I just figured you were saying what you wanted me to believe. Nick Banner's mom did that to him. She told him that his dad had died in a car accident when he was a baby, then one day he heard his grandpa tell somebody that his dad was alive and had another family someplace and that he didn't want Nick."

Shelly's breath caught in her throat. She felt an urgent need to take her son into her arms and assure him that unlike Nick's father, his father did want him. But she knew he was now at an age where mothers' hugs were no longer *cool*. Her heart felt heavy knowing that AJ had denied himself knowledge of his father in an attempt to save her from what he thought was embarrassment.

"Come on, let's sit at the table. I think it's time for us to have a long talk."

AJ hung his head thoughtfully then glanced back at her. His eyes were wary. "About him?"

"Yes about him. There are things I think you need to know, so come on."

He followed her over to the table and they sat down. Her gaze was steady as she met his. "Now then, just to set the record straight, everything I've ever told you about your father was true. He was someone I dated through high school and college while I lived here in College Park. Everyone in town thought we would marry, and I guess that had been my thought, too, but your father had a dream."

"A dream?"

"Yes, a dream of one day becoming an FBI agent. You have your dream to grow up and become an astronaut one day, don't you?"

"Yes."

"Well, your father had a similar dream, but his was one day to become an FBI agent, and I knew if I had told him that I was pregnant with you, he would have turned his back on his dream for us. I didn't want him to do that. I loved him too much. So, without telling him I was pregnant with you, I left town. So he never knew about you, AJ."

Shelly sighed. Everything she'd just told AJ was basically true. However, this next part would be a lie; a lie Dare was convinced AJ needed to believe. "Your father still doesn't know about you, and this is where I need your help."

AJ looked confused. "My help about what?"

"About what I should do." When his confusion didn't clear she said, "Since we moved back, I found out your father is still living here in College Park."

She could tell AJ was momentarily taken aback by what she'd said. He stared at her with wide, expressive eyes. "He's here? In this town?" he asked in a somewhat shaky yet excited voice.

"Yes. It seems that he moved back a few years ago after he stopped working for the FBI in Washington, D.C." Shelly leaned back in her chair. "I want to be fair to the both of you. You're getting older and so is he. I think it's time that I finally tell him about you, just like I'm telling you about him."

AJ nodded and looked at her and she saw uncertainty in his eyes. "But what if he doesn't want me?"

Shelly smiled and then chuckled. "Trust me, when he finds out about you he will definitely want you. In fact I'm a little concerned about what his reaction will be when he realizes that I've kept your existence from him. He is a man who strongly believes in family and he won't be a happy camper."

"Had he known about me, he would have married you?"

Shelly's smiled widened, knowing that was true. "Yes, in a heartbeat, which is the reason I didn't tell him. And although it's too late for either of us to think of ever having a life together again, because we've lived separate lives for so long, there's no doubt in my mind that once I tell him about you he'll want to become a part of your life. But I need to know how you feel about that."

AJ shrugged. "I'm okay with it, but how do you feel about it, Mom?"

"I'm okay with it, too."

AJ nodded. He then lowered his head as his finger made

designs across the tablecloth. Moments later he lifted his eyes and met her gaze. "So when can I get to meet him?"

Shelly took a deep breath and hoped that her next words sounded normal. "You've already met your father, AJ. You met him yesterday."

She inhaled deeply then broke it down further by saying, "Sheriff Dare Westmoreland is your father."

Chapter 5

"Sheriff Westmoreland!" AJ shouted as he jumped out of his seat. He stood in front of his mother and lifted his chin angrily, defiantly. "It can't be him. No way."

Shelly smiled slightly. "Trust me, it *is* him. I of all people should know."

"But—but, I don't want *him* to be my father," he huffed loudly.

Shelly looked directly at AJ, at how badly he was taking the news, which really wasn't unexpected, considering the way he and Dare had clashed. "I'm sorry you feel that way because he is and there's nothing you can do about it. Alisdare Julian Westmoreland *is* your father."

When she saw the look that crossed his face, she added. "And I didn't make up that part, either. You really were named after him, AJ. He merely shortens the Alisdare to Dare."

She felt AJ's need to deny what she'd just told him, but there was no way she could let him do that. "The question is, now that you know he's your father, what are we going to do about it?"

She watched his forehead scrunch into a frown, then he said, "We don't have to do anything about it since he doesn't have to know. We can continue with things the way they are."

She lifted a brow. "Don't you think he has every right to know about you?"

"Not if I don't want him to know."

Shelly shook her head. "Dare will be very hurt if he ever learns the truth." She studied her son. "Can you give me a good reason why he shouldn't be told?"

"Yes, because he doesn't like me and I don't like him."

Shelly met his gaze. "With your disrespectful attitude, you probably didn't make a good impression on him yesterday, AJ. However, Dare loves kids. And as far as you not liking him, you really don't know him, and I think you should get to know him. He's really a nice guy, otherwise I would not have fallen in love with him all those years ago." A small voice whispered that that part was true. Dare had always been a caring and loving person. "How did things go between the two of you today?"

AJ shrugged. "We still don't like each other, and I don't want to get to know him. So please don't tell him, Mom. You can't."

She paused for a moment knowing what she would say, knowing she would not press him anymore. "All right, AJ, since you feel so strongly about it, I won't tell him. But I'm hoping that one day *you* will be the one to tell him. I'm hoping that one day you'll see the importance of him knowing the truth."

She stood and walked over to AJ and placed her hand on his shoulder. "There's something else you need to think about."

"What?"

"Dare is a very smart man. Chances are he'll figure things out without either one of us telling him anything."

He frowned and his eyes grew round. "How?"

Shelly smiled. "You favor him and his four brothers. Although he hasn't noticed it yet, there's a good chance that he will. And then there's the question of your age. He knows I left town ten years ago, the same year you were born."

AJ nodded. "Did he ask you anything when you saw him yesterday?"

"No. I think he assumes your father is someone I met after leaving here, but as I said, there's a chance he might start putting two and two together."

AJ's features drew in a deeper frown at the thought of that happening. "But we can't let him figure it out."

She shook her head. Shelly hated lying to AJ although she knew it was for a good reason. She had to remember that. "Whoa. Don't include me in this, AJ. It's strictly your decision not to let Dare know about you, it isn't mine. I'm already in hot water for not having told him that you exist at all. But I'll keep my word and not tell him anything if that's the way you want it."

"Yes, that's the way I want it," AJ said, not hiding the relief on his face.

His lips were quivering, and Shelly knew he was fighting hard to keep his tears at bay. Right now he was feeling torn. A part of him wanted to be elated that his father did exist, but another part refused to accept the man who he'd discovered his father was, all because of that Westmoreland pride and stubbornness.

Shelly shook her head when she felt tears in the back of her own eyes. Dare's mission to win his son's love would not be easy.

Later that night, after AJ had gone to bed Shelly received a phone call from Dare.

"Did you tell him?"

She leaned against her kitchen sink. "Yes, I told him."

There was a pause. "And how did he take it?"

Shelly released a deep sigh. "Just as we expected. He doesn't want you to know that he's your son." When Dare didn't respond, she said, "Don't take it personally, Dare. I think he's more confused than anything right now. Tonight I discovered why he had stopped asking me about you."

"Why?"

"Because he didn't really believe you existed, at least not the way I'd told him. It seems that a friend of his had shared with him the fact that his mother had told him his father had died in a car accident when he was a baby, and then he'd discovered that his father was alive and well and living somewhere with another family. So AJ assumed what I had told him about you wasn't true and that I really didn't know how to contact you if he ever asked me to. And since he never wanted to place me in a position that showed me up as a liar, he just never bothered."

Again she released a sigh as she fought back the tears that threaten to fall. "And to think that he probably did want to know you all this time but refrained from asking to save me embarrassment in being caught in a lie."

A sob caught in her throat as she blinked back a tear. "Oh, Dare, I feel so bad for him, and what he's going through is all my fault. I thought I was making all the right decisions for all the right reasons and now it seems I caused more harm than good."

Dare lay in bed, his entire body tense. He could no longer hold back the anger he felt for Shelly, even knowing he had made a couple of mistakes himself in handling things ten years ago. Had he not chosen a career over her then, things would have worked out a whole lot differently. So, in reality, he was just as much to blame as Shelly, but together they had a chance to make things work to save their son.

"Things are going to work out in the end, Shell, you'll see. You've done your part tonight, now let me handle things from here. It might take months, but in the end I believe that AJ will accept me as his father. In my heart I believe that one day he'll want me to know the truth."

Shelly nodded, hearing the confidence in Dare's voice and hoping he was right. "So now we move to the second phase of your plan?"

"Now we move to the second phase of *our* plan."

The next morning, after AJ had left for school, a gentle knock on the door alerted Shelly that she had a visitor. Today was her day off and she had spent the last half hour or so on the computer paying her bills online, and was just about to walk into the kitchen for a cup of coffee.

Crossing the living room she glanced out of the peephole. Her breath caught. Dare was standing on her porch, and his tall, muscular frame was silhouetted by the mid-morning sunlight that was shining brightly behind him. He looked gorgeous; his uniform, which showcased his solid chest, firm stomach and strong flanks, made him look even more so.

She shivered as everything about her that was woman jolted upward from the soles of her feet, to settle in an area between her legs. She inhaled and commanded her body not to go there. Whatever had been between her and Dare had ended ten years ago, and now was not the time for her body to go horny on her. She'd done without sex for this long, and she could continue to go without it for a while longer. But damn if Dare Westmoreland didn't rattle and stir up those urges she'd kept dormant for ten years. She couldn't for the life of her forget how it had felt to run her hands over his chest, indulging in the crisp feel of his hair and the masculine texture of his skin.

She closed her eyes and took a deep breath at the memory of his firm stomach rubbing against her own and the feel of his calloused palm touching her intimately on the sensitive areas of her body. She remembered him awakening within her a passion that had almost startled her.

His second knock made her regain her mental balance, and warning signals against opening the door suddenly went off in her head as she opened her eyes. A silent voice reminded her that although she might want to, there was no way to put as much distance between herself and Dare as she'd like. No matter how much being around him got to her, their main concern was their son.

Inhaling deeply, she slowly opened the door and met his gaze. Once again she felt every sexual instinct she possessed spring to life. "Dare, what are you doing here?" she asked, pausing afterwards to take a deep, steadying breath.

He smiled, that enticingly sexy smile that always made her want to go to the nearest bed and get it on with him. There was no way she couldn't see him and not think of crawling into bed next to him amidst rumpled sheets while he reached out and took her into his arms and…

"I tried calling you at the agency where you worked and

they told me you were off today," he said as he leaned in her doorway, breaking into her wayward thoughts and sending her already sex-crazed mind into turmoil. Why did he still look so good after ten years? And why on earth was her body responding to the sheer essence of him this way? But then she and Dare always had had an abundant amount of overzealous hormones and it seemed that ten years hadn't done a thing to change that.

"Why were you trying to reach me?" she somehow found her voice to ask him. "Is something wrong?"

He shook his head, immediately putting her fears to rest. "No, but I thought it would be a good idea if we talked."

Shelly's eyebrows raised. "Talk? But we talked yesterday morning at Kate's Diner and again last night. What do we have to talk about now?" she asked, trying not to sound as frustrated as she felt.

"I thought you'd like to know how my meeting went with Jared yesterday."

"Oh." She had completely forgotten about his plans to meet with his attorney cousin for lunch. She'd always liked his cousin Jared Westmoreland, who, over the years, had become something of a hotshot attorney. "I would." She took a step back as she fought to remain composed. "Come in."

He stepped inside and closed the door behind him and then glanced around. "It's been years since I've been inside this house. It brings back memories," Dare said meeting her gaze once again.

She nodded, remembering how he used to stand in that same spot countless times as he waited for her to come down the stairs for their dates. And even then, when she breezed down the stairs her mind was filled with thoughts of their evening, especially how it would finish. "Yes, it does."

A long, seemingly endless moment of silence stretched between them before she finally cleared her throat. "I was about to have a cup of coffee and a Danish if you'd like to join me," she offered.

"That's a pretty tempting offer, one that I think I'll take you up on."

Shelly nodded. If he thought *that* was tempting he really didn't know what tempting was about. *Tempting* was Dare Westmoreland standing in the middle of her living room looking absolutely gorgeous. And it didn't help matters one iota when she glanced his way and saw a definite bulge behind his fly. Apparently he was just as hot and bothered as she was.

She quickly turned around. "Follow me," she said over her shoulder, wondering how she was going to handle being alone in the house with him.

Following Shelly was the last thing Dare thought he needed to do. He tried not to focus on the sway of the backside encased in denim shorts in front of him. He was suddenly besieged with memories of just how that backside had felt in his hands when he'd lifted it to thrust inside her. Those thoughts made his arousal harden even more. He suppressed a groan deep in his throat.

He tried to think of other things and glanced around. He liked the way she had decorated the place, totally different from the way her parents used to have it. Her mother's taste had been soft and quaint. Shelly's taste made a bold statement. She liked colors—bright cheery colors—evident in the vivid print of the sofa, loveseat and wingback chair. Then there were her walls, painted in a variety of colorful shades, so different from his plain off-white ones. He was amazed how she was able to tie everything together without anything clashing. She had managed to create a cozy and homey atmosphere for herself and AJ.

As they entered the kitchen, Dare quickly sat down at the table before she could note the fix his body was in, if she hadn't done so already. But he soon discovered that sitting at the table watching her move around the kitchen only intensified his problem. He was getting even more turned on by the fluid movements of her body as she reached into a cabinet to get their coffee cups. The shorts were snug, a perfect fit, and his entire body began throbbing in deep male appreciation.

"You still like your coffee black and your Danish with a lot of butter, Dare?"

"Yes," he managed to respond. He began to realize that he had made a mistake in dropping by. Over the past couple of days when they'd been together there had been other people around. Now it was just the two of them, alone in this house, in this room. He had to fight hard to dismiss the thought of taking her right there on the table.

He inhaled deeply. If Shelly knew what thoughts were running through his mind she would probably hightail it up the stairs, which wouldn't do her any good since he would only race up those same stairs after her and end up making love to her in one of the bedrooms.

That was something they had done once before when her parents had been out of town and he had dropped by unexpectedly. A slow, lazy smile touched the side of his mouth as he remembered the intensity of their lovemaking that day. That was the one time they hadn't used protection. Perhaps that was the time she had gotten pregnant with AJ?

"What are you smiling about?"

Her question invaded his thoughts and he shifted in the chair to alleviate some of the tension pressing at the zipper of his pants. He met her gaze and decided to be completely honest with her, something he had always done. "I was thinking about that time that we made love upstairs in your bedroom without protection, and wondered if that was the time you got pregnant."

"It was."

He regarded her for a second. "How do you know?"

She stared at the floor for a moment before meeting his gaze again. "Because after that was the first time I'd ever been late."

He nodded. The reason they had made love so recklessly and intensely that day was because he had received orders a few hours earlier to leave immediately for an area near Kuwait. It was a temporary assignment and he would only be gone for two months. But at the time, two months could have been two years for all she cared. Because of the danger of his assignment, the news had immediately sent her in a spin and she had raced up the stairs to her bedroom so he wouldn't see her cry. He had gone after her, only to end up placing her on the bed and making frantic, uncontrolled love to her.

"What did Jared have to say yesterday?" Shelly asked him rather than think about that particular day when they had unknowingly created their son. Straightening, she walked over to the table and placed the coffee and rolls in front of him, then sat down at the table.

He took a sip of coffee and responded, "Jared thinks that whatever we decide is the best way to handle letting AJ know I'm his father is fine as long as we're in agreement. But he strongly thinks I should do whatever needs to be done to compensate you from the time he was born. And I agree. As his father I had certain responsibilities to him."

"But you didn't know about him, Dare."

"But I know about him now, Shelly, and that makes a world of difference."

Shelly nodded. She knew that to argue with Dare would be a complete waste of her time. "All right, I have a college fund set up and if you'd like to contribute, I have no problem with that. That is definitely one way you can help."

Dare leaned back in his chair and met her gaze. "Are you sure there's no other way I can help?"

For a moment she wondered if he was asking for AJ or for her. Could he detect the deep longing within her, the sexual cravings, and knew he could help her there? She sighed, knowing she was letting her mind become cluttered. AJ was the only thing between them, and she had to remember that.

"Yes, I'm sure," she said softly. "My job pays well and I've always budgeted to live within my means. The cost of living isn't as high here as it is in L.A., and my parents aren't charging me any rent, so AJ and I are fine, Dare, but thanks for asking."

At that moment the telephone rang; she hoped he didn't see the relief on her face. "Excuse me," she said, standing quickly. "That's probably the agency calling to let me know my hours and clients for next week."

As Shelly listened to the agency's secretary tell her what her schedule would be for the following week, she tried to get her thoughts back together. Dare had stirred up emotions and needs that she'd thought were dead and buried until she'd seen him two days ago. His presence had blood racing through her body at an alarming speed.

"All right, thanks for calling," she said before hanging up the phone. She quickly turned and bumped into a massive solid chest. "Oh."

Dare reached out and quickly stopped Shelly from falling.

"Sorry, I didn't mean to scare you," he said, his words soft and gentle.

She took a step back when he released her. Each time he touched her she was reminded of the sensual feelings he could easily invoke. "I thought you were still sitting down."

"I thought it was time for me to leave. I don't want to take you from your work any longer."

She rubbed her hands across her arms, knowing it was best if he left. "Is that all Jared said?"

He nodded. That was all she needed to know. There was no need to tell her that Jared had suggested the possibility of him having legal visitation rights and petitioning for joint custody of AJ. Both suggestions he had squashed, since he and Shelly had devised what they considered a workable plan.

His gaze moved to her hands and he watched her fingers sliding back and forth across her arms. He remembered her doing that very thing on a certain part of his anatomy several times. The memory of the warmth of her fingers touching him so intimately slammed another arousal through his body that strengthened the one already there.

At that moment, he lost whatever control he had. Being around her stirred up memories and emotions he could no longer fight, nor did he want to. The only thing he wanted, he needed, was to kiss her, taste her and reacquaint the insides of his mouth, his tongue, with hers.

Shelly was having issues of her own and took a steadying breath, trying to get the heated desire racing through her body under control. She swallowed deeply when she saw that Dare's gaze was dead-centered on her mouth, and fought off the panic that seized her when he took a step forward.

"I wonder…" he said huskily, his gaze not leaving her lips.

She blinked, refocused on him. "You wonder about

what?" she asked softly, feeling the last shreds of her composure slipping.

"I wonder if your mouth still knows me."

His words cut through any control she had left. Those were the words he had always whispered whenever they were together after being apart for any length of time, just moments before he took her into his arms and kissed her senseless.

He leaned in closer, then lowered his mouth to hers. Immediately, his tongue went after hers in an attempt to lure her into the same rush of desire consuming him. But she was already there, a step ahead of him, so he tried forcing his body to calm down and settle into the taste he'd always been accustomed to. He had expected heat, but he hadn't expected the hot, fiery explosion that went off in his midsection. It made a groan erupt from deep in his throat.

His hands linked around her waist to hold her closer, thigh-to-thigh, breasts to chest. Sensation after sensation speared through him, making it hard to resist eating her alive, or at least trying to, and wanting to touch her everywhere, especially between her legs. Now that he had rediscovered this— the taste of her mouth—he wanted also to relive the feel of his fingers sliding over her heated flesh to find the hot core of her, swollen and wet.

That thought drove a primitive need through him and the erection pressing against her got longer and harder. The thought of using it to penetrate the very core of her made his mind reel and drugged his brain even more with her sensuality.

A shiver raced over Shelly and a semblance of control returned as she realized just how easily she had succumbed to his touch. She knew she had to put a halt to what they were doing. She had returned to College Park not for herself but for AJ.

She broke off their kiss and untangled herself from his arms. When he leaned toward her, to kiss her again, she pushed him back. "No, Dare," she said firmly. "We shouldn't have done that. This isn't about you or me or our inability to control overzealous hormones. It's about our son and doing what is best for him."

And why can't we simultaneously discover what is best for us, he wanted to ask but refrained from doing so. He understood her need to put AJ first and foremost, but what she would soon realize was that there was unfinished business between them as well. "I agree that AJ is our main concern, Shelly, but there's something you need to realize and accept."

"What?"

"Things aren't over between us, and we shouldn't deceive ourselves into thinking there won't be a next time, so be prepared for it."

He saw the frown that appeared in her eyes and the defiance that tilted her lips reminded him of AJ yesterday and the day before. "No, Dare, there won't be a next time because I won't let there be. You're AJ's father, but what was between us is over and has been for years. To me you're just another man."

He lifted a brow. He wondered if she had kissed many men the way she'd kissed him, and for some reason he doubted it. She had kissed him as though she hadn't kissed anyone in years. He had felt the hunger that had raged through her. He had felt it, explored it and, for the moment, satisfied it. "You're sure about that?"

"Yes, I'm positive, so I suggest you place all your concentration on winning your son over and forget about your son's mother."

As he turned to cross the room to leave, he knew that he would never be able to forget about his son's mother, not in a million years. Before walking out the door he looked back at her. "Oh, yeah, I almost forgot something."

She lifted a brow. "What?"

"The brothers four. They're dying to see you. I told them of our plans for AJ and they agreed to be patient about seeing him, but they refuse to be patient about seeing you, Shelly. They want to know if you'll meet them for lunch one day this week at Chase's restaurant in downtown Atlanta?"

She smiled. She wanted to see them as well. Dare's brothers had always been special to her. "Tell them I'd love to have lunch with them tomorrow since I'll be working in that area."

Dare nodded, then turned and walked out the door.

AJ saw the two boys standing next to his bike the moment he walked out the school door. Since his bike was locked, he wasn't worried about the pair taking it, but after his fight with Caleb Martin yesterday the last thing he wanted was trouble. Especially after the talks the sheriff and his mother had given him.

The sheriff.

He shook his head, not wanting to think about the fact that the sheriff was his father. But he had thought about it most of the day, and still, as he'd told his mother last night, he didn't want the sheriff to know he was his son.

"What are you two looking at?" he asked in a tough voice, ignoring the fact that one of the boys was a lot bigger than he was.

"Your bike," the smaller of the two said, turning to him. "We think it's cool. Where did you get it?"

AJ relaxed. He thought his bike was cool, too. "Not from any place around here. My mom bought it for me in California."

"Is that where you're from?" the largest boy asked.

"Yeah, L.A. That's where I was born, and I hope we move

back there." He sized up the two and decided they were harmless. He had seen them before around school, but neither had made an attempt to be friendly to him until now. "My name is AJ Brockman. What's yours?"

"My name is Morris Sears," the smaller of the two said, "and this is my friend Cornelius Thomas."

AJ nodded. "Do you live around here?"

"Yeah, just a few blocks, not far from Kate's Diner."

"I live just a few blocks from Kate's Diner, too, on Sycamore Street," AJ said, glad to know there were other kids living not far away.

"We saw what happened with you and Caleb Martin yesterday," Morris said, his eyes widening. "Boy! Did you teach him a lesson! No one has ever done that before and we're glad, since he's been messing with people for a long time for no reason. He's nothing but a bully."

AJ nodded, agreeing with them.

"Would you like to ride home with us today?" Cornelius asked, getting on his own bike. "We know a shortcut that goes through the Millers' land. We saw a couple of deer on their property yesterday."

AJ's eyes lit up. He'd never seen a deer before, at least not a real live one. He then remembered where he had to go after school. "I'm sorry but today I can't. I have to report directly to the sheriff's office now."

"For fighting yesterday?" Morris asked.

AJ shook his head. "No, for cutting school two days ago. I was throwing rocks at cars and the sheriff caught me and took me in."

Cornelius eyes widened. "You got to ride in the back of Sheriff Westmoreland's car?" he asked excitedly.

AJ raised a brow. "Yes."

"Boy, that's cool. Sheriff Westmoreland is a hero."

AJ gave a snort of laughter. "A hero? And what makes him a hero? He's nothing but a sheriff who probably does nothing but sit in his office all day."

Morris and Cornelius shook their head simultaneously.

"Not Sheriff Westmoreland," Morris said as if he knew that for a fact. "He was in all the newspapers last week for catching those two bad guys the FBI has been looking for. My dad says Sheriff Westmoreland got shot at bringing them in and that a bullet barely missed his head."

"Yeah, and my dad said," Cornelius piped in, "that those bad guys didn't know who they were messing with, since everyone knows the sheriff doesn't play. Why, he used to even be an FBI agent. My dad went to school with him and graduated the same year Thorn Westmoreland did."

AJ looked curiously at Cornelius. "What does Thorn Westmoreland have to do with anything?"

Cornelius lifted a shocked brow. "Don't you know who Thorn Westmoreland is?"

Of course AJ knew who Thorn Westmoreland was. What kid didn't? "Sure. He's the motorcycle racer who builds the baddest bikes on earth."

Cornelius and Morris nodded. "He's also the sheriff's brother," Morris said grinning, happy to be sharing such news with their new friend. "And have you ever heard of Rock Mason?"

"The man who writes those adventure-thriller books?" AJ asked, his mind still reeling from what he'd just been told— Thorn Westmoreland was the sheriff's brother!

"Yes, but Rock Mason's real name is Stone Westmoreland and he's the sheriff's brother, too. Then there are two more of them, Chase and Storm Westmoreland. Mr. Chase owns a big restaurant downtown and Mr. Storm is a fireman."

AJ nodded. He wondered how Morris and Cornelius knew so much about a family that he was supposed to be a part of, yet he didn't know a thing about.

"And I forgot to mention that their sister married a prince from one of those faraway countries," Morris added, interrupting AJ's thoughts.

"How do you two know so much about the Westmorelands?" AJ asked, wrinkling his forehead.

"Because the sheriff coaches our Little League team and his brothers often help out."

"The sheriff coaches a baseball team?" AJ asked, thinking now he'd heard just about everything. The only time the people in L.A. saw the sheriff was when something bad happened and he was needed to make a statement on TV.

"Yes, and we're on the team and bring home the trophies every year. If you're good he might let you join."

AJ shrugged, not wanting to be around the sheriff any more than he had to. "No thanks, I don't want to join," he said. "Well, I've got to go, since I can't be late."

"How long do you have to go there?" Morris asked, standing aside to let AJ get to his bike.

"The rest of the week, so I'll be free to ride home with you guys starting Monday if you still want me to," AJ said, getting on his bike.

"Yes," Cornelius answered. "We'll still want you to. What about this weekend? Will your parents let you go look at the deer with us this weekend? Usually Mr. Miller gives his permission for us to come on his property as long as we don't get into any trouble."

AJ was doubtful. "I'll let you know tomorrow if I can go. My mom is kind of protective. She doesn't like me going too far from home."

Morris and Cornelius nodded in understanding. "Our moms are that way, too," Morris said. "But everyone around here knows the Millers. Your mom can ask the sheriff about them if she wants. They're nice people."

"Do you want to ride to school with us tomorrow?" Cornelius asked anxiously. "We meet at Kate's Diner every morning at seven-thirty, and she gives us a carton of chocolate milk free as long as we're good in school."

"Free chocolate milk? Hey, I'd like that. I'll see you guys in the morning." AJ put his bike into gear and headed for the sheriff's office, determined not to be late for a second time.

Chapter 6

Her mouth still knew him.

A multitude of emotions tightened Dare's chest as he sat at his desk and thought about the kiss he and Shelly had shared. Very slowly and very deliberately, he took his finger and rubbed it across his lips, lips that a few hours ago had tasted sweetness of the most gut-wrenching kind. It was the kind of sweetness that made you crave something so delightful and pleasurable that it could become habit forming.

But what got to him more than anything was the fact that even after ten years, her mouth still knew him. That much was evident in the way her lips had molded to his, the familiarity of the way she had parted her mouth and the ease in which his tongue had slid inside, staking a claim he hadn't known he had a right to make until he had felt her response.

He leaned back in the chair. When it came to responding

to him, that was something Shelly could never hold back from doing. He'd always gotten the greatest pleasure and enjoyment from hearing the sound of her purring in bed. He used to know just what areas on her body to touch, to caress and to taste. Often, all it took was a look, him simply meeting her gaze with deep desire and longing in his eyes, and she would release an indrawn sigh that let him know she knew just what he wanted and what he considered necessary. Those had been the times he hadn't been able to keep his hands off her, and now it seemed, ten years later, he still couldn't. And it didn't help matters any that she had kissed him as though there hadn't been another man inside her mouth in the ten years they'd been apart. Her mouth had ached for his, demanded everything his tongue could deliver, and he'd given it all, holding nothing back. He could have kept on kissing her for days.

Dare ran his hand over his face trying to see if doing so would help him retain his senses. Kissing Shelly had affected him greatly. His body had been aching and throbbing since then, and the painful thing was that he didn't see any relief in sight.

Over the past ten years he had dated a number of women. His sister Delaney had even painted him and his brothers as womanizers. But he felt that was as far from the truth as it could be. After he and Shelly had broken up, he'd been very selective about what women he wanted in his bed. For years he had looked for Shelly's replacement, only to discover such a woman didn't exist. He hadn't met a woman who would hold a light to her, and he'd accepted that and moved on. The women he'd slept with had been there for the thrill, the adventure, but all he'd gotten was the agony of defeat upon realizing that none could make him feel in bed the way he'd always felt with Shelly. Oh, he had experienced pleasure, but not the kind that made you pound your chest with your fists and holler out for more. Not the kind that compelled you to go ahead and remain inside her body since another orgasm was there on the horizon. And not the kind you could still shudder from days later, just thinking about it.

He could only get those feelings with Shelly.

Closing his eyes, Dare remembered how she had broken off their kiss and the words she'd said before he'd left her house. *"You're AJ's father, but what was between us is over and has been for years. To me you're just another man."*

He sighed deeply and reopened his eyes. If Shelly believed that then she was wrong. Granted, AJ was their main concern, but what she didn't know and what he wouldn't tell her just yet was that his mission also included her. He hadn't realized until she had walked into his office two days ago that his life had been without direction for ten years. Seeing her, finding out about AJ and knowing that he and Shelly were still attracted to each other made him want something he thought he would never have again.

Peace and happiness.

The buzzer interrupted his thoughts. Leaning forward he pushed the button for the speakerphone. "Yeah, Holly, what is it?"

"That Brockman kid is here, Sheriff. Do you want me to send him in?"

Dare again sighed deeply. "Yes, send him in."

Dare felt AJ watching him. The kid had been doing so off and on since he'd finished the chores he'd been assigned and had come into his office to sit at a table in the corner and finish his homework.

Dare had sat behind his desk, reading over various reports.

The only sound in the room was AJ turning the pages of his science book and Dare shuffling the pages of the report. More than once Dare had glanced up and caught the kid looking at him, as if he were a puzzle he was trying to figure out. As soon as he'd been caught staring, the kid had quickly lowered his eyes.

Dare wondered what was going through AJ's mind now that he knew he was his father? The only reason Dare could come up with as to why he'd been studying him so intently was that he was trying to find similarities in their features. They were there. Even Holly had noticed them, although she hadn't said anything, merely moving her gaze between Dare and AJ several times before comprehension appeared on her face.

Dare glanced up and caught AJ staring again and decided to address the issue. "Is something wrong?" he asked.

AJ glanced up from his science book and glared at him. "What makes you think something is wrong?"

Dare shrugged. "Because I've caught you staring several times today like I've suddenly grown two heads or something."

He saw the corners of AJ lips being forced not to smile. "I hate being here. Why couldn't I just go home after I finished everything I had to do instead of hanging around here?"

"Because your punishment was to come here for an hour after school and I intend to get my hour. Besides, if I let you leave earlier, you might think I'm turning soft."

"That will be the day," AJ mumbled.

Dare chuckled and went back to reading his reports.

"Is Thorn Westmoreland really your brother?"

Dare lifted his head and gazed back across the room at AJ. My brother and your uncle, he wanted to say. Instead he responded by asking, "Who told you that?"

AJ shrugged. "Morris and Cornelius."

Dare nodded. He knew Morris and Cornelius. The two youngsters usually hung together and were the same age and went to the same school as AJ. "So you know Morris and Cornelius?"

AJ turned the page on his book before answering, pretending the response was being forced from him. "Yeah, I know them. We met today after school."

Dare nodded again. Morris and Cornelius were good kids. He knew their parents well and was glad the pair were developing a friendship with AJ, since he considered them a good influence. Both got good grades in school, sung in the youth choir at church and were active in a number of sports he and his brothers coached.

"Well, is he?"

Dare heard the anxiousness in AJ's voice, although the kid was trying to downplay it. "Yes, Thorn's my brother."

"And Rock Mason is, too?"

"Yes. I told you the other day I had four brothers and all of them live in this area."

AJ nodded. "And they help you coach your baseball team?"

Dare leaned back in his chair. "Yes, pretty much, although Thorn contributes to the youth of the community by teaching a special class at the high school on motorcycle safety and Stone is involved with the Teach People to Read program for both the young and old."

AJ nodded again. "What about the other two?"

Dare wondered at what point AJ would discover they were holding a conversation and revert back to his I-don't-like-cops syndrome? Well, until he did, Dare planned to milk the situation for all it was worth. "Chase owns a restaurant and coaches a youth basketball team during basketball season. His team won the state championship two years in a row."

Dare smiled when he thought of his younger brother Storm. "My youngest brother Storm hasn't found his niche yet." Other than with women, Dare decided not to add. "So he helps me coach my baseball team and he also helps Chase with his basketball team."

"And your sister married a prince?"

Dare's smile widened when he thought of the baby sister he and his brothers simply adored. "Yes, although at the time we weren't ready to give her up."

AJ's eyes grew wider. "Why? Girls don't marry princes every day."

Dare chuckled. "Yes, that may be true, but the Westmorelands have this unspoken code when it comes to family. We stick together and claim what's ours. Since Delaney was the only girl, we claimed her when she was born and weren't ready to give her up to anyone, including a prince."

AJ turned a few pages again, pretending further disinterest. A few moments later he asked, "What about your parents?"

Dare met AJ's stare. "What about them?"

"Do they live around here?"

"Yes, they live within walking distance. Their only complaint is that none of us, other than Delaney, have gotten married. They're anxious for grandkids and since they don't see Delaney's baby that often, they would like one of us to settle down and have a family."

Dare knew that what he'd just shared with AJ would get the kid to thinking. He was about to say something else when the buzzer on his desk sounded.

"Yes, McKade, what is it?"

"Ms. Brockman is here to see you."

Dare was surprised. He hadn't expected Shelly to drop by, since AJ had ridden his bike over from school. A quick glance across the room and he could tell by AJ's features that he was surprised by his mother's unexpected visit as well. "Send her in, McKade."

Dare stood as Shelly breezed into his office, dressed in a skirt and a printed blouse. "I hate to drop in like this, but I received an emergency call from one of my patients living in Stone Mountain and need to go out on a call. Ms. Kate has agreed to take care of AJ, and I have to drop him off at her place on my way out. I thought coming to pick him up would be okay since his hour is over."

Dare glanced at the clock on the wall which indicated AJ's hour had been over ten minutes ago. At some point the kid had stopped watching the clock and so had he.

"Since you're in a rush, I can save you the time by dropping him off at Ms. Kate's myself. I was getting ready to leave anyway."

Dare then remembered that since tonight was Wednesday night, his parents' usual routine was to have dinner with their five sons at Chase's restaurant before going to prayer meeting at church. He knew his family would love meeting AJ, and since they'd been told of his and Shelly's strategy about AJ knowing Dare was his father, there was no risk of someone giving anything away.

"And I have another idea," he said, meeting Shelly's gaze, trying not to notice how beautiful her eyes were, how beautiful she was, period. Just being in the same room with her had his mouth watering. She stood in the middle of his office silhouetted by the light coming in through his window and he thought he hadn't seen anything that looked this good in a long time.

"What?" she asked, interrupting his thoughts.

"AJ is probably hungry and I was on my way to Chase's

restaurant where my family is dining tonight. He's welcome to join us, and I can drop him off at Ms. Kate's later."

Shelly nodded. Evidently Dare felt he'd made some headway with AJ for him to suggest such a thing. She glanced across the room at AJ who had his eyes glued to his book, pretending not have heard Dare's comment, although she knew that he had.

"AJ, Dare has invited you to dine with his family before dropping you off at Ms. Kate's. All right?"

It seemed AJ stared at her for an endless moment, as if weighing her words. He then shifted his gaze to Dare, and Shelly felt the sudden clash of two very strong personalities, two strong-willed individuals, two people who were outright stubborn. But then she saw something else, something that made her breath catch and her heart do a flip—two individuals who, for whatever reason, were silently agreeing to a give a little, at least for this one particular time.

AJ then shifted his gaze back to her. He shrugged. "Whatever."

Shelly let out a deep sigh. "Okay, then, I'll see you later." She walked across the room to place a kiss on AJ's forehead; ignoring the frown he gave her. "Behave yourself tonight," she admonished.

She turned and smiled at Dare before walking out of his office.

"The only reason I decided to come with you is because I want to meet Thorn Westmoreland. I think he is so cool," AJ said, and then turned his attention back to the scenery outside the vehicle's window.

Instead of using the police cruiser, Dare had decided to drive his truck instead, the Chevy Avalanche he'd purchased a month ago. He glanced over at AJ when he brought the vehicle to a stop at a traffic light. He couldn't help but chuckle. "I figured as much, but you won't be the first kid who tried getting on my good side just to meet Thorn."

AJ scowled. "I'm not trying to get on your good side," he mumbled.

Dare chuckled again. "Oh, sorry. My mistake."

For the next couple of miles the inside of the vehicle was quiet as Dare navigated through evening traffic with complete ease.

"So, how was your day at school?" Dare decided to ask when the vehicle finally came to a complete standstill as he attempted to get on the interstate.

AJ glanced over at him. "It had its moments."

Dare smiled. "What kind of moments?"

AJ glared. "Why are you asking me all these questions?"

Dare met his gaze. "Because I'm interested."

AJ's glare deepened. "Are you interested in me or in my mother? I saw the way you were looking at her."

Dare decided the kid was too observant, although he was falling in nicely with their plans. "And what way was I looking at her?"

"One of those man-like-woman looks."

Dare chuckled, never having heard it phrased quite that way before. "What do you know about a man-like-woman look?"

"I wasn't born yesterday."

"Not for one minute did I think you had been." After a few moments he glanced back at AJ. "Did you know your mom used to be my girlfriend some years back?"

"So?"

"So, I thought you should know."

"Why?"

"Because she was very special to me then."

When Dare exited off the interstate, AJ spoke. "That was back then. My mother doesn't need a boyfriend, if that's what you're thinking."

Dare gave his son a smile when he brought the vehicle to a stop at a traffic light. "What I think, AJ, is that you should let your mom make her own decisions about those kinds of things."

AJ glared at him. "I don't like you."

Dare shrugged and gave his son a smile. "Then I guess that means nothing has changed." But he knew something *had* changed. As far as he was concerned, AJ consenting to go to dinner with him to meet his family was a major breakthrough. And although the kid claimed that Thorn was the only reason he was going, Dare had no problem using his brother to his advantage if that's what it took. Besides, AJ would soon discover that of all the Westmorelands, Thorn was the one who was biggest on family ties and devotion, and if you accepted one Westmoreland, you basically accepted them all, since they were just that thick.

At that moment Dare's cell phone rang and he answered it. After a few remarks and nods of his head, he said, "You're welcome to join us for dinner if you'd like. I know for a fact that everyone would love to see you." He nodded again and said, "All right. I'll see you later.

Moments later he glanced over at AJ when they came to a stop in front of Chase's restaurant. "That was your mother. The emergency wasn't as bad as she'd thought, and she is on her way back home. I'm to take you there after dinner instead of to Ms. Kate's house."

AJ narrowed his eyes at Dare. "Why did you do that?"

"Do what?" Dare asked, lifting a brow.

"Invite her to dinner?"

"Because I figured that like you, she has to eat sometime, and I know that my family would have loved seeing her again." He hesitated for a few moments, then added, "And I would have liked seeing her again myself. Like I said, your mom used to mean a lot to me a long time ago."

Their gazes locked for a brief moment, then AJ glared at him and said angrily, "Get over it."

Dare smiled slightly. "I don't know if I can." Before AJ had time to make a comeback, Dare unsnapped his seat belt. "Come on, it's time to go inside."

Shelly pulled onto the interstate, hoping and praying that AJ was on his best behavior. No matter what, she had to believe that all the lessons in obedience, honor and respect that he'd been taught at an early age were somewhere buried beneath all that hostility he exhibited at times. But right now she had to cope with the fact that he was still a child, a child who was getting older each day and enduring growing pains of the worst kind. But one thing was for certain, Dare was capable of dealing with it, and for that she was grateful.

When she thought of Dare, she had no choice but to think of her traitorous body and the way it had responded to him earlier that day at her house. As she'd told AJ, Dare was smart. He was also very receptive, and she knew he had picked up on the fact that she had wanted him. All it had taken was one mindblowing kiss and she'd been ready to get naked if he'd asked.

When she came to a traffic light she momentarily closed her eyes, asking for strength where Dare was concerned. If she allowed him to become a part of her life, she could be asking for potential heartbreak all over again, although she had to admit the new Dare seemed more settled, less likely to go chasing after some other dream. But whatever the two of them had once shared was in the past, and she refused to bring it to the present. She had enough to deal with in handling AJ without trying to take on his father, too.

She had to continue to make it clear to Dare that it was his son he needed to work on and win over and not her. Their first and foremost concern was AJ, and no matter how hot and bothered she got around Dare, she would not give in again. She had to watch her steps and not put any ideas into Dare's head. More than anything, she had to stop looking at him and thinking about sex.

Her body was doing a good job reminding her that ten years was a long time to go without. She'd been too busy for the abstinence to cross her mind, but today Dare had awakened desires she'd thought were long buried. Now she felt that her body was under attack—against her. It was demanding things she had no intention of delivering.

Her breath caught and she felt her nipples tingle as she again thought about the kiss they had shared. Once more she prayed for the strength and fortitude to deal with Alisdare Julian Westmoreland.

Chapter 7

"Dad, Mom, I'd like you to meet AJ. He's Shelly's boy." Dare knew his father wouldn't give anything away, but he wasn't so convinced about his mother as he saw the play of emotions that crossed her features. She was looking into the face of a grandson she hadn't known she'd had; a grandson she was very eager to claim.

Luckily for Dare, his father understood the strategy that he and Shelly were using with AJ and spoke up before his wife had a chance to react to the emotions she was trying to hold inside. "You're a fine-looking young man, but I would expect no less coming from Shelly." He reached out and touched AJ's shoulder and smiled. "I'm glad you're joining us for dinner. How's your mother?"

"She's fine," AJ said quietly, bowing his head and studying his shoes.

Dare wondered what kind of docile act the kid was performing, but then another part of him wondered if when taken out of his comfort zone, AJ had a tendency to feel uneasy around people he didn't know. Dare recalled a conversation he'd had with Shelly about AJ not being all that outgoing.

When Dare saw Thorn enter the restaurant he beckoned him over saying, "Thorn, I'd like you to meet someone. From what I gather, he's a big fan of yours."

AJ's mouth literally fell open and the size of his eyes increased. He tilted his head back to gaze up at the man towering over him. "Wow! You're Thorn Westmoreland!"

Thorn gave a slow grin. "Yes, I'm Thorn Westmoreland. Now who might you be?"

To Dare's surprise, AJ grinned right back. It was the first look of happiness he'd seen on his son's face, and a part of him regretted he hadn't been the one to put it there.

"I'm AJ Brockman."

Thorn tapped his chin with his finger a couple of times as if thinking about something. "Brockman. Brockman. I used to know a Shelly Brockman some years ago. In fact she used to be Dare's girlfriend. Are you related to that Brockman?"

"Yes, I'm her son."

Thorn chuckled. "Well, I'll be," he said, pretending he didn't already know that fact. "And how's your mother?"

"She's fine."

At that moment Dare looked up and saw his other brothers enter. More introductions were made, and, just like Thorn, they pretended they were surprised to see AJ, and no one gave anything away about knowing he was Dare's son.

When they all sat down to eat, with AJ sitting between Thorn and Dare, it was obvious to anyone who cared to notice that the boy was definitely a Westmoreland.

* * *

Shelly put aside the novel she'd been reading when she heard the doorbell ring. A glance out the peephole confirmed it was AJ, but he wasn't alone. Dare had walked him to the door, and with good reason. AJ was half asleep and barely standing on his feet.

She quickly opened the door to AJ's mumblings. "I told you I could walk to the door myself without your help," he was saying none too happily.

"Yeah, and I would have watched you fall on your face, too," was Dare's response.

Shelly stepped aside and let them both enter. "How was dinner?" she asked, closing the door behind them.

AJ didn't answer, instead he continued walking and headed for the stairs. She gave a quick glance to Dare, who was watching AJ as he tried maneuvering the stairs. "That kid is so sleepy he can't think straight," he said. "You might want to help him before he falls and breaks his neck. I would do it, but I think he's had enough of me for one evening."

Shelly nodded, then quickly provided AJ a shoulder to lean on while he climbed the stairs.

Dare moved to stand at the foot of the stairs and watched Shelly and AJ until they were no longer in sight. He sighed deeply, thinking how his adrenaline had pumped up when Shelly had opened the door. She'd been wearing the same outfit she'd worn to his office that evening, and his gaze had been glued to her backside all the while she'd moved up the stairs, totally appreciating the sway of her hips and the way the skirt intermittently slid up her thighs with each upward step she took.

He thought that he would do just about anything to be able to follow right behind her and tumble her straight into bed, but he knew that wasn't possible, especially with AJ in the house. Not to mention the fact that she was still acting rather cautiously around him.

He knew it would probably take her a while to get AJ ready for bed, and since he didn't intend leaving until they had talked, he decided to sit on the sofa and wait for her. He picked up the book she'd been reading, Stone's most recent bestseller, and smiled, thinking it was a coincidence that he was reading the same book.

Making sure he kept the spot where she'd stopped reading marked, he flipped a couple of chapters ahead and picked up where he'd left off last night before sleep had overtaken him.

Shelly paused on the middle stair when she noticed Dare sitting on her sofa reading the book she had begun reading earlier that day. She couldn't help noticing that her living room appeared quiet and seductive, and the light from a floor lamp next to where he sat illuminated his features and created an alluring scene that was too enticing to ignore.

She silently studied him for a long time, wondering just how many peaceful moments he was used to getting as sheriff. He looked comfortable, relaxed and just plain sexy as sin. His features were calm, yet she could tell by the way his eyes were glued to the page that he was deeply absorbed in the action-thriller novel his brother had written.

He shifted in his seat while turning the page and crossed one leg over the other. She knew they were strong legs, sturdy legs, legs that had held her body in place while his had pumped relentlessly into her, legs that had nudged hers apart again when he wanted a second round and a third.

Swallowing at the memory, she felt her heart rate increase, and decided the best way to handle Dare was to send him home—real quicklike. She didn't think she could handle another episode like the one they had shared earlier that day.

He must have heard the sound of her heavy breathing, or maybe she had let out a deep moan without realizing she'd uttered a single word. Something definitely gave her away, and she felt heat pool between her legs when he lifted his gaze from the book and looked at her. It wasn't just an ordinary look either. It was a hot look, a definite scorcher and a blatant, I-want-to-take-you-to-bed look.

She blinked, thinking she had misread the look, but then she knew she hadn't. He wouldn't say the words out loud, but he definitely wanted her to know what he was thinking. She breathed in deeply. Dare was trouble and she was determined to send him packing.

He stood when she took the last few steps down the stairs. "He's out like a light," she said quietly when he came to stand in front of her. "I could barely get him in the shower and in bed without him falling asleep again. Thanks for taking him to dinner and for making sure he got back home."

Shelly paused, knowing she had just said a mouthful, but she wasn't through yet. "I know you've had a busy day today and need your rest as much as I do, so I'll see you out now. In fact you didn't have to wait around for me to finish upstairs."

"Yes, I did."

She stared at him. "Why?"

"I thought you'd want to know how tonight went."

Shelly inwardly groaned. Of course she wanted to know how tonight went, but she'd been so intent on getting Dare out the door she had forgotten to ask. "Yes, of course. Did he behave himself? How did he take to your family?"

Dare glanced up at the top of the stairs then returned his gaze to her. "Is there somewhere we can talk privately?"

The first place Shelly thought about was the kitchen, and then she remembered what had happened between them earlier that day. She decided the best place to talk would be outside on the porch. That way he would definitely be out of the house. "We can talk outside on the porch," she said, moving in that direction.

Without waiting for his response, she took the few steps to the door and stepped outside.

The night air was crisp and clear. The first thing Shelly noticed was the full moon in the sky, and the next was the zillions of stars that sparkled like diamonds surrounding it. She went to stand next to a porch post, since it was the best spot for the glow of light from the moon. The last thing she needed was to stand in some dark area of the porch with Dare.

She heard him behind her when he joined her, however, instead of standing with her in the light, he went and sat in the porch swing that was located in a darkened corner. She sucked in a breath. If he thought for one minute that she would join him in that swing, he had another thought coming. As far as she was concerned, they could converse just fine right where they were.

"So how did AJ behave tonight?" she asked, deciding to plunge right in, since there was no reason to prolong the moment.

She heard the swing's slow rocking when he replied, "To my surprise, very well. In fact, his manners were impeccable, but then it was obvious that he was trying to impress Thorn." Dare chuckled. "He pretty much tried ignoring me, but my brothers picked up on what he was doing and wrecked those plans. Whenever he tried excluding me from the conversation, they counteracted and included me. Pretty soon he gave up, after finding out the hard way an important lesson about the Westmorelands."

"Which is?"

"We stick together, no matter what."

Shelly nodded. She'd known that from previous years.

"But I must admit there was this one time when they were ready to disclaim me as their brother," Dare said, chuckling.

Shelly rested her back against the post and crossed her legs. "And what time was that?"

"The night I ended things with you. They thought I was crazy to give you up for any reason. And that included a career."

She nervously rubbed her hands up and down her arms, not wanting to talk about what used to be between them. "Well, all that's in the past, Dare. Is there anything else about tonight I should know?" she asked, trying to keep their conversation moving along.

"Yes, there is something else."

She sought out his features, but could barely make them out in the darkened corner of the porch. "What?"

"I gave AJ reason to believe that I'm interested in you again."

Shelly nodded. "And how did he handle that?"

Dare smiled. "He had something to say about it, if that's what you're asking. Just how far he'll go to make sure nothing develops between us I can't rightly say."

Shelly nodded again. Neither could she. Personally, she thought AJ's dislike of Dare was a phase he was going through, but a very important phase in his life, and she didn't want to do anything to make things worse with him. "In that case, more than likely he'll have a talk with me about it."

Dare leaned back against the swing. "And what do you plan to say when he does?"

Shelly sighed. "Basically, everything we agreed I should

say. I'm to let him know he's the one who has a beef with you, not me, and therefore I don't have a problem with reestablishing our relationship."

Dare heard her words. Although they were fabricated for AJ's benefit, they sounded pretty damn good to him, and he wished they were true, because he certainly didn't have a problem reestablishing anything with her.

He looked over at Shelly and saw how she leaned against the post while silhouetted by the glow from the moon. His gaze zeroed in on the fact that she stood with her legs crossed. Tight. She had once told him that she had a tendency to stand with her legs crossed really tight whenever she felt a deep throbbing ache between them. Evidently she had forgotten sharing that piece of information with him some years ago.

"Well, if that about covers everything, then we'd best call it a night."

Her words interrupted his thought, and he figured they could do better than just call it a night. Calling it a "night of seduction" sounded more to his liking. Some inner part of him wanted to know if she wanted him as much as he wanted her, and there was only one way to find out.

"Come sit with me for a while, Shelly," he said, his voice husky.

Shelly swallowed and met his gaze. "I don't think that's a good idea, Dare."

"I do. It's a beautiful night and I think we should enjoy it before saying good-night."

Enjoy it or enjoy each other? Shelly was tempted to ask, but decided she wouldn't go there with Dare. Once he got her in that swing that would be the end of it. Or the beginning of it, depending on the way you looked at it. Her body was responding to him in the most unsettled and provocative way tonight. All he had to do was to touch her one time and…

"Let me give you what you need, Shelly."

He saw her chin lift defiantly, and he saw the way she frowned at him. "And what makes you think that you know what I need?"

"Your legs."

She raised a confused brow. "What about my legs?"

"They're crossed, and pretty damn tight."

Shelly's heart missed a beat and the throbbing between her legs increased. He had remembered. A long, seemingly endless moment of silence stretched out between them. She could see his features. They were as tight as her legs were crossed. And the gaze that held hers was like a magnet, drawing her in, second by tantalizing second.

She shook her head, trying to deny her body what it wanted, what it evidently needed, but it had a mind of its own and wasn't adhering to any protest she was making. The man sitting on the swing watching her, waiting for her, had a history of being able to pleasure her in every possible way. He knew it and she knew it as well.

Breathing deeply, she found herself slowly crossing the porch toward him, out of the light and into the darkness, out from temptation and into a straight path that led to seduction. She came to a stop between his spread knees and when their legs touched, she sucked in a deep breath at the same time she heard him suck in one, too. And when she felt his hand reach under her skirt skimming her inner thigh, her knees almost turned to mush.

His voice was husky and ultrasexy when he spoke. "This morning I had to know if your mouth still knew me. Now I want to find out if this," he said, gliding his warm hand upward, boldly touching the crotch of her panties, "knows me as well."

Her eyes fluttered closed and she automatically reached out and placed both hands on his shoulders for support. A part of her wanted to scream Yes! Her body knew him as the last man…the only man…to stake a claim in this territory, but she was incapable of speech. All she could do was stand there and wait to see what would happen next and hope she could handle it.

She didn't have to wait long; the tips of Dare's fingers slowly began massaging the essence of her as he relentlessly stroked his hand over the center of her panties.

"You're hot, Shelly," he said, his voice huskier than before. "Sit down in my lap facing me."

Dare had to move his body forward then sideways for her to accommodate his request. The arrangement brought her face just inches from his. His hand was still between her legs.

He leaned forward and captured her mouth, giving her a kiss that made the one they'd shared that morning seem complacent. Her senses became frenzied and aroused, and the feel of his hand stroking her only added to her turmoil. And when she felt his fingers inch past the edge of her bikini panties, she released a deep moan.

"Yeah, baby, that's the sound I want to hear," he said after releasing her lips. "Open your legs a little wider and tell me how you like this."

Before she could completely comply with his request, he slid three fingers inside her, and when he found that too tight a fit, backed out and went with two. "You're pretty snug in there, baby," he whispered as his fingers began moving in and out of her in a rhythm meant to drive her insane. "How do you like this?"

"I love it," she whispered, clenching his shoulders with her hands. "Oh, Dare, it's been so long."

He leaned closer and traced the tips of her lips with his tongue before moving to nibble at her ear. She was about to go up in smoke, and he couldn't help but wonder how long it had been for her, since this was making her come apart so quickly and easily. He asked, "How long has it been, Shelly?"

She met his gaze and drew in a trembling breath. "Not since you, Dare."

His fingers went still; his jaw tightened and his gaze locked with hers. "You mean that you haven't done this since we…"

She didn't let him finish as she closed her mouth over his, snatching his words and his next breath in the process. But the thought that no other man had touched her since him sent his mind escalating, his entire body trembling. No wonder her legs had been crossed so tightly and he intended to make it good for her.

His fingers began moving inside her again and her muscles automatically clenched around them. She was tight and wet and the scent of her arousal was driving him insane. He broke off the kiss, desperately needing to taste her.

"Unbutton your top, Shelly."

She released her hands from his shoulders and slowly unbuttoned her blouse, then unsnapped the front opening of her bra. As soon as her breasts poured forth, looming before him, he began sucking, nibbling and licking his way to heaven. He moved his fingers within her using the same rhythm his tongue was using on her breasts.

He felt the moment her body shook and placed his mouth over hers to absorb her moans of pleasure when spasms tore into her. Her fingernails dug into his shoulders as he continued using his fingers to pleasure her. And when it started all over again, and more spasms rammed through her, signaling a second orgasm, she pulled her mouth from his, closed her eyes and leaned forward to his chest, crying out into the cotton of his shirt.

"That's it, baby, let go and enjoy."

And as another turbulent wave of pleasure ripped through her and she fought to catch her breath, Shelly let go and enjoyed every single moment of what Dare was doing to her.

And she doubted that after tonight her life would ever be the same.

Chapter 8

"Mom? Mom? Are you okay?"

Shelly heard the sound of AJ's voice as he tried gently to shake her awake.

"Mom, wake up. Please say something."

She quickly opened her eyes when her mind registered the panic in his tone. She blinked, feeling dazed and disoriented, and tried to focus on him, but at the moment she felt completely wrung out. "AJ? What are you doing out of bed?"

Confusion appeared in his face. "Mom, I'm supposed to be out of bed. It's morning and I have to go to school today. You forgot to wake me up. And why did you sleep on the sofa all night in the same clothes you had on yesterday?"

Somehow, Shelly found the strength to sit up. She yawned, feeling bone-tired. "It's morning already?" The last thing she remembered was having her fourth orgasm in Dare's arms and slumping against him without any strength left even to hold up her head. He must have brought her into the house and placed her on the sofa, thinking she would eventually come around and go up the stairs. Instead, exhausted, depleted and totally satisfied, she had slept through the night.

"Mom, are you all right?"

She met AJ's concerned gaze. He had no idea just how all right she was. Dare had given her just what her body had needed. She had forgotten just what an ace he was with his fingers on a certain part of her. "Yes, AJ, I'm fine." She glanced at the coffee table and noticed the book both she and Dare had been reading and considered it the perfect alibi. "I must have fallen asleep reading. What time is it? You aren't late are you?" She leaned back against the sofa's cushions. After a night like last night, she could curl up and sleep for the entire day.

"No, I'm not late, but you might be if you have to go to work today."

Shelly shook her head. "I only have a couple of patients I need to see, and I hadn't planned on going anywhere until around ten." She decided not to mention that she was also having lunch with Dare's brothers today. She yawned again. "What would you like for breakfast?"

He shrugged. "I'll just have a bowl of cereal. I met these two guys at school yesterday and we're meeting up to ride our bikes together."

Shelly nodded. She hoped AJ hadn't associated himself with the wrong group again. "Who are these boys?"

"Morris Sears and Cornelius Thomas. And we're going to meet at Kate's Diner every morning for chocolate milk." As an afterthought he added. "And it's free if we let her know we've been good in school."

Shelly made a mental note to ask Dare about Morris and Cornelius when she saw him again. Being sheriff he probably knew if the two were troublemakers.

"They're real cool guys and they like my bike," AJ went on to say. "Yesterday they told me all about the sheriff and his brothers." His eyes grew wide. "Why didn't you tell me that Thorn Westmoreland is my uncle?"

"Because he's not."

At AJ's confused frown, Shelly decided to explain. "Until you accept Dare as your father you can't claim any of the Westmorelands as your uncles."

AJ glared. "That doesn't seem fair."

"And why doesn't it? You're the one who doesn't want Dare knowing he's your father, so how can you tell anyone that Thorn and the others are your uncles without explaining the connection? Until you decide differently, to the Westmorelands you're just another kid."

She stood. "Now, I'm going upstairs to shower while you eat breakfast."

AJ nodded as he slowly walked out of the room and headed for the kitchen. Shelly knew she had given him something to think about.

"Is it true?" Morris asked excitedly the moment AJ got off his bike at Ms. Kate's Diner.

AJ raised a brow. "Is what true?"

It was Cornelius who answered, his wide, blue eyes expressive. "That you had dinner with the sheriff and his family last night?"

AJ shrugged, wondering how they knew that. "Yeah, so what about it?"

"We think it's cool, that's what about it. The sheriff is the bomb. He makes sure everyone in this town is safe at night. My mom and dad say so," Cornelius responded without wasting any time.

AJ and the two boys opened the door and walked into the diner. "How did you know I had dinner with the sheriff?" he asked as they walked up to the counter where cartons of chocolate milk had been placed for them.

"Mr. and Mrs. Turner saw all of you and called my grandmother who then called my mom and dad. Everyone was wondering who you were and I told my mom that you were a kid who got in trouble and had to report to the sheriff's office after school every day. They thought you were a family member or something, but I told them you weren't."

AJ nodded. "My mom had to go to work unexpectedly last night and the sheriff offered to take me to dinner with him since I hadn't eaten."

"Wow! That was real nice of him, wasn't it?"

AJ hadn't really thought about it being an act of kindness and said, "Yeah, I guess so."

"Do you think he'll mind if we go with you to his office after school?" Morris asked excitedly.

AJ scrunched his face, thinking. "I guess not, but he might put you to work."

Morris shrugged. "That's all right if he does. I just want him to tell us about the time he was an FBI agent and did that undercover stuff to catch the bad guys."

AJ nodded. He didn't want to admit it, but he wouldn't mind hearing about that himself. He smiled when the nice lady behind the counter handed them each a donut to go along with their milk.

Shelly's hands tightened on the steering wheel after she brought her car to a stop next to the police cruiser marked

Sheriff. She'd had no idea Dare would be joining his brothers for lunch. How would she manage a straight face around him and not let anyone know they had spent close to an hour in a darkened area of her porch last night doing something deliriously naughty?

She opened the car door and took a deep breath, thinking that the things Dare had done to her had turned her inside out and whetted her appetite. To put it more bluntly, sixteen hours later she was still aroused. After having gone without sex for so long she now felt downright hungry. In fact *starving* was a better word to use. Would Dare look at her and detect her sexually excited state? If anyone could, it would be Dare, a man who'd once known her better than she'd known herself.

And to think she'd even admitted to him that she hadn't slept with another soul since their breakup ten years ago. Now that he knew, she had to keep her head on straight and keep Dare's focus on AJ and not her.

With a deep sigh she opened the door and went inside.

She paused and watched all five men stand the moment she entered the restaurant. They must have seen her drive up and were ready to greet her. Tears burned the back of her eyes. It had been too long. When she'd been Dare's girlfriend, the brothers had claimed her as an honorary sister, and since she'd been an only child, she'd held that attachment very dear. One of the hardest things about leaving College Park had been knowing that in addition to leaving Dare she'd also left behind a family she had grown very close to.

As she looked at them now, she began to smile. They stood in a line as if awaiting royalty and she walked up to them, one by one. "Thorn," she said to the one closest to Dare in age. She gladly accepted the kiss he boldly placed on her lips and the hug he fondly gave her.

"Ten years is a long time to be gone, Shelly," he said with a serious expression on his face. "Don't try it again."

She couldn't help but smile upon seeing that he was bossy as ever. "I won't, Thorn."

She then moved to Stone, the first Westmoreland she had come to know; the one who had introduced her to Dare. Without saying a word she reached for him, hugging him tightly. After they released each other, he placed a kiss on her lips as well.

"I'm so proud of your accomplishments, Stone," she said, smiling through her tears. "And I buy every book you write."

He chuckled. "Thanks, Shell." His face then grew serious. "And I ditto what Thorn said. Don't leave again." His gaze momentarily left hers and shifted to where Dare was standing. He glared at his brother before returning his gaze to hers and added, "No matter what the reason."

She nodded. "All right."

Then came the twins, who were a year younger than she. She remembered them getting into all sorts of mischief, and from the gleams in their eyes, it was evident they were still up to no good. After they both placed chaste pecks on her lips, Storm said, smiling. "We told Dare that he blew his chance with you, which means you're now available for us."

Shelly grinned. "Oh, am I?"

"Yeah, if you want to be," Chase said, teasingly, giving her another hug.

When Chase released her she drew a deep breath. Next came Dare.

"Dare," she acknowledged softly, nervously.

She figured since she'd already been in his company a few times, not to mention what they had done together last night, that he would not make a big production of seeing her. She soon discovered just how wrong that assumption was when he gently pulled her into his arms and captured her lips, nearly taking her breath in the process. There was nothing chaste about the kiss he gave her and she knew it had intentionally lasted long enough to cause his brothers to speculate and to give anyone who saw them kiss something to talk about.

When he released her mouth, it was Stone who decided to make light of what Dare had done by saying, "What was that about, Dare? Were you trying to prove to Shelly that you could still kiss?"

Dare answered as his gaze held hers. He smiled at Stone's comment and said, "Yeah, something like that."

Shelly never had problems getting through a meal before. But then she'd never had the likes of Dare Westmoreland on a mission to seduce her. And it didn't matter that she was sitting at a table in a restaurant next to him, surrounded by his brothers, or that the place was filled to lunch-crowd capacity.

She took several deep breaths to calm her racing heart, but it did nothing to soothe the ache throbbing through her. It all started when she caught herself staring at his hand as he lifted a water goblet to his lips. Seeing his fingers had reminded her how she had whimpered her way into ecstasy as those same fingers had stroked away ten years of sexual frustration.

She had caught his eyes dark with desire, over the water glass, and had realized he had read her thoughts. And, as smooth as silk, when he placed the glass down he took that same hand and without calling attention to what he was doing, placed it under the table on her thigh.

At first she'd almost jerked at the cool feel of his hand, then she'd relaxed when his hand just rested on her thigh without moving. But then, moments later, she had almost gasped when his hand moved to settle firmly between her legs. And amidst all conversations going on around them, as the brothers tried to bring her up to date on what had been going on in their lives over the past ten years, no one seemed to have noticed that one of Dare's hands was missing from the table while he gently stroked her slowly back and forth through the material of her shorts. He'd tried getting her zipper down, a zipper that, thanks to the way she was sitting, wouldn't budge.

Thinking that she had to do something, anything to stop this madness, she leaned forward and placed her elbows on the table and cupped her face in her hands as she tried to ignore the multitude of sensations flowing through her. She glanced around wondering if any of the brothers had any idea what Dare was up to, but from the way they were talking and eating, it seemed they had more on their minds than Dare not keeping his hands to himself.

"We want you to know that we'll do everything we can to help you with AJ, Shelly."

Shelly nodded at Stone's offer and then felt her cheeks grow warmer when another one of Dare's fingers wiggled its way inside her shorts. "I appreciate that, Stone."

"He's my responsibility," Dare spoke up and glanced at his brothers, keeping a straight face, not giving away just what sidebar activities he was engaged in.

"Yeah, but he belongs to us, too," Thorn said. "He's a Westmoreland, and I think that you did a wonderful job with him, Shelly, considering the fact that you've been a single parent for the past ten years. He's going through growing pains now, but once he sees that he has a family who cares deeply for him, he'll be just fine."

She nodded. She had to believe that as well. "Thanks, Thorn."

"Well, although I truly enjoyed all your company, it's time for me to get back to the station," Dare said, finally removing his hand from between her legs. When he stood she glanced up at him knowing that regardless of whether it was a dark, cozy corner on her porch at night or in a restaurant filled with people in broad daylight, Dare Westmoreland did just what he pleased, and it seemed that nothing pleased him more than touching her.

"So, what did you do next, Sheriff?"

Dare shook his head. When AJ had shown up after school, he had brought Morris and Cornelius with him and explained that the two had wanted to tag along. Dare had made it clear that if they had come to keep AJ company then they might as well help him with the work, and he had just the project for the three of them.

He had taken them to the basement where the police youth athletic league's equipment was stored, with instructions that they bring order to the place. That past year a number of balls, gloves and bats had been donated by one of the local sports stores.

Deciding to stay and help as well as to supervise, he had not been prepared for the multitude of questions that Morris and Cornelius were asking him. AJ didn't ask him anything, but Dare knew he was listening to everything that was being said.

"That's why it pays to be observant," Dare said, unloading another box. "It's always a clue when one guy goes inside and the other stays out in the car with the motor running. They had no idea I was with law enforcement. I pretended to finish filling my tank up with gas, and out of the corner of my eye I could see the man inside acting strangely and I knew without a doubt that a robbery was about to take place."

"Wow! Then what did you do?" Morris asked, with big, bright eyes.

"Although I worked for the Bureau, we had an unspoken agreement with the local authorities to make them aware of certain things and that's what I did. Pretending to be checking out a map, I used my cell phone to alert the local police of what was happening. The only reason I became involved was because I saw that one of the robbers intended to take a hostage, a woman who'd been inside paying for gas. At that point I knew I had to make a move."

"Weren't you afraid you might get hurt?" AJ asked.

Dare wondered if AJ was aware that he was now as engrossed in the story as Morris and Cornelius were. "No, AJ, at the time the only thing I could think about was that an innocent victim was at risk. Her safety became my main concern at that point, and whatever I did, I had to make sure that she wasn't hurt or injured."

"So what did you do?"

"In the pretense of paying for my gas, I entered the store at the same time the guy was forcing the woman out. I decided to use a few martial arts moves I had learned in the marines, and—"

"You used to be in the marines?" AJ asked.

Dare smiled. The look of total surprise and awe on his son's face was priceless. "Yes, I served in the marines for four years, right after college."

AJ smiled. "Wow!"

"My daddy says the marines only picks the most bravest and the best men," Morris said, also impressed.

Dare smiled. "I think all the branches of the military selects good men, but I do admit that marines are a very special breed." He glanced at his watch. "It's a little over an hour, guys. Do I need to call any of your parents to let them know that you're on your way home?"

All three boys shook their heads, indicating that Dare didn't have to. "All right."

"Sheriff, do you think you can teach us some simple martial arts moves?" Cornelius asked.

"Yeah, Sheriff, with bad people kidnapping kids we need to know how to protect ourselves, don't we?" Morris chimed in.

Dare grinned when he saw AJ vigorously nodding his head, agreeing with Morris. "Yes, I guess that's something all of you should know, some real simple moves. Just as long as you don't use it on your classmates for fun or to try to show off."

"We wouldn't do that," Morris said eagerly.

Dare nodded. "All right then. I'll try to map out some time this Saturday morning. How about checking with your parents, and if they say it's all right, then the three of you can meet me here."

He glanced at his watch again. Shelly didn't know it yet, but he intended to see her again tonight, no matter what excuse he had to make to do so. He smiled, pleased with the progress he felt he'd made with AJ today. "Okay, guys, let's get things moving so we can call it a day. The three of you did an outstanding job and I appreciate it."

"Mom, did you know that the sheriff used to be in the marines?"

Shelly glanced up from her book and met AJ's excited gaze. He was stretched out on the floor by the sofa doing his homework. "Yes, I knew that. We dated during that time."

"Wow!"

She lifted a brow. "What's so fantastic about him being a marine?"

AJ rolled his eyes to the ceiling. "Mom, everyone knows that marines are tough. They adapt, improvise and overcome!"

Shelly smiled at her son's Clint Eastwood imitation from one of his favorite movies. "Oh." She went back to reading her book.

"And, Mom, he told us about the time he caught two men trying to rob a convenience store and taking a hostage with them. It was real cool how he captured the bad guys."

"Yeah, I'm sure it was."

"And he offered to teach us martial arts moves on Saturday morning at the police station so we'll know how to protect ourselves," he added excitedly in a forward rush.

Shelly lifted her head from her book again. "Who?"

"The sheriff."

She nodded. "Oh, your father?"

Their gazes locked and Shelly waited for AJ's comeback, expecting a denial that he did not consider Dare his father. After a few minutes he shrugged his shoulders and said softly, "Yes." He then quickly looked away and went back to doing his homework.

Shelly inhaled deeply. AJ admitting Dare was his father was a start. It seemed the ice surrounding his heart was slowly beginning to melt, and he was beginning to see Dare in a whole new light.

Chapter 9

Dare walked into Coleman's Florist knowing that within ten minutes of the time he walked out, everyone in College Park would know he had sent flowers to Shelly. Luanne Coleman was one of the town's biggest gossips, but then he couldn't worry about that, especially since for once her penchant to gab would work in his favor. Before nightfall he wanted everyone to know that he was in hot pursuit of Shelly Brockman.

Due to the escape of a convict in another county, he had spent the last day and a half helping the sheriff of Stone Mountain track down the man. Now, thirty-six hours after the man had been recaptured, Dare was bone tired and regretted he had missed the opportunity to see Shelly two nights ago as he'd planned. The best he could do was go home and get some sleep to be ready for the martial arts training he had promised the boys in the morning.

He also regretted that he had not been there when AJ had arrived after school yesterday. It had officially been the last time he was to report to him. According to McKade, AJ had come alone and had been on time. He had also done the assignment Dare had left for him to do without having much to say. However, McKade had said AJ questioned him a couple of times as to why he wasn't there.

Dare walked around the shop, wondering just what kind of flowers Shelly would like, then decided on roses. According to Storm, roses, especially red ones, said everything. And everyone knew that Storm was an ace when it came to wooing women.

"Have you decided on what you want, Sheriff?"

He turned toward Mrs. Coleman. A woman in her early sixties, she attended the same church as his parents and he'd known her all of his life. "Yes, I'd like a dozen roses."

"All right. What color?"

"Red."

She smiled and nodded as if his selection was a good one, so evidently Storm was right. "Any particular type vase you have in mind?"

He shrugged. "I haven't thought about that."

"Well, you might want to. The flowers say one thing and the vase says another. You want to make sure you select something worthy of holding your flowers."

Dare frowned. He hadn't thought ordering flowers would be so much trouble. "Do you have a selection I can take a look at?"

"Certainly. There's an entire group over on that back wall. If you see something that catches your fancy, bring it to me."

Dare nodded again. Knowing she was watching him with those keen eyes of hers, he crossed the room to stand in front of a shelf containing different vases. As far as he was concerned one vase was just as good as any, but he decided to try and look at them from a woman's point of view.

A woman like Shelly would like something that looked special, soft yet colorful. His gaze immediately went to a white ceramic vase that had flowers of different colors painted at the top. For some reason he immediately liked it and could see the dozen roses arranged really prettily in it. Without dallying any further, he picked up his choice and walked back over to the counter.

"This is the one I want."

Luanne Coleman nodded. "This is beautiful, and I'm sure she'll love it. Now, to whom will this be delivered?"

Dare inwardly smiled, knowing she was just itching to bits to know that piece of information. "Shelly Brockman."

Her brows lifted. "Shelly? Yes, I heard she was back in town, and it doesn't surprise me any that you would be hot on her heels, Dare Westmoreland. I hope you know that I was really upset with you when you broke things off with her all those years ago."

You and everybody else in this town, Dare thought, leaning against the counter.

"And she was such a nice girl," Luanne continued. "And everyone knew she was so much in love with you. Poor thing had to leave town after that and her parents left not long after she did."

As Luanne accepted his charge card she glanced at him and said, "I understand she has a son."

Dare pretended not to find her subject of conversation much to his interest. He began fidgeting with several key rings she had on display. "Yes, she does."

"Someone said he's about eight or nine."

Dare knew nobody had said any such thing. The woman

was fishing, and he knew it. He might as well set himself up to get caught. "He's ten."

"Ten?"

"Yes." Like you didn't already know.

"That would mean he was born soon after she left here, wouldn't it?"

Dare smiled. He liked how this woman's mind worked. "Yes, it would seem that way."

"Any ideas about his father?"

"No."

"No?"

Dare wanted to chuckle. "None."

She frowned at him. "Aren't you curious?"

"No. What Shelly did with her life after she left here is none of my business."

Dare couldn't help but notice that Luanne's frown deepened. She handed his charge card back to him and said, "I have Shelly's address, Sheriff, since she's staying at her parents' old place."

Dare nodded, not surprised that she knew that. "When will the flowers be delivered?"

"Within a few hours. Will that be soon enough?"

"Yes."

"Sheriff, can I offer you a few words of advice?"

He wondered what she would do if he said no. She would probably give him the advice anyway. He could tell she was just that upset with him right now. "Why sure, Ms. Luanne. What words of advice would you like to offer me?"

She met his gaze without blinking. "Get your head out of the sand and stop overlooking the obvious."

"Meaning?"

She frowned. "That's for you to figure out."

* * *

Shelly looked at Mr. Coleman in surprise. She then looked at the beautiful arrangement of flowers he held in his hand. "Are you sure these are for me?"

The older man beamed. "Yes, I'm positive. Luanne said for me to get them to you right away," he said handing them to her.

"Thanks, and if you just wait a few minutes I'd like to give you a tip."

Mr. Coleman waved his hand as he went down the steps. "No need. I've already been tipped real nice for delivering them," he said with a grin that said he had a secret that he wouldn't be sharing with her.

"All right. Thanks, Mr. Coleman." She watched as he climbed into his van and drove off. Closing the door she went into the living room and placed the flowers on the first table she came to. Someone had sent her a dozen of the most beautiful red roses that she had ever seen. And the vase they were in was simply gorgeous; she could tell the vase alone had cost a pretty penny.

She quickly pulled off the card and read it aloud. "You're in my thoughts. Dare."

Her heart skipped a beat as she lightly ran her fingers over the card. Even the card and envelope weren't the standard kind that you received with a floral arrangement. They had a rich, glossy finish that caused Dare's bold signature to stand out even more.

For a moment, Shelly could only stare at the roses, the vase they were in and the card and envelope. It was obvious that a lot of time and attention had gone into their selection, and a part of her quivered inside that Dare would do something that special for her.

You're in my thoughts.

She suddenly felt tears sting her eyes. She didn't know what was wrong with her. It seemed that lately her emotions were wired and would go off at the least little thing. Ever since that day of Dare's visit and what he'd done to her on the porch, not to mention that little episode he'd orchestrated at the restaurant, she'd been battling the worst kind of drama inside her body. He had done more than open Pandora's box. He had opened a cookie jar that had been kept closed for ten years, and now she wanted Dare in the worst possible way.

"Who sent the flowers, Mom?"

Shelly lifted her head and met her son's gaze. "Your father."

He shrugged. "The sheriff?"

"One and the same." She glanced back over at the flowers. "Aren't they beautiful?"

AJ came to stand next to her. It was obvious they couldn't see the arrangement through the same eyes when he said, "Looks like a bunch of flowers to me."

She couldn't help but laugh. "Well, I think they're special, and it was thoughtful for him to send them to let me know I was in his thoughts."

AJ shrugged again. "He's looking for a girlfriend, but I told him you weren't interested in a boyfriend."

Shelly arched a brow. "AJ, you had no right to say that."

His chin jutted out. "Why not? You've never had a boyfriend before, so why would you care about one now? It's just been me and you, Mom. Isn't that enough?"

Shelly shook her head. Her son had years to learn about human sexuality and how it worked. She was just finding out herself what ten years of abstinence could do to a person. "AJ, don't you think I can get lonely sometimes?" she asked him softly.

He didn't say anything for a little while. Then he said, "But you never got lonely before."

"Yes, and I worked a lot before. That's how you got into all that trouble. I was putting in extra hours at the hospital when the cost of living got high. I needed additional money so the two of us could afford to live in the better part of town. I didn't have time to get lonely. Now with my new job, I can basically make my own hours so I can spend more time with you. But you're away in school a lot during the days, and pretty soon you'll have friends you'll want to spend time with, won't you?"

AJ thought of Morris and Cornelius and the fun they'd had on the playground that day at school. "Yes."

"Well, don't you think I need friends, too?"

"Yes, but what's wrong with having girlfriends?"

"There's nothing wrong with it, but most of the girls I went to school with have moved away, and although I'm sure I'll meet others, right now I feel comfortable associating with people I already know, like Dare and his brothers."

"But it's the sheriff who wants you as his girlfriend. He likes you."

She smiled. Dare must have laid it on rather thick. "You think so?"

"Yes. He said you used to be his special girl. His brothers and parents said so, too. And I've got a feeling he wants you to be his special girl again. But if you let him, he'll find out about me."

"And you still see that as a bad thing, AJ?"

He remained silent for a long time, then he hunched his shoulders. "I'm still not sure he would want me."

Shelly felt a knot forming in her stomach. She wondered if he was using his supposed dislike of Dare as an excuse to shield himself from getting hurt. "And why wouldn't he want you?"

"I told you that he didn't like me."

And you also said you didn't like him, she wanted to remind him, but decided to keep quiet about that. "Well, I know Dare, and I know that he likes you. He wouldn't have invited you to dinner with him and his family if he didn't. He would have taken you straight to Ms. Kate's house knowing she would have fed you."

She watched AJ's shoulders relax. "You think so?"

If you only knew, she thought. "Yes, I think so. I believe you remind Dare of himself when he was your age. I heard he was a handful for his parents. All the brothers were."

AJ nodded. "Yes, he said that once. He has a nice family."

She smiled. "Yes, he has."

AJ stuck his hands inside his pockets. "So, he's back now?"

"Who?"

"The sheriff. He left town to help another sheriff catch a guy who escaped from jail. Deputy McKade said so."

"Oh." Shelly had wondered why she hadn't heard from him since the luncheon on Thursday. Not that she had been looking for him, mind you. "Well, in that case, yes, I would say that he's back, since he ordered these flowers."

"Then our lessons for tomorrow morning are still on."

"Your lessons?"

"Yeah, remember, I told you he had said he would teach me, Morris and Cornelius how to protect ourselves at the police station in the morning."

"Oh, I'd almost forgotten about that." She wanted to meet her son's new playmates and ask Dare about them. "Will they need a ride or will their parents bring them?"

"Their parents will be bringing them. They have to go to the barbershop in the morning."

Shelly nodded, looking at the long hair on her son's head.

She'd allowed him to wear it in twists, as long as they were neat-looking. Maybe in time she would suggest that he pay a visit to the barbershop as well.

"And after our class they have to go to church for choir practice."

AJ's words recaptured Shelly's attention. Morris and Cornelius were active in church? The two were sounding better and better every minute. "All right then. Go get cleaned up for dinner."

He nodded. "Do you think the sheriff will call tonight or come by?" AJ asked as he trotted up the stairs.

I wish. "I'm not sure. If he just got back into town he's probably tired, so I doubt it."

"Oh."

Although she was sure he hadn't wanted her to, she had heard the disappointment in his voice anyway. He sounded just how she felt.

Dare couldn't sleep. He felt restless. Agitated. Horny.

He threw back the covers and got out of bed, yanked a T-shirt over his head and pulled on his jeans. His body was a nagging ache, it was throbbing relentlessly and his arousal strained painfully against his jeans. He knew what his problem was, and he knew just how he could fix it.

He sighed deeply, thinking he definitely had a problem, and wondered if at two in the morning, Shelly was willing to help him solve it.

Shelly couldn't sleep and heard the sound of a pebble the moment it hit her window. At first she'd thought she was hearing things, but when a second pebble hit the window she knew she wasn't. She also knew who was sending her the signal to come to the backyard.

That had always been Dare's secret sign to let her know he was back in town. She would then sneak past her parents' bedroom and slip down the stairs and through the back door to race outside to his arms.

She immediately got out of bed, tugged on her robe and slipped her feet into her slippers. Not even thinking about why he would be outside her window this time of night, she quickly tiptoed down the stairs. Without turning on a light, she entered the kitchen and opened the back door, and, although it was too dark for her to see, she knew he was there. Her nostrils immediately picked up his scent.

"Dare?" she whispered, squinting her eyes to see him.

"I'm here."

And he was, suddenly looming over her, gazing down at her with a look in his eyes that couldn't be disguised. It was desperate, hot, intense, and it made her own eyes sizzle at the same time the area between her legs began to throb. "I heard the pebbles," she said, swallowing deeply.

He nodded as he continued to hold her gaze. "I was hoping you would remember what it meant."

Oh, she remembered all right. Her body remembered, too. "Why are you here?" she asked softly, feeling her insides heat up and an incredible sensation flow between her legs. Desire was surging through every part of her body and she was barely able to stand it. "What do you want, Dare?"

He reached out and placed both hands at her waist, intentionally pulling her closer so she could feel his large, hard erection straining against his jeans. "I think that's a big indication of what I want, Shelly," he murmured huskily, leaning down as his mouth drew closer to hers.

Chapter 10

Shelly felt a moment of panic. One part of her mind tried telling her that she didn't want this, but another part, the one ruled by her body, quickly convinced her that she did. Her mind was swamped with the belief that it didn't matter that it hadn't been a full week since she laid eyes on Dare again after ten years. Nor did it matter that there were issues yet unresolved between them. The only thing that mattered was that this was the man she had once loved to distraction, the man she had given her virginity to at seventeen; the man who had taught her all the pleasures a man and woman could share, and the man who had given her a son. And, she inwardly told herself, this has nothing to do with love but with gratifying our needs.

Realizing that and accepting it, her body trembled as she lifted her face to meet his, and at that moment everything, in-

cluding the ten years that had separated them, evaporated
and was replaced by hunger, intense, sexual hunger that was
waiting to explode within her. He felt it, too, and his body re-
acted, drawing her closer and making a groan escape from her
lips.

He covered her mouth with his, zapping her senses in a way
that only he could do. Fueled by the greed they both felt, his kiss
wasn't gentle. It displayed all the insatiability he was feeling.

And then some.

Dare didn't think he could get enough. He wanted to get
inside her, reacquaint her body with his and give her the satisfaction she had denied herself for ten years. He wanted to
give her *him*. He felt his blood boil as he pulled his mouth
from hers with a labored breath. She was shaking almost vi-
olently. So was he.

"Come with me. I've got a place set up for us."

Nodding, she let him lead her off the back porch and
through a thicket of trees to a spot hidden by low overhanging branches, a place they had once considered theirs. It was
dark, but she was able to make out the blanket that had been
spread on the ground. As always, he had thought ahead. He
had planned her seduction well this night.

"Where did you park your car?" she asked wondering how
he had managed things.

"At the station. I walked from there, using the back way.
And nobody saw me."

She nodded. Evidently he had read her mind. From the information she had gotten from Ms. Kate earlier today, the
town was buzzing about AJ, wondering if Dare was actually
too dim-witted to figure out her son was his.

She met his gaze, which was illuminated by the moonlight.

"Thanks for the flowers. They're beautiful. You didn't have to send them."

"I wanted to send them, Shelly."

He drew in a deep breath, and she saw that his gaze was glued to her mouth just as hers was glued to his. She couldn't help but think of the way he tasted, the hunger and intense desire that was still blatant in his loins, making his erection even bigger. Their need for each other had never been this sharp, all-consuming.

"I want you, Shelly," he whispered gently, pulling her down to the blanket with him.

She went willingly, without any resistance, letting him know that she wanted the intimacy of this night as much as he did. She wanted to lose herself in him in the same way he wanted to lose himself in her. Totally. Completely.

She didn't say a word as he gently pushed her robe from her shoulders, and then pulled her nightgown over her head. Nor did she utter a sound when his fingers caressed her breasts then tweaked her nipples before moving lower, past her rib cage and her stomach until he reached the area between her legs.

When he touched her there, dipped into her warmth, her breathing quickened and strained and she almost cried out.

"You're so wet," his voice rumbled against her lips. "All I could think about over the last couple of days is devouring you, wanting the taste of you on my tongue."

Heat built within her body as he pushed her even more over the edge, making her whimper in pleasure. And when pleasure erupted inside her with the force of a tidal wave, he was there to intensify it.

He kissed the scream of his name from her lips, again taking control of her mouth. The kiss was sensual, the taste erotic and it fueled her fire even more. She had ten years to make up for, and somehow, she knew, he was well aware of that.

When her body ceased its trembling, he pulled back, ending their kiss, and stood to remove his clothes. She looked up at him as he tossed his T-shirt aside. He appeared cool and in control as he undressed in front of her, but she knew he was not. His gaze was on her, and she again connected with it. It felt like a hot caress.

She watched as he eased down his jeans, and she gasped. Her mouth became moist, her body got hungrier. He wasn't wearing any underwear and his erection sprang forth—full of life, eager to please and ready to go. The tip seemed to point straight at her, and the only thing she could think about was the gigantic orgasm she knew Dare would give her.

Anticipation surged within her when he kicked his jeans aside and stood before her completely naked. And her senses began overflowing with the scent of an aroused man.

An aroused man who was ready to mate with an aroused woman.

She then noticed the condom packet he held in his hand. It seemed he had planned her seduction down to the last detail. She watched as he readied himself to keep her safe. Inhaling deeply when the task was done, he lifted his head and met her gaze.

"This is where you tell me to stop, Shelly, and I will."

She knew him, trusted him and realized that what he'd said was true. No matter how much he wanted her, he would never force himself on her. But then, he need not worry about her turning him down. Her body was on fire for him, the area between her legs throbbed. He had given her relief earlier, but that hadn't been enough. She wanted the same thing he wanted.

Deep penetration.

They had discovered a long time ago that they were two intensely sexual human beings. Anytime he had wanted her, all he had to do was touch her and he would have her hot, wet and pulsing within minutes. And anytime they mated, neither had control other than to make sure she was protected from pregnancy, except for that one time when they hadn't even had control for that.

When he dropped down to rejoin her on the blanket, she drew in a deep breath and automatically wrapped her arms around him as he poised his body over hers. He leaned down and placed a kiss on her lips.

"Thank you for my son."

A groan gently left her throat when she felt the head of him pressed against her entrance. Hot and swollen. He nudged her legs apart a little wider with his knees as his gaze continued to hold hers. "Ten years of missing you and not sharing this, Shelly."

And then he entered her, slowly, methodically, trembling as his body continued to push into hers as he lifted her hips. He let out a deep guttural moan. In no time at all he was planted within her to the hilt. The muscles of her body were clenching him. Milking him. Reclaiming him.

She held his gaze and when he smiled, so did she.

And then he began an easy rhythm. Slowly, painstakingly, he increased the pace. And with each deep thrust, he reminded her of just how things used to be between them, and how things still were now.

Hungry. Intense. Overpowering.

His gaze became keen, concentrated and potently dark each time he thrust forward, drove deeper into her, and she felt her body dissolve, dissipate then fuse into his. She felt the muscles of his shoulders bunch beneath her hands, heard the masculine sound of his growl and knew he was fighting reaching sexual fulfillment, waiting for her, refusing to leave her behind. But he couldn't hold back any longer, and, with one last, hard, deep thrust his body began shaking as he reached the pinnacle of satisfaction.

His orgasm triggered hers, and when her mouth formed a chilling scream, he quickly covered it with his, denying her the chance to wake the entire neighborhood. But he couldn't stop her body from quivering uncontrollably. Nor could he stop her legs from wrapping around him, locking their bodies together, determined that they continue to share this. She closed her eyes as a feeling of unspeakable joy and gratification claimed her in the most provocative way, restitution, compensation for ten years of not having access to any of this.

And when the last of the shudders subsided and they both continued to shiver in the aftermath, he sank down, lowered his head to the curve of her neck, released a deep satisfied sigh, and wondered what words he could say to let her know just how overwhelmed he felt.

He forced himself to lift up, to meet her gaze, and she opened her eyes and looked at him. And at that moment, in that instant, he knew words weren't needed. There was no way she couldn't know how he felt.

And as he leaned down and kissed her, he knew that the rest of the night belonged to them.

"Mom? Mom? Are you all right?"

Shelly opened her eyes as she felt AJ nudge her awake. Once again he had found her sleeping on the sofa. After several more bouts of intense lovemaking, they had redressed, then Dare had gathered her into his arms and carried her inside the house. Not wanting to risk taking her upstairs to her

own bed and running into AJ, just in case he had awakened
during the night to use the bathroom or something, she had
asked Dare to place her on the sofa.

Now she turned over to meet AJ's gaze and felt the soreness
between her legs as she did so. She had used muscles last night
that she hadn't used in over ten years. "Yes, sweetheart, I'm
fine."

He lifted a brow. "You slept on the sofa again."

She glanced at the book that was still where it had been
the last time she had used it for an alibi. "I guess I fell asleep
reading again." She glanced at the clock on the wall. It was
Saturday which meant it wasn't a school day so why was he
up so early? "Isn't this your day to sleep late?"

He smiled sheepishly, and that smile reminded her so much
of Dare that her breath almost caught. "Yeah, but the sheriff
is giving us martial arts lessons today, remember?"

Yes, she remembered, then she wondered if after last night
Dare would be in any physical shape to give the boys anything
today. But then he was a man, and men recovered from intense sessions of lovemaking a lot quicker than most women.
Besides, she doubted if he'd gone without sex for ten years
as she had. She forced the thought from her mind, not wanting to think about Dare making love to other women.

She shifted her attention back to AJ. "You're excited about
taking lessons from Dare, aren't you?"

He shrugged. "Yes, I guess. I've always wanted to learn
some type of martial arts, but you never would let me take
any classes. Morris said his father told him that the sheriff is
an ace when it comes to that sort of stuff, and I'm hoping he'll
be willing to give us more than one lesson."

Shelly wondered if AJ would ever stop referring to Dare

as "the sheriff." But then, to call him Dare was even less re-
spectful. "All right, do you want pancakes this morning?"

"Yes! With lots and lots of butter!"

She smiled as she stood, wincing in the process. Her sore
muscles definitely reminded her of last night. "Not with lots
and lots of butter, AJ, but I'll make sure you get enough."

Shelly saw Dare the moment she pulled her car into the
parking lot at the sheriff's office. He walked over to the car
and met them. She wasn't surprised to discover that he'd
been waiting for them.

"Are we late?" AJ asked quickly, meeting Dare's gaze.

Dare smiled at him. "No, Cornelius isn't here yet, but I understand he's on his way. Morris's mother just dropped him
off a few minutes ago. He's waiting inside."

He then looked at Shelly, and his smile widened. "And how
are you doing this morning, Shelly?"

She returned his smile, thinking about all the things the two
of them had done last night while most of College Park slept.
"I'm fine, Dare, what about you?"

"This is the best I've felt in years." He wanted to say ten
years to be exact, but didn't want AJ to catch on to anything.

Shelly glanced at her watch. "How long will the lessons
last today?"

"At least an hour or so. Why? Is there something you need
to do?"

Shelly placed an arm around AJ's shoulders. "Well, I was
hoping I'd have enough time to get my nails done in addition
to getting my hair taken care of."

"Then do it. I'm going over to Thorn's shop when I leave
here to check out the new bike that he's building. AJ is wel-

come to go with me if he likes and I can bring him home later."

He shifted his glance from Shelly to AJ. "Would you like to go to Thorn's shop to see how he puts a motorcycle together?"

The expression in AJ's eyes told Dare that he would. "Yes, I'd love to go!" He turned to Shelly. "Can I, Mom?"

Shelly met Dare's gaze. "Are you sure, Dare? I wouldn't want to put you out with having to—"

"No, I'd like his company."

AJ's eyes widened in surprise. "You would?"

Dare grinned. "Sure, I would. You did a great job with all the chores that I assigned to you this week, and I doubt that you'll be playing hooky from school anytime soon, right?"

AJ lowered his head to study his sneakers. "Right."

"Then that does it. My brothers will be there and I know for a fact they'd like to see you again."

AJ smiled. "They would?"

"Yes, they would. They said they enjoyed having you at dinner the other night. Usually on Saturday we all pitch in to give Thorn a hand to make sure any bike he's building is ready to be delivered on time. The one he's working on now is for Sylvester Stallone."

"Wow!"

Dare laughed at the astonishment he heard in AJ's voice and the look of awe on his face. What he'd said about his brothers wanting to see AJ again was true. They were biting at the bit for a chance to spend more time with their nephew.

"Well, I guess that's settled," Shelly said, smiling at Dare and the son he had given her. "I'd better get going if I want to make my hair appointment on time." She turned to leave.

"Shelly?"

She turned back around. "Yes?"

"I almost forgot to mention that Mom called this morning. She heard from Laney last night. She, Jamal and the baby are coming for a visit in a couple of weeks and will stay for about two months. Then they will be moving to stay at their place in Bowling Green, Kentucky, while Laney completes her residency at the hospital there."

Shelly smiled. When she'd last seen Dare's baby sister, Delaney was just about to turn sixteen and the brothers were having a time keeping the young men away. Now she had graduated from medical school and had landed herself a prince from the Middle East. She was a princess and the mother to a son who would one day grow up to be a king. "That's wonderful! I can't wait to see her again."

Dare grinned. "And she can't wait to see you, either. Mom told her that you had moved back and she was excited about it."

Without having to worry about AJ, Shelly decided to throw in a pedicure after getting her hair and nails done. Upon returning home, she collapsed on the bed and took a nap. The lack of sleep the night before still had her tired. After waking up, she was about to go outside on the porch and sit in the swing when she heard a knock at the door. She glanced through the peephole and saw it was Dare and AJ. Both of them had their hands and faces smeared with what looked like motor oil. She frowned. If they thought they were coming inside her house looking like that, they had another thought coming.

"Go around back," she instructed, opening the door just a little ways. "I'll bring you washcloths and a scrub brush to clean up. You can also use the hose." She then quickly closed the door.

She met them in the backyard where they were using the

hose to wash oil from their hair. It was then that she noticed several oil spots on AJ's outfit as well. "What on earth happened?"

"Storm happened," Dare grumbled, taking the shampoo and towel she handed him. His frown indicated he wasn't all that happy about it, either. "You know how he likes to play around? Well, for some reason he decided to fill a water gun with motor oil, and AJ and I became his victims."

She shifted her gaze from Dare to AJ. Whereas Dare was not a happy camper because of Storm's childish antics, it seemed AJ was just the opposite. "Storm is so much fun!" He said, laughing, "He told me all about how he had to save this little old lady from a burning house once."

Shelly smiled. "Well, I'm glad you enjoyed yourself, but those clothes can stay out here. In fact, we may as well trash them."

AJ nodded. "Storm said to tell you that he's going to buy me another outfit and he'll call to find out when he can take me shopping."

Shelly crossed her arms over her chest and lifted a brow. "Oh, he did, did he?"

"Yes."

She shifted her gaze back to Dare. "What are we going to do about that brother of yours?"

Dare shrugged, smiling. "What can I do? I guess we could try marrying him off, except so far there's not a woman around who suits his fancy except for Tara, but she's Thorn's challenge."

A bemused look covered Shelly's face. "What?"

"Tara Matthews. She's Laney's friend—a doctor who works at the same hospital in Kentucky where Delaney plans to complete her residency. I'll explain about her being Thorn's challenge at another time."

Shelly nodded, planning to hold him to that. She glanced down at her watch. "I was about to cook burgers and fries, if anyone is interested."

Dare looked pleased. "Only if you let me grill the burgers."

"And I'll help," AJ chimed in, volunteering his services.

Shelly shook her head. "All right, and I'll cook the fries and make some potato salad and baked beans to go along with it. How does that sound?"

"That sounds great, Mom."

Shelly nodded, liking the excitement she heard in her son's voice. "Dare?"

He chuckled. "I agree with AJ. That sounds great."

Dare remained through dinner. He got a call that he had to take care of, but returned later with Chase and Storm close on his heels. They brought a checkers game, intent on showing AJ how to play. It was almost eleven before AJ finally admitted he was too tired to play another game. Chase and Storm left after AJ went to bed, leaving Dare to follow later after they mentioned they were headed over to Thorn's place to wake him up to play a game of poker.

An hour or so later, Shelly walked Dare to the door. He had spent some time telling her how Tara Matthews was a feisty woman that only Thorn could tame and that was why the brothers referred to her as Thorn's challenge. "So you think this Tara Matthews has captured the eye of Thorn Westmoreland?"

Dare chuckled. "Yes, although he doesn't know it yet, and I feel sorry for Tara when he does."

Shelly nodded. Moments later she said, "I hope you know your leaving late is giving the neighbors a lot to say."

He smiled. "Yeah, I heard from McKade that a lot of

people around town are questioning my intelligence. They think I haven't figured out that AJ's my son."

Shelly nodded. "Yes, that's what I'm hearing, too, from Ms. Kate."

"How do you think AJ is handling things?"

"I don't think anyone has said anything to him directly, but I know a couple of people have asked him about his father in a roundabout way."

Dare lifted a brow. "When?"

"A couple of days ago at Kate's Diner. He goes there every morning on his way to school."

Dare nodded. "Damn, Shelly, I'm ready to end this farce and let this whole damn town know AJ's mine."

"I know, Dare, but remember we decided to let him be the one to determine when that would be. Personally, I think it'll be sooner than you think, because he's slowly coming around."

Dare raised a questioning brow. "You think so?"

"Yes. The two of you are interacting together a lot better. That's obvious. I can tell, and I know your brothers picked up on it tonight as well."

"Yes, but for some reason he still holds himself back from me," Dare said in a frustrated tone. "I sense it, Shelly, and it bothers the heck out of me. I don't know why he's doing it."

Shelly smiled slightly. "I think I do."

Dare met her gaze. "Then tell me—why?"

She sighed. "I think AJ is beginning to wonder if he's good enough to be your son."

Dare frowned. "Why would he wonder about a thing like that?"

"Because basically he's beginning to see you through a new set of eyes, the same eyes Morris and Cornelius see you with, and AJ's concerned about the way the two of you met. He knows it wasn't a good start and that you were disappointed with him. Now he's afraid that he won't be able to wipe the slate clean with you."

Dare rubbed a hand down his face. "There'll never be a time that I wouldn't want my son, Shelly."

She wrapped her arms around his waist upon hearing the frustration in his voice. She heard the love there as well. "I know that and you know that, but he has to know that, too. Now that you've broken the ice with him, it's time for you to get to know him and for him to get to know you. Then he'll see that no matter what, you'll always be there for him."

Dare let out a deep sigh. "And I thought winning him over would be easy."

She smiled. "In a way, it has been. To be honest with you, I really didn't expect him to come around this soon. Like you, he has somewhat of a stubborn streak about certain things. Him coming around the way he has just goes to show that you evidently have a way with people."

Dare smiled and brought her closer to him. "And do I have a way with you, Shelly?" The only reason he wasn't making love to her again tonight was that he was well aware of the fact that her body was sore. He couldn't help noticing how stiff her movements were when she'd dropped AJ off that morning and again this evening at dinner.

"After last night how can you even ask that, Dare? You know I was putty in your hands," she said, recapturing his attention.

"Then that makes us even, because I was definitely putty in yours as well." He leaned down and kissed her, thinking of just how right she felt in his arms.

Just like always.

Chapter 11

Shelly stretched out in her bed with a sensuous sigh. Almost two weeks had passed since she and Dare had spent the night together on a blanket in her backyard. Since then, nightly meetings in the backyard on a blanket had become almost a ritual. He had become almost a fixture in her home, dropping by for dinner, and inviting her and AJ to a movie or some other function in town.

AJ was beginning to let his guard down around Dare, but as yet he had not acknowledged him as his father. Shelly knew Dare's patience was wearing thin; he was eager to claim his son, but as she had explained to Dare weeks ago, AJ had to believe in his heart that his father wanted him for a son before he could give Dare his complete love and trust.

She then thought about her own feelings for Dare. She had to fight hard to keep from falling in love with Dare all over again. She had to remember they were playacting for AJ's sake.

To anyone observing them, it seemed that he was wooing her. He was giving the townspeople something to talk about with the different flower arrangements that he sent her each week.

A couple of people had taken her aside and warned her not to be setting herself up for heartbreak all over again, since everyone knew Dare Westmoreland was a staunch bachelor. But there were others who truly felt he was worthy of another chance, and they tried convincing her that if anyone could change Dare's bachelor status, she could.

What she couldn't tell them was that she was not interested in changing Dare's bachelor status. Although she had detected some changes in him, she could not forget that at one time he had been a man driven to reach out for dreams that had not included her. And she could never let herself become vulnerable to that type of pain again. For six years she had believed she was the most important thing in Dare's life, and to find out that she hadn't been had nearly destroyed her. She had enough common sense to know that what she and Dare were sharing in the backyard at night was not based on emotional but on physical needs, and as long as she was able to continue to know the difference, she would be all right.

She pulled herself up in bed when she heard the knock on her bedroom door. "Come in, AJ."

It was early still, an hour before daybreak, but she knew he was excited. Today was the day that Dare's sister Delaney and her family were arriving from the Middle East. The Westmoreland brothers were ecstatic and had talked about their one and only sister so much over the past two weeks that AJ had gotten caught up in their excitement; after all, the woman was his aunt, although he assumed Delaney didn't know it.

He opened the door and stood just within the shadows of the light coming in from the hallway. Again, Shelly couldn't help but notice just how much he looked like Dare. No wonder the town was buzzing. "What is it, AJ?"

He shrugged. "I wanted to talk to you about something, Mom."

She nodded and scooted over in bed, but he went and sat in the chair. Evidently, he thought he was past the age to get into his mother's bed. Shelly's heart caught. Her son was becoming a young man and with his budding maturity came a lot of issues that Dare would be there to help her with. Not only Dare but the entire Westmoreland family.

He remained silent for a few minutes, then he spoke. "I've decided to tell the sheriff I'm his son."

Shelly's heart did a flip, and she swallowed slowly. "When did you decide that?"

"Yesterday."

"And what made you change your mind?"

"I've been watching him, Mom. I was in Kate's Diner one morning last week when he came in, but he didn't see me at first. When he walked in, all the people there acted like they were glad to see him, and he knew all their names and asked them how they were doing. Then it hit me that he really wasn't a bad cop or a mean cop at all. No one would like him if he was, and everybody likes him, Mom."

Shelly blinked away the tears from her eyes. AJ was right. Everyone liked Dare and thought well of him. AJ had had to discover that on his own, and it seemed that he had. "Yes, everyone likes Dare. He's a good sheriff and he's fair, AJ."

"Most of the kids at school think he's the bomb and feel that I'm lucky because you're his girlfriend."

Shelly made a surprised face. "The kids at your school think I'm his girlfriend?"

AJ nodded. "Well, aren't you?"

Shelly smiled slightly. She didn't want to give him hope that things would work out between her and Dare, and that once he admitted to being Dare's son they would miraculously become a loving family. "No, AJ, although we're close, Dare and I are nothing more than good friends. We always have been and always will be."

"But he wants you for his girlfriend, I can tell. Everyone can tell and they're all talking about it, as well as the fact they think I'm his son, although they don't want me to hear that part, but I do. The sheriff spends a lot of time with us and takes us places with him. The kids at school say their parents think it's time for him to settle down and marry, and I can tell that he really likes you, Mom. He always treats you special and I like that."

Shelly inhaled deeply. She liked it, too, but she knew a lot more about why Dare was spending time with her than AJ did. It was all part of his plan to gain his son's love and trust. She refused to put too much stock into anything else, not even the many times they had slept together. She knew it had to do with their raging hormones and nothing more. "So, when are you going to tell him?" she asked quietly.

AJ shrugged. "I still don't know that yet. But I wanted to let you know that I would be telling him."

She nodded. "Don't take too long. Like I said, Dare won't be a happy camper knowing we kept it from him, but I believe he'll be so happy about you that he'll quickly come around."

AJ's eyes lit up. "You think so?"

"Yes, sweetheart, I do."

He nodded. "Then I might tell him today. He asked if I'd like to go with him to meet his sister and her family at the airport. I might tell him then."

Shelly nodded again, knowing that if he did, it would certainly make Dare's day.

AJ thought Dare's truck was really cool. He had ridden in it a couple of times before, and just like the other times, he thought it was a nice vehicle for a sheriff to have when you wanted to stop being sheriff for a little while. But as he looked at Dare out of the corner of his eyes, he knew that the sheriff was always the sheriff. There was probably never a time when he wasn't on the job, and that included times like now when he wasn't wearing his uniform.

"So are you looking forward to that day out of school next Friday for teachers' planning day?" Dare asked the moment he'd made sure AJ had snapped his seat belt in place. Once that was done, he started the engine.

"Yes, although Mom will probably find a lot of work for me to do that day." He didn't say anything else for a little while, then he asked quickly, "Do you like kids?"

Dare glanced over at him and smiled. "Yes, I like kids."

"Do you ever plan to have any?"

Dare lifted his brow. "Yeah, one day. Why do you ask?"

AJ shrugged. "No reason."

Dare checked the rearview mirror as he began backing out of Shelly's driveway. He was headed for the airport like the rest of his family to welcome his sister home. He couldn't help wondering if AJ had started quizzing him for some reason and inwardly smiled, ready for any questions that his son felt he needed to ask.

Princess Delaney Westmoreland Yasir clutched her son to her breast and inhaled sharply. She leaned against her husband's side for support. Her mother had said Shelly's son favored Dare, but what she was seeing was uncanny. There was no way anyone could take a look at the boy standing next to Dare and not immediately know they were father and son. They had the same coffee coloring, the same dark intense eyes and the same shape mouth and nose. AJ Brockman was a little Dare; a small replica of his father, there was no doubt of that.

"And who do we have here?" she asked after regaining her composure and giving her parents and brothers hugs.

"This is AJ," Dare said, meeting his sister's astonished gaze. "Shelly Brockman's son. I think Mom mentioned to you that she had returned to town."

Delaney nodded. "Yes, that's what I heard." She smiled down at AJ and immediately fell in love. He was a Westmoreland, and she was happy to claim him. "And how are you, AJ?" she asked her nephew, offering him her hand.

"I'm fine, thank you," he said somewhat shyly.

"And how is your mother?"

"She's doing fine. She said she couldn't wait to see you later today."

Delaney smiled. "And I can't wait to see her. She was like a big sister to me."

With love shining in her eyes, Delaney then glanced at the imposing figure at her side and smiled. "AJ, this is my husband, Jamal Ari Yasir."

AJ switched his gaze from Delaney to the tall man standing next to her. He wasn't sure what he should do. Was he supposed to bow or something? He let out a deep sigh of relief when the man stooped down to his level and met his gaze. "And how are you, AJ?" he asked in a deep voice, smiling.

AJ couldn't help but return the man's smile, suddenly feeling at ease. "I'm fine, sir."

When the man straightened back up, AJ switched his gaze to the baby Delaney held in her arms. "May I see him?"

Delaney beamed. "Sure. His name is Ari Terek Yasir." She leaned down and uncovered her son for AJ to see. The baby glanced at AJ and smiled. AJ smiled back, and so did everyone else standing around them at the airport. Delaney looked over at her mother, in whose eyes tears of happiness shone at seeing her two grandsons together, getting acquainted.

Suddenly Prince Jamal Ari Yasir cleared his throat. Everyone had become misty-eyed and silent, and he decided to put the spark and excitement back into the welcome gathering. This was the family he had come to love, thanks to his wife who he truly cherished. His dark eyes shone with amusement as he addressed the one brother who he hadn't completely won over yet. "So, Thorn, are you still being a thorn in everyone's side these days?" he asked, smiling.

Chapter 12

Shelly smiled as she looked at the young woman sitting in the chair across from her on the patio at Dare's parents' home. The last time she had seen Delaney Westmoreland she'd been a teenager, a few months shy of her sixteenth birthday, a rebellious, feisty opponent who'd been trying to stand up to her five overprotective and oftentimes overbearing brothers.

Now she was a self-assured, confident young woman, a medical doctor, mother to a beautiful baby boy and wife to a gorgeous sheikh from a country in the Middle East called Tahran. And from the looks the prince was constantly giving his wife, there was no doubt in her mind that Delaney was also a woman well loved and desired.

And, Shelly thought further, Delaney was breathtakingly stunning. Even all those years back there had never been any doubt in Shelly's mind that Delaney would grow up to become a beauty. She was sure there hadn't been any doubt in the brothers' minds of that as well, which was probably the reason they had tried keeping such a tight rein on her. But clearly they had not been a match for Prince Jamal Ari Yasir.

Delaney and Shelly were alone on the patio. Mrs. Westmoreland was inside, singing Ari to sleep, and AJ had gone with his father and grandfather to the store to buy more charcoal. The brothers and Jamal had taken a quick run to Thorn's shop for Jamal to take a look at Thorn's latest beauty of a bike.

"I'm glad you returned, Shelly, to bring AJ home to Dare and to us. I don't think you know how happy you've made my parents. They thought Ari was their only grandchild and were fretting over the fact they wouldn't be able to see him as often as they wanted to. I felt awful about that, but knew my place was with Jamal, which meant living in his country the majority of the time. One good thing is that as long as his father is king, we have the luxury of traveling as much as we want. But things will change once Jamal becomes king."

When Shelly nodded, she continued, "We hope that won't happen for a while. His father is in excellent health and has no plans to turn things over to Jamal just yet."

After a long moment of silence, Shelly said, "I want to apologize for leaving the way I did ten years ago, Delaney, and for not staying in touch."

Delaney's eyes shone in understanding. "Trust me, we all understood your need to put distance between you and Dare. Everyone got on his case after you left, and for a while there was friction between him and my brothers."

Shelly nodded. Dare had told her as much.

"Mom explained the situation to me about AJ," Delaney added, breaking into Shelly's thoughts. "She told me how you and Dare have decided to let him be the one to tell Dare the truth. What's the latest on that? Is he softening any toward Dare? As someone just arriving on the scene, I'd say they seem to be getting along just fine."

Shelly nodded, remembering AJ's intense dislike of Dare in the beginning. "I think he's discovered Dare isn't the mean cop that he thought he was, and yes, he is definitely softening. He even told me this morning that he plans to tell Dare that he's his father."

A huge smile touched Delaney's features. "When?"

"Now, that I don't know. From what I gather he'll tell Dare when they get a private moment and when he feels the time is right. He's battling his fear that Dare may not want him because of the way he behaved in the beginning."

Delaney shook her head. "There's no way Dare would not want his son."

"Yes, I know, but AJ has to realize that for himself."

Delaney nodded, knowing Shelly was right.

AJ stood next to Dare in the supermarket line. He watched as the sheriff pulled money from his wallet to pay for his purchases. When they walked outside to wait for Mr. Westmoreland, who was still inside buying a few additional items he'd discovered he needed, AJ decided to use that time to ask Dare a couple more questions.

"Can I ask you something?"

Dare looked at him. "Sure. Ask me anything you want to know, AJ."

"Earlier today you said you liked kids. If you ever marry, do you think you'd want more than one child?"

Dare wondered about the reason for that question. Was AJ contented being an only child? Would he feel threatened if

Dare told him that he relished the thought of having other children—if Shelly would be their mother? He sighed, deciding to be completely honest with his son.

"Yes, I'd want more than one child. I'd like as many as my wife would agree to give me."

AJ's face remained expressionless, and Dare didn't have a clue if the answer he'd given would help him or hang him. "Any more questions?"

For a long moment, AJ didn't say anything. Then he met Dare's gaze and asked, "Is Dare your real name?"

Dare shook his head. "No, my real name is Alisdare Julian Westmoreland." He continued to hold his son's gaze. "Why do you ask?"

AJ placed his hands into his pockets. "Because my name is Alisdare Julian, too. That's what the AJ stands for."

Dare wasn't sure exactly what he was supposed to say, but knew he should act surprised, so he did. He raised his dark brows as if somewhat astonished. "Your mother named you after me?"

AJ nodded. "Yes."

Dare stared at AJ for a moment before asking. "Why did she do that?"

He watched as his son drew a deep breath. "Because—"

"Sorry I took so long. I bet your mom thinks the three of us have been kidnapped."

Both Dare and AJ turned to see Mr. Westmoreland walking toward them. But Dare was determined his son would finish what he'd been about to say. He returned his gaze to AJ. "Because—?"

AJ looked at the older man walking toward them, and then at Dare and, after losing his nerve, quickly said, "Because she liked your name."

* * *

"Because she liked your name."

Later that night Dare shook his head, remembering the reason AJ had given him for Shelly's choice of his name. He knew without a shadow of a doubt that AJ had come within a second of finally telling him he was his son before his father had unintentionally interrupted them, destroying that chance. But Dare was determined he would get it again.

Once they'd returned to his parents' home, there had been no private time, and on more than one occasion he'd been tempted to suggest that the two of them go back to the store and pick up some item his mother just had to have, but since his brothers and Jamal hadn't yet returned, his mother put him to work helping his father grill the ribs and steaks.

Now it was past eleven and Shelly was gathering her things to take a tired and sleepy AJ home. He had gotten worn out playing table tennis with his uncles for the past couple of hours.

Dare studied Shelly, as he'd been doing most of the night. She was wearing a pair of jeans that molded to her curvaceous hips and a blue pullover top that, to him, emphasized her lush breasts. Breasts he'd been kissing and tasting quite a lot over the past few weeks. Her body had always been a complete turn-on to him, and nothing had changed. He'd been fighting an arousal all night. The last thing he needed was for his brothers to detect what a bad way he was in, although from the smirks they had sent him most of the evening, he was well aware that they knew.

"AJ and I are going to have to say good-night to everyone," Shelly said smiling. "Thanks again for inviting us." She met Dare's gaze and blinked at his unspoken message. He was letting her know that he would be seeing her later tonight.

He slowly crossed the room to her. "I'll walk the two of you out."

She nodded before turning to give Delaney and Jamal, the elder Westmorelands and finally the brothers hugs.

Dare frowned at Storm when he deliberately kissed Shelly on the lips, trying to get a rise out of him and knowing it had worked. As far as Dare was concerned Shelly was his, and he didn't appreciate anyone mauling her. He had put up with it the first time they'd seen her at Chase's restaurant, but now he figured that it was time Storm learned to keep his hands and his lips to himself.

When Shelly and AJ walked ahead of him going out the door, he hung back and growled to Storm. "If you ever do that again, I'll break your arm."

He ignored Storm's burst of laughter and followed Shelly and AJ outside.

It was a beautiful night. The air felt crisp, pleasantly cool as Shelly closed the back door behind her and raced across the backyard to the place where she knew Dare was waiting for her. She hadn't bothered to put on a robe, since he would be taking it off her anyway, and she hadn't bothered to put on a gown, preferring to slip into an oversized T-shirt instead.

It had taken her some time to get AJ settled and into bed after arriving home from the Westmorelands. They had talked; he had told her that he'd come close to telling Dare the truth tonight, but that he'd been interrupted. She knew the longer he put it off, the harder it was going to be for him.

"Shelly?"

She sucked in a deep breath when Dare emerged from the shadows, dazzling her senses beneath the glow of a full moon. She immediately walked into his arms. Dark, penetrating eyes met hers and then, in a deep, ragged breath, he tipped her head back as his lips captured hers.

The whimpered sounds erupting from deep within her throat propelled him forward, making the urge for them to mate that much more intense, urgent, imperative. He gently lifted her T-shirt and touched her, discovering she was completely bare underneath. With unerring speed he lifted her off her feet, wrapped her legs around his waist and walked a few steps to a nearby tree.

She saw it was another seduction, planned down to every detail. Evidently he'd kept himself busy while waiting for her, she thought, noticing he had securely tied a huge pillow around the tree trunk. It served as a cushion for her backside when he pressed her against it. And then he was breathing hard and heavy while unzipping his pants and reaching inside to free himself. "I knew I couldn't wait, so I've already taken care of protection," he whispered as he thrust forward, entering her.

At her quick intake of breath, he covered her mouth with his, sipping the nectar of surprise from her lips, playing around in her mouth with his tongue as if relishing the taste of her. How long ago had they last kissed? Hadn't it been just last night? You couldn't tell by the way he was eating away at her mouth and the way she eagerly responded, wanting, needing and desiring him with a vengeance.

She opened her legs wider, wrapped them around his waist tighter when he went deeper, sending shock waves of pleasure racing through her. She felt close, so very close to the edge, and she knew she wanted him to be with her when she fell.

She broke off their kiss. "Now, Dare!"

Dare began moving. Throwing his head back he inhaled a

deep whiff of her scent—hot, enticing, sensually hers—and totally lost it. His jaw clenched as he thrust deeper, moved faster, when she arched her back. Desperately, he mated with her with quick, precise strokes, giving her all he had and taking all she had to give.

He was past the point of no return and she was right there with him. And when he felt her body tighten and the spasm rip through her, bringing with it an orgasm so powerful that he felt the earth shake beneath his feet, he held her gaze and thrust into her one final time as he joined her in a climax that just wouldn't stop. The sensations started at the top of his head and moved downward at lightning speed, building intense pressure in that part of his body nestled deep inside her, and making him clench his teeth to keep from screaming out her name and stomping his feet.

The sensations kept coming and coming and he leaned forward to kiss her again, capturing the essence of what they were sharing. As his body continued to tremble while buried deep inside of her, he knew that even after ten long years, he was still seductively, passionately and irrevocably hers. She was the only woman he would ever want. The only woman he would ever need. The only woman who could make him understand and appreciate the difference between having mindblowing sex and making earth-shattering, soul-stirring, deep-down-in-your-gut love.

She was the only woman.

And he also knew that she was the only woman he would ever love and that he still loved her.

Moments later, Dare pulled his body from Shelly's and, gathering her gently into his arms, walked over to place her on the blanket. He stretched out on his side facing her as he waited for the air to return back to his lungs and the blood to stop rushing fast and furious through his veins.

"I was beginning to think you weren't coming," he finally said some time later, the tone of his voice still quivering from the afterglow of what they'd just shared.

He couldn't help touching her again, so he slid his hand across her stomach, gently stroking her. He remembered the question AJ had asked him about wanting other children, and he remembered thinking that he'd want more children only if Shelly were their mother. He wouldn't hesitate putting another child of his inside her, in the womb he knew he had touched tonight. Not only had he touched it, he had branded it his.

Shelly slowly opened her eyes as her world settled, and the explosion she'd felt moments ago subsided. She gazed up at him and wondered how was it possible that each time they did this it was better than the time before. She always felt cherished in his arms.

Treasured.

Loved.

She silently shook that last thought away, refusing to let her mind go there; refusing to live on false hope. And she refused to give in to the want, need and desire to give him her heart again, no matter how strong the pull was to do so. She broke eye contact with him and looked away.

"Shelly?"

She returned her gaze to him, to respond to what he'd said. "It took a little longer than expected to get AJ settled tonight. He wanted us to have a long talk."

Dare asked, "Is he all right?"

"Yes. But I think he's somewhat disappointed that he

didn't get the chance to tell you the truth today. He had planned to do so."

Dare sighed deeply. His gut instincts had been right. "Do you think I should talk to him tomorrow?"

Shelly shook her head. "No, I think the best thing to do is to wait until he gets up his courage again. But I suggest you make things a bit easier on him by making sure the two of you have absolute privacy without any interruptions. However, you're also going to have to make sure he doesn't think things are being orchestrated for that purpose. He still has to feel as though he's in control for a while longer, Dare, especially with this. Right now, telling you that he's your son is very important to him."

Dare nodded. It was important to him as well. He slumped down on his back beside her and looked up at the stars. "I think I have an idea."

"What?"

"The brothers and I, along with Jamal, had planned on going to the cabin in the North Carolina mountains to go fishing. AJ knows about it since he heard us planning the trip, so he won't think anything about it. What if I invite him to come along?"

Shelly raised a brow. "Why would you want to take AJ with you guys? I'd think the six of you had planned it as a sort of guys' weekend, right?"

"Right. But I remember AJ mentioning to Thorn that he'd never gone fishing before, and I know that Thorn came close to inviting him. The only reason he didn't was because he knew we would be playing poker in addition to fishing and Storm's mouth can get rather filthy when he starts losing."

Shelly nodded. "But how will this help your situation with AJ? The two of you still won't have any privacy?"

"Yes, we will if the others don't come. After AJ and I arrive, the others can come up with an excuse as to why they couldn't make it."

Shelly raised a doubtful brow. "All five of them?"

"Yes. It has to be a believable reason for all of them though, otherwise AJ will suspect something."

Shelly had to agree. "And while you and AJ are there alone for those three days, you think he'll open up to you?"

Dare sighed deeply. "I'm hoping that he will. At least I'm giving him the opportunity to do so." He met Shelly's stare. "What do you think?"

Shelly shrugged. "I don't know, Dare. It might be just the thing, but I don't want you to get your hopes up and be disappointed. I know for a fact that AJ wants you to know the truth, but I also know that for him the timing has to be perfect."

Dare nodded as he pulled her into his arms. "Then I'm going to do everything in my power to make sure that it is."

Chapter 13

Dare hung up the phone and met AJ's expectant gaze.

"That was Chase. One of his waitresses called in sick. He'll have to pitch in for the weekend and won't be able to make it."

He saw the disappointment cloud AJ's eyes. So far since arriving at the cabin they had received no-show calls from everyone except Thorn, and he expected Thorn to call any minute.

"Does that mean we have to cancel this weekend?" AJ asked in such a disappointed voice that a part of Dare felt like a heel.

"Not unless you want to. There's still a possibility that Thorn might show."

Although he'd said the words, Dare knew they weren't true. His brothers and Jamal had understood his need to be alone with AJ this weekend and had agreed to bow out of the picture and plan something else to do.

When AJ didn't say anything, Dare said. "You know what I think we should do?"

AJ lifted a brow. "What?"

"Enjoy the three days anyway. I've been looking forward to a few days of rest and relaxation, and I'm sure you're glad to have an extra day off school, as well, right?"

AJ nodded. "Right."

"Then I say that we make the most of it. I can teach you how to fish in the morning and tomorrow night we can camp outside. Have you ever gone camping?"

"No."

Dare sadly shook his head at the thought. When they were kids his father had occasionally taken him and his brothers camping for the weekend just to get them out of their mother's hair for a while. "We can still do all the things that we'd planned to do anyway. How's that?"

AJ was clearly surprised. "You'll want to stay here with just me?"

A lump formed in Dare's throat at the hope he heard in his son's voice. He swallowed deeply. *If only you knew how much I want to stay here with just you,* he thought. "Yes," he answered. "I guess I should be asking you if you're sure that you want to stay here with just me."

AJ smiled. "Yes, I want to stay."

Dare returned that smile. "Good. Then come on. Let's get the rest of the things out of the truck."

The next morning Dare got up bright and early and stood on the porch enjoying a cup of coffee. AJ was still asleep, which was fine, since the two of them had stayed up late the night before. Thorn had finally called to say he couldn't make it due to a deadline he had to meet for a bike he had to deliver. So it was final that it would only be the two of them.

After loading up the supplies in the kitchen after Thorn's call, they'd gathered wood for a fire. Nights in the mountains meant wood for the fireplace and they had gathered enough to last all three days. Then, while he left AJ with the task of stacking the wood, Dare had gone into the kitchen to prepare chili and sandwiches for their dinner.

They hadn't said much over their meal, but AJ'd really started talking while they washed dishes. He'd told him about the friends he had left behind in California, and how he had written to them. They hadn't written back. He'd also talked about his grandparents, the Brockmans, and how he had planned to spend Christmas with them.

Now, Dare glanced around, deciding he really liked this place. It had once been jointly owned by one of their cousins and a friend of his, but Jamal had talked the two men into selling it to him and had then presented it to Delaney as one of her wedding gifts. It was at this cabin that Delaney and Jamal had met. While she was out of the country, Delaney had graciously given her brothers unlimited use of it, and all five had enjoyed getting away and spending time together here every once in a while.

Dare turned when he heard a noise behind him and smiled. "Good morning, AJ."

AJ wiped sleep from his eyes. "Good morning. You're up early."

Dare laughed. "This is the best time to catch fish."

AJ's eyes widened. "Then I'll be ready to go in a second." He rushed back into the house.

Dare chuckled and hoped his son remembered not only to

get dressed but to wash his face and brush his teeth. He inhaled deeply, definitely taking a liking to this father business.

Dare smiled as he looked at the sink filled with fish. AJ had been an ace with the fishing pole and had caught just as many fish as he had. He began rolling up his sleeves to start cleaning them. They would enjoy some for dinner today and tomorrow and what was left they would take home with them and split between his mother and Shelly. Maybe he could talk Shelly into having a fish fry and inviting the family over.

His gaze softened as he thought how easy it was to want to include Shelly in his daily activities. He suppressed a groan thinking of all their nighttime activities and smiled as it occurred to him they had yet to make love in a bed. He had to think of a way to get her over to his place for the entire night. Sneaking off to make love in her backyard under the stars had started off being romantic, but now he wanted more than romance, he wanted permanence…forever. He wanted them to talk and plan their future, and he wanted her to know just how greatly she had enriched his life since she had returned.

He shifted his thoughts to AJ. So far they'd been together over twenty-four hours and he hadn't brought up the topic of their relationship. They had spent a quiet, leisurely day at the lake talking mostly about school and the Williams sisters. It seemed his son had a crush on the two tennis players in a big way, especially Serena Williams. Dare was glad he'd let Chase talk him into taking tennis lessons with him last summer; at least he knew a little something about the game and had been able to contribute to AJ's conversation.

Dare sighed, anxious to get things out in the open with AJ, but as Shelly had said, AJ would have to be the one to bring it up. He glanced over his shoulder when he heard his son enter the kitchen. He had been outside putting away their fishing gear.

"You did a good job today with that fishing rod, AJ," Dare said, smiling over his shoulder. "I can't wait to tell Stone. The rod and reel you used belongs to him. He swears only a Westmoreland can have that kind of luck with it," he added absently.

"Then that explains things."

Dare turned around. "That explains what?"

"That explains why I did so good today—I *am* a Westmoreland."

Dare's breath caught and he swallowed deeply. He leaned back against the sink and stared at AJ long and hard, waiting for him to stop studying his sneakers and look at him. Moments later, AJ finally lifted his head and met his gaze.

"And how are you a Westmoreland, AJ?" Dare asked quietly, already knowing the answer but desperately wanting to hear his son say it anyway.

AJ cleared his throat. "I—I really don't know how to tell you this, but I have to tell you. And I have to first say that my mom wanted to tell you sooner, but I asked her not to, so it's not her fault so please don't be mad at her about it. You have to promise that you won't be mad at my mom."

Dare nodded. At that moment he would promise almost anything. "All right. I won't be mad at your mom. Now tell me what you meant about being a Westmoreland."

AJ put his hands into his pockets. "You may want to sit down for this."

Dare watched AJ's face and noticed how nervous he'd become. He didn't want to make him any more nervous than he already was, so he sat at the kitchen table. "Now tell me," he coaxed gently.

AJ hesitated, then met Dare's gaze, and said, "Although

my last name is Brockman, I'm really a Westmoreland…because I'm your son."

Dare's breath got lodged in his throat. He blinked. Of course, the news AJ was delivering to him didn't surprise him, but the uncertainty and the caution he saw in his son's gaze did. Shelly had been right. AJ wasn't sure if he would accept him as his son, and Dare knew he had to tread lightly here.

"You're my son?" he asked quietly, as if for clarification.

"Yes. That's why I'm ten and that's why we have the same name." He looked down at his sneakers again as he added, "And that's why I look like you a little, although you haven't seemed to notice but I'll understand if you don't want me."

Dare stood. He slowly crossed the room to AJ and placed what he hoped was a comforting hand, a reassuring hand, a loving hand on his shoulder. AJ looked up and met his gaze, and Dare knew he had to do everything within his power to make his son believe that he wanted him and that he loved him.

Choosing his words carefully and speaking straight from his heart and his soul, he said, "Whether you know it or not, you have just said words that have made me the happiest man in the entire world. The very thought that Shelly gave me a son fills me with such joy that it's overwhelming."

AJ searched his father's gaze. "Does that mean you want me?"

Dare chuckled, beside himself in happiness. "That means that not only do I want you, but I intend to keep you, and now that you're in my life I don't ever intend to let you out of it."

A huge smile crept over AJ's features. "Really?"

"Yes, really."

"And will my name get changed to Westmoreland?"

Dare smiled. "Do you want your name changed to Westmoreland?"

AJ nodded his head excitedly. "Yes, I'd like that."

"And I'd like that, too. We'll discuss it with your mother and see what her feelings are on the matter, all right?"

"All right."

They stared at each other as the reality of what had taken place revolved around them. Then AJ asked quietly, "And may I call you Dad?"

Dare's chest tightened, his throat thickened and he became filled with emotions to overpowering capacity. He knew he would remember this moment for as long as he lived. What AJ was asking, and so soon, was more than he could ever have hoped for. He had prayed for this. A smile dusted across his face as parental pride and all the love he felt for the child standing in front of him poured forth.

"Yes, you can call me Dad," he said, as he reached out and pulled his son to him, needing the contact of father to son, parent to offspring, Westmoreland to Westmoreland. They shared a hug of acceptance, affirmation and acknowledgement as Dare fought back the tears in his eyes. "I'd be honored for you to call me that," he said in a strained voice.

Moments later, Dare sighed, thinking his mission should have been completed, but it wasn't. Now that he had his son, he realized more than ever just how much he wanted, loved and needed his son's mother. His mission wouldn't be accomplished until he had her permanently in his life as well.

Later that night Dare placed calls to his parents and siblings and told them the good news. They took turns talking with AJ, each welcoming him to the family. After dinner Dare and AJ had talked while they cleaned up the kitchen. Already plans were made for them to return to the cabin in a few months, and Dare suggested that they invite Shelly to come with them.

"She won't come," AJ said, drying the dish his father had handed him.

Dare raised a brow. "Why wouldn't she?"

"Because she's not going to be your girlfriend," he said softly. "Although now I wish that she would."

Dare turned and folded his arms across his chest and looked at his son. "And what makes you think your mother won't be my girlfriend, AJ?" he asked, although the title of wife was more in line with what he was aiming for.

"She told me," he said wryly. "That same night we had a cookout at Grandma and Grandpa Westmoreland's house. After we got home we talked for a long time, and I told her that I had come close to telling you that night that I was your son. I asked if the three of us would be a family after I told you and she said no."

Dare remembered that night well. Shelly had been late coming to the backyard and had mentioned she and AJ had had a long talk. He sighed deeply as he tilted his head to the side to think about what AJ had said, then asked, "Did she happen to say why?"

AJ shook his head. "Yes. She said that although the two of you had been in love when you made me, that now you weren't in love anymore and were just friends. She also said that chances were that one day you would marry someone nice and I'd have a second mother who would treat me like her son."

Dare frowned. He and Shelly not being in love was a crock. How could she fix her lips to say such a thing, let alone think it? And what gave her the right to try and marry him off to some other woman? Didn't she know how he felt about her? That he loved her?

Then it suddenly hit him, right in the gut that, no, Shelly had no idea how he felt, because at no time had he told her. For the past month they had spent most of their time alone together, at night in her backyard under the stars making love. Did she think all they'd been doing was having sex? But then why would she think otherwise? He sucked in a breath, thinking that he sure had missed the mark.

"Is that true, Dad? Will you marry someone else and give me a second mother?"

Dare shook his head. "No, son. Your mother is the only mother you'll have, and she's the only woman I ever plan to marry."

Mimicking his father, AJ placed his arms across his chest and leaned against the sink. "Well, I don't think she knows that."

Dare smiled. "Then I guess I'm just the person to convince her." He leaned closer to his son and with a conspiratorial tone, he said. "Listen up. I have a plan."

Chapter 14

The first thing Shelly noticed as she entered the subdivision where Dare's home was located was that all the houses were stately and huge and sat on beautiful acreages. This was a newly developed section of town that had several shopping outlets and grocery stores. She could vividly remember it being a thickly wooded area when she had left town ten years ago.

She glanced at her watch. Dare had called and said that he and AJ had decided to return a day early and asked that she come over to his place and pick up AJ because Dare needed to stay at home and wait for the arrival of some important package. All of it sounded rather secretive, and the only thing she could come up with was that it pertained to some police business.

After reading the number posted on the front of the mailbox, she knew the regal-looking house that sat on a hill with a long, circular driveway belonged to Dare. She and Delaney had spent the day shopping yesterday and one of the things Delaney had mentioned was that Dare had banked most of his salary while working as a federal agent, and when he moved back home he had built a beautiful home.

Moments later, after parking her car Shelly strolled up the walkway and rang the doorbell. It didn't take long for Dare to answer.

"Hi, Shelly."

"Hi, Dare." Her heart began beating rapidly, thinking she would never tire of seeing him dressed casually in a pair of jeans and a chambray shirt. As she met his gaze, she thought that she had definitely missed him during the two days he and AJ had gone to North Carolina.

"Come on in," he invited, stepping aside.

"Thanks." She glanced around Dare's home when he closed the door behind her. Nice, she thought. The layout was open and she couldn't help noticing how chic and expensive everything looked. "Your home is beautiful, Dare."

"Thanks, and I'm glad you like it."

Shelly saw that he was leaning against the closed door staring at her. She cleared her throat. "You mentioned AJ finally got around to admitting that you're his father."

Dare shook his head. "Yes."

Shelly nodded. "I'm happy about that, Dare. I know how much you wanted that to happen."

"Yes, I did."

A long silence followed, and, with nothing else to say, Shelly cleared her throat again, suddenly feeling nervous in Dare's presence, mainly because he was still leaning against the door staring at her with those dark penetrating eyes of his.

Breaking eye contact, she glanced at her watch and decided to end the silence. "Speaking of AJ, where is he?"

Dare didn't say anything for a moment, then he spoke. "He isn't here."

Shelly raised a brow. "Oh? Where is he?"

"Over at my parents'. They dropped by and asked if he could visit with them for a while. I didn't think you would mind, so I told them he could."

Shelly nodded. "Of course I don't mind." After a few minutes she cleared her throat for the third time and said, "Well, I'm sure you have things to do so I'll—"

"No, I don't have anything to do, since the important package I was waiting for arrived already."

"Oh."

"In fact, I was hoping that you and I could take in a movie and have dinner later."

Her dark gaze sank into his. "Dinner? A movie?"

"Yes, and you don't have to worry about AJ. He'll be in good hands."

With a slight shrug, she said, "I know that, Dare. Your parents are the greatest."

Dare smiled. "Well, right now they think their oldest grandson is the greatest. Now that the secret is out, you should have seen my mom. She can't wait to go around bragging to everyone about him since it's safe to do so."

Shelly's stomach tightened. Now that the secret was out, things would be changing…especially her relationship with Dare. He wouldn't have to pretend interest in her any longer. Even now, she knew that probably the only reason he was inviting her to the movies and to dinner was out of kindness.

"Well, what about the movies and dinner?" Dare asked, reclaiming her attention.

She met his gaze. This would probably be the last time they would be together, at least out in public. There was no doubt in her mind that until they got their sexual needs under control they would still find the time to see each other at night in private.

"Yes, Dare. I'll go out to the movies and to dinner with you."

"Thanks for going out with me tonight, Shelly."

"Thanks for inviting me, Dare. I really enjoyed myself." And she had. They had seen a comedy featuring Eddie Murphy at the Magic Johnson Movie Theater near the Greenbriar Mall. Afterward, they had gone to a restaurant that had served the best-tasting seafood she'd ever eaten. Now they were walking around the huge shopping mall that brought back memories of when they had dated all those years ago and had spent a lot of their time there on the weekends.

Dare claimed the reason he was in no hurry to end their evening was because he wanted to give his parents and siblings a chance to bond with AJ, and he thought the stroll through Greenbriar Mall would kill some time.

"How do you like the type of work you're doing now, working outside the hospital versus working inside?"

This was the first time he had ever asked her anything about her job since she'd moved back. "It took some getting used to, but I'm enjoying it. I get to meet a lot of nice people and because of the hours I work, I'm home with AJ more."

Dare nodded. "I never did tell you why I stopped being an agent for the Bureau, did I?"

Shelly shook her head. "No, you didn't."

Dare nodded again. He then told her all the things he had liked about working for the FBI and those things he had begun to dislike. Finally he told her the reason he had returned home.

"And do you like what you're doing now, Dare?" she couldn't help but ask him, since she of all people knew what a career with the FBI had meant to him.

"Yes, I like what I'm doing now. I feel I'm making more of a difference here than I was making with the Bureau. It's like I'm giving back to a community that gave so much to my brothers and me while we were growing up. It's a good feeling to live in a place where you have history."

Shelly had to agree. She enjoyed being back home and couldn't bear the thought of ever leaving again. Although she had lived in L.A. for ten years, deep down she had never considered it as her home.

She sighed and glanced down at her watch. "It's getting late. Don't you think it's time for us to pick up AJ? I don't want him to wear out his welcome with your folks."

Dare laughed, and the sound sent sensations up Shelly's body, making her shiver slightly. He thought she had shivered for a totally different reason and placed his arm around her shoulders, pulling her closer to him for warmth. "He'll never be able to wear out his welcome with my family, Shelly. Come on, let's go collect our son."

Three weeks later, Shelly sat outside alone on her porch swing as it slowly rocked back and forth. It was the third week in October and the night air was cool. She had put on a sweater, but the stars and the full moon were so beautiful she couldn't resist sitting and appreciating them both. Besides, she needed to think.

Ever since that night Dare had taken her to a movie and to dinner, he had come by every evening to spend time with AJ. But AJ wasn't the only person he made sure he spent time with. Over the past few weeks he had often asked her out, either to a movie, dinner or both. Then there was the time he had asked her to go with him to the wedding of one of his deputies.

She sighed deeply. Each time she had tried putting distance between them, he would succeed in erasing the distance. Then there were the flowers he continued to send each week. When she had asked him why he was still sending them, he had merely smiled and said because he enjoyed doing so. And she had to admit that she enjoyed receiving them. But still, she didn't want to put too much stock in Dare's actions and continued to see what he was doing as merely an act of kindness on his part. It was evident that he wanted them to get along and establish some sort of friendly relationship for AJ's sake.

The other thing that confused her was the fact that he no longer sought her out at night. Their late-night rendezvous in her backyard had abruptly come to an end the night Dare had taken her on their first date. He had offered her no explanation as to why he no longer came by late at night, and she had too much pride to ask him.

He came by each afternoon around dinnertime and she would invite him to stay, so she still saw him constantly. And at night, after AJ went to bed, he would sit outside on the porch swing with her and talk about how her day had gone, and she would ask him about his. Their talks had become a nightly routine, and she had to admit that she rather enjoyed them.

She shifted her thoughts to AJ. He was simply basking in the love that his father and the entire Westmoreland family were giving him. Dare had been right when he'd said all AJ had needed was to feel that he belonged. Each time she saw her son in one of his happy moods, she knew that he was glad as well as proud to be a part of the Westmoreland clan, and that she had made the right decision to return to College Park.

She stood, deciding to go inside and get ready for bed.

Dare had left immediately after dinner saying he had to go to the station and finish up a report he was working on. As usual, before he left he had kissed her deeply, but otherwise he had kept his hands to himself. However, whenever he pulled her into his arms, she knew he wanted her. His erection was always a sure indicator of that fact. But she knew he was fighting his desire for her, which made things confusing, because she didn't understand why.

As she got ready for bed she continued to wonder what was going on with Dare. Why had he ended all sexual ties between them? Had he assumed she thought things were more serious between them than they really were because of their nightly meetings in her backyard?

As she closed her eyes she knew that if reality could not find her in his arms making love, that she would be there with him in the dreams she knew she would have that night.

Shelly smiled at Ms. Mamie. The older woman had broken her ankle two weeks ago and Shelly had been assigned as her home healthcare nurse. "I thought we had talked about you staying off your foot for a while, Ms. Mamie."

Ms. Mamie smiled. "I tried, but it isn't easy when I have so much to do."

Shelly shook her head. "Well, your ankle will heal a lot quicker if you follow my instructions," she said, rewrapping the woman's leg. She made it a point to check on Ms. Mamie at least twice a week, and she enjoyed her visits. Even with only one good leg, the older woman still managed to get around in her kitchen and always had fresh cookies baked when Shelly arrived.

"So, how are things going with you and the sheriff?"

Shelly looked up. "Excuse me?"

"You and the sheriff. How are the two of you doing? Everyone is talking about it."

Shelly frowned, not understanding. "They are talking about Dare and AJ or about me and Dare?"

"They are talking about you and Dare. Dare and AJ is old news. Everyone knew that boy was Dare's son even if Dare was a little slow in coming around and realizing that fact." Shelly's mind immediately took in what Ms. Mamie had said. She'd had no idea that she and Dare were now the focus of the townspeoples' attention. "Why are people talking about me and Dare?"

"Because everyone knows how hard he's trying to woo you."

Shelly stilled in her task and looked at Ms. Mamie. She couldn't help but grin at something so ridiculous. "Why would people think Dare is trying to woo me?"

"Because he is, dear."

The grin was immediately wiped from Shelly's face. Woo her? Dare? She shook her head. "I think you're mistaken."

"No, I'm not," Ms. Mamie answered matter-of-factly. "In fact, me and the ladies in my sewing club are taking bets."

Shelly raised a brow. "Bets?"

"Yes, bets as to whether or not you're going to give him a second chance. All of us know how much he hurt you before."

Shelly's head started spinning. "But I still don't understand why you all would think he was wooing me."

Ms. Mamie smiled. "Because it's obvious, Shelly. Luanne tells us each time he sends you flowers, which I understand is once, sometimes twice a week. Then, according to Clara, who lives across the street from you, he comes to dinner every evening and he takes you out on a date occasionally." The woman's smile widened. "Clara also mentioned that he's protecting your reputation by leaving your house at a reasonable time every night so he won't give the neighbors something to talk about."

Shelly shook her head. "But none of that means anything."

Ms. Mamie gently patted her hand. "That's where you're wrong, Shelly. It means everything, especially for a man like Dare. The ladies and I have watched him over the years ignore one woman after another, women who threw themselves at him. He never got serious about any of them. When you came back things were different. Anyone with eyes can see that he is smitten with you. That boy has always loved you, and I'll be the first to say he made a mistake ten years ago, but I feel good knowing he's trying real hard to win you back." She then grinned conspiratorially. "It even makes me feel good knowing that you're making it hard for him."

Making it hard for him? She hadn't even picked up on the fact that he was trying to win her back. Shelly opened her mouth to say something, then closed it, deciding that she needed to think about what Ms. Mamie had said. Was it true? Was Dare actually wooing her?

That question was still on her mind half an hour later when she pulled out of Ms. Mamie's driveway. She sighed deeply. The only person who could answer that question was Dare, and she decided it was time that he did.

Thunder rumbled in the distance as Dare placed a lid on the pot of chili he'd just made. He had tried keeping himself busy that afternoon since thoughts of Shelly weighed so heavily on his mind.

He knew one of the main reasons for this was that AJ would be spending the weekend with Morris and Cornelius, which meant Shelly would be home all alone, and Shelly all alone was too much of a temptation to think about. He sighed deeply, wondering just how much longer he could hold out in his plan to prove to her that what was between them was more than sex and that he cared deeply for her. For the past three weeks he had been the ardent suitor as he tried easing his way back into her heart. The only thing about it was that he wasn't sure whether his plan was working and exactly where he stood with her.

He paused in what he was doing when he heard his doorbell ring and wondered which of his brothers had decided to pay him a visit. It would be just like them to show up in time for dinner. Leaving the kitchen, he made his way through the living room to open the front door. His chest tightened with emotion when he looked through his peephole and saw that it wasn't one of his brothers standing outside on his porch, but Shelly.

He quickly opened the door and recognized her nervousness. A man in his profession was trained to detect when someone was fidgety or uneasy about something. "Shelly," he greeted her, wondering what had brought her to his place.

"Dare," she said returning the greeting in what he considered a slightly skittish voice. "May I come in and talk to you about something?"

He nodded and said, "Sure thing," before stepping aside to let her enter.

His gaze skimmed over her as she passed him, and he thought there was no way a woman could look better than this, dressed in something as simple as a pullover V-neck sweater and a long flowing skirt; especially if that skirt appeared to have been tailor-made just for her body. It flowed easily and fluidly down all her womanly curves.

He locked the door and turned to find her standing in the middle of his foyer as though she belonged in his house, every day and every night. "We can go into the living room if you like," he said, trying not to let it show just how much he had missed being alone with her.

"All right."

He led her toward the living room and asked; "Are you hungry? I just finished making a pot of chili."

"No, thanks, I'm not hungry."

"What about thirsty? Would you like something to drink?"

She smiled at him. "No, I don't want anything to drink. I'm fine."

He nodded. Yes, she was definitely fine. He didn't know another woman with a body quite like hers, and the memories of being inside that body made his hands feel damp. The room suddenly felt warmer than it should be.

He inhaled as he watched her take a seat on the sofa. He, in turn, took the chair across from her. Once she had gotten settled, he asked, "What is it you want to talk to me about, Shelly? Is something wrong with AJ?"

She shook her head. "Oh, no, everything with AJ is fine. I dropped him off at the Sears's house. I think he's excited about spending the weekend."

Dare nodded. He thought AJ was excited about spending the weekend as well. "If it's not about AJ then what do you want to talk about?"

His gaze held hers, and she hesitated only a moment before responding. "I paid a visit to Ms. Mamie today to check on her ankle. I'll be her home healthcare nurse for a while."

Dare nodded again, thinking there had to be more to her visit than to tell him that. "And?"

She hesitated again. "And she mentioned something that I found unbelievable, but I was concerned since it seems that a lot of the older women in this town think it's true."

He searched her features and detected more nervousness than before. "What do they think is true?"

Dare became concerned when seconds passed and Shelly didn't answer. Instead, she moved her gaze away from his to focus on some object on his coffee table. He frowned slightly. There had never been a time that Shelly had felt the need to be shy in his presence, so why was she now?

Standing, he crossed the room to sit next to her on the sofa. "All right, Shelly, what's this about? What do Ms. Mamie and her senior citizens' club think is true?"

Shelly swallowed deeply and took note of how close Dare was sitting next to her. Every time she took a breath she inhaled his hot male scent, a scent she had grown used to and one she would never tire of.

She breathed in and decided to come clean. Making light of the situation would probably make it easier, she thought, especially if he decided to laugh at something so absurd. She smiled slightly. "For some reason they think you're trying to woo me."

His gaze didn't flicker, but remained steadily on her face when he asked. "Woo you?"

She nodded. "Yes, you know—pursue me, court me."

Sitting so close to her, Dare could feel her tension. He also felt her uncertainty. "In other words," he said softly, "they think I'm trying to win you over, find favor in your eyes, in your heart and in your mind and break down your resistance."

Shelly nodded, although she didn't think Dare needed to break down her resistance since he had successfully done that a month or so ago. "Yes, that's it. That's what they believe. Isn't that silly?"

Dare shifted his position and draped his arms across the back of the sofa. He met Shelly's gaze, suddenly feeling hungry and greedy with an appetite that only she could appease.

He studied her face for a little while longer, then calmly replied. "No, I don't think there's anything silly about it, Shelly. In fact, their assumptions are right on target."

She blinked once, twice, as the meaning of his words sank in. He watched as her eyebrows raised about as high as they could go, and then she said, "But why?"

Keeping his gaze fixed on hers, he asked, "Why what?"

"Why would you waste your time doing something like that?"

Dare drew in a deep breath. "Mainly because I don't consider it a waste of my time, Shelly. Other than winning my son's love and respect, winning your heart back is the most important thing I've ever had to do."

Shelly swallowed, and for the first time in weeks she felt a bubble of hope grow inside her. Her heart began beating rapidly against her ribs. Was Dare saying what she thought he was saying? There was only one way to find out. "Tell me why, Dare."

He leaned farther back against the sofa and smiled. His smile was so sexy, so enticing and so downright seductive that it almost took her breath away. "Because I wanted to prove to you that I knew the difference between having sex and making love. And I had the feeling that you were beginning to think I didn't know the difference, and that all those times we spent in your backyard on that blanket were about sex and had nothing to do with emotions. But emotions were what it was all about, Shelly, each and every time I took you into my arms those nights. I have never just had sex with you in my life. There has never been a time that I didn't make love to you. For us there will always be a difference."

Tears misted Shelly's eyes. He was so absolutely right. For them there would always be a difference. She had tried convincing herself that there wasn't a difference and that each time they made love it was about satisfying hormones and nothing more. But she'd only been fooling herself. She loved Dare. She had always loved him and would always love him.

"AJ made me realize what you might have been thinking when we spent time at the cabin together," Dare said, interrupting Shelly's thoughts.

"He told me what you had said about the possibility of me getting married one day, and I knew then what you must have been thinking to assume that you and AJ and I would never be a family."

Shelly nodded. "But we will be a family?" she asked quietly, wanting to reach out and touch Dare, just to make sure this entire episode was real and that she wasn't dreaming any of it.

"Yes, we will be a family, Shelly. I made a mistake ten years ago by letting you go, but I won't make the same mistake twice. I love you and I intend to spend the remainder of my days proving just how much." Sitting forward, his smile was tender and filled with warmth and love when he added, "That is, if you trust me enough to give me another chance."

Shelly reached out and cupped his jaw with her hands. She met the gaze of the man she had always loved and who would forever have her heart. "Are you sure that is what you want, Dare?"

"Yes, I haven't been more sure of anything in my life, Shelly, so make me the happiest man in the world. I love you. I always have and always will, and more than anything, I want you for my wife. Will you marry me?"

"Oh, Dare, I love you, too, and yes, I will marry you." She automatically went into his arms when he leaned forward and kissed her. His kiss started off gentle, but soon it began stoking a gnawing hunger that was seeping through both of their bodies and became hard and demanding. And then suddenly Dare broke the kiss as he stood and Shelly found herself lifted off the sofa and cradled close to his body.

While she slowly ran her lips along his jaw, the corners of his mouth and his neck, he took the stairs two at a time, his breath ragged, as he carried her to his bedroom. Once there, he placed her in the middle of his bed and began removing his shirt. Her mouth began watering as he exposed a hard-muscled chest. All the other times since she'd been back they had made love in the dark, and although she had felt his chest she hadn't actually seen it. At least not like this. It was daylight and she was seeing it all, the thatch of hair that covered his chest then tapered down into a thin line as it trailed lower to his…

She swallowed and realized that his hand had moved to the snap on his jeans. He slowly began taking them off. She swallowed again. Seeing him like this, in the light, a more mature and older Dare, made her see just how much his body had changed, just how much more physical, masculine and totally male he was.

And just how much she appreciated being the woman he wanted.

She watched as he reached into the nightstand next to the bed to retrieve a condom packet, and how he took the time to prepare himself to keep her safe. With that task done, he lifted his gaze and met hers. "I'd like other children, Shelly."

She smiled and said, "So would I, and I know for a fact that AJ doesn't like being an only child, so he would welcome a sister or brother as well."

Dare nodded, remembering the question AJ had asked about whether he wanted other children. He was glad to hear

AJ would welcome the idea. Dare walked the few steps back over to the bed and, leaning down, he began removing every stitch of clothing from Shelly's body, almost unable to handle the rush of desire when he saw her exposed skin.

"You're beautiful, Shelly," he whispered breathlessly, smiling down at her when he had finished undressing her and she lay before him completely naked.

She returned his smile, glowing with his compliment. As he joined her in bed and took her into his arms, she knew that this was where she had always been meant to be.

Shelly felt the heat of desire warm her throat the moment Dare joined his mouth to hers, and all the love she had for him seeped through every part of her body as his kiss issued a promise she knew he would fulfill.

They hadn't made love in over a month so she wasn't surprised or shocked by the powerful emotions surging through her that only intensified with Dare's kiss. He wasn't just kissing her, he was using his tongue to stroke a need, deliver a promise and strip away any doubt that it was meant for them to be together.

Dare dragged his mouth from hers, his breath hard, shaky and harsh. "I need you now, baby," he said, reaching down and checking her readiness and finding her hot and wet. He settled his body over hers as fire licked through his veins, love flowed from his heart and a need to be joined with her drove everything within him.

He inhaled sharply as the tip of his erection pressed her wet and swollen flesh and it seemed that every part of his being was focused there, and when she opened her legs wider for him, arched her back, pushed her hips up and sank her nails deep in his shoulder blades, he couldn't help but groan and surge forward. The sensation of him filling her to the hilt only made him that much more hungry, greedy. And she was there with him all the way.

He thrust into her again and again, each stroke more hard and determined than the one before; the need to mate life sustaining, elemental, a necessity. And when he felt her thighs begin to quiver with the impact of her release, he followed her, right over the edge into oblivion. This woman who had given him a little Dare, who gave him more love than he rightly deserved would have his heart forever.

A shiver of awareness coursed down the length of Shelly's spine when Dare placed several kisses there. She opened her eyes and met his warm gaze.

"Do you know this is the first time we've made love in a bed since you've been back," he said huskily, as an amused smile touched his lips.

She tipped her head to the side and smiled. "Is that good or bad?"

His long fingers reached out and began skimming a path from her waist toward the center of her legs. "It's better." He leaned down and placed a kiss on her lips. "Stay with me tonight."

The heat shimmering in his eyes made her body feverish. With AJ spending the weekend away there was no problem with her staying with him. "Umm, what do I get if I stay?" She closed her eyes and sighed when his fingers touched her, caressed her, intent on a mission to drive her insane.

"Do you have to ask?" he rasped, his voice low and teasing against her lips.

"No, I don't," she replied in breathless anticipation.

She trembled as Dare began inflaming her body the

same way he had inflamed her heart. They had endured a lot, but through it all their love had survived and for the first time since returning to College Park, she felt she had finally come home.

Epilogue

A month later

Shelly couldn't help but notice the frown on Dare's face. It was a frown directed at Storm, who had just kissed her on the lips.

"I thought I warned you about doing that, Storm," Dare said in a very irritated tone of voice.

"But I can get away with it today because she's the bride and any well-wisher can kiss a bride on her wedding day."

Dare raised a brow. "Are you also willing to kiss the groom?"

Now it was Storm who frowned. "Kiss you? Hell, no!"

Dare smiled. "Then I suggest you keep your lips off the bride," he said, bringing Shelly closer to his side. "And there's enough single women here for you to kiss so go try your lips on someone else."

Storm chuckled. "The only other woman I'd want to kiss is Tara and I'm not crazy enough to try it. You're all talk, but Thorn really *would* kill me."

Shelly chuckled at Storm's comment as her gaze went to the woman the brothers had labeled Thorn's challenge, Tara Matthews. She was standing across the room talking to Delaney. Shelly thought that Tara was strikingly beautiful in an awe-inspiring, simply breathtaking way, and she couldn't help noticing that most of the men at the reception, both young and old, were finding it hard to keep their eyes off her. Every man except for Thorn. He was merely standing alone on the other side of the room looking bored.

"How can the two of you think that Thorn is interested in Tara when he hasn't said anything to her at all, other than giving her a courtesy nod? And he's not paying her any attention."

Dare chuckled. "Oh, don't let that nonchalant look fool you. He's paying her plenty of attention, right down to her painted toenails. He's just doing a good job of pretending not to."

"Yeah," Storm chimed in, grinning. "And he's been brooding ever since Delaney mentioned at breakfast this morning that Tara is moving to Atlanta to finish up her residency at a hospital here. The fact that she'll be in such close proximity has Thorn sweating. The heat is on and he doesn't like it at all."

A short while later Dare and Shelly had a talk with their son. "It's almost time for us to leave for our cruise, AJ. We want you on your best behavior with Grandma and Grandpa Westmoreland."

"All right." AJ looked at his father with bright eyes. "Dad, Uncle Chase and Uncle Storm said all of us are going fishing when you get back."

Dare smiled. He had news for his brothers. If they thought

for one minute that he would prefer spending a weekend with them rather than somewhere in bed with his wife, they had another thought coming. "Oh, they did, did they?"

"Yes."

He nodded as he glanced over at his brothers who were talking to Tara—all of them except for Thorn. He also noted the Westmoreland cousins—brothers Jared, Durango, Spencer, Ian and Reggie—were standing in the group as well. The only one missing was Quade, and because of his covert activities for the government, there was no telling where that particular Westmoreland was or what he was doing at any given moment. "We'll talk about it when I get back," Dare said absently to AJ, wondering at the same time just where Thorn had gone off to. Although he didn't see him, he would bet any amount of money that he was somewhere close by with his eyes on Tara.

Dare shrugged. He was glad Tara was Thorn's challenge and not his. He then returned his full attention to his son. "When school is out for the holidays, your mom and I are thinking about taking you to Disney World."

"Wow!"

Dare chuckled. "I take it you'd like that?"

"Yes, I'd love it. I've been to Disneyland before but not Disney World and I've been wanting to go there."

"Good." Dare pulled Shelly into his arms after checking his watch. It was time for them to leave for the airport. They would be flying to Miami to board the cruise ship to St. Thomas. "And keep an eye on your uncles, AJ, while I'm gone. They have a tendency to get a little rowdy when I'm not here to keep them in line."

AJ laughed. "Sure, Dad."

Dare clutched AJ's shoulder and pulled him closer. "Thanks. I knew that I could count on you."

He breathed in deeply as he gathered his family close. With Shelly on one side and AJ on the other, he felt intensely happy on this day, his wedding day, and hoped that each of his brothers and cousins would one day find this same happiness. It was well worth all the time and effort he had put into it.

When he met Shelly's gaze one side of his mouth tilted into a hopelessly I-love-you-so much smile, and the one she returned said likewise. And Dare knew in his heart that he was a very happy man.

His mission had been accomplished. He had won the hearts of his son and of the woman that he loved.

* * * * *

THORN'S CHALLENGE

Prologue

Tara Matthews hated weddings.

She had done a pretty good job of avoiding them until she had met the Westmorelands. Since then she had attended two weddings within an eighteen-month period. She had even been maid of honor when her good friend, Delaney Westmoreland, had married a desert sheikh almost a year and a half ago.

And today, like everyone else in the grand ballroom of the Sheraton Hotel in downtown Atlanta, she had come to celebrate the wedding of Delaney's brother, Dare Westmoreland, to the woman he loved, Shelly Brockman.

The worst part, Tara thought as she glanced around her, was that she couldn't really complain about having to attend the weddings. Not when the Westmorelands had become the closest thing to a family she'd had since that fateful day in June two years ago. It was to have been her wedding day, but she had stood at the altar in complete shock after the groom, the man she had loved, who she thought had loved her, had announced to all three hundred guests that he couldn't go through with the wedding because he was in love with her maid of honor—the woman she'd considered her best friend for over fifteen years. That day Tara had left Bunnell, Florida, hurt and humiliated, and vowing to her family that she would never return.

And so far she hadn't.

A few days later she'd accepted a position as a resident pediatrician at a hospital in Bowling Green, Kentucky. Leaving her hometown had destroyed her and her father's dream of working together in his pediatric practice.

While working at the hospital in Kentucky, she had met Delaney Westmoreland, another pediatrician, and they had become the best of friends. She had also become good friends with four of Delaney's five older brothers, Dare, Stone and the twins, Chase and Storm. The initial meeting between her and the fifth brother, Thorn, had been rather rocky. She'd "gone off" on him about his unpleasant mood. Since then, they had pretty much avoided each other, which suited her just fine. At six-foot-four, thirty-five years of age, ruggedly handsome and sexy as sin, Thorn Westmoreland was the last man she needed to be around; especially since whenever she saw him she thought of scented candles, naked bodies and silken sheets.

"I'm going to the ladies' room," she whispered to Delaney, who turned to her, nodded and smiled. Tara smiled back, understanding that the older woman Delaney was talking to wasn't letting her get a word in. Glancing at her watch to see how much longer she needed to put in an appearance, Tara made her way down a long, empty hallway to the restrooms.

Her thoughts drifted to the fact that next month she would be moving from Kentucky to the Atlanta area. She was moving because an older married doctor with clout at the Kentucky hospital had been obsessed with having her in his bed. When she'd rebuffed his advances, he'd tried making her work environment difficult. To avoid the sexual harassment lawsuit she'd threatened to file, the hospital had decided to relocate her and Atlanta had been her first choice.

Tara was so busy putting her lipstick case back in her purse after leaving the restroom that she didn't notice the man coming out of the men's room at the same time, until they collided head-on.

"Oh, I'm so sorry. I wasn't looking where I was—"

Any further words died on her lips when she saw that the man she had bumped into was Thorn Westmoreland. He seemed as surprised to see her as she was to see him.

"Thorn."

"Tara."

He returned her greeting in an irritated tone as his intense dark eyes held her gaze. She frowned, wondering what he was upset about. He hadn't been looking where he was going any more than she had, so the blame wasn't all hers. But she decided to be cordial for once where he was concerned. "I apologize for not looking where I was going."

When he didn't say anything, but frowned and narrowed his eyes at her, Tara decided not to wait for a response that undoubtedly wasn't coming. She made a move to pass him, and it was then that she noticed he had not removed his hand from her arm. She looked down at his hand and then back at him.

"Thanks for keeping me from falling, Thorn, but you can let go of me now."

Instead of releasing her, his hold tightened and then he muttered something deep in his throat, which to Tara's ears sounded pretty much like, "I doubt if I can." Then, suddenly, without any warning, he leaned down and captured her lips with his.

The first thought that came to Tara's mind was that she had to resist him. But a second thought quickly followed; she should go ahead and get him out of her system since he had been there from the day they'd met. Shamefully she admitted that the attraction she'd felt for him was stronger than any she'd ever felt for a man, and that included Derrick Hayes, the man she had planned to marry.

The third thought that whipped through her mind was that Thorn Westmoreland definitely knew how to kiss. The touch of his tongue to hers sent a jolt through her so intense, her midsection suddenly felt like a flaming torch. Emotions, powerful and overwhelming, shot through her, and she whimpered softly as he deepened the kiss with bold strokes of his tongue, seizing any sound she made, effectively and efficiently staking a claim on her mouth.

A claim she didn't want him to make, but one he was making anyway.

He used his hands to cup her bottom boldly and instinctively she moved closer to him, coming into contact with his straining arousal. When she placed her arms around his neck, he arched his back, lifted her off the floor and brought her more snugly to him, hip-to-hip, thigh-to-thigh, and breast-to-breast. His taste, tinged with the slight hint of champagne, went right to her head, and a dizzy rush of need she couldn't explain sent blood rushing through all parts of her.

When he finally released her mouth and placed her back down on solid ground, they were both breathless. He didn't let go of her. He continued to hold her in his arms, nibbling on her neck, her chin and her lips before recapturing her mouth with his for another bone-melting kiss.

He sucked on her tongue tenderly, passionately, slowly, as though he had all the time in the world to drive her mad with desire. It was a madness that flooded her insides and made her moan out a pleasure she had never experienced before. Potent desire, stimulating pleasure, radiated from his hands, his tongue and the hard body pressed to hers. When he finally broke off the kiss, she slumped weakly against his chest thinking that in all her twenty-seven years, she had never been kissed like that.

She slowly regained her senses as she felt him remove his hands from her. She slid her hands from his shoulders and looked up into his eyes, seeing anger radiating there. He apparently was mad at himself for having kissed her, and even madder with her for letting him. Without saying a word he turned and walked off. He didn't look back. When he was no longer in sight she breathed deeply, still feeling the heat from his kiss.

Tara nervously moistened her lips as she tried to regain control of her senses. She felt it was fairly safe to assume, after a kiss like that, that Thorn was now out of her system. In any case, she was determined more than ever to continue to avoid him like the plague.

Two years ago she had learned a hard lesson; love, the happily-ever-after kind, was not meant for her.

Chapter 1

Three months later

She had a body to die for and Thorn Westmoreland was slowly drawing his last breath.

A slow, easy smile spread across his face. She was exquisite, every man's fantasy come true. Everything about her was a total turn-on, guaranteed to get your adrenaline flowing, and his blood was so incredibly fired up he could barely stand it.

He took his time and studied every magnificent line of her. The sight lured him closer for an even better inspection. She was definitely a work of art, sleek, well built with all the right angles and curves, and tempted him beyond belief. He wanted to mount her and give her the ride of her life…or possibly get the ride of his.

He felt a distinct tingle in his stomach. Reaching out, his fingers gently touched her. She was ready for him.

As ready as he was for her...

"Hey, Thorn, you've been standing there salivating over that bike for at least ten minutes. Don't you think you should give it a rest?"

The smile on Thorn's face faded and without turning around to see who had spoken he said. "The shop's closed, Stone."

"You're here, so that means it's open," Stone Westmoreland said, coming into his brother's line of vision. Thorn was standing ogling the motorcycle he had built, his latest creation, the Thorn-Byrd RX1860. Rumors were spreading like wildfire that a Harley couldn't touch the Thorn-Byrd RX1860 for style and a Honda had nothing on it for speed. Stone didn't doubt both things were true. After all, this was another one of Thorn's babies. It had taken Thorn an entire year to build it; five months longer than it usually took him to put together one of his motorcycles. People came from all over the country to special order a Thorn-Byrd. They were willing to pay the hefty price tag to own the custom-built style and class only Thorn could deliver. You got what you paid for and everyone knew Thorn put not only his reputation and name behind each bike he built, but also his heart and soul.

"And why are you closing up early?" Stone asked, ignoring his brother's deep frown. He knew Thorn well enough to overlook his grouchiness.

"I thought I would be getting a few moments of privacy. I regret the day I gave all of you keys to this place."

Stone grinned, knowing Thorn was referring to him and their three brothers. "Well, it was best that you did. No telling when we might drop in and find you trapped beneath a pile of chrome and metal."

Thorn raised his eyes to the ceiling. "Has the thought ever occurred to you that you could also find me in bed with a woman?"

"No."

"Well, there is that possibility. Next time try knocking first instead of just barging in," Thorn snapped. Because he spent so many hours at the shop, his office had all the comforts of home including a room in the back with a bed. He also had a workout room that he used regularly to stay in shape.

"I'll try and remember that," Stone said, chuckling. His brother was known for his bark as well as his bite. Thorn could be a real pain in the rear end when he wanted to. There was that episode with Patrice Canady a few years back. It seemed Thorn had been mad at the whole world because of one woman. On top of that, there was Thorn's policy of not indulging in sex while training for a race. And since he'd been involved in a number of races so far this year, he'd been grouchier than usual. Like a number of athletes, Thorn believed that sex before an event would drain your body and break your concentration. As far as Stone was concerned, race or no race, to improve his mood Thorn definitely needed to get laid.

"What are you doing here, Stone? Don't you have a book to write?" Thorn asked. Stone, at thirty-three, was a nationally known bestselling author of several action-thriller novels. He wrote under the pen name of Rock Mason.

Thorn's question reminded Stone why he had dared enter the lion's den. "No, I just finished a book and mailed it to my publisher this morning. I'm here to remind you about tonight's card game at seven-thirty."

"I remember—"

"And to let you know the location has changed. It's not

going to be over at Dare's place as planned since AJ's camping trip was cancelled. The last thing we need is for Storm to be cursing all over the place when he starts losing and tempting our nephew to add a few of those choice words to his vocabulary."

Thorn nodded in agreement. "So where will it be?"

"Tara's place."

Thorn turned and narrowed his gaze at his brother. "Why the hell are we playing cards at Tara's place?"

Stone hoped the amusement dancing in his eyes didn't show. He and the other brothers had taken Tara up on her offer to have the card game at her place mainly because they knew it would rile Thorn. They were well aware of how hard he went out of his way to avoid her. "The reason we're having the card game at her place is because she invited us over as a way to thank us for helping her move in."

"I didn't help."

"Only because you were out of town for a race that weekend."

Thorn propped his hip against a table and decided not to tell Stone that even if he'd been in town he would not have helped. Being around Tara Matthews was pure torture and the last thing he wanted to remember was the time he'd lost his head and gotten a real good taste of her at Dare's wedding. If his brothers knew the two of them had kissed, he would never hear the last of it.

Sighing deeply, Thorn slanted his brother a hard look. "Why can't we play cards at your place?"

"It's being painted."

"What about Chase's place?" He asked about the brother who owned a soul food restaurant in downtown Atlanta. Chase was a twin to his brother Storm.

"Too junky."

"And Storm's?"

"There'll be too many interruptions from women calling him on the phone."

Thorn sighed deeply. At thirty-two, Storm, who was the younger of the twins, was a fireman by day and a devout ladies' man at night.

"Then what about my place?"

Stone laughed and shook his head. "Forget it. You never have any food in the fridge or enough beer to drink. So are you coming?"

Thorn frowned. "I'll think about it."

Stone inwardly smiled. It was hard for Thorn to miss a Westmoreland card game "Okay, if we see you, that's fine, and if we don't see you that will be fine, too. I'll just win all of Storm's money by myself."

Thorn's frown deepened. "Like hell you will."

Stone smile. "And like hell you would even if you're there," he said throwing out the challenge, knowing just how much Thorn liked challenges. Whether Thorn admitted it or not, his brothers knew that his biggest challenge was a good-looking woman by the name of Tara Matthews.

The buzzing of Tara Matthews's intercom captured her attention. "Yes, Susan?"

"Mrs. Lori Chadwick is here to see you, Dr. Matthews."

Tara lifted a brow, wondering what had brought Lori Chadwick to her office. Her husband, Dr. Martin Chadwick, was Head of Pediatrics and a very important man around the hospital. He was also her boss. "Please send her in."

Tara smiled when the door opened and Lori Chadwick walked in. As usual the older woman looked stunning. It was a known fact that Lori Chadwick enjoyed raising money for the hospital, and if the new children's wing was any indication, she was very good at it.

"Mrs. Chadwick," Tara greeted respectfully, offering her hand.

"Dr. Matthews, it's good seeing you again, dear."

"Thanks," Tara said, gesturing to a chair across from her desk. "It's good seeing you again, too." The last time she'd seen Mrs. Chadwick had been at a charity function a few weeks ago. It had been the first such function she had attended since moving to Atlanta and joining the staff at Emory University Hospital.

Lori Chadwick smiled. "I know how busy you are, Dr. Matthews, so I'll get straight to the point. I'm here to solicit your help in a fundraiser I'm planning."

Tara sat down behind her desk and returned Lori Chadwick's smile, flattered that the older woman had sought her assistance. One of the first things she'd been told by the other doctors when she had first arrived was not to get on Lori Chadwick's bad side. The woman loved her pet projects and expected everyone else to have the same enthusiasm for them as well. "I'd be glad to help. What sort of project do you have in mind?"

"I thought a charity calendar would be nice and would generate a lot of interest. The money that we'll make from the sale of the calendars will help Kids' World."

Tara nodded. Kids' World was a foundation that gave terminally ill children the chance to make their ultimate dream—such as a visit to any place in the world—come true. All proceeds for the foundation came from money raised through numerous charity events.

"Any ideas for this calendar?" Tara asked, thinking she really liked what Mrs. Chadwick was proposing.

"Yes. It will be a calendar of good-looking men," the older

woman said chuckling. "I'm not too old to appreciate a fine masculine physique. And a 'beefcake' calendar, tastefully done of course, would sell like hotcakes. But I want a variety of men from all walks of life," she added excitedly. "So far, I've already gotten a number of firm commitments. But there are still a few spots open and that's why I'm here. There's one name that keeps popping up as a suggestion from a number of the women I've talked to, and from what I understand he's a friend of yours."

Tara raised a brow. "A friend of mine?"

"Yes."

"Who?"

"Thorn Westmoreland, the motorcycle racer. I understand that he's something of a daredevil, a risk-taker on that motorcycle of his. He would definitely do the calendar justice."

Before Tara could gather her wits and tell Lori Chadwick that Thorn was definitely not a friend of hers, the woman smiled radiantly and said. "And I'm counting on you, Dr. Matthews, to convince Mr. Westmoreland to pose for the charity calendar. I know you won't let me and Kids' World down."

Later that evening Tara glanced up at a knock at her front door. Wiping the cookie dough from her hands she looked at the clock on the stove. It was only a little past seven and the card game wouldn't start until nine. She crossed her living room to the door and peeped out.

Thorn!

She thought Stone had said that Thorn wouldn't be coming tonight. Her heart suddenly began pounding fast and furious. Adrenaline mixed with overheated hormones gave her a quick rush, and the first thought that entered her mind was of the kiss she and Thorn had shared at his brother's wedding three months before; a kiss she'd been certain would get him out of her system.

But it hadn't.

In fact he was more in her thoughts than ever before.

She slowly opened the door, wondering why, if he had come to play cards, he had arrived so early. There was just something about the way he stood there with his helmet in his hand that really did crazy things to Tara's entire body. She felt breathless and her pulse actually ached low in her stomach as he adopted the sexiest pose she had ever seen in a man. It was a stance that would have any woman salivating if it was captured on a calendar; especially the kind Lori Chadwick proposed.

The thumb of his right hand was in his pocket and his left hand held his helmet by his side. He had shifted most of his weight to his right leg which made his jeans stretch tight, firmly across his thighs. They were masculine thighs, lean and powerful looking. The broad shoulders under the leather bomber jacket revealed a beautiful proportioned upper body and from the first, she had been acutely conscious of his tall, athletic physique. He was so devilishly handsome she could barely stand it. She lowered her gaze to his black leather motorcycle boots before returning to his eyes. The man was definitely gorgeous with his brooding good looks. There was no other way to describe him.

His gaze made intense heat settle in the pit of her stomach, and her heart began pounding even harder. She tried not to concentrate on his tight jeans, his leather bomber jacket or the diamond stud earring in his left ear. But that only left his face, which in itself was a total turn-on. His hair was cut close to his head and his skin was a smooth coppery brown. His eyes were so dark they appeared to be black satin. His nose was firm and his cheekbones chiseled. But it was his mouth that had her full attention. She was flooded with memories of how that mouth had felt against hers and how it had tasted. It was full, generously curved, and enticing with a capital *E*. It suddenly occurred to her that she had never seen him smile. Around her he always wore a frown.

Even now.

Even that night he had kissed her.

She sighed, not wanting to remember that night although she knew she'd never forget it. "Thorn, what are you doing here?" she cleared her throat and asked.

"Isn't there a card game here tonight?" he responded in a voice too good to be real. A deep huskiness lingered in its tone and the throaty depth of it held a sensuality that was like a silken thread wrapping all around her, increasing the rhythm of her heart.

She cleared her throat again when he raised his brow, waiting for her response. "Yes, but you're early. It doesn't start until nine."

"Nine?" he lifted a dark, brooding brow. "I could have sworn Stone said the game started at seven-thirty." He glanced down at his watch. "All right, I'll be back later," he said curtly and turned to leave.

"Thorn?"

He turned back around and met her gaze. He was still frowning. "Yes?"

Tara knew that now would be a good time to talk to him about Lori Chadwick's calendar. She had mentioned it to Chase Westmoreland when he'd stopped by the hospital after Mrs. Chadwick's visit, and he'd said there was no reason for her not to ask Thorn if he'd do it. After all, the calendar was for charity. He had warned her upfront, however, that she had her work cut out for her in persuading Thorn to do the calendar. Thorn, he'd said, detested a lot of publicity about himself. According to Chase, the last time Thorn had been involved in a publicity stunt had ended up being a love affair from hell. No amount of further probing had made Chase give her any more information than that. He had said that if she wanted to know the whole story, Thorn would have to be the one to tell her.

"You're welcome to hang around until the others arrive if you'd like. You won't have that long to wait. It's only an hour and a half," she said.

"No thanks," he didn't hesitate in saying. "In fact, tell my brothers that I've changed my mind and won't be playing cards tonight after all."

Tara watched as Thorn walked over to his bike, straddled his thighs over it, placed the shiny black helmet over his head, started the engine and took off as if the devil himself was chasing him.

This, Thorn thought, *is the next best thing to making love to a woman.*

Bearing down, he leaned onto the bike as he took a sharp curve. The smooth humming sound of the bike's engine soothed his mind and reminded him of a woman purring out her pleasure in bed. It was the same purring sound he would love to hear from Tara Matthews's lips.

Even with Atlanta's cool January air hitting him, his body felt hot, as a slow burning sensation moved down his spine. He was experiencing that deep, cutting, biting awareness he encountered every time he saw Tara. His hands tightened their grip on the handlebars as he remembered how she had looked standing in the doorway wearing a pair of jeans and a tank top. He found her petite, curvy body, dark mahogany skin, light brown eyes and dark brown shoulder-length hair too distracting on one hand and too attracting on the other. It rattled him to no end that he was so physically aware of everything about her as a woman.

Even when she'd lived in Kentucky she had invaded his sleep. His dreams had been filled with forbidden and invigorating sex. Cold showers had become a habit with him. No woman had been able to invade his space at work, but she had been there, too, more times than he could count. Building motorcycles and preparing for races had always gotten his total concentration—until he'd met Tara Matthews.

He'd constantly been reminded of the first time they had met. He had arrived at his sister Delaney's apartment late one night with his four brothers playing cards and no one had a clue where Delany had gone or when she would return. At least no one had felt the need to tell him. He had lost his cool and had been one step away from murdering his brothers. Tara had stormed out of Delaney's kitchen, with all her luscious curves fitting snugly in a short denim skirt, sexier than any woman had a right to be. And with more courage than anyone had a right to have, she had gotten all in his face. She had straightened her spine, lifted her chin and read him the riot act about the way he had questioned his brothers over Delaney's whereabouts. She'd told him in no uncertain terms what she thought of his foul mood. All the while she'd been setting him straight, his lust had stirred to maximum proportions, and the only thing he could think about was getting her to the nearest bedroom and zapping her anger by making love to her.

The quick intensity of his desire had frightened the hell out of him, and he had resented feeling that way. After Patrice, he had vowed that no woman would be his downfall again and he'd meant it. He wasn't having any of that.

An ache suddenly gripped his midsection when he thought of just what he *would* like to have. A piece of Tara would do him just fine; just enough so that he could get her out of his system, something the kiss hadn't accomplished. He wanted to bury himself inside her as deeply as he could and not come out until he had gotten his fill, over and over again. Such a feat might take days, weeks, even months. He had never been in this predicament before and was working hard not to let his brothers know. If they had any idea that he had the hots for their baby sister's best friend, they would give him pure hell and he would never hear the last of it. Even now the reminder of Tara's taste was causing his mouth to water.

And to think she had invited him to hang around her place for an hour and a half and wait for his brothers tonight. He couldn't imagine himself alone with her for any length of time and especially not for longer than an hour. There was no way he could have done that and kept his sanity. That would have been asking for even more trouble than he had gotten into with her at Dare's wedding.

Squaring his shoulders he leaned onto his bike as he took another sharp curve with indulgent precision, relishing the freedom and thrill of letting go in a totally uninhibited way. It was the same way he wanted to take Tara when he made love to her.

The way he *would* take her.

That simple acceptance strengthened his resolve and made the decision he'd just made that much easier to deal with. The restraint and control he'd tried holding on to since first meeting Tara was slowly loosening. A completely physical, emotionally free affair is what he wanted with her. It was time to stop running and meet his challenge head-on.

His next race was during Bike Week in Daytona Beach and

was only seven weeks from now. Seven more weeks of celibacy to go.

While waiting he intended to get Tara primed, ripe and ready, much like this very machine he was riding. However, even with all the similarities, there was no doubt in his mind that getting Tara in his bed would be a unique experience. He would get the ride of his life and centrifugal force would definitely be the last thing on his mind.

He smiled. Yes, it was time he and Tara stopped avoiding each other and started making plans to put all that wasted energy to good use.

Chapter 2

Tara heard the doorbell ring the minute she opened the oven to take out another batch of cookies. "Stone, can you get that for me, please?" she called out to one of the men busy setting up the card table in her dining room.

"Sure thing," Stone said, making his way to Tara's front door.

Opening the door, Stone lifted a brow when he saw Thorn standing on the other side. "I thought you told Tara that you'd changed your mind about tonight," he said, stepping aside to let his brother enter.

"And I changed it back," Thorn said curtly, meeting Stone's curious gaze. "Why are you the one opening the door instead of Tara?"

Stone smiled. It was hard getting used to Thorn's jealous streak; especially since it was a streak Thorn wasn't even aware he had. "Because she's busy in the kitchen. Come on. You can help get the card table set up in the dining room."

"And didn't you tell me the card game started at seven-thirty instead of nine?" Thorn asked meeting his brother's gaze.

Keeping a straight face, Stone said. "I don't think so. You must have misunderstood me."

The moment Thorn walked into the kitchen, Tara turned away from the sink and met his gaze. Surprise flared in her eyes and increased the rhythm of her heart. She swallowed deeply and looked at him for a moment then said. "I thought you weren't coming back."

Thorn leaned against a kitchen counter and stared at her. It was apparent seeing him again had rattled her. The way she was pulling in a ragged breath as well as the nervous way she was gripping the dish towel were telling signs. "I changed my mind," he said, not taking his gaze from hers, beginning to feel galvanized by the multitude of sensations coursing through him.

Now that he had decided that he would no longer avoid her, he immediately realized what was happening between them and wondered if she realized it, too. He inwardly smiled, feeling that she did. She broke eye contact with him and quickly looked down at the kitchen floor, but it hadn't been quick enough. He had seen the blush coloring her cheeks as well as the contemplative look in her eyes.

"There's a lot of money to be won here tonight and I decided that I may as well be the one to win it," he added.

Stone rolled his eyes to the ceiling. "Are you going to help set up the table or are you going to stay in here and engage in wishful thinking?"

Thorn turned to his brother and frowned slightly. "Since you want to be such a smart-mouth, Stone, I'm going to make sure your money is the first that I win, just to send you home broke."

"Yeah, yeah, whatever," Stone said.

Thorn's gaze then moved back to Tara with a force he knew she felt. He could feel her response all the way across the room. Satisfied with her reaction, he followed Stone out of the kitchen.

As soon as Thorn and Stone left the room, Tara leaned back against the kitchen counter feeling breathless, and wondered if Stone had picked up on the silent byplay that had passed between her and Thorn. Staring at him while he had stared at her had almost been too much for her fast-beating heart. The intensity of his gaze had been like a physical contact and she hadn't quite yet recovered from it.

But she would.

Ever since Derrick, she had instituted a policy of not letting any man get too close. She had male friends and she hadn't stopped dating altogether, but, as soon as one showed interest beyond friendship she hadn't hesitated to show him the door. She'd been aware from the first that Thorn was dangerous. Even though her intense attraction to him had set off all kinds of warning signs, she had felt pretty safe and in control of the situation.

Until their kiss a few months back.

Now she didn't feel safe and wasn't sure she was in control of anything. The man was temptation at its finest and sin at its worse. There was something about him that was nothing short of addictive. She had no plans to get hooked on him and knew what she needed to do, but more importantly, she also knew what she needed *not* to do; she couldn't let Thorn Westmoreland think she was interested in him.

Curious, yes. Interested, no.

Well, that was partly true. She *was* interested in him for Mrs. Chadwick's calendar, but Tara was determined not to let her interest go any further than that.

* * *

Where is she?

Thorn glanced around the room once again and wondered where Tara had gone. After they had gotten things set up in her dining room, she had shown them her refrigerator filled with beer, and the sandwiches and cookies she had placed on the kitchen counter. Since then he had seen her only once, and that was when she had come into the room to tell them she had also made coffee.

That had been almost two hours ago.

He couldn't help but think about what had transpired between them in her kitchen, even in Stone's presence, although he felt certain his brother hadn't had a clue as to what had been going on. Stone had a tendency sometimes to overlook the obvious. And the obvious in this case was the fact that just being in the same room with Tara made him hot and aroused. Judging from her reaction to him, she'd also been affected. Since it seemed they were on the same wave length, he saw no reason to fight the attraction any longer.

He wanted her, plain and simple.

First he wanted to start off kissing her, to reacquaint himself with her mouth until he knew it just as well as he knew his own. Then he wanted to get to know her body real well. He had always admired it from a distance, but now he wanted to really get into it, literally. He'd had nearly two years to reconcile himself to the reality that Tara Matthews was not just a bump-and-grind kind of woman. He hadn't needed to get up close and personal with her to realize that fact. He could easily tell that she was the kind of woman who could stimulate everything male about him, and fate had given him the opportunity to discover what it was about her that made his senses reel and heated up his blood. The relationship he wanted to share with her would be different from the one he had shared with any woman, including Patrice. This time his heart would not be involved, only certain body parts.

"Are you in this game or not, Thorn?"

Dare's question captured his attention and judging from his brother's smile, Dare found Thorn's lack of concentration amusing. Dare, the oldest brother at thirty-seven, was sheriff of College Park, a suburb of Atlanta, and didn't miss much. "Yes, I'm in the game," Thorn stated with annoyance, studying the cards he held in his hand once more.

"Just thought I'd ask, since you've lost a whole lot of money tonight."

Dare's words made him suddenly realize that he *had* lost a lot of money, three hundred dollars, to Stone who was looking at him with a downright silly grin on his face.

"It seems Thorn's mind is on other things tonight," Stone said chuckling. "You know what they say—you snooze, you lose—and you've been snoozing a lot tonight, bro."

Thorn leaned back in his chair and glared at his brother. "Don't get too attached to my money. I'll recoup my losses before the night's over." He pushed back his chair and stood. "I think I'll stretch my legs by walking to the living room and back."

"Tara's not in there, Thorn. She's upstairs reading," his brother Storm said, smiling as he threw out his last card. At Thorn's frown he chuckled and said. "And please don't insult my intelligence by giving me that I-don't-know-what-you're-talking-about look. We're not stupid. We all know you have this thing for her."

Thorn's frown deepened. He wondered how long they'd known. His brothers were too damn observant for their own good. Even Stone, whom he'd always considered the less observant one, seemed to have sensed the tension between him and Tara. "So what if I do?" he snapped in an agitated voice. "Any of you have a problem with it?"

Dare leaned back in his chair. "No, but evidently you do since you've been fighting it for nearly two years now," he said, meeting Thorn's frown with one of his own. "We knew from the beginning that she was your challenge and even told you so. It's about time you come to terms with it."

Thorn leaned forward, both palms on the table, and met his brothers' gazes. "I haven't come to terms with anything," he snapped.

"But you will once you put that nasty episode with Patrice behind you," Dare responded. "Damn, Thorn, it's been three years since that woman. Let it go. To my way of thinking you never actually loved her anyway, you just considered her your possession and got pissed to find out you weren't the only man who thought that. As far as I'm concerned she was bad news and I'm glad you found out her true colors when you did. You're a smart man and I don't think you're into self-torture, so relax and stop being stubborn and uptight and get over what she did to you. And for Pete's sake, please do something about your sexual frustrations. You're driving us crazy and it's gotten so bad we hate to see you coming."

Chase laughed. "Yeah, Thorn, it's obvious you haven't gotten laid in a while. Don't you think that rule you have of not indulging in sex while racing is a bit much? By my calculations it's been way over a year, possibly two. Don't you think you're carrying this celibacy thing a bit too far?"

"Not if he's waiting on a particular woman that he's set his sights on and he wants with a fierce Westmoreland hunger," Stone said smiling, knowing the others knew the gist of his meaning. "Since we all have a good idea what he wants from

Tara, maybe now would be a good time to tell Thorn just what Tara wants from him, Chase."

The room got quiet and all eyes turned to Chase. But the ones that unsettled Chase more than the others belonged to Thorn as he sat back down. Chase smiled, seeing Thorn's annoyance as well as his curiosity. He had shared the news with Stone about Tara wanting Thorn to pose for the charity calendar but hadn't gotten around to telling the others yet.

"I stopped by the hospital today to visit Ms. Amanda, who's had hip surgery," he said, mentioning the older woman who worked as a cook at his soul food restaurant. "While I was there I decided to drop in on Tara to see if there was anything she needed for tonight. She mentioned that some lady who's a big wheel around the hospital had stopped by her office earlier asking about you, Thorn. The lady wants you to pose for a charity calendar," Chase said in a calm voice, explaining things to everyone.

"After talking to Tara, I got the distinct impression that somehow the lady found out Tara knew you. She wanted Tara to use her influence to get you to do it," Chase added.

"Thorn doesn't 'do it,'" Storm said, chuckling. "Didn't we just establish the fact that he's still celibate?"

Chase frowned and swung his glance toward his twin. "Can't you think about anything but sex, Storm? I'm talking about posing for the calendar."

"Oh."

Chase refocused his gaze on Thorn. "So, will you do it?"

Thorn frowned. "Are you asking me on Tara's behalf?"

"No. But does it matter? If Tara were to ask you, would you do it?"

"No," Thorn said without hesitation while throwing a card out, remembering how he and Patrice had first met. She was a photographer who had wanted to do a calendar of what she considered sexy, sweaty, muscle-bound hunks, and in the process had ended up being his bed partner. His and a few others, he'd later found out.

Chase frowned. "It's for a good cause."

"All charities are," Thorn said, studying his hand.

"This one is for children, Thorn."

Thorn looked up and met Chase's gaze. Anyone knowing Thorn knew that on occasion he might give an adult pure hell, but when it came to children, he was as soft as a marshmallow. "The racing team I'm affiliated with already works closely with the Children's Miracle Network, Chase."

Chase nodded. "I know that, Thorn, but that's on a national level. This is more local and will benefit Kids' World."

Everyone living in the Atlanta area was familiar with Kids' World and the benefits it provided to terminally ill children. "All I'm asking is for you to think about it and be prepared when Tara finally gets up enough nerve to ask you," Chase added.

Thorn frowned. "Why would she need to get up nerve to ask me anything?"

It was Dare who chuckled. "Well, ahh, it's like this, Thorn," he said, throwing a card out. "You aren't the friendliest person toward her, but we all know the reason why, even if you refuse to acknowledge it."

Glancing around the room to make sure Tara hadn't come back downstairs, Dare continued. "The plain and simple fact is that you have a bad case of the hots for her and it's been going on now for almost two solid years. And as far as I'm concerned, you need to do something about it or learn to live with it. And if you choose to live with it, then please adjust your attitude so the four of us can live with you."

Thorn glared at Dare. "I don't need an attitude adjustment."

"The hell you don't. Face it, Thorn. You're not like the rest of us. Storm, Chase, Stone and I can go a long time without a woman and it doesn't bother us. But if you go without one for too long, it makes you hornier than sin, which for you equates to being meaner than hell. And it seems that you're deliberately holding out while deciding what to do about Tara, and it's making you worse than ever. Don't you think that in two years you should have made some decisions?"

Thorn's intense dark eyes held his brothers'; they were all watching him like hawks, waiting for his response. "I *have* made decisions regarding what I'm going to do about Tara," he said slowly, seeing the looks of comprehension slowly unfolding in their eyes.

"About damn time you stop backing away from the inevitable," Storm said, smiling broadly. "I knew you would come to your senses sooner or later."

"Uh, I hate to be the voice of reason at a time like this," Chase said grinning. "But I'd think twice about whatever decisions you've made about Tara without her consent, Thorn. She's quite a handful. I've seen her rebellious side and bringing her around won't be easy. Personally, I don't think you can handle her."

"Neither do I," Stone chimed in.

Thorn's face darkened as he gazed at all of them. "I can handle Tara."

"Don't be so sure about that," Stone said smiling. "Her first impression of you wasn't a good one, and I don't think she likes you much, which means you'll definitely have your hands full trying to win her over. I'm not so sure you're up for the challenge."

"I bet you any amount of money that he is," Storm said

grinning. "Thorn can do anything he wants to do, including taming Tara."

"Don't hold your breath for that to happen," Chase said chuckling. "Have you ever really noticed the two of them around each other? They're both stubborn and strong-willed. I say he can't hang."

"Okay you guys, pull back," Storm said, slowly stroking his chin. "Thorn's a smart man who plans his strategies well. Hell, look how he has trained for those races he's won. If he goes after Tara with the same determination, then there won't be anything to it. Therefore, I say taming Tara will be a piece of cake for Thorn."

"No, it won't," Chase said chuckling. "In fact, I'll be willing to bet a case of Jack Daniel's that it won't."

"And I bet you a new set of tools that it won't be, too," Stone added, shaking his head with a grin.

"And I bet you a day's wage and work for no pay in your restaurant as a waiter that it will, Chase. And I also bet you that same set of tools that it will, Stone. Thorn can handle any challenge he faces," Storm said, with confidence in his voice as he gathered up everyone's cards to start a new game.

Thorn had been sitting back listening to his brothers make their bets. He looked over at Dare who just shrugged his shoulders. "Making those kinds of bets aren't legal, and since as a sheriff I'm duty-bound to uphold the law, I'll pass," he said jokingly. "However, if I *were* a betting man, I'd say you *could* pull it off, but it wouldn't be as easy as Storm thinks. Calendar or no calendar, Tara's not going to let you just waltz in and sweep her off her feet. You'll have to set yourself up on a mission," he said, grinning as he remembered the tactic he'd used to win the heart of the woman he loved. "Then you can't play fair," he added, thinking of the technique his brother-in-law, Prince Jamal Ari Yasir, had used to woo their baby sister, Delaney.

Thorn nodded. *Set myself up on a mission and then play unfair.* He could handle that. He'd put his plans into action later tonight when everyone left. Tara wouldn't know what had hit her until it was too late.

Way too late.

Chapter 3

Tara's heart, beating twice as fast as it should have, slammed against her rib cage when, after the card game was over, it became obvious that, unlike his brothers, Thorn had no intentions of leaving.

She closed the door and turned to him. The air in the room suddenly seemed charged. "Aren't you leaving?" she asked, as she leaned against the closed door.

"No. I think we need to talk."

Tara inhaled deeply, wondering what he thought they needed to discuss. While upstairs in her bedroom she had managed to get her thoughts and her aroused senses under control after convincing herself that her earlier reaction to Thorn had been expected. After all, from the first she had been physically attracted to him and memories of the kiss they had shared a few months back hadn't helped matters. Then there was the way he always looked at her with that penetrating gaze of his. After thinking things through logically, she felt confident that the next time he looked at her as if he would love to gobble her up in one scrumptious bite, things would be different. She would be more in control of the situation as well as her senses.

"What do you want to talk about?" she asked, wondering if Chase had mentioned anything to him about the charity calendar.

He met her gaze. "About us."

She lifted an arched brow. There was no "us" and decided to tell him so. "There's no us, Thorn. In fact I've always gotten the distinct impression that you don't even like me."

Boy, was she wrong, Thorn thought. If anything he liked her too damn much. There were several emotions he'd always felt toward Tara Matthews from the first and dislike hadn't been one of them.

He took a couple of steps forward, bringing him right in front of her. "I've never disliked you, Tara."

She swallowed deeply against the timbre in his voice and the look of melting steel in his eyes. That's the same thing his brothers had claimed when she'd told them how she felt last year. They had argued that Thorn was just a moody person and told her not to take it personally. But a part of her *had* taken it personally.

"My brothers think you're my challenge," he added, not taking his eyes off her.

"Why would they think that?" she asked. She had wondered about it the first time the brothers had mentioned that very same thing to her. But none of them had given her any further explanation.

"Because they don't think I can handle you."

She frowned. "Handle me? In what way?"

His gaze ran provocatively down her full length before

coming back to meet hers. "Evidently not the way I originally thought," he said, thinking just how much he had underestimated his brothers' cleverness. They had set him up from the first.

"Of the five of us, I'm the one who'd always had a better handle on Laney than anyone, so I assumed they meant that I couldn't handle you because you were as headstrong, willful and unmanageable as she could be at times. And although you seem to have those traits, too, I now believe they meant you were my challenge for a totally different reason. I think they meant that I couldn't handle you as a woman. There's a big difference in the two."

They gazed at each other for a long, intense moment and then she asked. "And what's the difference?" She knew she might be asking for trouble, but at the moment she didn't care.

The room crackled and popped with what she now recognized as sexual tension and physical attraction. It hadn't been dislike the two of them had been battling since they'd met. It had been primal animal lust of the strongest kind.

He took another step closer. "If I were to group you in the same category as Laney, I'd have no choice but to think of you with brotherly affections since I'm almost eight years older than you. But if I were to forget about the age thing and place you in the same category as I do any other woman, then that would make you available."

Tara frowned. "Available?"

"Yes, available for me."

Tara swallowed again and ran her sweaty palms down over her slender waist to settle on her hips. She wondered what his reaction would be if he knew that in all her twenty-seven years she had never been available for any man. Although she and Derrick had dated for a number of years, they had never slept together, which meant she was probably the oldest living virgin in the state of Georgia. But that certainly didn't make her open game and she resented any man thinking she was his for the taking. Derrick had taught her a lesson and she had no desire to forget it any time soon. "Sorry to burst your bubble, but I'm not available for any man, Thorn."

Thorn continued to stare at her. Yes, she was definitely his challenge, and he liked challenges. "I think differently," he finally said.

Tara blinked once, then twice when she actually saw the corners of Thorn's lips move and his mouth suddenly creased into a smile. It was definitely a rare Kodak moment and she would have given anything to capture it on film. He had the most irresistibly, devastating smile she had ever seen. It contained a spark of eroticism that sent her pulses racing.

"You are definitely my challenge, Tara," he added in a raspy voice.

Too late she realized he had taken another step forward, bringing her thigh-to-thigh, chest-to-chest with him. Her breath caught when the sexy sound of his voice and the heat from his smile set her body on fire. But she fought to hold on to every ounce of control she had and refused to go up in flames. "I'm not anyone's challenge, Thorn," she said, barely above a whisper.

He began lowering his head toward hers and said huskily, "You are definitely *mine*, Tara."

The impact of Thorn's statement, his words of possession, made a degree of lust, stronger and more potent than she'd ever experienced before, fill the air; the room suddenly felt hot. A distinct, seductive warmth flooded the area between her legs. She wanted to fight him and the emotions he was causing her to feel. She tried convincing herself that he was just a man and she had promised herself that she would never lose her head over a man again. She had to admit that Thorn was the type of man who would make it hard to keep that promise, but she was determined to do so.

The one thing Thorn didn't know about her was that she didn't need a man, physically or mentally. As far as she was concerned, you couldn't miss what you'd never had. Besides, like most men who didn't have marriage on their minds, the only thing Thorn would ever give her was a whirlwind, meaningless affair that centered on sex.

Feeling more in control she took a step back, away from him, out of the way of temptation. "The hour is late and we're through talking."

"Yes, we're through talking."

Tara swallowed deeply, suddenly aware that his tone of voice was a low, seductive whisper and the intensity of his gaze had darkened. She stood rooted in place as he slowly recovered the distance she had put between them. He was so close that she could actually see her reflection in his eyes. So close she was sure that he heard the irregular beat of her heart.

She swallowed deeply. He was staring at her and his face was filled with such intense desire, that even a novice like herself could recognize it for what it was. It then occurred to her that her earlier assumption that you couldn't miss what you'd never had had no meaning when it came to basic human nature, and tonight, between them, animal magnetism was at an all-time high. Other than the kiss they had shared before, she had never felt so wired, so hungry for something she'd never had and so ripe for the picking.

The part of her that made her a woman felt thick, pouty and naughty. It was as if it had a mind of its own and was responding to Thorn as though he had some sort of mysterious telepathic connection to it. The absurdity of such a thing made her want to take a step back but she couldn't. His gaze was holding her still. Her entire concentration was on him and his was centered on her.

"I should probably get the hell out of here," he whispered in a low, sexy rumble of a voice as he placed his arms at her waist and shifted his gaze to her lips.

"Yes, you should," she whispered back, as a shiver passed from his touch at her waist all the way to her toes. She shifted her gaze to his lips as well and felt the intensity, the desires that were building up within her. Blood rushed to every part of her body.

"And I will," he said in a sensually charged voice, bringing her body closer to his. "After I've gotten a real good taste of you again."

Tara blinked and her mouth fell open. Thorn swiftly descended on it like an eagle swooping down on its prey. The feel of his mouth closing on hers was warm, startling, a direct hit. His lips were seductive against hers and gently yet thoroughly coaxed her into a response, a response she had no trouble giving him.

The sensations, acute and volatile, were a replay of the last time they had kissed, but, as she settled against him, she immediately decided that this kiss was destined to be in a class by itself. If he was bold before, this time he was confidently assertive. There was nothing timid about the way he was feasting on her mouth. The intensity of it made her body tremble. It was heat and sensuality rolled into one and her body tightened in hunger, unaccustomed to such nourishment. Her pulse points pounded, right in sync with the turbulent beating of her heart.

When she felt his hands moving over her body with an expertise that overwhelmed her, Tara knew she had to put a stop to this madness and slowly, regretfully, she eased her lips from Thorn's.

But he continued to touch her, gently rubbing her back. For the longest time neither of them said anything. They couldn't. The act of breathing alone took too much effort.

When she found the ability to lift her head, she met his gaze. It was so intense it nearly made the words she was about to say catch in her throat. She swallowed then forced herself to speak. "Why?"

She saw comprehension in the dark eyes that were locked with hers. He knew what she was asking and understood her need to know. "Because I want you and have from the first time I saw you. I tried denying it but I can't any longer. You may not accept it or acknowledge it, but your response proves to me that you want me just as much as I want you, Tara."

She knew his words were true, but she wasn't ready to accept what he was saying. "But I don't want this."

He nodded. "I know, but I refuse to give up or walk away. I want you more than I've wanted any woman in a long time."

A spark of anger lit her features. "And I'm supposed to feel good about that?"

Thorn lifted a brow. "I would hope that you do."

"Well, I don't. The last thing I want is an involvement with a man."

Thorn's frown deepened. "You're saying one thing but your kiss said another."

Her eyes filled with anger. "Imagine what you want, but I prefer doing the solo act. There's less chance of being played a fool that way. Once bitten you have a tendency to avoid a second bite."

Thorn sighed deeply, remembering what one of his brothers had told him about how Tara's fiancé had hurt and humiliated her on what was supposed to have been their wedding day. Tara's words touched a part of him that hadn't been touched in a long time. He reached out and caressed her cheek tenderly, mesmerized by the smoothness of her flesh and the pained yet angry look in her eyes.

He wanted to kiss her again but forced himself to speak instead. "You will never get a bite of pain from me, Tara. But you will get nibbles of passion and pleasure of the most profound kind. That I promise you." Walking away while he had the mind to do so, he picked his helmet up off the table.

He paused before opening the door, seeing the confused look on her face. As he'd hoped, he had her thinking. The Tara that had been feeding his nightly fantasies for almost two years was a woman who was as turbulent as the storm of sensations she stirred within him. Now that he'd finally admitted to himself that he wanted her, he intended to have her. And if she thought she was going to put distance between them then she had another thought coming.

"I'll be by tomorrow," he said calmly. He could tell by the way she narrowed her eyes that she intended to rebuild that wall between them. Little did she know he had every intention of keeping it torn down. He watched as she folded her arms beneath her breasts. They were breasts he intended to know the taste of before too long.

"You have no reason to come by tomorrow, Thorn."

"Yes I do," he responded easily. "I want to take you for a ride on my bike." He saw something flicker in her eyes. First surprise, then stubbornness, followed by unyielding resistance.

She lifted her chin. "I have no intention of doing anything with you."

Thorn sighed good-naturedly, thinking that she liked talking tough, and a part of him couldn't help but admire her spunk, which was something you rarely saw in a woman these days. Most were too eager to please. But even with all her feistiness, in good time she would discover that he was a man who appreciated a good fight more often than most people, so her willfulness didn't bother him any. In fact it made her just that much more desirable.

"And I intend to see that you do anything and everything with me, Tara," he said throatily, assuredly, before opening the door, walking out and closing it behind him.

Tara leaned against the closed door as the soft hum of Thorn's motorcycle faded into the distance. Taking a deep breath she tried to get her pulse rate and heartbeat back to normal. There was no denying that Thorn Westmoreland had the ability to rock her world. But the problem was that she didn't want her world rocked. Nor did she want the changes he was putting her through. And she definitely didn't want to remember the kiss they had just shared. The memory of it sent a tingling feeling through every part of her body. She had discovered three months ago that the man was an expert kisser and had a feeling he was probably an expert at making love as well. And she believed if given the chance he would do whatever it took to get her mind and body primed for sex.

She pulled in a deep breath trying to get her mind back in focus. It was late, but she doubted she would be able to sleep much tonight. She thought that it was a good thing she didn't have to work tomorrow. She was having lunch with Delaney and was looking forward to it.

Pushing away from the door she headed for the kitchen hoping she would find something there to keep her busy. She stopped in the doorway. There was nothing for her to do since the Westmoreland brothers had left everything spotless. But one brother in particular had gone a step further. Tonight Thorn had invaded her space and gotten closer to her than any man since Derrick had dumped her.

That realization disturbed her. Her fantasies of Thorn had been rather tame compared to the real thing and she hated to admit it but she had found kissing him the most exciting thing she had done since leaving Bunnell.

As she climbed the stairs to her bedroom, it suddenly dawned on her that she hadn't mentioned anything about the calendar to Thorn, which meant she would have to see him again this week. And since he claimed he would be coming by tomorrow she would bring it up then.

Thorn had a difficult time sleeping that night. Whenever he tried closing his eyes, memories of his kiss with Tara were so vivid he could still actually taste her. Tonight's kiss had been much better than the previous one. That kiss had had an element of surprise. Tonight their kiss had been fueled by desire—basic and fundamental.

Muttering something unintelligible, he rolled out of bed knowing that sleep was out of the question. Making his way through the living room and into the kitchen he opened the refrigerator, needing a beer. With his present state of mind, he might need more than one.

As he pulled a beer from the six-pack and popped the tab, a low moan formed in his throat. He took a long, pleasurable gulp. At that moment, unexpectedly, huge drops of rain splattered on his rooftop and he was glad he had made it home before the downpour. He had gotten caught on his bike during storms enough times to know it wasn't something he relished.

A smile worked at his mouth when he thought of something he did relish. Thorn couldn't wait until he saw Tara again. The thought that she would try to avoid him made the challenge that much more sweet.

Tonight he had made a decision and it hadn't been easy, but kissing her had helped to put things into the right perspective. Tara was a pure challenge if he'd ever seen one, and although she had fought what they shared and would continue to fight it, he was convinced more than ever that she was just the woman he needed.

They had been attracted to each other from the first, and tonight had exposed numerous possibilities, all of them definitely worth pursuing.

Finishing off his beer and placing the empty can in the bin, he headed back up the stairs to the bedroom. He was hot. He was hard. He was horny. And the sound of the rain pounding against his roof didn't help matters. It only made him want to pound his body into Tara's with the same steady yet urgent rhythm. The thought of doing so made his gut clench with need. A vivid, sensuous scene flashed in his mind. The impact almost took his breath away. Thorn quickly sucked in air. This was not good. Tara Matthews fascinated him. She intrigued him and filled him with intense desire and made him think of unbridled passion.

Unless he did something about his predicament, she would be the death of him and he wasn't ready to die just yet.

Chapter 4

"There's only one word to describe your brother, Laney, and that's stubborn."

The two women were sitting at a table on the terrace of the restaurant. They had enjoyed lunch and were now enjoying a glass of wine. A smile tilted the corners of Delaney's lips and her eyes sparkled as she glanced over at her friend. "Let me guess. You must be referring to brother number two, none other than Thorn Westmoreland."

Tara couldn't help but return Delaney's smile. "Yes. Who else? Your other brothers are simply adorable and don't have a grumpy bone in their bodies. But that Thorn…"

Delaney chuckled. "I don't know why you continue to let him get next to you, Tara," she said, taking another sip of her wine, although she had a pretty good idea. She had been keeping a close eye on Thorn and Tara since they'd met and knew better than anyone that the spark of annoyance flying between two individuals was a sure sign of attraction. She and her husband Jamal could certainly attest to that. When they'd first met there had been sparks, too, but then the sparks had turned into fiery embers that had fed another kind of fire. Delaney hated that she hadn't been around more to prod Thorn and Tara in the right direction. She and Jamal had spent more time in his homeland during their son Ari's first year of life. They had returned to the States a few months ago so that she could complete the rest of her residency at a hospital in Kentucky. They would be remaining in the States for at least another year.

"I know I shouldn't let him get under my skin, Laney, but I can't help it. For instance, last night, when the others left my house after the card game, Thorn hung back just to rattle me."

Delaney lifted a brow. "Thorn hung back? I'm surprised he wasn't the first to leave."

Tara had been surprised, too. Usually, he avoided her like the plague. "Well, for once he decided to stick around."

"And?"

"And he said we needed to talk."

Delaney shook her head. "About Mrs. Chadwick wanting him to do that calendar?"

"No, I never got around to mentioning that."

"Oh. Then what did the two of you have to talk about?"

A rush of color suffused Tara's mahogany skin when she thought of just what they had done in addition to talking. Aftereffects of their kiss still had her feeling warm and tingly in certain places.

"Tara?"

Tara met Delaney's gaze. "Ahh…he wants to take me bike-riding today and we talked about that," she said, not telling Delaney everything because she figured she really didn't have to. No doubt there was a telltale sign all over her face that Thorn had kissed her.

"Are you?"

Tara blinked as Delaney's question broke into her thoughts. "Am I what?"

"Are you going bike-riding with Thorn?"

Tara shrugged. "I told him I wouldn't, but that didn't mean a thing to him since he indicated he would drop by today anyway. At first I had planned to make sure I wasn't home when he arrived, but then I remembered Mrs. Chadwick and that darned calendar."

"So, you're going?"

Tara breathed in a deep sigh. "I guess so. I'm only going so that I can ask him about the charity calendar."

Delaney smiled. It seemed things were finally beginning to happen between Thorn and Tara; after two years it was definitely about time. But still she decided she needed to leave her friend with a warning. "Look, Tara, I know my brothers probably better than anyone and Thorn is the one I can read the best. He was involved in an affair a few years back that left him with a bad taste in his mouth, and heaven knows that was the last thing Thorn needed, since he was moody enough. He's an ace when it comes to doing whatever it takes to get whatever it is he wants. He'll pull out all stops and take any risks necessary if the final result suits him. There's only one way I know to get the best of him."

"And what way is that?"

Delaney smiled, her eyes crinkling attractively as she thought of the brother who loved being a thorn in everyone's side most of the time. "Don't try beating Thorn at his game, since he's a pro. What you should do is to come up with a game plan of your own."

Tara arched an eyebrow. "A game plan of my own?"

Delaney nodded. "Yes. One that will get you what yo
want, while making him think he has accomplished his goal–
getting whatever it is he wants from you."

Tara frowned. For the past two years Thorn had avoide
her space and now suddenly he was determined to invade i
She didn't have to think twice as to what he wanted from he
since he had pretty much spelled things out last night. H
wanted her! "A game plan of my own. Umm, I think that's
wonderful idea."

Thorn sat astride his motorcycle and gazed at Tara's house
wondering if she was home. He had heard from Stone that sh
had had lunch with Laney earlier that day.

He should have called first but he hadn't wanted to giv
her the chance to refuse his invitation. He'd figured that th
best thing to do was to catch her with her guard down sinc
chances were she probably thought she had made hersel
clear and he wouldn't show up today.

Shutting off the engine he began walking toward her doc
with two helmets in his hands. He was determined that the
would go today. He hadn't slept most of the night for thinkin
of how it would feel when she leaned into his back with he
arms wrapped around him, while the vibrations of the moto
cycle's powerful engine hummed through her.

He rang the doorbell and heard the faint sound of footstep
approaching. Moments later Tara opened the door. And sh
was smiling.

"I was beginning to wonder if you were going to show uj
Thorn. I've been ready for over an hour."

He blinked and a look of indecision filled his eyes. Th
woman certainly looked like Tara but the one standing befor

him didn't appear surprised to see him. In fact, from her statement it seemed she had been expecting him. His gaze darkened dangerously as he wondered just what the hell she was up to.

"I thought you weren't going riding with me," he said, meeting her gaze and holding it with an intensity that should have made her nervous. Instead she waved her hand, dismissing his words and stood aside to let him enter.

"If you really thought that then why are you here?" she asked, closing the door behind him and leaning against it to look at him. The suspicious look on his face, his pensive and forever brooding expression had Tara wanting to go up to him and wrap her arms around his neck and assure him that he wasn't imagining things, and that she had thrown him a curve. She had a feeling that few people did that to him. And she had another feeling that she should savor this rare moment of having the upper hand with Thorn.

Then, to her astonishment and complete surprise, the corner of his mouth quirked into a seductive grin. "Because I've learned when most women say one thing they really mean another."

She frowned. "When I say I won't do something, usually I won't. The only reason I changed my mind is because I remembered I needed to talk to you about something."

Thorn continued to meet her gaze. He knew just what she wanted to talk to him about—that charity calendar. He quickly decided he would prefer turning her down after their bike ride rather than before it. "All right. I plan for us to have dinner at a restaurant I think you'll like. We'll be able to talk then."

She raised a brow. "Dinner? You didn't mention anything about dinner."

He shrugged. "Didn't I? It must have slipped my mind."

He then studied her outfit, a pair of jeans, a lightweig pullover sweater and a pair of short leather boots. It was t perfect riding attire and the outfit looked perfect on her. "It m get chilly later so you might want to grab a jacket," he su gested.

Tara sighed. He had intentionally not mentioned dinner her last night. A part of her thought of resisting, but s quickly decided not to start fighting him just yet. There wou be plenty of time for that later. There was no doubt in her mi that after telling him what she needed from him, he wou prove to be difficult. "Okay, I'll be right back."

Thorn went completely still and held his breath when Ta passed him to go up the stairs. He'd seen her in jeans a numb of times before and always thought she knew how to we them well, but today he couldn't help but pay close attentic to how the jeans fit her, especially the way the denim cuppe her curvy backside.

And she was wearing her hair down and he liked that. H wanted to know how the silken strands would feel blowin in the wind as he tore up the road with her clinging to him

"All right, I'm ready."

He glanced back to the stairs and watched her come dow He looked at her intently before saying. "So am I."

"Here, let me help you with that," Thorn said, easing th helmet on Tara's head and adjusting the straps to keep firmly in place. "Have you ever ridden on a motorcycl before?" he asked as he tried to ignore how his body was re sponding to her closeness. As usual, whenever he was aroun her, a deep, sexual hunger stirred to life in his midsection. was only at times like these that he remembered just how lon he had been celibate, which didn't help matters.

"No, I've never ridden on one before."

He swallowed deeply. The low, seductive tone of her voice was only adding to his misery.

"But I have ridden on a moped. Does that count?" she asked.

He shook his head. "No, that doesn't count, so consider this your first experience," he said as he assisted her in straddling the seat behind him. He tried not to think of how good she looked with her legs spread wide across the padded seat or how well her body fit onto it. Today he was riding the Thorn-Byrd 1725, a huge bike that had a passenger armrest and backrest to give a second rider added comfort.

"You, okay?" he asked as he placed his own helmet on his head and strapped it on.

"Yes, I'm fine, just a little nervous. This bike is huge."

He chuckled. "Yeah, and I prefer building them that way."

"I'm truly amazed."

"About what?"

"The skill and craftsmanship that went into building this bike. You truly have gifted hands."

A pleased smile curved the corners of his lips. He was glad she thought so and intended that she find out real soon just how gifted his hands were. But at the moment his main thoughts were on *her* hands. "Place your arms around me and hold on tight with your hands. And don't hesitate to lean into me for an easier ride. Okay?"

"Why would leaning into you provide an easier ride?" she asked, in a confused tone of voice.

"You'll see."

Tara nodded, preferring to try and sit up straight with her arms around Thorn's waist. But when he turned on the engine to a low, rumbling purr that escalated to a much louder growl, she automatically leaned forward, tightened her grip around

him and pressed her body against the wide expanse of hi
back. His leather bomber jacket felt warm, cushiony, and s
much a part of him. Pressing her face against his solid back
she breathed in the scent of leather and the scent of man. It wa
masculine and a mixture of shaving cream and a real nice
smelling cologne. This wasn't the first time she had been awar
of his scent. That first time he had kissed her at Dare's weddin
she had gone to bed later that night with his scent embedde
in her nostrils. It had been both alluring and arousing.

It still was.

"Ready?" she heard him ask her over his shoulder.

She sighed deeply and closed her eyes. "Yes, I'm ready.
The next thing she knew he shifted gears and the two of then
went flying into the wind.

Tara opened her eyes as her nervousness began easin;
away. It was plain to see that in addition to being a gifte
craftsman, Thorn was also a skilled biker. He took the shar;
curves with ease as he expertly controlled the large an
powerful machine.

Her breasts felt tight and achy, so she leaned forward and
pressed her body even more to his. He'd been right. This wa
the best position. She wondered if, with her sitting so close, h
could feel the frantic pounding of her heart. But that question
and others were suddenly zapped from her mind when she too|
a look at the countryside they passed. Instead of traveling on th
busy interstate, Thorn had maneuvered the bike onto a sceni
two-lane road that had very few cars. She liked the view. An
she liked the feel of the man she was clutching for dear life.

"Am I holding you too tight?" she decided to ask. Sh
wondered if he heard her question or if the sound of her voic
had been swept away with the wind.

"No."

She smiled. He *had* heard her, and she was glad she hadn't caused him any discomfort.

Thorn tried to keep his concentration on the road ahead of him and not on the woman behind him, but her breasts were pressing against his back and arousing him no end. Everything about her was arousing. He had ridden other women on his bike but never had he felt such excitement and exhilaration before. Riding with Tara was seduction at its best, temptation at its finest.

He pulled his concentration back in as he maneuvered the bike around a curvy mountain road. This was the part of Atlanta that he loved seeing on his bike and he wanted to share the view with Tara. It was a part of the city that had escaped the developer's bulldozer. The Westmoreland family intended to keep it that way.

He slowed the bike as he left the highway and steered to a single-lane gravel road that led to a huge lake in a wooded area surrounded by large overhanging trees. Moments later, he brought the motorcycle to a stop and shut off the engine. Before she could ask, he said. "I think this is one of the most beautiful spots in Atlanta and thought you might enjoy seeing it."

Tara glanced around and her breath caught. He was right. It *was* breathtaking. She gazed back at him. She would never have guessed that he was a man in sync with nature, but from the look in his eyes as he glanced around, she could tell that he was.

"You come here often," she said. It wasn't a question but a statement. She could detect deep appreciation in his gaze as he viewed his surroundings.

"Yes. This is Westmoreland land. The ruins of my grandparents' house isn't far from here and we visited this place a

lot while growing up. My father's youngest brother, the on
who has never been married, Corey Westmoreland, spent
lot of his time teaching us to appreciate the natural world an
its environment here. I believe you've met my uncle."

Tara nodded. "Yes, twice—at both Laney's and Dare'
weddings. He's the one who's a park ranger at Yellowston
National Park. Right?"

Thorn nodded. "Yes, and so is my cousin Durango. In fac
when Durango finished high school he decided to move t
Montana to attend college to be near our uncle. Now I doub
you could get either of them to return here to live. They'r
Montana men through and through."

He kicked down the motorcycle stand and removed hi
helmet. "Come on, let's take a walk."

Tara slowly slid off the bike and had to steady herself s
she wouldn't lose her balance. Thorn appeared at her side t
assist and to help her take off her helmet. He stared down a
her when he held her helmet in his hand.

"What?" she asked, wondering if she had something on he
face since he was looking at her so intently.

"Nothing. I'd been wondering why your hair hadn't bee
blowing in the wind. I had forgotten that the helmet woul
hold it in place."

She lifted a brow. He had been thinking of her hair blowin
in the wind? Before she could think about that further, he too
her hand in his. "Come on, let me show you around."

Tara knew she was seeing another side of Thorn Westmore
land. For some reason he wasn't his usual grumpy self, an
she decided to take full advantage of his current kinder an
gentler disposition. She knew it would probably be best fo
the both of them if they were to continue to avoid each other

but then she thought of Mrs. Chadwick's request. Somehow and someway she had to get Thorn to agree to pose for that calendar.

Together they silently walked the surrounding land. She saw more wild animals than she had ever seen before. There was a family of deer, numerous rabbits and wild turkeys. There was even a fox skirting across the overbrush. In soft tones Thorn pointed out to her the spot where he had learned to ride his first motorcycle. His grandparents had bought it for him when he was twelve years old. It had been a dirt bike, one not meant for the road.

"Ready to go?" he finally asked her.

Tara glanced up at him. "Yes, I'm ready."

Thorn leaned toward her to place her helmet back on her head and suddenly he stopped. He traced her jawline with the tip of his finger and met her gaze. She took a slow, deep breath to calm the erratic beating of her heart when it became crystal-clear what he was about to do. He was going to kiss her and she couldn't form the words to tell him not to.

Instead, a need, a hunger, flared to life inside her when her gaze settled on his lips as his gaze had settled on hers. Memories filled her mind of the last two kisses they had shared. Hot. Mind-boggling kisses.

She quickly decided that she would question the sensibility of her actions later, but for now she needed this kiss as much as she needed her next breath.

She shuddered when she thought of the intensity of that need and felt a quickening in her stomach when he lowered his mouth to hers. Her lips automatically parted the second their mouths touched, and she breathed a sigh of pleasure as her arms reached out to hold him.

As it had been the other times, his mouth was skillful, and

another soft sigh escaped her lips when he deepened the kiss and thoroughly explored the warm recesses of her mouth with his tongue. Then he captured hers and gently mated with it, the sensations rocking her all the way to her toes.

She knew the taste of him, had never forgotten it and refused to consider the possibility it was becoming addictive. However, she did concede that this kiss, the hunger behind it and all the enticements in front of it, were causing a deep ache between her legs. This openmouthed exploration of tongues and teeth was flooding her with sensations she had never felt before. She heard one of them whimper and moan and realized the sounds were coming from her. She shouldn't expect any less when the blood was running so hot and heavy in her veins.

She felt his hand run provocatively down her back to settle on her hips, then slowly to her backside, and she moved her body closer to the fit of his. Her belly was pressed against his front and she could feel an incredible hardness straining against the crotch of his jeans. For the moment, she didn't care. The only thing she did care about was the fact that she was enjoying kissing him. Their tongues continued to tangle and their breaths steadily mingled.

Reluctantly, he ended the kiss, struggling for control. She saw his jaw tense and knew he was regretting kissing her already. Without saying anything he placed her helmet back on her head, adjusted the straps and helped her straddle the bike.

He had gone from tender to moody in just that instant and she didn't like it. When he got back on the bike and had his own helmet in place, she asked, in a fairly angry voice, "Why did you kiss me if you're going to get all huffy and puffy about it? Next time keep your mouth to yourself, Thorn Westmoreland."

For the longest moment he didn't say anything, then finally he turned to her on the bike and said. "That's the problem, Tara. When it comes to you I don't think I can keep my mouth to myself. It seems to always want to find its way to yours."

He sighed deeply and added. "My brothers think you're my challenge, but now I'm beginning to think you're something else all together."

She lifted a brow. "What?"

"My sweetest temptation."

Chapter 5

"So what did you want to talk to me about?"

Tara nervously nibbled on her bottom lip. She and Thorn had just finished the best chili she had ever eaten. The building that housed the restaurant was rustic, made of logs with tall, moss-covered oak trees surrounding it. The place resembled a roadside café more than a restaurant and was positioned almost in seclusion off the two-lane highway.

Due to its lack of visibility, Tara could only assume that those who frequented the restaurant were regular customers since the place was taking in a high degree of business. It also appeared that a lot of those customers were bikers. She found the atmosphere comfortable and had almost forgotten the discussion she needed to have with Thorn.

"I want to ask a favor of you."

He met her gaze over his cup of coffee. "What kind of favor?"

She sighed. "Have you ever heard of Lori Chadwick?"

He frowned as if searching his brain, then moments later said, "No."

Tara nodded. "Well, she is well-known around the city for her charity work. Mrs. Chadwick has come up with this great idea for a project to raise funds for Kids' World. You have heard of Kids' World, haven't you?"

"Yes."

"Well, she has decided what she wants to do to raise money for that particular charity this year. She wants to do a calendar of good-looking men from different professions, and would like you to be one of the models. She wanted me to ask you about it."

He placed his coffee cup down. "You can go back and let her know that you asked me."

She met his gaze. "And?"

"And that I turned you down."

Tara narrowed her eyes. "I think it was wonderful that you were one of the men she wanted."

"Then I'm flattered."

"From what I understand, they will pay you."

"It's not about the money."

"Then what is it about, Thorn? I know for a fact you're involved with a number of charities for children. Why not this one?"

He leaned back in his chair. "I don't like having my picture taken."

She frowned. "That's a crock and you know it, considering the number of times newspaper photographers have taken your picture when you've won a motorcycle race or built a bike for some celebrity."

He shrugged. "Newspaper reporters are different. I don't

like having my picture taken in a private session, in a studio or anything like that."

"In that case you won't have anything to worry about. It's my understanding they want to capture you in your element—probably outside standing next to your bike."

"The answer is still no, Tara."

She glared at him. "Why are you being so difficult, Thorn?"

"I have my reasons," he said, glaring back at her as he threw money on the table for their meal. "It's getting late so we should head back."

Tara sighed. He had to be the most stubborn man she had ever met. "I need to make a pit stop at the ladies' room before we leave," she said softly, disappointed that he had flatly refused to do the calendar.

Moments later, when she walked outside to where he stood next to the bike, she couldn't help but wonder why he didn't want to be photographed by a professional photographer. "I'm ready now."

Without saying anything, he helped put her helmet on again and adjusted the straps. She swung her leg across the huge bike without his help and glared up at him. "I said I was ready, Thorn."

He stood there and looked at her for a few moments before finally getting on the bike in front of her, revving the engine and riding off.

Tara was mad and he knew it, but there was nothing he could do about it since he would *not* be doing the calendar. The sooner she accepted that the better.

"You're in la-la land again, Thorn. Are you in this game or not?"

Thorn glared at Chase. "Yes, I'm in."

Chase chuckled as he studied his hand. "Yes, you may be in this game but from what I hear you're definitely out with Tara since you turned her down for that calendar."

Thorn tossed out a card. "She'll get over it."

"Possibly. However, it may take a while since she feels she let someone down."

Thorn decided not to ask, but curiosity got the best of Storm and he did the asking. "Who did Tara let down?"

"The children."

"Oh." Storm glared at Thorn after throwing out a card. "I'd forgotten about Kids' World. So I guess that also means I'm going to lose the bet. Thorn will never make any points with Tara by pissing her off."

Thorn decided he needed a break and placed his cards face-down on the table. "Where is Shelly, Dare? I need a drink of water."

Dare didn't look up from studying his hand. "She's probably upstairs watching a movie or something, but you know where the refrigerator is. Help yourself. There's beer and soda in there as well."

Thorn stood up from the dining-room table as all of the brothers except for Dare glared at him. He walked into the kitchen and pulled out a pitcher of water from the refrigerator. He'd reached the max for beers he could consume and still ride his bike.

After reaching into the cabinet for a glass, he filled it with cold water and glanced across the way at a framed photograph that was on Dare and Shelly's living-room table. It was a photograph of Shelly, Tara and Delaney taken during a shopping trip the three women had taken to New York a few months ago.

Tara.

He hadn't seen her or talked to her since the day of their bike ride almost a week ago, but there hadn't been a day that passed when she hadn't crossed his mind. He had called her and left her a couple of messages, but she hadn't returned his calls, not that he had really expected her to. He hated admitting it, but Storm was right. It would be hard for him to garner any points with her because she was totally pissed off with him. But still, the thought of standing in front of a camera, posing for a photographer—as he'd done for Patrice—was something he was hell-bent against doing.

"Thorn! If you're still in the game, we need you out here!"

He recognized Stone's voice. "Keep your underwear on. I'm coming."

As he went back to the card game, Thorn returned his brothers' glares.

"I don't like losing, Thorn," Storm said as he watched him intently.

Thorn knew Storm was talking about the bet his brothers had made and not about the card game. He sighed. He knew what Tara wanted from him, and he knew what he wanted from her. Suddenly, he had an idea how they could both get what they wanted. Satisfied he had come up with a workable plan, one he thought was strategically sound, he met Storm's intense stare. "Don't give up on me yet, bro."

Storm's lips eased into a relieved smile. "Thanks, Thorn. I knew I could count on you."

Thorn pulled his bike to a stop in front of Tara's apartment. A number of lights were still on inside which must mean she hadn't gone to bed yet. He quickly shut off the bike's engine and made his way to her door, wondering if she would agree to the offer he intended to make.

He rang her doorbell and waited for her to answer. He didn't wait long. First he registered her surprise and then her frown. "Thorn. What are you doing here?"

He leaned against the doorjamb. "I needed to talk to you about something."

He saw the lifting of her brow. He also noticed that although she hadn't gone to bed, she was wearing a white velour bathrobe. He couldn't help but wonder what, if anything, she wore underneath the robe.

"Talk to me about what?"

"The possibility of me doing that calendar."

She met his gaze and he saw uncertainty. "You've changed your mind about doing it?"

He shook his head. "No, not yet. However, I think the two of us can work something out where I might be able to swing it."

The uncertainty in her gaze changed to hope. "All right. Come in," she invited, opening the door to him and standing back.

He entered and closed the door behind him. More than anything, he wanted to take her into his arms and kiss her senseless. He had missed her taste, her scent and every damn thing about her. But he didn't think she would appreciate him touching her just yet.

"Would you like something to drink?"

Her voice, soft and delicate, captured his attention. "No, I just left a card game at Dare's. I'm on the bike and don't want anything else to drink."

She nodded. "I was sitting in the kitchen drinking a cup of coffee while reading a medical report if you want to join me there."

"All right."

He'd always thought her kitchen was large...until the two

of them were in it alone. Now it seemed small. And for some reason her kitchen table seemed to have shrunk.

"Are you sure I can't at least pour you a cup of coffee?"

He sighed as he sat down. "Now that I think about it, a cup of coffee would be nice."

"And how would you like it?"

"Black with two sugars."

Silence closed around them as she stood at the counter and prepared his coffee. "I called you a couple of times and you never returned my calls," he decided to say to break the silence in the room.

"I really didn't think we had anything to say, Thorn."

He nodded. Yes, he could see her thinking that way.

She came back to the table with his cup of coffee. He took a slow sip. He was particular about how he liked his coffee but found that she had made it just right. "Ahh, this is delicious."

"Thanks. Now if you'll excuse me, I need to slip into some clothes."

He slowly looked her up and down. He liked what she was wearing. "Don't go to any trouble on my account."

"It's no trouble. Please excuse me, I'll be back in a few minutes."

When she left him in the kitchen he glanced over at the medical journal she'd been reading. After making sure she had marked the page where she had left off, he closed it. When she came back he wanted her full attention. He had given his proposal much thought and didn't know how she would take it but he hoped she would keep an open mind. He intended to be honest with her, up-front, and not to pull any punches. He needed to make sure she understood just what he expected from her...if she went along with things.

"Okay, Thorn. What did you want to talk to me about?"

He turned in his seat. She was back already. He met her gaze after checking out her outfit: a pair of capri pants and a midriff top. She looked good, he thought. But what really grabbed his attention was the portion of her bare belly that showed beneath the short top. Damn if her navel didn't look good enough to taste. He cleared his throat to get his mind back to the business at hand. "I have a proposition for you," he said, barely able to get the words out of his mouth.

He watched as she arched a brow. He leaned back in the chair when she came to stand in the middle of the kitchen, a few feet from him and propped her hips against the counter near the sink. "What sort of a proposition?"

He had to force his attention away from her navel and back to the subject at hand. He cleared his throat again. "You still want me to do that calendar?"

"Yes, that would be nice."

He nodded. "Then I hope what I'm proposing will be acceptable."

She inclined her head and tilted it somewhat as a cautious smile touched her lips. "You still haven't told me just what this proposition is, Thorn."

He slowly stood and walked over to her. He leaned forward, braced his hands on the counter behind her, trapping her in. He moved his face close to hers. "I will agree to do the calendar if you do a favor for me, Tara."

He watched as she nervously licked her lips. "What kind of favor, Thorn?"

He felt his pulse quicken as desire for what he wanted from her filled his entire being. "I've been without a woman for over two years."

She blinked. He saw her throat move as she swallowed deeply. "You have?"

"Yes."

"Why?"

"Because I always take an oath of celibacy right before a race, and during the past couple of years I've been involved in a number of races. But I have to admit that had I really wanted to, I could have found the time to squeeze a woman or two in during the off-season when there were no races, but I didn't."

She nervously licked her lips again. "Why not?"

"Because I had met you and from the first time I laid eyes on you I wanted you and no one else."

Tara shook her head as if what he was saying didn't make much sense. "But—but you didn't like me. You avoided me. You were downright moody and grumpy."

He smiled. "Yes, I was. I'm usually moody and grumpy whenever I've gone without sex for a long period of time. My bad moods have become a habit and most people who know me get used to them. I avoided you because I had no intention of getting involved with you. But now I've changed my mind."

She swallowed again. "How so?"

"I want to make a deal. I'll give you what you want from me if you'll give me what I want from you."

Tara stared at him. "And just what is it that you want from me?"

He leaned closer. "My next race is in Daytona during Bike Week, five weeks from now. Once the race is over, I want you to share my bed for a week."

He saw the startled look in her eyes. He then saw that look turn to anger. He quickly placed his finger to her lips to shut off whatever words she was about to say. "One week is all I'm asking for, one week in a completely physical and emotionally free affair. I need to get you out of my system as well as make up for what I haven't had in over two years."

He felt her breathing become unsteady as what he was proposing became crystal clear in her mind. For one week they would share a bed and take part in nothing short of a sexual marathon. He decided not to worry her mind by also telling her that during the five weeks leading up to the race, he intended to use that time to get her primed, ripe and ready for what he planned to do. By the time they slept together, she would want him just as much as he wanted her.

Just to prove a point he removed his finger from her lips and quickly placed his mouth there, swiping away any words she wanted to say. In no time at all he had her panting and whimpering under the onslaught of his mouth as he kissed her with everything he had inside him, mating relentlessly with her tongue.

He placed a hand on the bare section of her belly, feeling the warmth of her skin, smooth as silk, and felt her shudder from his touch. Deciding to take things further, his fingers breached the elastic of her capri pants and went deeper until he could feel the silky material of her underpants.

He didn't stop there.

While he continued to make love to her mouth, he slipped his fingers past the elastic of her panties until he found just what he was seeking, that part of her that was hot, plump and damp.

Inhaling the very essence of her womanly scent, he let his fingers go to work as he centered on that part of her that he knew would bring her pleasure. She had told him last week that she thought he had gifted hands and she was about to experience just how gifted his hands were. He intended to use his fingers to drive her over the edge.

Desire was blatant in their kiss, the way their tongues mingled, fused, mated, as his fingers entered her. Her body felt extremely tight but that didn't stop him from using his fingers to make her shudder, tremble, shiver. Then there were those sounds she was making that were driving him insane.

He felt her knees weaken as though she could no longer stand, and with his other hand he held on to her, keeping her upright while his fingers worked inside her. Then he felt her scream into his mouth, shudder in his arms, as an orgasm rocked her body, shaking her to the core.

He pulled his mouth away and looked at her, wanting to see her in the throes of passion, but she quickly pulled his mouth back down to hers, needing the contact. He didn't let his fingers stop what they were doing. He intended to keep going until it was all over for her. Until he heard her very last sigh of ecstasy.

When he saw she was gradually coming back down to earth, he slowly removed his hand and spread her dampness on her bare belly, letting it get absorbed into her skin. He inhaled deeply, loving her scent and knowing the next five weeks would be tortuous for him, but definitely well worth the wait.

He took a step back and watched as she slowly opened her eyes and met his gaze, realizing that he had just given her an orgasm while she stood in the middle of her kitchen. He knew she wanted to say something, but no words came from her mouth. So he leaned forward and placed a kiss on her lips.

"That's just a sample, Tara," he whispered softly. "Agree to have an affair with me for a week and I'll do the calendar thing for you. Think about it and let me know your decision."

Without saying anything else, he turned and left.

As soon as Thorn got home he went straight to the kitchen, grabbed a beer from the refrigerator and sank into the nearest chair. He quickly popped open the can and took a sip. Hell, he took more than a sip; he took a gulp. He needed it.

No other woman had ever affected him the way Tara did. Even now the potent scent of her still clung to him and he had an erection so huge it was about to burst out of his jeans. The only thing his mind could remember, the only thing his mind could not forget was the sound of her letting go; the sound of her reaching the pinnacle of pleasure under his hands.

He took another gulp of beer. He had almost lost it as a result of the sounds she had made. He knew she wasn't dating anyone. In fact, according to one of his brothers, after what had happened with her and that jerk she was supposed to marry, she had pretty much sworn off men.

And although no one had given him the full story, he knew she had moved to Atlanta because some married doctor with clout at her last job had gotten obsessed with her and had tried to force her to become his mistress. Although he hadn't tried forcing her, Thorn had to admit that he had pretty much made her the same offer. He hoped like hell that she would see the difference between his pursuit and that doctor's harassment. They would be good together in bed; tonight she'd got a sample of just how good they would be. From the way she had come apart against him, he had a feeling she had not even been aware of the full extent of her sensuality as a woman. She hadn't known the desires of the body could be so intense, so strong or so damn stimulating. And there had been something else he had found rather strange, but tonight he didn't want to think about that possibility.

The only thing he wanted to think about was the fact that he wanted her.

That was the bottom line. He wanted her in a way he had never wanted another woman. He wanted her in positions his mind was creating; in ways he had taken her in his dreams, his fantasies. And as he had told her, had blatantly warned her, by the time the motorcycle race was over in Daytona, he would have more than two years' worth of pent-up sexual needs.

He hadn't wanted to scare her, but he had wanted her to know up front just what she would be facing. He owed her that piece of honesty.

He groaned, feeling himself get harder, straining even more against his jeans at the thought of them making love. If she agreed to what he wanted, he would make all the plans. He wanted a hotel for a week, in seclusion, in privacy and all he would need was food, something to drink and Tara in his bed.

Tara in his bed.

What he had told her last week was true. She had become his sweetest temptation and, he hoped, in a few weeks she would also be his greatest pleasure.

Chapter 6

Tara got to the hospital almost thirty minutes later than usual after enjoying the best sleep she remembered ever having. It was only with the brightness of morning that she had allowed herself to think of Thorn's proposition. Last night, after he'd left, she had been too exhausted and too satiated to do anything but strip naked, take a shower, slip into a nightgown and get into bed.

That morning while she had taken another shower, brushed her teeth, dressed for work and grabbed a small carton of apple juice as she raced out of the door, she was feeling angry all over again.

First it was Derrick, then Dr. Moyer and now Thorn. Did she have a sign on her forehead that said, Go Ahead And Use Me?

Not that she was even considering Thorn's ridiculous offer, but if she did go with him to Daytona, she would be close to home. Her hometown of Bunnell, Florida, was less than an hour from Daytona Beach, and it had been two years since she'd been home. She frequently talked to her family on the telephone, but she hadn't visited them. Luckily they had understood her need to stay away from the place that conjured up such painful memories. Instead of her going home, her family often visited her. Since Bunnell was a small town, everyone knew what had happened with Derrick on their wedding day.

Her thoughts shifted back to Thorn. Funny, but no matter how mad she got, she could not discount the pleasure Thorn had given her last night. A penetrating heat settled deep in her stomach just thinking about it, and she still felt this awesome tingle between her legs. She knew all about climaxes and orgasms, although she had never experienced one before last night. But still, a part of her couldn't help but think that if Thorn could make her orgasm so explosively with his hands, what would happen when they really made love?

And she hated admitting it, but a part of her was dying to find out.

She sighed deeply, getting as mad with herself as she was with Thorn. He should never have introduced her to something like that. All this time she had been operating under the premise that you couldn't miss what you never had, and now that he had given her a sampling, she couldn't get it out of her mind. Already she was anticipating the possibility of a repeat performance.

"Dr. Matthews, Mrs. Chadwick left a message asking that you give her a call," Tara's secretary informed her the moment she stepped off the elevator.

She briefly closed her eyes, having a good guess what the woman wanted. She needed to know if Thorn would be posing for the calendar. Oh, he would be posing, Tara thought, as she opened the door to her office and placed her medical bag on her desk. He would willingly pose if she agreed to his "completely physical, emotionally free affair."

Only a man could assume there was such a thing!

And what was this nonsense about him not engaging in sexual activities while training for a race? Not to mention his claim that he hadn't slept with a woman in over two years. Could that really be true? If it was then no wonder he was in a bad mood most of the time.

She had read enough medical books to know how the lack of intimate physical contact could play on some people's mind. No doubt Thorn was expecting a sexual marathon once his long, self-imposed wait was over. He had even mentioned he wanted to get her out of his system.

Tara's head began spinning and she sat down at her desk knowing she had to make decisions and soon. Suddenly, Delaney's words came back to her mind... *Don't try to beat Thorn at his game since he's a pro. What you should do is to come up with a game plan of your own.*

Tara sighed deeply. She had tried that very thing the day they had gone bike-riding and had failed, miserably. Maybe it was time she made another attempt.

Thorn thought he could hold out and not sleep with her until after the race. She couldn't help but wonder just how far he would go not to yield to temptation. Chances were if his willpower and control were tested or pushed to the limit, he would go away and leave her alone. There was no way he would let his sexual need for her interfere with the possibility of him losing a race. And if he really believed that nonsense that he needed to remain celibate before a race, then she would make it hard on him and do everything in her power to try and un-celibate him.

If he thought he was the one calling all the shots he needed to think again. Thorn Westmoreland would soon discover that he had met his match.

Tara shook her head as she entered what Stone had referred to as "the lion's den."

She slipped the key he had given her back into her purse as she stepped inside and glanced around. According to the brothers, this is where Thorn spent most of his evenings. He would usually close shop and work on the special bike he was building. And in this case, he was putting together a dirt bike that he planned to give his nephew, AJ. AJ was the son Dare hadn't known he had until last year when both mother and son had moved back into town. Now Dare, Shelly and AJ were a very happy family.

At first Tara hadn't wanted to take the key Stone had offered her, but he had assured her that it was all right and that Thorn could probably use the company. But they had warned her to watch out for his bark as well as his bite. The closer the time got to a race, the moodier he became.

After what Thorn had told her the other night, she now understood why.

It had been three days since she had seen Thorn. Even now, the episode in her kitchen was still on her mind and was the cause of many sleepless nights. She would wake up restless. Agitated. Hot.

And Thorn was to blame.

But somehow, she had found the courage to brave the lion in his den to let him know of her decision about his proposition. She hoped like the dickens she wasn't making a mistake and the plan she had concocted wouldn't backfire on her.

She glanced around after quietly closing the door. Inside

the building, the side entrance led into a huge office area with file cabinets on both sides of the wall. There was also a huge desk that was cluttered with metal and chrome instead of with paper. But what caught her attention were the framed photographs hanging on the wall. She walked farther into the room to take a closer look.

The first was a photo of Thorn and former president Bill Clinton. In the photo the two men were smiling as they stood beside a beautiful motorcycle. Tara then remembered that Thorn had built a motorcycle for the former president last year.

She then glanced at the other photographs, all of Thorn and Hollywood and sports celebrities. She couldn't stop the feeling of pride that suddenly flooded her as she viewed the evidence of Thorn's accomplishments. What she had told him the day they had gone bike-riding was true. He had gifted hands.

A shudder ran through her when she thought that the same hands that skillfully shaped chrome and metal into a motor-cycle could also bring a woman to the epitome of sexual release. She shook her head, not wanting to go there, but re-membering that the main reason she was here was because she *had* gone there…too many times lately. There wasn't a single day that went by that she didn't think of her and Thorn's kitchen encounter. She wanted to believe that although he had kept his control, he had been just as affected as she had been.

With that belief, she had made a decision to show him that he had bitten off more than he could chew and she was more trouble than she was worth. She intended to turn up the heat by tempting him so badly that he would want to break things off with her before their relationship interfered with his race.

She saw it as the battle of wills, Mr. Experience against Miss Innocence. Thorn's brothers thought she was his challenge. He thought she was his sweetest temptation. She was determined to become Thorn's ultimate downfall.

The screwdriver Thorn was using to tighten a bolt on the bike's fender nearly slipped from his fingers. His nostrils flared and his entire body went on alert. He swore he'd picked up Tara's scent although he knew that wasn't possible. But still, the mere thought of her had blood pumping into every part of his body and shoved the beating of his heart into overdrive.

He couldn't help but groan under a tightly held breath. Boy, did he have it bad! He hadn't seen her in three days and already he was imagining her presence and inhaling the essence of her scent.

He had tried not to think about her; tried not to wonder what she'd been doing since he'd last seen her, and if she'd given any thought to his proposal. A light shudder raced down his spine at the possibility that she would consider it. The very idea of Tara in his bed for a week nearly made it impossible for him to breathe.

He placed his work tools aside. With her so deeply embedded in his mind, it would be impossible to get any work done. He decided to call it quits for the night and grab a beer. And he may as well spend the night at the shop since there was definitely no one waiting for him at home.

Thorn had turned and headed toward the refrigerator that sat on the other side of the room when he thought he heard something. He stopped and his gaze took a slow scan of the room, lingering on the area where the hallway led to his office.

Only his brothers had keys to his shop. He wondered if one

of them had dropped by. It wouldn't be the first time one of them had found refuge in his office to read his latest issue of *Cycle World* magazine and raid his candy jar.

He suddenly caught Tara's scent again. The smell was both alluring and seductive. He narrowed his eyes curiously as he began walking toward his office.

The air inside the building began to sizzle with each step he took. His skin began to get warm, his hands felt damp and pressure began escalating deep in his chest. Tension within him mounted at the sheer possibility, the inkling of any notion that Tara had stepped into his domain. His shop was more than just his place of business. It was more than somewhere he hung out most of the time. It was his lair. His sphere. His space.

The sharp edge of that thought cut deep into his brain. But not for one moment did it cut into his increasing desire. If anything, his body was struggling to get back the cool it had lost a while ago. He tried to keep his face solemn as he slowly and quietly rounded a corner. Tara's scent was becoming more overpowering.

And then he saw her.

Tara Matthews. His challenge. His sweetest temptation. Thorn watched as she studied the pictures he had hanging on the wall, not believing she was really there.

He wondered which one of his brothers had given her a key, not that it mattered. However, they had been with him earlier and knew the state of his mind…and his body. They were very well aware that lately he had been a man on the edge, a man in a state of pure funk with an attitude that was more biting and cutting than they had seen in a long time. Yet they had sent Tara here! At least, they hadn't tried talking her out of coming. If this was their idea of a joke, then he didn't see a damn thing funny about it. He just had to keep his mind on the prize. At the moment his mind was slightly foggy about whether that prize was the trophy he sought in Daytona or the woman standing across the room from him.

He shook his head, not believing he had thought such a thing. No woman, and that included Patrice, had ever come between him and his motorcycle, his desire to win, his need to take risks.

The corners of his lips quirked upward, as he admitted that Tara came pretty damn close to ruining his focus. His gaze took her in from head to toe, from behind, since her back was to him as she continued to study the pictures on his office wall. But that was okay. Checking out the back of her was just fine. He'd always like the shape of her backside anyway.

Her head was thrown back as she tried viewing a photograph that was positioned at a high angle. That made her hair fan across her shoulders, and the way the light in the room was hitting it gave the strands a brilliant glow.

She was wearing a dress. A rather short one but her curves were meant for the dress and the dress was meant for her curves. His gaze roamed down her body to her legs. They were long, shapely and he bet they would feel like heaven wrapped around his waist, holding him inside her real tight while he made love to her with no intention of ever stopping.

Something made her go still. He could tell the exact moment she knew he was in the room although she didn't turn around. It didn't matter to him that she wasn't ready to acknowledge his presence. Eventually she would have to. What really mattered to him was that she was there. Alone with him and looking sexier than any woman had a right to look.

But he inwardly admitted that there was a lot more to Tara than her being pleasing to the eyes. There were things about her that went beyond the physical. There was the way she had captured the love, admiration and respect of his family, especially his four brothers. For some reason, none of them had taken a liking to Patrice; however, with Tara it was an entirely different story. Then there was the love and dedication she had for her job as a pediatrician. He happened to be at the hospital one day and had seen first hand what a warm, loving and caring approach she had with a sick child. He had known at that moment while watching her that she would make a fantastic mother to any man's child…even his.

A warning bell went off in his head and he got the uneasy feeling that he was losing control and shouldn't be thinking such thoughts, even if Tara was proving to be the most captivating woman he'd ever met.

He drew in a deep breath. The coming weeks would test his willpower, his determination and definitely his control. The only thing that would make any of it worth a damn was the possibility of her being his, completely his, in the end. And that was what he needed to know more than anything. He had to know if she would accept the proposal he had offered her.

"If I'd known you were stopping by, I would have tidied up the place," he finally said as moments continued to tick by.

She turned slightly and gestured around the room that all of a sudden looked small and felt cramped. "I wouldn't have wanted you to go to any trouble on my account. Besides, I don't plan to stay that long anyway. I only stopped by to let you know of my decision."

He pushed away from the door and walked into the center of the room, needing to be closer to her. "And what is your decision, Tara?"

She turned and met his inquiring gaze. Damn, she looked good, and he fought the urge to reach out and pull her into

his arms, to taste her in a kiss that had his mouth watering at
the thought of it.

Awareness flashed in her eyes. They were heated, compelling, and he watched as emotions flickered through them.
For a long moment the two of them stood in the center of his
office feeding off each other's needs, wants and desires. And
the sad thing about it was that they couldn't control their reactions to each other. It seemed they were both suffering from
a unique brand of animal lust.

Thorn let out a deep breath and took a step back. Nothing
of this magnitude had ever happened to him. He was within
a few feet of jumping her bones. He had a mind to take her
right there in his office, on his desk. Right then, at that
moment, he saw her as a means to an end, a way to get intense
pleasure and a way to give pleasure as well.

He shook his head, reminding himself that he would have
to wait another five weeks, until after the race. He cursed
inwardly. As far as he was concerned the first week of March
couldn't get there soon enough.

He then remembered he was assuming things. She hadn't
said she would go along with what he had proposed. For all
he knew she could have come to tell him to go to hell and to
take his proposal with him.

He swallowed deeply. The suspense was killing him as much
as his lust was. "What's it going to be?" he had to ask her.

He watched her study him with dark eyes before saying,
"I want to make sure I understand what you're proposing,
Thorn. You will pose for the calendar if I agree to sleep with
you in a completely physical, emotionally free affair once
your race at Bike Week is over. I'm supposed to be at your
disposal, your beck and call for a week."

He smiled. Everything she had said sounded pretty damn

right to him. It had also painted one hell of a tempting picture in his mind. "Yeah, that about sums it up."

"And you won't touch me until *after* the race?" she said, as if to clarify.

Thorn crossed his arms over his chest. "Oh, I will touch you, I just won't make love to you in the traditional sense until *after* the race. As far as I'm concerned, anything else is game."

Tara lifted a brow. "Anything…like what?"

Now it was Thorn's turn to lift a brow. "A variety of things, and I'm surprised you would have to ask."

Tara nodded, deciding to leave well enough alone before he became suspicious about just how much experience she had. Knowing she was a virgin would really scare him off and probably anger him to the point of not posing for the calendar. "I fully understand my part in all of this."

Thorn inwardly smiled. He doubted that she fully understood anything, especially her part in it. But her duties would be clearly defined over the coming weeks. "So what's your answer?"

Tara prayed things worked out as she had planned. "Yes. I'll go along with your proposition."

Thorn released a deep breath, relieved.

"So how soon can you be available to do the calendar?"

Her question broke into his thoughts, just as well, since they were about to go somewhere they shouldn't be going. "How soon would they want me?"

"Probably within the next couple of weeks."

He nodded. "Just let me know when and where and I'll be there."

She blinked, and he could tell she couldn't believe he was being so accommodating. "What are your plans for this weekend?" he asked her.

She raised a brow before answering. "I'm working at the hospital on Saturday but I'll be off on Sunday. Why?"

"Chase is having a Super Bowl party at his restaurant Sunday evening. I'd like you to go with me."

She blinked again. "Me? You? As a couple?" she asked, as if clearly amazed.

"Yes. Don't you think we should let my family get used to seeing us together as a couple? Otherwise, what will they think when we take off for Daytona together?" he asked.

In all honesty, Thorn really didn't give a hoot what his brothers thought, since they assumed they had things pretty much figured out to suit their fancy anyway. His main concern was his parents. They considered Tara as another daughter and would give him plenty of hell if they thought for one minute his intentions toward her weren't honorable. Since his intentions weren't honorable, he had to at least pretend they were for his parents' benefit. Then there was Delaney to consider. She definitely wouldn't like it if she knew his plans for Tara.

He watched as she nervously bit her bottom lip before saying. "Yes, I guess you're right. In that case, yes, I'll go to Chase's party with you on Sunday."

He nodded, pleased with himself.

"It's getting late and I'd better go."

Her leaving wasn't such a bad idea considering his body's reaction to her presence. There was only so much temptation he could handle. "All right. I'll walk you to your car." He thought of something. "How did you get in here anyway?"

"Stone let me use his key. He told me it would be best to come in quietly through the side door and not the front so as not to disturb you."

Thorn nodded, knowing that wasn't the true reason Stone

had told her that. He had wanted him to be surprised by her presence; he definitely had been.

They didn't talk as he walked her to her car. A couple of times he came close to asking her to stay and let him show her around his shop. But he couldn't do that. He had to play by the rules he had established to keep his sanity, and at the moment the temptation to bed her was too great. After she left he would spend time working out, getting his blood flowing to all the parts of his body, especially to his brain.

He had to think clearly and tread lightly with Tara. Now that she had agreed to his proposal, he had to make sure he was the one in the driver's seat and she was only along for the ride. And in the end, he intended to give her the ride of her life.

But temptation being what it was, he couldn't stop himself from inching closer to her as they walked toward her car, intentionally allowing his thigh and hip occasionally to brush against hers. Her sharp intake of breath at each contact sent shivers down his spine. When they did sleep together, there was no doubt in his mind they would go up in smoke. They were just that hot.

He stood back and watched her open the door to her compact sedan. She turned to him before getting inside. "Thanks for walking me to my car, Thorn."

"Don't mention it." His gaze was devouring her but he couldn't help it. He blew out a long breath before taking a step toward her. He could tell that she was ready for his kiss, and he was more than happy to oblige her. He leaned forward and placed his mouth on hers, lightly tracing the tip of his tongue along the line of her lips, repeating the gesture several times before she easily parted her lips and drew his tongue inside her mouth with her own. His heart thudded deep in his chest at the way she was eager for the mating with his tongue, something that seemed a necessity for both of them. At this moment in time, it all made sense. He would probably think he was crazy later, but for now, standing in the middle of his parking lot, devouring her mouth like there was no tomorrow seemed perfectly normal to him. As far as he was concerned, it was the sanest thing he had done in a long time.

Her taste seduced him. It made his mind concentrate on things it shouldn't be thinking about this close to competition time. He needed to pull back, but he was steadily convincing himself otherwise.

He only brought the kiss to an end when he detected her need to breathe and wondered just how long their mouths had been joined. He stared into her eyes, watching the play of emotions that crossed her face. Confusion? Curiosity? Caution?

He took a step back. They had shared enough for tonight. The next time they were together they would be around family and friends who would serve as the buffer he needed between them.

"Drive home safely, Tara," he said, deciding she needed to leave now so he could pull himself together before he was tempted to do something he would later regret.

She nodded and without saying anything, she got into the car. His heart skipped a beat when he got a glimpse of her thighs. The hem of her dress inched up as she slid into the driver's seat. Forcing breath into his lungs, he watched as she slowly drove off, all the while thinking that he had five weeks of pure hell to endure. Five whole weeks he somehow intended to survive.

Chapter 7

"Okay, Mr. Westmoreland, I only need a few more shots and then this session will be all over," the photographer said as she adjusted the lighting.

Thank God, Thorn thought as he sat astride his bike once again. He had plenty of work to do back at the shop and had been at this photo session for three hours. The photographer, Lois Kent, had decided the best place to shoot the photos was outside to better show the man, his bike and the open road.

They had taken over a hundred shots already and Thorn's patience was beginning to wear thin. The only thing that kept him going was knowing that he was living up to his end of the bargain, which meant he could make damn sure Tara lived up to hers. This past week he'd been restless, agitated and moodier than ever.

"It will only take a minute while I reload the film."

Thorn nodded. Things hadn't gone as badly as he'd

thought they would. Lois Kent was strictly a professional, unlike Patrice. To Lois this was a job and nothing more and he appreciated that.

He glimpsed behind her and saw a car pull up. His heart quickened when he recognized the driver.

He watched as Tara got out of her car and walked toward them. She was wearing a pair of white slacks and a pullover blue sweater.

And as usual she looked good.

It had been a week since he had seen her; a week since he had taken her to his brother's restaurant for the Super Bowl party. Even surrounded by family and friends, he hadn't been able to keep his eyes off her. His interest in Tara hadn't gone unnoticed by his brothers. And they had been teasing him about it ever since, which only pissed him off even more.

He raised a brow, wondering why she was here, not that he had any complaints. It was only that he had been trying to keep his distance from her so that he could retain his sanity and his control. He had decided it would only take a week or two to get her primed to the level he wanted her to be. He now had four weeks left.

He watched as she spoke to Lois, and then she glanced over at him. "Hi, Thorn."

"Tara," he acknowledged, taking a deep breath. He had been the perfect gentleman that Super Bowl Sunday, even when he had taken her home. He had kissed her on her doorstep, made sure she had gotten safely inside and left. Doing more than that would have been suicide.

"I'm surprised to see you here," he said, not taking his eyes off her as he drank in her beauty. It was one of those days when the air was brisk with a slight chill although the sun was shining high overhead. The sun's rays made her look that much more gorgeous.

"Today was my day off. I wasn't doing anything special so I thought I would come and check things out. I had lunch at Chase's place, and when I asked about you, he told me where you were."

Thorn nodded. He just bet his brother was happy to give her any information about him that she wanted. They would do anything to get him out of his foul mood. But what surprised him was that Tara had asked Chase about him. Thorn wondered if perhaps she had sought him out about anything in particular. He sighed, deciding he would find out soon enough.

"All right, Mr. Westmoreland, I'm ready to start shooting again," Lois said, recapturing his attention.

He slid his gaze from Tara's to Lois's. "Okay," he said, ready to get the photo session over with. "Let your camera roll."

Tara's breath got lodged in her throat as she watched Thorn before the camera. He looked magnificent.

Thorn and his motorcycle.

Together they were a natural, and she knew that he would be the highlight in any woman's calendar as Mr. July. In a month that was known to be hot anyway, he would definitely make things explosive.

She should have her head examined even for being here. She had known that today was the day for Thorn's photo session and when Chase had mentioned just where it would be, she couldn't help being pulled to this place to seek him out. On the drive over she kept asking herself why she needed to see him, but she hadn't come up with an answer.

"That's right, Mr. Westmoreland, give me another one of those sexy smiles for the camera. That's it. Just think about all those women who'll be looking at you on that calendar and panting. I'm sure some of them will even find a way to contact you. You'll certainly have your pick of any of them," Lois said, as she moved around in front of Thorn and snapped picture after picture.

Tara frowned. The photographer's words didn't sit too well with her. Just the thought of other women contacting Thorn after seeing the calendar bothered her. It shouldn't have. She met his gaze and saw he was watching her intently. Had he read the displeasure on her face when the photographer had mentioned other women?

She sighed deeply, getting aggravated with herself. What Thorn did with his free time did not concern her. At least it shouldn't, but it did.

"Okay, that's it, Mr. Westmoreland. You were a wonderful subject to capture on film and I can't wait for the calendar to come out. I know it will be a huge success and will benefit Kids' World greatly."

Lois then added. "And not to impose but I have a friend who asked me to give you her phone number. She is a huge fan of yours and would love to get together with you some time. She's a flight attendant who usually attends Bike Week in Daytona each year and was wondering if perhaps—"

"Thanks, but I'm not interested," Thorn said, getting off his bike. He didn't even glance at the surprised look on Lois's face when he walked toward Tara. "I have all the woman I need right here."

Thorn saw surprise in Tara's face just seconds before he leaned down and kissed her in a full open-mouth caress that left no one guessing about their relationship. At least no one other than Tara.

"Oops, sorry," Lois said when Thorn released Tara's mouth

from his. "I didn't know the two of you were an item, Dr. Matthews." She smiled apologetically. "I assumed you had dropped by as a member of the committee to see how things were going. Besides, from everything I'd always heard or read, Thorn Westmoreland has never made a claim on any woman," she said, chuckling. "Evidently, I'm wrong."

Before Tara could open her mouth, the one that had just been thoroughly kissed by Thorn, to tell Lois that she had not been wrong and had misread things, Thorn spoke up.

"Yeah, you were wrong because I'm definitely staking a claim on this woman."

Tara raised a brow and decided that now was not the time or the place to set Thorn straight. No man staked a claim on her. "I gather things went well," she found herself saying instead.

"Better than I thought they would. Lois is good at her job. I just hope all those photographs she took come out the way she wants them to."

Tara nodded. There was no doubt in her mind they would. What Lois had said was true. Thorn was definitely a wonderful subject to capture on film. "Well, I'd better go. I dropped by out of curiosity," she said, easing away.

He nodded. "What are your plans for the rest of the day?"

Tara's heart thudded in her chest with his question. "I don't have any. Why?"

"Would you like to go bike-riding with me and have dinner at that restaurant again?"

Tara really would have liked that but wondered if it was wise. But then, if she planned to seduce Thorn into breaking his vow of celibacy, she had to get things rolling.

"All right. Just give me an hour to go home and change clothes."

His gaze was steadily focused on hers when he said, "Okay."

* * *

Thorn didn't have to encourage Tara this time to lean into him. Her body automatically did so after straddling the bike behind him and fitting her rear end comfortably on the seat. She placed her chest against his back, delighting in the feel of her body pressed against his. She inhaled the pleasant scent of him as she rested her head against his jacket, and, at the moment, without understanding what was going on with her, she felt being this close to him was a necessity to her very existence. It didn't make sense. She had vowed never to feel that way about any man again.

But she admitted that Thorn was her challenge.

Although she knew a future wasn't in the cards for them, and any involvement would be just as he wanted—completely physical and emotionally free—she still couldn't help but be cautious. There was something about Thorn that could become addictive. But then she reminded herself quickly that she didn't intend things to go that far between them. Thorn would have to choose between her and the race, and she was banking that it would be the race. It was an ego thing. He could get another woman in his bed any time, but a chance to be victorious at Bike Week, to reign supreme, was something he had been working years to achieve.

So she decided to do whatever was needed to increase his physical craving and make sure he was tempted beyond his control. She scooted closer to him and leaned more into him. Her arms around his waist tightened. She planted her cheek against his back and again inhaled his scent—manly, robust and sensual.

Closing her eyes, she remembered that night in her kitchen, the skill of his exploring fingers and the sensations he had made her feel. She then imagined how things might be if they were to make it beyond the four weeks, although she knew they wouldn't. But still she decided there was nothing wrong with having wild fun in her imagination.

What would happen if her plan to seduce Thorn failed? He would probably win the race—only because he was arrogant and cocky enough to do so—and then he would celebrate his victory, but not for long. He would turn his attention to her with one thought on his mind; taking her to bed.

The thought of that happening was almost too much to think about. But she did so anyway. In the dark recesses of her mind, she could picture the two of them wrapped in silken sheets in a huge bed, making out like there was no tomorrow. *For an entire week.*

She opened her eyes and tried to shove the thoughts away. Too late. There were too many of them firmly planted in her mind. After two years of going without he would no doubt take her at a level that bordered on desperation. He would be like a starving man eating his favorite meal for the first time in a long while. She shuddered slightly as she imagined how his first thrust would feel. Probably painful, considering her virginal state. But then, any that followed would be…

She blinked, noticing Thorn had slowed the bike down. She glanced around, wondering if they had arrived at their destination, and was surprised to see he had brought her back to the wooded area he had said was Westmoreland land. Why? They had taken a walk around the property the last time they were here a couple of weeks ago. Why was he bringing her back here?

Thorn breathed in deeply as he brought his bike to a stop. All he had planned to do was take Tara out to eat and then back home. But the feel of her arms wrapped tightly around his waist, the feel of her pressed so close to his back and the scent of her surrounding him had been too much.

He angled his head over his shoulder and came very close to her face. "We need to talk."

Tara lifted a brow. "Couldn't we have waited until we got to the restaurant?"

He shook his head. "No, it's rather private and not a topic we would want to discuss over dinner."

"Oh," she said, wondering just what topic that could be.

She climbed off the bike and stood back as he turned off the engine, kicked down the motorcycle stand and then swung his leg over the bike. She tried not to look at how tightly stretched his jeans were across his body, especially over his midsection, as he slowly covered the distance that separated them. She met his gaze. He had said that he wanted to talk, but the look in his eyes told another story.

She swallowed when he came to a stop in front of her. "What did you want to talk about?"

Thorn blinked. For a moment he had completely forgotten just what he had wanted to discuss with her. His concentration had gone to her mouth and his desire to devour it. Savor it. Taste it.

"It's about birth control," he finally said.

Now it was Tara's turn to blink. "Birth control?"

"Yes," Thorn answered in a husky voice. "I need to know if you're using any?"

Tara blinked again. "Excuse me?"

Thorn's voice got huskier when he explained. "I need to know if you plan on using birth control when we make love because I don't intend to use anything."

Tara stared at him, momentarily speechless. Never in a million years would she have thought that he was the kind of man who would be the selfish type in the bedroom. They were men who thought all they had to do was to enjoy the act of making love and not contribute to the responsibility of making sure there was not an unwanted pregnancy. She had heard about such men and couldn't believe that Thorn was one of them. She couldn't believe he was actually standing in front of her dumping something like that in her lap.

Looking him squarely in the eye she placed her hands on her hips. "No, I'm not on any type of birth control," she said, deciding not to add that she had started taking the pill six months before her wedding was to take place. She had stopped when the marriage hadn't happened and had not given any thought to going back on them since there had not been a need. As far as she was concerned there still was no need since she had no intention of sleeping with Thorn, although he didn't know that.

Her gaze sharpened and angry fire appeared in her eyes. The expression on her face would probably have killed lesser men. "So if you plan to sleep with me, Thorn Westmoreland, then it will be up to you to wear a condom."

Thorn crossed his arms over his chest. Oh, he intended to sleep with her all right. But sleep was only a portion of what they would do, a very small portion. He watched her glare at him. Damn, but he liked her feistiness and had from the first time they had met. He knew he had ventured into territory that was probably off-limits by the way she was acting, but the sooner she knew the score, the better. First he had to clarify things with her.

"Don't misunderstand me, Tara. If it were any woman other than you, I wouldn't even dream of taking them to bed without my own brand of protection no matter what type of protection they claimed to be using. In addition to that, I would make sure we both knew the state of our health. Safe sex means a lot to me, and I need to be certain it also means a lot to the woman I'm sleeping with. When it comes to bed partners, I'm extremely selective. Because of racing, I routinely take physicals, and I'm sure since you're involved in the medical field, things are probably the same way with you. I apologize if I came off just now as being a man who leaves the responsibility of birth control strictly in the hands of the woman. That is far from the truth. I'm not that selfish nor am I that stupid."

Confusion clouded Tara's eyes. "Then why did you ask me that? I still don't understand."

He decided it was time to make her understand. "Because I have wanted you for so long, and my desire for you is so great, I want to explode inside you and know it's happening and actually feel it happening. I want to be skin to skin with you when it happens. More than anything, I desire it to be that way with you."

Tara's chest rose as she took a deep breath, removed her hands from her hips and clenched them by her sides. She met the eyes that bored into hers and whispered in a soft voice the single word that immediately came to her mind. "Why?"

He took a step closer. "Because I want to share more pleasure with you than I've ever shared with another woman. For one solid week I don't want to know where your body begins and where mine ends. And at that moment when I am inside of you, making love to you over and over again, I want to be able to feel, actually feel, you getting wet for me. I want the full effect of reaching the ultimate climax with you."

He reached out and touched her waist and felt the tremors that his words had caused. He pulled her to him, wanting her to feel just what he was feeling, too. She was the reason for his constant state of arousal and had been the reason for quite some time. No other woman had been able to do this to him. Only her. He had two years of pent-up sexual frustrations to release and he wanted to do it inside of her. He could think of making love to no one else.

He saw an involvement with someone else as a sexual act that would be empty, meaningless and unfulfilling. Maybe it was a mind game he had gotten caught up in, but there was no help for it. He was convinced that Tara was not only his challenge and his sweetest temptation, he truly believed that she was also his passion and the two of them would connect in bed in a special way. They would be fantastic together. He had no illusions that they would not be.

Tara licked her bottom lip. She wondered what Thorn would say if she told him she was a virgin. And better yet, what would he say if she told him she didn't intend to get on any type of birth control just for a week that wouldn't happen? But she couldn't tell him either of those things.

Instead, she said. "And what if I told you I couldn't take the pill due to medical reasons and that I don't feel comfortable using any other type of birth control? Would you use a condom then?"

Without hesitating he said. "Yes."

She nodded, believing that he would. But then, after what he had just told her, she knew that if they ever made love— although there was a very slim chance of that happening— they both knew what it would take to give him the ultimate in sexual satisfaction when he slept with her. He wanted it all and had engrained into his mind that he wanted things to be different with her than they had been with any other woman he had been with.

Tara didn't know whether to be flattered or frightened.

A part of her knew she had nothing to fear from Thorn. Even when he had come across as moodier than hell, she hadn't been afraid of him. The reason she had avoided him for the past two years was for the very thing he was talking to her about now.

Wants and desires.

She had always wanted him, from the first. Even now she wanted him. She was woman enough to admit that. But wanting something and having something were two totally different things. Derrick had pretty much killed her emotions, but Thorn had easily brought them back to life. If she was afraid of anything, it was of losing her heart to someone else and getting hurt once more. But she couldn't think about any of that when Thorn was looking at her as if she was a treat he wanted to savor, over and over again.

"Thanks for letting me know what I'm up against, Thorn," she said softly. She watched a slow smile touch the corners of his lips. Everyone knew Thorn's smiles were infrequent, and whenever he smiled, especially at her, pleasant emotions always flooded her body.

"That's not the only thing you will be up against, Tara."

She heard the little hitch in his voice and followed the path of his gaze downward as it settled on his midsection. She shuddered when she saw his arousal straining against the zipper of his jeans.

"But there's no doubt in my mind that you can handle me."

Tara blinked. She wasn't so sure when she saw how large he was. A mixture of desire and anticipation rammed through her mind as well as her body. It didn't do any good to try and convince herself that she didn't have a thing to worry about since she and Thorn would never make love. Seeing him standing before her with a determined look on his face made her realize just what she really *was* up against. His mind was pretty made up. He would be competing in the race, and he would have her at the end of four weeks and nothing would deter him from his goals.

She would have to see about that. She needed to test his control and let him know just what he was up against as well.

Determined to make a point, she leaned up on tiptoe and placed her mouth to his. After overcoming his surprise, he immediately captured her lips with his. At the first touch of his tongue to hers she began to shudder, and he placed his arms around her and brought her closer into the fit of him to thoroughly taste her and devour her mouth. A keen ache throbbed deep within her. She slipped her arms around his neck and held on as his kiss became more demanding. Arching against him she felt the hardness of his erection more firmly against her belly, igniting heat and a deep sense of yearning.

He was giving her just what she wanted, and she suddenly pushed aside her need to make a point. At the moment nothing mattered to her, except the sensation of him against her stomach, and the feel of his hands cupping her backside to secure a closer fit.

Breath whooshed from her lungs the moment he broke off the kiss, and he held her in his arms as they both panted their way back to reality. For the longest moment, neither of them moved. Instead they stood there, on Westmoreland land, with their arms wrapped around each other trying their best to breathe and regain control of their minds and bodies.

Doing so wasn't easy and they both knew, for totally different reasons, they were in deep trouble.

"I understand you were once engaged to be married."

Tara stopped eating abruptly and glanced up at Thorn,

startled by his statement. There was a serious glint in the depths of the dark eyes looking at her. Trying to keep her features expressionless, she met his gaze and asked. "Who told you that?"

Thorn contemplated her for a long moment before saying, "One of my brothers. I can't remember which one, though. Was it supposed to have been a secret?"

Tara gave him a considering glance. "No."

He studied her. "So, what happened?"

Tara figured he already knew the full story and wondered why he was asking. The night of Delaney's wedding she had been the one to catch the bouquet, and when the Westmoreland brothers had remarked that she would be next, she'd immediately told them she would never marry and had ended up telling them why.

She sighed. "Derrick, the man I was to marry, decided on my wedding day at the church, in front of over three hundred guests, that he loved my maid of honor instead of me. So he stopped the wedding, asked for my forgiveness and he and the woman I'd always considered my best friend took off. They drove to Georgia and got married that same day."

"He was a fool," Thorn didn't hesitate in saying before taking a sip of his coffee. He met her gaze then asked, "Are you over him?"

His question and the way he was looking at her quickened her pulse. "Yes. Why?"

"Curious."

Tara continued eating, wondering why Thorn would be curious about her feelings for Derrick. Deciding she had given him enough information about her past, she decided she wanted to know about the woman who'd been in his past. The one who'd made him leery of getting serious about a woman.

"What about you, Thorn? Have you ever been in love?"

He met her gaze over the rim of the coffee cup he held to his lips. "Why do you ask?"

"Curious."

He set down his cup. "I don't know. I may have thought I was at one time, but when I take the time to analyze the situation, I don't think I've ever been in love."

Tara nodded. "But a woman has hurt you." It was more a statement than a question.

"I think it was more disappointment than hurt. It's hard for anyone to discover they were deceived by someone they cared about, Tara."

She of all people knew how right he was on that one. She thought of how many times Derrick and Danielle had written to her, asking her forgiveness for deceiving her, and how many times she had tossed their letters in the trash.

"But she meant a lot to you?"

He picked up his cup and took another sip before answering. "Yes, at the time I thought she did, but I can say it was nothing but lust. What disappointed me the most was finding out I wasn't the only man she was sleeping with, and I'm glad I used protection to the max with her. I make it a point to stay away from women who routinely have multiple bed partners."

Tara nodded. "What did she do for a living?"

He signaled for a waitress to refill his coffee. "She's a freelance photographer."

"Oh." No wonder he hadn't been anxious to do that photo shoot, she thought. "And are you over her?"

He chuckled. Evidently he thought she had scored with that question. She was following the same line of questioning he had used on her earlier.

"Yes, I am definitely over her." He leaned over the table,

closer to her and whispered. "You, Tara Matthews, are the only woman on my agenda, and I'm counting the days until I have you in bed with me while I do all kinds of wild and wicked things to you."

Tara swallowed as her pulse rate increased. She dropped her gaze to her plate, but the sensations that swept through her with his words forced her to meet his gaze again. The look he was giving her was dark, sexy and brooding and she knew that if things worked out the way he planned, he would have her in his bed after the race so fast it would make her head spin.

She lowered her gaze and began eating her food again. Thorn was seducing her and she couldn't let him do that. They had already played their love games for the day. She needed to think smart and stay in control. She decided to maneuver their conversation to a safer topic.

"Why do you race?"

His mouth twitched, and a smile appeared. She knew he saw through her ploy but decided to go along with her. "I like the excitement of taking risks. I've always liked to compete. Motorcycle racing stimulates that side of me."

For the next twenty minutes she listened while he talked about racing and what benefits, promotions and recognition his company would receive if he won the first race of the year, the one during Bike Week at the Daytona Speedway. He also told her about his desire one day to compete on the European circuit.

"Do you race a lot?"

"I do my share. Last year I was in a total of twelve races. That averaged out to be a race a month, so I was on the road quite a bit. The men who're my crew chief and mechanic are the best in the business. And I also have the best damn wrench around."

"Wrench?"

"Yeah, just like a wrench is a mechanic's basic tool, the same holds true of a human wrench in racing. He's the person I most depend on. I have an eighteen-wheeler that transports my bikes from race to race and wherever I go, my wrench travels with me. Racing is a team sport and if I win, my team wins."

By the time the evening was over, Tara had received a very extensive education on motorcycle racing. For most of an hour, they had avoided bringing sex into their conversation and when they left the restaurant to head home, Tara looked at Thorn and smiled before getting on the motorcycle. Unlike the last time, when they had ended their meal with tempers flaring, tonight she had thoroughly enjoyed the time she had spent with him.

Later that night, as she lay in bed, half asleep with thoughts of Thorn running through her head, she couldn't help but remember their conversation about birth control.

She inhaled a lengthy, deep, fortifying breath when she thought of what Thorn wanted to do to her. Closing her eyes she thought of the picture Thorn had painted at the restaurant of them in bed together. She imagined him climbing on her, straddling her and burying himself deep within her, stroking her insides, making it last while his desire raged for her at a level that wasn't normally possible. Then finally, as she imagined him climaxing inside her, with nothing separating them, feeling everything, the complete essence of him, she felt the area around the juncture of her legs get hot and sensitive.

Tara opened her eyes. She'd better play it safe. Just in case there was a slim possibility that she and Thorn ever actually did make love, she knew she would want it just as he described. Tara decided to make an appointment with her gynecologist this week.

Chapter 8

Tara glanced at the clock on the wall. Thorn would be arriving any minute.

She had called him at the shop asking if he knew anything about repairing a leaking faucet. It was the perfect ploy since his brothers had gone on a camping trip for the weekend. Had they been available, he would wonder why she had summoned him instead of one of them.

She nearly jumped at the sound of the doorbell. It had been a couple of days since she had seen him, and today she had a plan. She was intent on testing his control to the limit, with the hope that he would finally see that she was more trouble than she was worth and a threat to his winning his race; especially if he strongly believed in this celibacy thing.

She looked down at herself before walking to the door. Although her outfit wasn't outright provocative, she thought t would definitely grab his attention. After glancing out of he peephole in the door, she opened it.

"Thorn, thanks for coming. I really hated to bother you but hat dripping faucet was driving me crazy and I knew if I lidn't get it taken care of, I wouldn't be able to sleep tonight."

"No problem," he said, stepping inside with a toolbox in his hand. "I'm sure this will only take a minute."

His gaze traveled down the length of her, taking in her very short cut-off jeans and her barely-there, thin tank top. It wasn't transparent but it might as well have been the way her nipples showed through. It left very little to the imagination.

His face turned into a frown. "You went somewhere dressed like that?"

She glanced down at herself. "What's wrong with the way I'm dressed?"

"Nothing, unless you're looking for trouble."

She thought about telling him that the only trouble she was looking for was standing right in front of her. Instead she rolled her eyes. "Back off, Thorn. You're beginning to sound like Stone."

He raised a brow. "Stone?"

"Yes, Stone. He's on this big-brother kick."

Thorn met her gaze. "I'm sure he is concerned about your welfare."

"Trust me, I can take care of myself. Now, if you don't mind, will you take a look at my faucet?"

He sighed. "Lead the way."

Thorn wished he could take back those three words when she walked off in front of him. His blood raced fast and furiously through all parts of his body when his gaze slid to her backside. Damn, her shorts were short. Way too short. And they were as tight as tight could be. She would probably get arrested if she wore something that short and tight out in public. They stopped barely at the end of her cheeks and each step she took showed him a little of a bare behind. When she headed up the stairs he decided to stop her.

"Hey, wait. Where are we going?"

She stopped and glanced back at him over her shoulder. "Up to my room."

He swallowed. "Why?"

Tara turned around and tried to keep her expression bland and innocent. "To fix the leaking faucet in the master bathroom."

Thorn didn't move. He had assumed she needed the faucet in her kitchen fixed. Hell, his control would be tested to the limit if he had to go anywhere near her bedroom.

"Is there something wrong, Thorn?"

Yes, there's a lot of things wrong, and two years of abstinence heads the list, he thought. He reached down within to drum up some self-control that he didn't think he had. "No, there's nothing wrong. Show me the way," he said.

He inhaled slowly as he followed her up the stairs and almost choked on his own breath when he walked into her bedroom. It was decorated in black, silver-gray and mauve, and everything matched—the floral print on the bedcovers, curtains and the loveseat. The room looked like her, feminine and sensuous. Even the huge bed looked like a bed intended for lovemaking more than for sleeping. He could imagine rolling around the sheets with her in that bed.

"The bathroom is this way."

He quickly pushed the thoughts out of his mind as he followed her into the connecting bathroom.

"Do you need my help with anything?" she asked, leaning against the vanity.

His gaze moved from her face to her chest, settling on what could be seen of her breasts through the thin material of her top. At the moment, the only thing she could do for him was to give him breathing space. "No, I'll be fine. Just give me a couple of minutes."

"All right. I'll be in my bedroom if you need anything."

He lifted a brow. He'd much prefer it if she went downstairs to the kitchen, as far away from him as she could, but he decided not to tell her that. After all, it wasn't her fault that he wanted to jump her bones.

As soon as she left, he went about checking out her faucet while trying to ignore the sound of her moving around in the bedroom. It didn't take him any time at all to repair the faucet and he was glad of that. Now he could concentrate on getting the hell out of here. He worked his way from under her sink and stood. It had been rather quiet in her bedroom for the past couple of minutes and he hoped she was downstairs.

Wrong.

He walked out of the bathroom and saw her standing on the other side of the room wearing nothing but her skimpy top and a pair of black thong panties. Her back was to him, and as soon as he cleared his throat she snatched a short silk robe off the bed and quickly put it on.

Too late. He had seen more than he should have.

"Sorry. I thought you would be a while and decided to change into something comfortable," she said, apologetically, looking down as she tied the belt of her robe around her waist.

He didn't say anything. He couldn't say anything. All he could think about was just how much of her naked skin he had seen. Damn, she looked good in a thong. His entire body began aching.

"Is it fixed?"

Her question reminded him why he was there, but couldn't quite bring him back around. His mind was still glued to the bottom part of her although she was now decently covered. But nothing could erase from his memory what he had seen.

"Well, is it?"

He slowly moved his gaze up to her face, and without thinking twice about what he was doing, he placed his toolbox on the table in her room and quickly crossed the space separating them. He stood staring at her then took her mouth with his, and she didn't try to resist when he thrust his tongue between her lips, tasting her with a force that shook him to the very core. And when he felt her return his kiss, mating her tongue with his, he totally lost it and began feasting greedily on her mouth.

He felt her tremble as he slid his hand down her body, reached under the short robe, spread her legs apart and then began moving his hand between them, needing to touch her in the same intimate way he had done before.

Moments later he discovered that wasn't enough. He had to have her. He needed to ease his thick, hot arousal into the very place he was touching.

With his free hand he began undoing his zipper while his mouth continued to plunder hers. Suddenly, she broke off the kiss.

"Thorn, we can't. No protection. The race."

Sanity quickly returned to Thorn with her words. He breathed in deeply and took a step back and rezipped his pants. For a moment he hadn't cared about anything. Nothing had mattered, definitely not the fact he didn't have any protection with him or the fact that he had completely forgotten about his vow of celibacy.

He raked a hand down his face then wished he hadn't done that. She had been primed, ready and wet; her scent was on his hand and made his nostrils flare with wanting and desire. Her scent was woman. Hot, enticing woman.

He closed his eyes for a moment then reopened them as he slowly began backing toward the door. He picked his toolbox up off the table. "Your faucet should be working just fine now," he said, huskily. "I'll call you."

And as quick as she could bat an eye, he was gone.

During the following weeks, Tara threw her heart and soul into her work.

After that first attempt, she had discovered that getting Thorn to break his vow of celibacy—finding an opportunity to put her plan into action and getting him to cooperate—was not easy.

He had taken her out to dinner several times and they had even gone to the movies together twice, but whenever he returned her home, he deposited her on her doorstep, kissed her goodnight and quickly got on his bike or into his car and took off. Getting under Thorn's skin was turning out to be a monumental task.

A stomach virus that was going around kept her busy as frantic mothers lined the emergency room seeking medical care for their little ones. Twice during the past week she had worked longer hours than she normally did, but Tara was grateful to stay busy.

Nighttime for her was torture at its best. She was restless, her mind returned to the kiss she'd shared with Thorn again and again. In an effort to help her sleep or just to occupy her mind, Delaney had given her plenty of reading material in the way of romance novels.

That only made matters worse.

She enjoyed reading about how the hero and heroine found their way to everlasting love, but the searing passion and profound intimacy the fictional characters shared always left Tara breathless, wondering if things like that could really happen between two people.

Pushing the covers aside, Tara got out of bed. Tonight was one of those nights she felt restless. She had gone to bed early, before eight o'clock, with a book to read, and had tried falling asleep. Instead, it was almost midnight and she was still wide awake.

It was a good thing that she was off work tomorrow. She knew Thorn was spending a lot of time at his shop working on his nephew's motorbike. Tara couldn't wait to see the expression on AJ's face when he received the sporty dirt bike Thorn was building especially for him. She hadn't seen it yet, but according to the brothers it was a sweet piece of machinery. All the Westmoreland men owned motorcycles. At eleven it was time AJ got his.

More than once Tara had thought of using the pretense of wanting to see the dirt bike as an excuse to drop by Thorn's shop unexpectedly again, but each time she got in her car and headed in that direction, she would change her mind and turn around. She'd had lunch with the brothers at Chase's restaurant earlier in the week and they had joked among themselves about how Thorn's mood had gone from bad to worse.

She had sat quietly, eating her meal while listening to their chatter. It seemed they knew the reason for Thorn's mean disposition these days and openly said they wished like hell that Bike Week would hurry up and come before he drove them, as well as himself, crazy.

From the conversation around her it appeared Thorn hadn't mentioned to his brothers that she would be going with him to Bike Week, because no one, including Delaney, had mentioned it.

Tara headed for the kitchen, deciding to get a glass of the iced tea she had made earlier that day. Maybe the drink would cool her off because tonight her body definitely felt hot.

Thorn brought his motorcycle to a complete stop and shut off the engine. The lights were still on in Tara's home, which meant she hadn't gone to bed yet. He had worked at the shop until he couldn't get his mind to concentrate on what he was doing. He kept thinking of Tara and what he wanted to do to her.

He'd never gone into a race this tense and restless over a woman before. Usually, one was the last thing on his mind this close to competition. This time that was not the case. Now that he knew how she tasted, he couldn't get the sweet flavor of her mouth and her body from his mind. And a day didn't go by when he didn't think about what they'd almost done that day in her bedroom. He had zipped down his pants, been ready to take her right then and there had her words not reclaimed his senses.

And his brothers were making matters worse with that stupid bet of theirs. He had refused to tell them anything; his relationship with Tara was not up for discussion. No one knew about their agreement, and other than the time they'd been seen together at Chase's Super Bowl party, no one knew what was going on with them. He wanted to keep it that way for as long as he could. The family would find out soon enough that she was going to Bike Week.

Earlier, when he'd seen he would not get any work done, he had tossed his tools aside, stripped off his clothes and had taken a shower to cool off his heated body. That hadn't worked. He got dressed and decided to go for a ride on his bike to let the wind and the chilly night air cool him down and take the edge off. But that hadn't worked either.

There was only one way he could relieve what ailed him and he couldn't risk going that far. Breaking his vow of celibacy before the race was not an option. Therefore, with Bike Week only a couple of weeks away, he needed to put as much distance between himself and Tara as possible. She was becoming too much of a temptation. That was why he had made the decision tonight to leave for Daytona earlier than planned and have Tara ride down later with one of his brothers.

The most important thing was that she be in Daytona when the race was over. There was no way he could hang around and run the risk of making love to her. But he was determined to leave them both with something to anticipate while he was gone.

Moments later he walked up to her door and rang the doorbell. He knew it was late but he had to see her. His body pulsed with something he had never felt before…urgency.

The sound of her soft voice hummed through the door. "Who is it?"

He took a deep breath and responded, "Thorn."

He watched as the door slowly opened, exposing the surprise on her features. "Thorn, what are you doing here?"

He swallowed as his gaze took in all of her. She was wearing a short silk nightgown that only covered her to midthigh. Her hair was in disarray—as if she had tossed and turned while trying to sleep, and one of the spaghetti straps of her gown hung down off her shoulder. The total picture was ultrasexy, enticing, a product of any man's fantasy.

"Thorn?"

He blinked, realizing he hadn't answered her question. "There's been a change in my plans about Bike Week and I thought I should share it with you."

He saw the indecision that appeared in her features. It was as if she was trying to make up her mind about whether to let him in. She was probably wondering why he hadn't picked up a phone and called her instead of dropping by unexpectedly.

"I apologize for showing up without calling first, but I wanted to tell you about the change in person," he added, hoping that would explain things to her although he was still confused as to what had driven him to seek her out tonight. All he knew was that he had to be alone with her if only for a few minutes. Hell, he would take a few seconds if that were all she would spare.

"All right, come in," she said, then stood aside to let him enter.

The moment he walked into her home and closed the door behind him, he was engulfed with desire so thick he was having difficulty breathing. He had to force air through his lungs.

This wasn't normal, but nothing, he reasoned, had been normal for him since he had first laid eyes on Tara. His life hadn't been the same since that day. And watching her bare legs and the way her hips swayed under the nightgown she was wearing as she walked across the room before turning around to face him wasn't helping matters.

For two years he had battled what he had felt for her, his desire, but most importantly, his growing affection. He hadn't wanted to care about her. He hadn't wanted to care about any woman for that matter. Other than his family, his love for motorcycles was the only thing he felt that he needed in his life. But Tara had come into it and messed up things really well. The more he'd found himself attracted to her, the more he had tried to resist, but to no avail.

"Thorn, what is the change in your plans?"

He leaned back against the closed door. "I've decided to leave for Daytona early."

Tara raised an arched brow. "How early?"

"I'm leaving Sunday if I can arrange everything."

"This Sunday?" When he nodded, she said. "That's only three days away. I can't take off work and—"

"And I don't expect you to. I'll talk to one of my brothers about you coming down with them later at the beginning of Bike Week."

"But—but why are you leaving so early?" she asked.

He shifted his helmet to his other hand, thinking there was no way he could tell her the absolute truth. So instead he said. "There are a few things I need to do to get ready for the race, like getting my mind in check," he said, which wasn't a total lie. With any type of race, concentration was the key and he couldn't do it here, not in the same town where she lived.

He placed his helmet on the table. "Tara?"

She met his gaze. "Yes?"

He held out his hand to her. "Come here," he said in a voice he didn't recognize as his own. The only thing he did recognize and acknowledge was his need to touch her, to taste her and hold her in his arms. Two weeks without seeing her would be absolute torture for him.

He watched her stare at his outstretched hand, moments longer than he had hoped, before she slowly closed the distance that separated them, taking his fingers and entwining them with her smaller ones. The heat from her touch was automatic. Sensual heat moved from his hand and quickly spread throughout his body. Even his blood simmered with their touch. He gently pulled her to him, letting her body come to rest against the hardness of his.

"Do you have any idea how much I want you, Tara?" he asked huskily, his lips only a few inches from hers.

Desire formed in her eyes before she said softly, "Yes, I think I do."

"I want you to know for certain. The moment you step foot in Daytona I want you to know just what to expect after the race is over and I turn my full attention to you. I don't want you to be surprised at the magnitude of my hunger and desire, and I want to give you a sample of what is to come. May I?"

As far as she was concerned he had given her plenty of samples already and she had a pretty good idea what she was in for. But still, the very thought that he asked permission almost made Tara come apart then and there. With all his roughness, and even when he'd been in his worse mood, Thorn had always remained a gentleman in his dealings with her. Sensuous, irresistible and sexy, yet a gentleman just the same.

Tara swallowed the lump in her throat, not knowing what she should do or more importantly, what she should say. If she granted him what he wanted, it wouldn't help matters where she was concerned. She was in the thick of things and didn't see a way out, not with Thorn hightailing it out of town on Sunday. With him leaving for Daytona earlier than planned, there was no way she could tempt him the way she needed in order to get him to call off their agreement. He would expect her to keep her end of the bargain and give him the week she had promised him.

But then she decided she had to be completely honest with herself and admit that she wanted that week, as well. Thorn Westmoreland had needs and a part of her could not imagine him making love to another woman. She refused to think about that. And standing before him now, she knew why.

She was in love with him.

The thought that he could end up hurting her the way Derrick had made her want to cover her heart and protect it from pain, to escape into her bedroom and hide. But it was too late for that. She had tried avoiding Thorn for two years, had tried protecting her heart and her soul from him. Yet in the end, he had gotten them anyway. He had asked her if she knew how much he wanted her; well she had a question for him. Did he have any idea how much she loved him?

However, that was a question she couldn't ask him.

Before getting lost in deep thoughts of how much she loved him, she decided to turn her attention back to the issue at hand. She met his gaze and knew he was waiting for an answer to his question of whether or not he could give her a sample of what was to come. And she would give him the only answer she could; there was no way she could deny his request. "Yes, you may."

Wordlessly, without wasting any time, in the next moment, the next breath, he covered her lips with his. He immediately deepened the kiss and she automatically draped her arms around his neck for support. He pulled her closer to him, molding both his mouth and his body to hers as his hands stroked downward, cupping her behind and pulling her closer.

Thorn's mouth fed off hers; he was like the hungriest of men, ravaging, taking possession. In a way this was different from all their other kisses, and for a second she felt his control slipping as the kiss became more intense. When she felt weak in the knees, he picked her up into his arms and carried her over to the sofa and sat down with her in his lap.

Tara looked up at the man holding her gently in his arms. Her gaze took in his dark brooding eyes, his chiseled jaw and the firmness of his lips. His breathing was irregular and he was staring down at her as if she was a morsel he wanted to devour. Now. Tonight.

She swallowed. She was cradled in his lap practically

naked. She wasn't wearing a bra or panties, just a nightgown, a short one at that. And she knew that even if he wasn't fully aware of it before, he was now aware of the state of her dress since she was sitting in his lap and her bare bottom was coming into contact with his aroused body.

Tara felt the air surrounding them heighten to full sexual awareness as she stared at Thorn the same way he was staring at her. She saw a muscle tick in his jaw as if he was fighting hard for control. She realized just how hard this had to be for him—a man who had gone without sex for two years—and she knew the only way to make things easier for him was to send him away, but she couldn't do that.

She licked her bottom lip and decided to tell him without words just how much she wanted his touch, how much she desired it. Her body was aching for him. And when she thought she couldn't stand it any longer, he leaned down and kissed her again.

Her breath caught when she felt his hand beneath her nightgown, touching her at the juncture of her thighs. And then he began stroking her. She whimpered her pleasure into his mouth as her body came alive to his intimate touch. She remembered how it had been the last time he had touched her this way, and she clutched at the front of his shirt while his mouth made love to hers and his skillful fingers stroked her until she thought she would scream.

He suddenly broke off the kiss, and before she could let out a whimper of protest, he eased her gown down from her shoulders, giving him a good view of her neck and exposing her breasts. His hand lightly caressed her neck and then he leaned forward, and slowly lowered his head. He captured a budding dark nipple in his mouth and began licking and sucking.

"Thorn," was the only word she could think to say as

pleasure beyond her control vanquished any further words. The only thing she could do was close her eyes and savor the moment in Thorn's arms. She moaned as his mouth continued to greedily taste her breasts and his hands stroked her wetness.

"I want to taste you," he mouthed against her breast, and she didn't get the full meaning of just what he meant until he gently laid her down on the sofa.

"Close your eyes, baby," he said in a deep, husky voice, kneeling over her.

She met his gaze and saw the deep desire lodged in their dark depths. She couldn't help but wonder how much control he had left and knew she couldn't do this to him. She couldn't do anything to jeopardize his chance of winning the race. "Thorn, we can't," she managed to get out the words. "Remember, no birth control."

His hand was still touching her between the legs. His fingers were stroking her, entering her, driving her mad with desire. "Shh, I know, sweetheart, but we don't need protection for what I want to do. I need this for good luck. Taking your taste with me makes me a sure winner in more ways than one. This is what I need right now more than anything."

And then he lifted her gown, dipped his head and kissed her stomach at the same moment that she closed her eyes to concentrate on what he was doing. Her breath caught when his mouth lowered to replace his stroking fingers.

"Thorn!"

She cried out his name then sucked in a deep breath, never having been kissed this way before. Her mind went blank of all conscious thought except for him and what he was doing to her. She felt pleasure, deep and profound, all the way to her bones. She groaned aloud when he deepened the intimate kiss. His tongue, she discovered, was just as skillful as his hands, and was drugging her into an intimacy she had never shared with any man. Sensations beyond belief with his seductive ministrations were making her realize and accept the extent and magnitude of her love for him.

She whimpered deep within her throat when the first wave of ecstasy washed over her, more powerful than the last time, and she cried out as she held his head to her, his tongue increasing its strokes and tasting her greedily while tremor after tremor raced through her body. Her body shook with the pleasure he was giving her, and moments later, when the tremors had stopped and her body had quieted, he picked her up and cradled her in his lap while gently stroking her back.

"Thank you," she heard him whisper in her ear.

She shifted in his arms slightly and pulled back, wondering why he was thanking her when she should be the one thanking him. From the feel of his arousal it was evident that he still was in a state of need, but had pushed his need aside to take care of hers.

"But—but you didn't—"

He placed a finger to her lips to seal off any further words. "That's okay. My day will come, trust me. I'm thanking you for giving me something to look forward to, something to anticipate, and whether I win the race or not, I have the prize I desire the most right here in my arms."

His words touched her deeply, and before she could find her voice to respond, he kissed away any words she was about to say, and she knew that the man who held her so tenderly in his arms would have her heart for always.

The next morning, Tara stirred then rolled over in bed. She slowly opened her eyes as she remembered last night. After

Thorn had kissed her, he had taken her upstairs and placed her in bed, then he had left.

She moaned deep in her throat as she recalled what they had done. He had created more passion in her than she had thought was possible, and he had unselfishly satisfied a need she didn't know she had. Even now, the memory sent delicious tremors all the way down to her womanly core. Thorn had branded a part of her as his in the most provocative and intimate way.

She loved him, and no matter how things turned out in Daytona, she knew that she would always love him.

The four men crossed their arms over their chests and glared at the one who stood before them, making a request they intended to refuse.

"What do you mean you're not in love with Tara? If that's the case then there's no way one of us will bring her to you, Thorn. We won't allow you to take advantage of her that way," Stone Westmoreland said angrily. "And you can forget the damn bet."

Thorn inhaled deeply, deciding not to knock the hell out of his brother just yet. He was about to leave for Daytona and had found all four of them having breakfast at Storm's house as they got ready to head out to go fishing. He had merely asked that one of them bring Tara to Bike Week. When Stone had grinned and asked him how it felt being in love, he'd been quick to set him straight and had told him he wasn't in love, and that what he and Tara shared was a completely physical, emotionally free affair. That's when all hell had broken loose.

"That bet wasn't my idea and shouldn't have been made in the first place. And regardless of what you say, Stone, one way or the other, Tara will be coming to Bike Week," Thorn said, barely holding on to his anger.

"No, she won't. I agree with Stone," Chase Westmoreland said with a frown on his face. "When we made that bet we thought it was to make you see how much you cared for Tara. But instead, you've concocted some plan to use her. Dammit, man, if Tara was Laney, we would beat the crap out of any man with your intentions. So whatever plans you've made for Tara you can scrap them until you fall in love with her."

"I won't be using her," Thorn growled through gritted teeth. Ready to knock the hell out of Chase as well. Other than Dare, he didn't see any of them falling in love with anyone, so why were they trying to shove this love thing down his throat?

Storm chuckled. "And you want us to believe that? Hell, you haven't had a woman in over two years and you want us just to stand aside while you get your fill knowing you don't care a damn thing about her?"

Thorn felt steam coming out of his ears. "I do care about Tara. I just don't love her. Besides, what Tara and I do is our business and none of you have a damn thing to say about it."

"That's where you are wrong, Thorn," Stone said angrily, rolling up his sleeves and taking a step forward.

Dare Westmoreland decided it was time to intercede before there was bloodshed. "It seems you guys are a little hot under the collar. Keep it up and I'll be forced to throw all four of you behind bars just for the hell of it, so back up, Stone."

He then turned his full attention to Thorn. "And as far as Tara goes, I'll bring her to Daytona when Shelly and I drive up."

"What!"

Dare ignored the simultaneous exclamations from his brothers, as well as the cursing. Instead his gaze stayed glued to Thorn, who was visibly relieved.

"Thanks, Dare," Thorn said, and without giving his other brothers a parting glance, he turned and walked out of the house.

It didn't take long for the other three Westmoreland brothers to turn on Dare.

"Sheriff or no sheriff, we ought to kick your ass, Dare," Chase said angrily. "How can you even think about doing that to Tara? Thorn doesn't mean her any good and she doesn't deserve something like this. Thorn is planning on using her and—"

"He loves her too much to use her," Dare said softly, as he heard the roar of Thorn's motorcycle pulling off.

"Love? Dammit, Dare, weren't you listening to anything Thorn said? He said he wasn't in love with Tara," Stone said angrily.

Dare smiled. "Yes, I heard everything he said. But I believe differently. Take it from someone who's been there, who's still there. Thorn is so much in love with Tara that he can't think straight. However, he needs total concentration for that race, which is why I'm glad he's leaving for Daytona early. Thorn needs Tara at that race, but once the race is over there is no doubt in my mind he'll begin seeing things clearly. It won't take long for him to realize just how much he loves her."

Chase frowned. "We all know just what a stubborn cuss Thorn can be. What if he never realizes it? Where does that leave Tara?"

Dare chuckled. "Right where she's been for the past two years, deeply embedded in Thorn's heart. But it's my guess that Tara's not going to settle for being any man's bed partner and will force Thorn to face his feelings."

"And if he doesn't?" Storm asked, still not convinced.

A smile tilted the corners of Sheriff Dare Westmoreland's lips. "Then we beat the crap out of him. One way or the other, he's going to accept that Tara is no longer his challenge. She's the woman he loves. But I don't think we have to take things that far. Rumor has it that he's sent Tara flowers for Valentine's Day. Chase raised a shocked brow. "Flowers? Thorn?"

Dare chuckled. "Yes, Thorn. You know Luanne Coleman can't hold water, and word is out that Thorn went into her florist shop yesterday, ordered flowers for Tara and wrote out the card himself. I heard he even sealed it before nosey Luanne could take a peek at it."

"Damn," Stone said, with disbelief on his face. He'd never known his brother to send flowers to any woman before, and that included Patrice. Everyone knew Thorn hadn't really loved Patrice, but had merely considered her as his possession, and when it came to the things Thorn considered his, he had a tendency to get downright selfish and wasn't into sharing. Being in love was a totally new avenue for Thorn, and Stone couldn't help wondering how his brother would handle things once the discovery was made. Knowing Thorn, he would be a tough nut to crack, but he agreed with Dare; Tara was just the woman to set him straight. In Thorn's case she might need a full-fledged nutcracker.

"Hey, guys, I bet there will be a wedding in June," Stone said to his brothers.

"I think it will be before June. I doubt he'll wait that long. I'll say sometime in May, close to his birthday," Chase threw in.

Storm rolled his eyes. "Love or no love, Thorn is going to kick and scream all the way down the aisle. He's going to be difficult, that's just his nature, so I bet he won't be tying the knot before September."

All three glanced at Dare to see what he had to say about it. "All of you know I'm not a betting man." A smile touched his lips. "But if I were to bet, I'd have to agree with Chase. Thorn won't last until June."

Tara walked down the busy hospital corridor, glad she was finally able to take a break in her hectic schedule. It only took a few minutes to slip into the small chamber that led away from the crowded hallway lined with patients, as she made her way toward her office.

Once inside she closed the door behind her, walked across the room and collapsed into the chair behind her desk. She had been at the hospital since six that morning and had agreed to make it a fourteen-hour day instead of a ten. One of her fellow doctors had asked her to cover for her while she treated her husband to a special dinner for Valentine's Day. Since Tara hadn't made any plans for the evening herself, she decided she could be flexible and help her coworker out.

She leaned back against her chair and closed her eyes and immediately remembered what had happened two nights ago when Thorn had come to see her to let her know of his change of plans.

After days of little sleep, her body had needed the release he had given to it, and she had been sleeping like a baby since. But now she was feeling downright guilty at the thought that in a few weeks, after the race, she would be letting him down. He thought he would be getting an experienced woman in his bed, when in truth he would be getting the complete opposite.

Twice she had thought of calling him before he left to tell him the truth, so he could make additional changes in his plans if he needed to make them. Chances were, after a two-year abstinence, he would want to share a bed with a woman who would know what she was doing. And the truth of the matter was that she didn't know squat. At least not enough to handle a man like Thorn Westmoreland.

He would be leaving sometime tomorrow for Daytona, so today was her last chance to come clean. Somehow she had to tell him that she'd never thought things would actually get this far. She'd assumed from the get-go that she would get him to the point where he would have to choose between her and celibacy.

That day in her bedroom hadn't even put a dent in the situation. He had merely given them a couple of days' breathing space then he had called to take her out, but he'd made sure the two of them had never been completely alone in her house again. And except for the other night, they hadn't been.

Okay, so she'd been stupid to count on such a thing happening, but she *had* counted on it, and now she was in a real fix. Delaney would be just the person to talk to about her dilemma, and to help her look at things more objectively, but unfortunately, Jamal had whisked her friend off to Rome where Valentine's Day was reputed to have originated. No doubt the prince intended to wine and dine his wife in style.

Tara smiled, thinking how much in love the couple were, as were Dare and Shelly. Love always seemed to radiate between them, and she always felt strong affectionate emotions whenever she was around them. On Super Bowl Sunday at Chase's restaurant it had been hard not to notice the intimate smiles the couples had exchanged, as well as the discreet touches.

She often wondered whether, if things had gone according to plan, she and Derrick would have shared that kind of loving relationship. For some reason she believed they would eventually have become a divorce statistic. It was only after she had finally stopped wallowing in bitterness and self-pity that she had decided not marrying Derrick had really been for the best. Still, she could not let go of the fact that he had betrayed and humiliated her the way he had.

Her thoughts shifted back to Thorn. When she had met him two years ago, her heart was recovering from being brutally battered. But still she knew, just as sure as she knew there were still a lot of patients yet to be seen, that she had fallen in love with Thorn that night they'd first met. It had been the same night she had stormed out of Delaney's kitchen to give him a piece of her mind. Instead, he had gotten a piece of her heart, a pretty big chunk. She had known the exact moment it had happened. At that time she had fled to the safety of her apartment.

Now she had nowhere to run to. The die was cast. A bargain made. He had kept his end of things and now she had to keep hers.

She loved him.

And the sad thing about it was that he had done nothing to encourage her emotional involvement. In fact, he had been more than up-front with her by letting her know he only wanted a physical relationship. She had known from the very beginning that his attraction to her had been based on lust and not love, and although it had been her intentions never to fall in love with another man after Derrick, she had done so anyway.

She opened her eyes at the sound of the knock on her office door. "Yes? Come in."

A fellow pediatrician, Dr. Pamela Wentworth, walked in carrying a huge vase of the most beautiful flowers Tara had ever seen. Tara smiled. "Wow, Pam, those are gorgeous. Aren't you special?"

Pam grinned. "No, in fact, you are, since these are for you."

Tara sat up straight in her chair. Her eyes instantly widened. "Excuse me. Did you say those were for me?"

"Yes. They were just delivered at the nurses' station, and I told Nurse Meadows that I would bring them to you myself," she said, setting the huge container in the middle of Tara's desk. "Hey, girlfriend, whatever you're doing, you must be doing it right to get flowers like these." She smiled brightly. "Well, I've got to get back. It's like a zoo out there so enjoy your break while it lasts."

Pam breezed out of her office just as quickly as she had breezed in, leaving Tara to stare at the huge arrangement of flowers sitting in the middle of her desk.

She frowned. "Who on earth would send these?" Tara wondered, leaning forward and pulling off the card that was attached. What man would remember her on Valentine's Day by sending her something like this?

She quickly opened the envelope and blinked at the message, then reread it again.

Be mine, Thorn.

A knot formed in Tara's throat. Be his what? His lover? His one-night stand? His bedmate for a week? His true love? His baby's mommy? What?

She sighed deeply. Only Thorn knew the answer to that question, and she intended to ask him when she saw him again.

Chapter 9

Tara scanned all the activities through Dare's SUV's window as the vehicle rolled into the heart of Daytona Beach where Bike Week would be held. Squinting against the glare of the sun shining brightly through the window, she was amazed at what she saw billed as the World's Largest Motorcycle Event. And to think that Thorn was a major part of it.

It had been a little more than two weeks since she had seen him and she couldn't forget the night he had shown up unexpectedly at her house. It had been the same night she had come to terms with her feelings for him. It had also been the same night he had given her a sample of what he had in store for her.

But what had arrived two days after his visit still weighed more heavily on her mind—the flowers he had sent her for Valentine's Day. The message on the card had been personal, and she still found herself wondering just what he'd meant.

"Ready to get settled so we can do some shopping, Tara?"

Shelly's question got her attention. She had enjoyed the company of Dare and his wife during the seven-hour drive from Atlanta. Since school was still in session in Atlanta, their son AJ had not been able to make the trip. He was staying with Dare's parents.

"I'm always ready to shop," Tara said, smiling. When she glanced out the window and saw the numerous vendors, she wondered if there was anything for sale other than bike wear and leather.

"As soon as we get settled into our hotel rooms we can hit the malls," Shelly said, turning around in her car seat to smile at Tara.

Tara nodded her head in agreement. A few months ago, before Shelly's wedding, she, Shelly and Delaney had flown to New York for a girls' weekend and had enjoyed themselves immensely. The one thing the three of them discovered they had in common was their obsession with shopping.

"I hope I see Thorn sometime today," she said honestly, not caring what Shelly or Dare thought, although she did wonder whether they thought she was making a mistake even coming here to spend time with Thorn. However, if they thought such a thing, neither said so. Even Delaney hadn't tried talking her out of coming, nor had Thorn's other brothers.

"It shouldn't be too hard to find Thorn," Dare said, meeting her gaze in the rearview mirror. "He rode his bike from Atlanta, but his work crew arrived by eighteen-wheeler a few days ago to set up shop and put his Thorn-Byrds on display. You wouldn't believe the number of people who're here to buy bikes. But then, within a few days of the race, be prepared not to see Thorn for a while. He usually goes off by himself to train. Going more than 180 mph while tackling the high banks of Daytona International Speedway on two wheels is no joke. Thorn needs total concentration for what he'll be doing, and I mean *total* concentration."

Tara nodded, understanding what Dare was saying. She had talked enough with the brothers over the past two weeks to know that what Thorn would be doing was risky. But she couldn't allow her mind to think about that. She had to believe that he would be fine.

She sighed deeply. From what Stone had told her, beside the races, the other activities lined up for the week included motorcycle shows and exhibits and concerts. There would be vendors at practically every corner who would try to sell anything they thought you needed, even a few things you didn't need.

When Dare pulled into the parking lot of their hotel, the only thing Tara could think about was Thorn and her need to see him before he went into seclusion.

Storm glanced down at his watch. "Dare, Shelly and Tara have probably arrived by now. Aren't you going over to the hotel to see them?"

Thorn was crouched down in front of one of his motorcycles and didn't miss a beat as he continued to put a shine on the immaculate machine. "Not now. Maybe later."

Storm frowned, thinking Thorn was definitely not acting like the man Dare had painted him to be, a man deeply in love. In fact he hadn't even mentioned Tara since Storm, Stone and Chase had arrived a few days ago.

Storm decided to try something. "Maybe it's just as well."

Thorn glanced up. "Why is that?"

Storm shrugged. "There's a chance Tara didn't come," he lied. "The last I heard she hadn't made up her mind whether she was coming or not."

Thorn frowned and he immediately stopped what he was doing. "What do you mean she hadn't made up her mind about coming? The last time I talked to her it was a sure thing."

"And how long ago was that, Thorn?"

Thorn's frown deepened as he tried to remember. Moments later he said, "A couple of days before I left town."

Storm shook his head. "Damn, Thorn, that was over two weeks ago. You mean to say that you haven't called or spoken to her since you left Atlanta?"

"No."

Storm crossed his arms over his chest. "Then it would serve you right if she didn't come. Even I know that women don't like being ignored."

"I wasn't ignoring her. I was giving both of us space."

"Space? Hell, there's nothing wrong with space if you keep in touch and let them know you're thinking about them. Women like to know they're on your mind at least every once in a while. I hate to say it, man, but you may have blown it. What on earth were you thinking about?"

Thorn stood and threw down the cloth in his hand. "How to keep my sanity." He grabbed his helmet off the seat of his bike and quickly put it on. "I'll be back later."

Storm chuckled as he watched his brother take off with the speed of lightning. He shook his head. Damn, Dare had been right. Thorn was in love and didn't even know it yet.

Tara had taken a shower and changed into comfortable clothing. Dare and Shelly's room was on the tenth floor and, like her hotel room, it had a beautiful ocean view. Stepping out on the balcony, she decided the sight was breathtaking. Down below, the boardwalk was filled with people having a good time.

She and Shelly had decided to postpone their trip to the mall. It was quite obvious that Dare wanted to spend time with his wife alone for a while, and Tara couldn't find fault with that. The two were still newlyweds. They wanted to put to good use their week without having to worry about AJ popping up unexpectedly.

Stepping back inside her hotel room, Tara glanced at the clock, wondering why Thorn hadn't at least called to make sure she had arrived. She knew he was probably busy and all, but still, she would have thought he'd have made time to see her, especially since they hadn't talked to or seen each other in over two weeks. Evidently, she'd been wrong.

She had to face the fact that as far as he was concerned, her sole purpose in being there took place *after* the race and not before. The hotel room she'd been given was in his name and he had seen to her every comfort by providing her with a suite, a suite he would eventually share with her. The bedroom was enormous and the bed was king-size. She could just imagine the two of them in that bed making love.

She nervously licked her lips. She needed to talk to Thorn and let him know before things went too far that she was not the experienced woman he thought she was. Chances were when he found out she was a twenty-seven-year-old virgin, he would put a quick halt to his plans and run for cover. She had overheard enough conversations between the single male doctors to know that most men preferred experienced women. No man wanted to waste time teaching a woman how to please him in bed.

Tara sighed. She'd intended to tell Thorn the truth when she saw him, but after hearing what Dare had said about Thorn needing total concentration, she'd decided not to tell him until after the race. That wouldn't be the best time but there was nothing she could do about it.

She glanced around when she heard a knock at the door. Thinking Shelly had changed her mind about going shopping, she quickly crossed the room to the door and glanced out the peephole.

"Thorn!"

She didn't waste any time in opening the door, and he didn't waste any time in stepping inside the room and closing the door behind him. Nor did he waste any time in pulling her into his arms and kissing her.

And she didn't waste any time in kissing him back.

His tongue was stroking hers with relentless precision and his hands were roaming all over her body as if to make sure she was really there. And when she wrapped her arms around him, he deepened the kiss.

She held on to him tight as he evoked sensations within her that were beyond anything she could have ever imagined from a kiss.

She thought he tasted of desire so hot she could feel it in the pit of her stomach, and pleasure points spread throughout every limb in her body. His kiss was overpowering, and she felt their controls slipping. Tara knew she should pull away from the kiss before they got carried away, but the more their tongues dueled and feasted, the more her mouth refused to do anything but stay put and get everything that Thorn was offering. Thorn was laying it on thick and she was enjoying every single minute of it.

Moments later, he pulled back, but didn't end the kiss completely. Instead he continued to torture her with tiny flicks of his tongue on her mouth. A moan escaped her lips and he captured it with his.

"I missed you," Thorn's voice whispered throatily as a hot throbbing sensation settled in her midsection. "Damn this celibacy thing. I want you now. Hell, I might not be around later. Anything could happen."

Thorn's words reminded her of the danger inherent in Sunday's race. She groaned as she pulled back from his touch. She could not, she would not, be responsible for him losing the race or possibly getting hurt. She loved him too much for that. One of them had to see reason and it seemed it would have to be her at the moment.

She exhaled a bone-deep sigh when they stood facing each other. Her heart was beating way out of control as her gaze took in everything about him, from the jeans and T-shirt that he wore to the biker boots on his feet. But she mostly zeroed in on his desire-glazed gaze that hadn't yet left hers.

For the longest time he didn't say anything, but neither did she. They continued to stand there, looking at each other, until finally, Thorn spoke in a voice that was husky and deep. "I want you, Tara. Not after the race but *now*."

She swallowed. Lust had temporarily taken over Thorn's mind, and it was up to her to put it back on track. If they did what he wanted and he lost the race, he would despise her for the rest of his days, and she couldn't handle that. She knew her next words would sound cold and indifferent, but he'd left her no choice.

She tilted her head back and frowned up at him. "It doesn't matter what you want now. Need I remind you that we have an agreement, Thorn? My purpose for being here is to fill your needs *after* the race and not before. I think it would be best if you kept your hands and lips to yourself until then."

He didn't say anything but stared at her with a look that went from desire to anger in a second, and seeing the transformation made Tara's heart thump so hard in her chest that it hurt. Her tone of voice had intentionally been like a dose of ice water on a burning flame, and the effect was unmistakably scorching.

Thorn took a step forward and looked Tara squarely in the eye. "Thanks for reminding me of your purpose for being here, Tara, and you won't have to worry about me keeping my hands and mouth to myself. But make no mistake about it, I've kept my end of the deal, and after the race I fully expect you to keep yours."

Without saying anything else he turned and walked out the door, slamming it behind him.

Gravel flew from the tires of Thorn's motorcycle as he leaned into a sharp curve, tearing up the road in front of him. He shuddered from the force of the anger consuming him as he tightened his grip on the handlebars.

Tara's words had burned, although quite frankly, he supposed he should be grateful that she had helped him to come to his senses before he'd done something he would later regret. But instead of wanting to thank her he felt the need to throttle her instead.

Damn, just like that day in her bedroom, he'd been ready to zip down his pants and have his way with her, race or no race. He'd been that hungry for sex. No, it wasn't just about sex. It was about her. He had been just that hungry for her. But leave it to her to remind him of their arrangement and to make him remember the only thing between them would be a no-strings-attached affair.

His spine tightened as he took another curve. Damn the agreement, he wanted more. During the past two weeks he had come to realize just how much Tara meant to him. He had discovered she was goodness and sweetness all rolled into one—on her good days—and tart and tingly on her bad days, but he enjoyed her just the same.

Letting her get under his skin had definitely not been part of the plan. But it had happened anyway. His thoughts went back to the harsh words she'd spoken. Did she really see her sole reason for being here as she had described it? But then, how could she not, when he had pretty much spelled out why he wanted her here?

He wondered just when his thoughts on the matter had changed. When had he decided that he wanted more from Tara than a week in bed? When had he decided he wanted more from her than sex?

He sighed deeply. He had been in denial for two long years, but he wouldn't lie to himself any longer. It had taken him long enough to come to grips with his feelings for her. He could now admit that he loved her and had from the first time he'd seen her. He had lied through his teeth when he'd told his brothers he didn't love her. At this very moment he was faced with the truth. He desperately loved her and didn't want her to pick now to start getting temperamental and difficult.

The last of his pent-up anger floated away in the wind as he rounded another curve at high speed. Now was not the time to get mad; he would get even and teach a certain doctor a lesson. Tara would soon discover that Thorn the celibate was moodier and grumpier than hell, but Thorn in love was a force to be reckoned with.

"Enjoying yourself, Tara?"

Tara glanced up from her drink and met Stone Westmoreland's curious stare. She then glanced around the table and met the gazes of the other Westmoreland brothers and smiled. It seemed every one of them was interested in her response.

"Yes, I'm enjoying myself," she responded cheerfully. She knew they weren't fooled and were well aware she was having a lousy time. The only thing she enjoyed was seeing Dare and Shelly and how they interacted with each other. The two were so much in love they practically glowed. Even now she couldn't help but watch as they danced together. It was a slow number and Dare was holding his wife as though she meant the world to him.

It touched Tara's heart deeply, the thought of a woman being loved that much by a man. She sighed. No man had ever loved her that much, certainly not Derrick.

"You want to dance, Tara?"

She glanced up at Chase. She wasn't fooled either. She was well aware that the brothers knew the one person she wanted to dance with wasn't around. What they probably didn't know was that she was intentionally keeping Thorn at bay.

"No, but thanks for asking." They were all seated around a table in a nightclub that had live entertainment. All the Westmoreland brothers were present except for Thorn.

She hadn't seen him since he had paid her a visit at the hotel three days ago. Each day she had made it a point to drop by the booth where his Thorn-Byrds were on display, hoping that he would be there, but he never was. According to Dare, Thorn was keeping a low profile and would probably be doing so until the day of the race.

"Tara?"

She smiled and glanced around, wondering what question one of the Westmoreland brothers had for her now, when suddenly she realized it hadn't been one of them who had called her name. Her name had been spoken by the man who stood next to their table.

Derrick!

Surprised, she met his gaze and wondered what on earth Derrick was doing in Daytona during Bike Week. Although Bunnell was less than sixty miles away, she had never known him to show an interest in motorcycles. But then she had to remember many people came to Bike Week just to check out the festivities.

She had planned to rent a car and drive to Bunnell to see her family tomorrow. It had been two years and it was time she finally went home for a visit. The main reason she had stayed away was now standing next to her table.

She plastered a smile on her face as she reached for the glass of soda in front of her. "Derrick, what are you doing here? This is certainly a surprise."

He was nervous, she could tell. But then after glancing around the table she understood why. Stone, Chase and Storm were glaring, facing him down, and letting Derrick know without saying a word that they didn't appreciate his presence. Evidently, it hadn't taken much to figure out who he was and to remember what he had done.

"Yes, well, me and a couple of the guys from town decided to come check things out," he said after nervously clearing his throat.

Tara nodded. She couldn't help but be openly amused by his nervousness. "And how is Danielle?"

Derrick cleared his throat again. "She's fine. She's expecting. Our baby is due to be born in a few weeks."

Surprisingly, that bit of news didn't have the effect on her it would have had a year ago. She found herself genuinely smiling. "Congratulations. I'm glad the two of you are happy and have decided to add to your family and wish you both the best."

Derrick nodded and then asked. "What about you, Tara? Are you happy?"

Tara opened her mouth to answer, but instead a deep male voice sounded from the shadows behind where Derrick stood.

"Yes, she's happy."

When the person came into view, Tara's heart began beating fast. She held her breath as Thorn moved around Derrick and came straight to her, leaned down and placed an openmouthed kiss on her lips, publicly declaring before Derrick, his brothers and anyone who saw him, that Tara was his.

After releasing her mouth Thorn straightened to his full height and turned back to Derrick. He glared at the man. "I make it my business to see that she's happy."

Tara wanted to scream out "Since when?" but decided to go along with whatever game Thorn was playing. Besides, what he'd done had effectively squashed any notion Derrick might have that there was a chance she was still pining away for him. She was grateful for that. According to her parents, the rumor still floating around Bunnell was that she hadn't been home because she hadn't gotten over Derrick.

Derrick met Thorn's stare. "I'm glad to know that." He then blinked as recognition hit. "Hey, aren't you Thorn Westmoreland?"

"Last I heard." Thorn crossed his arms over his chest and studied the man who'd had the nerve to betray and humiliate Tara on her wedding day. As far as Thorn was concerned, this man's loss was certainly his gain.

A look of adoration appeared in Derrick's eyes and a smile tipped the corners of his mouth. "Wow. Your bikes are the bomb."

Usually Thorn was appreciative of anyone who admired his work, but not this man. "Thanks. Now if you don't mind,

I'd like to dance with my lady. The race is in two days and I want to spend as much time with her as I can before then."

"Oh, sure, man," Derrick said awkwardly. He then met Tara's gaze again. "Take care, Tara, and I'll tell your family that I saw you."

Tara shrugged. "There's really no need since I plan to visit them tomorrow. There's no reason to be this close and not visit."

Derrick nodded. "Yeah, right. I'll be seeing you." He then moved on.

"Glad you could find the time to grace us with your presence tonight, Thorn," Dare said sarcastically to his brother when he and Shelly sat down at the table after dancing. He then glanced across the room at Derrick's retreating back after seeing his brothers' glares. "Who was that?"

Thorn met his brother's gaze. "Some fool who didn't know a good thing when he had it."

Without waiting for Dare, or anyone else for that matter, to make another comment, Thorn reached out and gave Tara's hand a gentle tug and brought her to her feet. "Dance with me."

Whatever words Tara wanted to say died in her throat the moment Thorn touched her. She offered no resistance when he led her to the dance floor where a slow number had just started. An uncomfortable glance over her shoulder verified that Derrick was sitting at a table with his friends, staring at her and Thorn. She quickly glanced around the crowded room. It seemed everyone was staring, especially the Westmoreland brothers. But they were doing more than just staring; they were all grinning from ear to ear. Why?

"Okay, what's going on with your brothers?" she asked Thorn the moment he pulled her into his arms.

He glanced over at the table where his four brothers sat, then back at her, meeting her gaze. "I have no idea. They tend to act ignorant while out in public. Ignore them."

That wouldn't be hard to do, Tara thought, since her concentration was mainly on him. "What are you doing here, Thorn? I thought with only two days left before the race you would be somewhere in seclusion."

Thorn frowned. "Yeah, you would probably think that. But don't worry, I'm more than ready for the race." He met her stare and his hands moved gently down to the small of her back and drew her closer into his arms. "In fact, I'm looking forward to it being over. And I don't want you to worry your pretty little head any, because I'm also ready for you after the race."

His words gave her pause, and she nervously licked her bottom lip with the tip of her tongue. Maybe now was a good time to tell him about her virginal state. She opened her mouth to speak, but before she could get any words out, he kissed her. In the middle of the dance floor he gave her a full-blown, nothing-held-back, full-mouth kiss, just the thing to make her lose all rational thought.

She ignored the catcalls she heard, the whistles, as well as the flashing bulbs from several sports reporters' cameras. Instead, she held on to Thorn to receive the mind-blowing kiss he was giving her.

He reluctantly pulled away when someone tapped him on his shoulder. He glared and turned to meet Dare's amused features. He and Shelly had returned to the dance floor. "You're making a scene, Thorn, and your song stopped playing moments ago. Maybe you ought to take that outside."

"No problem," Thorn said, and without waiting for Tara to say anything, he pulled her across the room and out the door.

* * *

Tara snatched her hand from Thorn's the moment Florida's night air hit her in the face, returning her to her senses. "Hold on, Thorn. What do you think you're doing?"

"Taking you somewhere," he said, pulling her out of the doorway to a secluded area.

She refused to move an inch. "Where?"

"To show you my bike."

Tara frowned. "I've seen your bike. I've even ridden on it, remember?"

He smiled. "Not this one. The bike I want to show you is the one I'll be using in the race."

For a moment it seemed as though Tara had forgotten to breathe. She had been around the Westmorelands enough to know how they joked with Thorn about not letting anyone see the bike he would race. Since he owned so many for racing, it was anyone's guess as to which one he would use to compete in any given race.

"But I thought that other than your racing team, no one is supposed to know about which bike you'd be using."

He gave a small shrug as he leaned one shoulder against a brick wall. "Usually that's true, but I want you to see it." He met her gaze. "In fact, I want you to christen it."

Tara lifted a brow. "Christen it? You want me to hit it with a bottle of champagne or something?"

Thorn shook his head and smiled. "No, that would put a dent in it. There's more than one way to christen something. If you come with me, I'll show you another way."

Indecisively, Tara just stared at him, not knowing what she should do. Being somewhere alone with Thorn was not a good idea, especially when he had told her just two days ago that he would be keeping his hands and his lips to himself.

Already tonight he had touched her and had kissed her twice and there was no telling what else he had in store.

Evidently she took too long to say anything because he covered the distance separating them, took her face in his hands and lowered his head to capture her lips with his.

Kiss number three, Tara thought, closing her eyes as his mouth totally devoured hers. She shuddered when she felt his hands pull her T-shirt from her shorts and slowly began caressing her bare skin underneath. Her tongue automatically mated with his, relishing in the taste of him.

Moments later, when he released her mouth, she pressed her face to his chest and sighed deeply into his T-shirt. The manly scent of him made her groan at the same time her midsection became flooded with warmth. She felt his hands gently caressing her back as he pulled her closer to him, letting him feel the hardness of the erection that stirred against her belly.

She forced her eyes upward and met his. They were so dark and filled with so much desire it made her tremble. "I thought you said you wouldn't touch me or kiss me, Thorn, until *after* the race."

He sighed deeply and reached up to thread his fingers through her hair, pushing it away from her face. "Lord knows I tried, but I don't think I can not touch you or kiss you, Tara," he said truthfully.

A part of him wanted to tell her more. He wanted to let her know that he loved her and that no matter whether he won the race or not, he knew his most valued prize was standing right here in front of him. But he couldn't tell her any of that yet. He would wait and tell her later, when he felt the time was right.

He inclined his head to take a good look at her and let her take a good look at him. "Will you come with me, Tara? I won't do anything you don't want me to do."

Oh, hell, Tara thought. Didn't he know she was human, and so far, whatever he'd done to her had been just fine and dandy with her. She couldn't imagine turning him down for anything unless it meant going all the way. She would not allow him to break his vow of celibacy two days before the race, but he was definitely testing her control.

"Tara? Will you come with me?"

Tara heaved an enormous sigh. If he thought she was his sweetest temptation, then he was her most tantalizing weakness. A chocolate bar with almonds had nothing on him.

She leaned back far enough to gaze into his eyes. And she knew at that moment that no matter what he claimed, he intended to do more than show her his bike. But heaven help her, she didn't have the strength to turn and walk away.

Instead she gave him the only answer she could. "Yes, Thorn. I'll go with you."

Tara glanced around, not believing that she was standing in the back of an eighteen-wheeler. Thorn had explained that he used the fifty-three-foot-long semi-tractor trailer whenever he traveled with his bikes. The back of the trailer had been separated into three sections. The back section, the one closest to the ramp-style door, was where the bikes were stored. The middle section served as Thorn's office and work area. The third section, the one closest to the cab of the truck, was set up like a mini motor home and included a comfortable-looking bed, a bathroom with a shower, a refrigerator, microwave, television and VCR—all the comforts of home.

After being shown around, Tara decided to play it safe and remain in the section where the motorcycles were stored. She moved around the trailer admiring all the bikes; some she had seen before and others she had not.

"This is the one I'll be racing," Thorn said, getting her attention.

She walked over to stand next to him to check out the motorcycle he was showing her. It was definitely a beauty and she told him so.

"Thanks. I began building it last year." He met her gaze. "It reminds me a lot of you."

Tara lifted a brow. She'd never been compared to a motorcycle before and was curious why it had reminded him of her. "Would you like to explain that one, Thorn?"

He smiled. "Sure. This beauty was designed to be every man's dream as well as fantasy. So were you. She's well-built, with all the right angles and curves, temptation at its best. And so are you." His eyes held hers, shining with blatant desire when he added, "And she gives a man a good, hard ride and there's no doubt in my mind that you'll do the same."

Tara swallowed thickly. She wasn't sure about that. The only riding she'd ever done was on her bicycle, and even then she could have used a lot more practice. She had preferred staying inside the house, playing doctor on her baby dolls.

Having no idea what comment she could make to Thorn's statement, she cleared her throat and pretended to give the immaculate riding machine her full attention.

"Tara?"

The sound of her name from Thorn's lips was like a warm caress, and it sent sensations flowing through her body. "Yes?"

His gaze held hers and the look in his eyes was dark, intense. "Do you want to ride?"

She blinked, wondering if this was a trick question. "Ride?"

He nodded, not breaking eye contact with her. "Yes, ride."

She swallowed again, thickly, then said. "But you've already put your bikes up for the night."

He nodded again. "Yes, but there's another way we can ride while my bike stays right here. I want you to christen it for me. Then there's no doubt in my mind that I'll be a sure winner on Sunday."

Tara released a deep sigh. He was confusing her, which wasn't hard to do when the subject was about sex, considering how little she knew. But she was smart enough to have an idea of what he was suggesting. "You want us to make out on your bike?"

He smiled. "Yes."

Her stomach clenched from his smile and his answer. "Call me crazy for not knowing the answer to this, but is such a thing possible?"

His smile widened. "Anything is possible with us, Tara, and I promise we won't go all the way. I'll take you part of the way, just like the other times." He took a step toward his bike and reached out his hand. "Let me do that, baby."

Tara wondered if he was into self-torture, because any time they made out, it was she who was left satisfied and not he. She couldn't help but wonder what Thorn was getting out of this. "But I won't be doing anything for you. Why are you doing this to yourself? Whenever we come together that way I'm the only one who's satisfied."

He thought about her question, trying to decide the best way to answer it, and decided to be as honest with her as he could. "I get my satisfaction from watching you reach an orgasm in my arms, Tara. I get a natural stone high knowing that under my ministrations you come apart, lose control and soar to the stars. And right now that's all the satisfaction I need. My time will come later."

There was a question she had to ask him. "When you sent those flowers to me for Valentine's Day, the card read, Be mine. What did you mean?"

In the confines of the trailer, Thorn smelled the way she thought a man was supposed to, masculine, robust and sexy. The warm solid strength of him surrounded her, touched her, and made a foreign need tingle at the juncture of her legs. She swallowed deeply when he reached out and curled a finger beneath her chin and tipped her head back to meet his gaze.

For a moment they just stood there, staring at each other. Then he finally said, "Even if it's for only a week, Tara, I won't take the time we spend together lightly. I know I have no right to ask for exclusiveness beyond that point, but until then, I want to know that no other man is on your mind, in your heart or a part of your soul. When I make love to you, I want you to be mine in every way a woman can belong to a man." And then he lowered his head, and Tara's mouth became his.

She melted into him, into his kiss, into everything that was essentially Thorn Westmoreland. He opened his mouth wider over hers, absorbing any and every sound of pleasure she made. Disregarding the warning bells going off in her head, she clung to him thinking this was where she wanted to be, in his arms, and at the moment, that was all that mattered.

Thorn broke the kiss and lifted her into his arms. She didn't resist him when he sat her in the bike's passenger seat. Instead of straddling his seat with his back to her, he straddled it facing her, then leaned forward and kissed her.

His hands touched her everywhere before going to her T-shirt. He pulled it off over her head and looked down. He had discovered she wasn't wearing a bra while dancing with her and had been anticipating this moment since then. The sight of her hard little nipples thrusting upward made him moan.

Taking her legs he wrapped them around his waist as he eased her back while leaning over and capturing a tight dark bud between his lips, letting his tongue caress it, then sucking greedily, enjoying the taste of her breasts.

But there was another taste he wanted. Another taste he needed.

Easing back up he slowly pulled down the zipper of her shorts, then, lifting her hips, he slid them down her body, taking them off completely. He gave an admiring glance to her sexy, black lace panties before taking them off as well.

He reached out and caressed her inner thigh with his fingers, then slowly traced a path across her feminine folds, already wet and hot for him. He lifted her, removed her legs from around his waist and lifted them high on his shoulders.

Then Thorn lifted her to him and leaned forward toward her body, seeking what he wanted the most. No matter how loudly Tara moaned and groaned, his mouth refused to let up as he gave her soul deep pleasure. Her body began trembling uncontrollably while his tongue thrust back and forth inside her, sending her over the edge.

"Thorn—"

"It's okay, baby, let it go," he said, as his fingers momentarily replaced his mouth. "I need to have you this way. When I'm taking the curves with this bike on Sunday, I'm going to remember just how it felt loving you like this. My pleasure is knowing I've given you pleasure."

And he did give her pleasure. Moments after his mouth once again replaced his fingers, she let out a mind-blowing scream and came apart, lost control and soared to the stars in his arms.

Chapter 10

Tara glanced around at the many spectators in the grandstands. Excitement was all around as everyone waited for the race to begin. She nervously bit her bottom lip as the scent of burnt rubber and fuel exhaust permeated the air. The weather was picture-perfect with sunny skies. It was a beautiful day for a motorcycle race.

The Westmoreland brothers had talked to her that morning and had gone out of their way to assure her that Thorn would be fine. But a part of her still felt antsy. She'd seen the preliminary races and knew how fast the riders would be going. Any incorrect riding technique of braking, cornering, sliding and passing could mean injury to a rider.

She tried not to think about the numerous laps around the speedway that Thorn and his bike would be taking, as well as the sharp curves; instead she tried to think about what had happened that night she had "christened" his bike. Even now

she blushed thinking about it. Afterward, Thorn had taken her
to the hotel and had walked her to her room. He hadn't come
inside. Instead he had kissed her tenderly in front of her door
before turning to leave.

The next morning he had surprised her when he'd unexpectedly shown up to take her to breakfast. The meal had been
delicious and she had enjoyed his company. They avoided dis-
cussing anything about the previous night; instead, he had
listened while she did most of the talking. She had told him
of her plans to visit her family, and he'd said he thought it
would be a good idea.

She smiled when she remembered how glad her family had
been to see her. Derrick hadn't wasted any time calling
everyone he knew to let them know he had seen her at Bike
Week with Thorn Westmoreland. Since Thorn was something
of a racing celebrity, her parents, siblings and many of their
friends in Bunnell had had a lot of questions about their alleged
affair. Her two brothers were still in college and were home
for the weekend, and her baby sister was a senior in high
school.

In a way she was glad everyone's attention had shifted
from her and Derrick and was now focused on her and Thorn's
relationship. She'd told anyone who asked—and it seemed
just about everybody did—that she and Thorn were seeing
each other and had left it at that. She'd let them draw their
own conclusions.

Sighing deeply, she glanced down below at Pit Road
where the Westmoreland brothers had become part of
Thorn's racing team. She couldn't help but admire how they
had made this a family affair with each helping out any way
he could. Everyone, including her, was sporting a black
T-shirt with the colorful huge Thorn-Byrd emblem on the

front and back, as well as a matching black Thorn-Byrd cap. Like the other riders, Thorn was dressed in leather. She had seen him from a distance and thought he looked good in his riding outfit.

She thought it would be best if she remained out of sight for now. He had spent the last two days getting psychologically prepared for today's race and she didn't want to do anything to mess with his concentration.

Tomorrow she and Thorn would be heading for West Palm Beach for a week and she didn't want to think about what he had in store for her. Already his luggage had been delivered to her suite. He had told her that night in his eighteen-wheeler that he intended to spend tonight with her at the hotel with a Do Not Disturb sign on the door. And there was no doubt in her mind that he would do that very thing…if he decided to keep her.

She couldn't help remembering what Delaney had told her about Jamal's reaction when he'd discovered she was a virgin right in the middle of their lovemaking. Delaney had decided not to tell Jamal beforehand, but let him find out for himself. According to Delaney, Prince Jamal Ari Yasir had been angrier than hell, but had soon gotten over it with a little female persuasion.

Tara couldn't help wondering if Thorn would get over it. Unlike Delaney, Tara planned to remove the element of surprise and tell him before anything got started. Considering his current state of mind after having being celibate for almost two years, she prayed he wouldn't be too upset by her news.

The announcer's loud voice over the intercom drowned out any further thoughts, and she settled back in her seat and smiled at Shelly, who was sitting next to her. Nervousness and anxiety laced with excitement raced down her spine. The green flag was dropped and the race began.

* * *

Everyone was on their feet as the cyclists rounded the curve, making the last lap around Lake Lloyd. Tara and Shelly had left their seats in the stands to join the Westmoreland brothers on Pit Road. Thorn's bike had performed with the precision that everyone had expected. There had been no mechanical problems such as those that had caused a number of other riders to drop from competition.

Thorn was three bikes behind, but the Thorn-Byrd was holding its own as the bikers made their way down the final stretch. Coming in fourth wouldn't be so bad, Tara thought, although according to Chase, this was Thorn's sixth time competing in this particular race, and he was determined to come home a winner this time.

All of a sudden Dare let out a humongous yell of excitement and started jumping up and down. The other Westmoreland brothers joined him, screaming at the tops of their lungs.

Tara squinted against the glare from the sun to see what had caused all the commotion. Using the binoculars she'd borrowed from Storm, she watched the proceedings unfold. Thorn was beginning to gain ground in a big way. He began moving forward as the bikers headed toward the finish line. The grandstands erupted into pure exhilaration as everyone focused their attention on motorcycle number thirty-four, Thorn and the Thorn-Byrd, as man and machine took center stage and eased past the bikes holding the second and third position coming neck to neck with the cyclist in the lead.

"Come on, Thorn, you can do it," Dare screamed, as if his brother would be able to hear him across the width of the track.

And then it happened: Thorn appeared to be giving the Thorn-Byrd all he had as man and machine inched past bike one and took the lead.

Tara's breath caught in her throat. Thorn had given the spectators at Daytona International Speedway something to talk about for years to come. Everyone was screaming as Thorn crossed the finish line, becoming the winner of this year's Bike Week.

Thorn barely had time to bring the Thorn-Byrd to a stop when everyone descended upon him. A reporter from CNN was there with the first question after a round of congratulations.

"Thorn, after six years of competing, you've finally won your first Daytona Speedway Bike Week, how do you feel?"

Thorn smiled. Thinking it wouldn't be appropriate to answer, "still horny," instead, he said, "It feels wonderful." He glanced around for Tara; though he didn't see her anywhere, somehow he felt her presence and knew Dare would follow his instructions to the letter.

"That was an excellent display of skill and sportsmanship when you took over the lead. What was the main thing on your mind as you inched your way across the finish line?"

Again, Thorn thought it wouldn't be kosher to give a truthful answer, at least not one with all the full details. His thoughts and emotions were too consumed with a certain woman. He smiled at the reporter and responded truthfully. "My woman."

"Thorn asked me to make sure you got back to the hotel, Tara," Dare Westmoreland said, smiling cheerfully. It was evident that he and his brothers were proud of Thorn.

"All right."

From the number of reporters crowding around Thorn, Tara knew it would be a while before he would be free. In a way that was good. She needed time to think. A proud smile touched her lips as she watched from a distance as Thorn was presented the winning trophy. He was happy and she was happy for him. She was glad she'd been able to share this special moment with him.

As she began walking away with Dare and Shelly, she couldn't help but think that her moment of reckoning had arrived.

Tara nervously paced her hotel room waiting for Thorn. The race had been over more than two hours. Because she had felt hot and sticky, she had showered and changed into a floral sundress with spaghetti straps.

The air-conditioning in the room was set at a reasonable temperature, but still she felt hot and was about to step outside on the balcony when she heard the sound of the door opening.

She turned and met Thorn's gaze the moment he stepped into the room. He had also showered and changed clothes. Gone was the leather outfit he had competed in. He was wearing a pair of jeans, a blue denim shirt and his biker boots.

Tara stood rooted in place and watched him watch her. A part of her wanted to go to him and kiss him and tell him just how proud she was of him, but another part of her held back. There was a possibility that Thorn wouldn't want to have anything to do with her after what she had to say. But still, she had to let him know of her pride in him.

"Congratulations, Thorn. I was so proud of you today."

He leaned against the closed door and continued to stare at her. His hands were pushed deep into his denim pockets and from the look on his face, winning the race, although a major accomplishment, was not at the moment what his thoughts were on.

His full attention was focused on her.

His next statement proved she was right. "You still have clothes on."

His words caught her off guard and for a moment she didn't know what to say. "Oh, boy," she finally whispered on an uneven sigh. "Did you really expect to find me here naked waiting for you?"

A slow, cocky smile curved his lips. "Yes, that would have been nice."

Tara couldn't help but return his smile. She guessed after a two-year abstinence, for him that *would* have been nice. "We need to talk, Thorn," she said, deciding not to beat around the bush.

She swallowed when he moved away from the door and walked toward her, like a hawk eyeing its prey. When he came to a stop less than a foot away, she inhaled his scent. He smelled of soap and shampoo as well as the manly fragrance that was so much a part of him.

He reached out and touched her chin with his finger. "We'll talk tomorrow."

Tara raised a brow. *Tomorrow?* Did he think he would be keeping her so busy this afternoon and tonight that she would have neither the time nor the strength to get a word out? She couldn't help it when the thought of that sent a tremor throughout her body.

She was suddenly swamped with memories of all the dreams she'd ever had of him, her need for him as well as her love for him. But still, none of that mattered if there was not complete honestly between them. He was entitled to know the truth about her.

"What I have to tell you can't wait until tomorrow." *After what I have to say there might not be a tomorrow for us,* she thought.

"Okay, you talk," he said huskily. And as if he needed to touch her as much as he needed to breathe, he reached out and placed his hand at her waist, then slowly began caressing her side, flooding her sensitive flesh with sensations through the material of her dress. She didn't bother to resist him since she wanted his touch as much as it seemed that he wanted hers.

She cleared her throat and covered his hand with hers to stop the movement so she could think straight. "There's something I think you ought to know about me, Thorn. Something that will determine whether you want to take this any further."

While she held fast to his one hand, before she realized what he was about to do, his free hand reached out and pushed the straps of her dress completely off her shoulders, exposing her black lace bra.

He stood quietly for a moment, not saying anything but just looking at her. "I don't think there's anything you can say that would make me think of not taking this any further, Tara," he said huskily, not taking his eyes off her.

Tara wasn't so sure of that. Thorn was an experienced man and more than likely he wouldn't want a novice in his bed.

Moving with the speed he'd displayed on the speedway, he flicked the front closure of her bra and bared her breasts. Just as quickly he moved his hand to her naked flesh, cupped her breast in his hand and muttered the word, "Nice."

Tara's breathing escalated and she felt her body go limp at his touch. Her entire being was becoming a feverish heat. She leaned back and tipped her head, suddenly realizing that at some point Thorn had backed her against a wall. Literally. It was a solid wall that prevented her from going any farther, neatly trapping her. She was caught, it seemed, between a rock and a hard place.

And when he leaned down and clamped his damp open

mouth to a nipple and began caressing it gently with the tip of his tongue, she lost her train of thought.

Almost, but not quite. She had to have her say.

"Thorn?"

"Umm?"

She swallowed hard and drew in a deep breath. She closed her eyes, not wanting to see his expression when she said the words. "I'm a virgin."

She braced, waited for his fury and when minutes passed and he didn't say anything, she opened her eyes. He seemed not to have heard her since he had left one nipple and was now concentrating on the other. She inhaled a long, fortifying breath at the way his mouth was nibbling her as though she was a treat he had gone without for too long.

"Thorn? Did you hear what I said?" She finally decided to ask, fighting against the astounding sensations that were running through her body.

He lifted his head and met her gaze. "Yes, I heard you."

Tara lifted a brow, thinking that if he had heard her, he was taking her news rather well. Too well. She frowned as things became obvious to her. "You knew, didn't you?" The question was a scant whisper in the room.

He gazed at her for a long moment before saying. "Yes, I knew."

Tara's eyebrows bunched. How had he known? She hadn't told another soul other than Delaney, and she knew his sister would not have shared that information with him. "But—but how…?" she asked, barely able to speak.

He shrugged. "I touched you there, several times, and on that first night I found you extremely tight and when my fingers couldn't go any farther, I suspected as much. But the next time when I touched you, I knew for sure."

She blinked. You asked Thorn a question and he would definitely give you a straight answer. She then felt a spark of anger that he'd known all this time and she had worried for nothing. But her anger was replaced by curiosity when she wondered why he wasn't upset. "But aren't you mad?"

He quirked a brow. "No, I'm not mad, Tara…I'm horny," he said with a sly chuckle.

"Yes, but I thought most men preferred experienced women in their beds."

He let out a frustrated sigh. "I want *you* in my bed, Tara, experienced or not. And as far as you being a virgin, I guess there's a good reason you waited this long, and I guess there's a good reason why it was meant for me to do the honor."

She looked up at him. "And you're sure about this? Are you sure this is what you want?"

He breathed in deeply. "Baby, this is what I want," he said, before exhibiting another quick move by placing his hand beneath her dress and gently clutching her feminine mound through the silky material of her panties. "This is what I need."

He leaned down and their lips touched and Tara knew at that very moment that she loved him more than she thought was humanly possible.

"I promise to be gentle the first time," he whispered against her moist lips. "And I promise to be gentle the second time. But all the times after that, I plan to ride you hard."

"Oh," she said in a soft and tremulous voice, moments before being swept effortlessly up into his arms.

Thorn placed Tara on the bed and his gaze swept down the full length of her half-clad body. She was still wearing her sundress, but barely. The straps were off her arms and the dress was bunched up to her waist showing her panties and her hips and thighs.

He began removing his shirt. When that was done, he met her gaze again and simply said, "I want you."

She swallowed and decided to be honest with him. "And I want you, too."

He smiled, seemingly pleased with what she had said and slowly unbuckled his belt. She blinked. She hadn't expected him to be this bold, to take off his clothes in front of her, but should not have been surprised. He was Thorn Westmoreland, a man who took risks, a man who lived on the edge, the man she loved.

Tara continued watching as he removed his boots then eased his jeans down his hips. She was enjoying this striptease show he had started. When he kicked his jeans aside and stood before her in a pair of black low-rise briefs that were contoured for a snug fit and supported his over-aroused erection, she almost lost her breath.

He was perfect in every way.

His body exemplified everything she had come to expect of him: power, endurance and strength. Lifting slowly, she eased toward the end of the bed where he was standing, wanting to touch his firm stomach. She knew his scent was masculine and robust, but she needed to know the texture of his skin under her fingers and her mouth.

Making a move before she lost her nerve, she felt her own cheeks become heated as she reached out and touched his belly, marveling at how his skin felt, solid and hard. She heard his sharp intake of breath and glanced up and met his gaze.

Potent desire pooled in his eyes and she felt her body become completely hot. Wanting to taste the texture of his skin she leaned forward and with the tip of her tongue traced a path around his navel.

"Oh, man," he uttered, tangling his hand in her hair as she continued laving her tongue across his stomach.

She knew what she was doing was torture, but he hadn't seen anything yet. She might be new at this, but those romance novels Delaney had given her to read had educated as well as entertained her. And tonight she felt bold enough to go for it, to show Thorn just what he meant to her.

Thorn was losing control and he knew had to slow down. When he felt Tara's tongue inch lower and she scooted her hand inside his briefs and touched him, he knew he had to take control.

Aroused beyond belief, he pulled her up to him and claimed her mouth, kissing her with the urgency of a starving man as their mouths mated intensely, on the edge of total madness. It was the taste of forbidden fruit, the sweetest temptation and the ultimate fulfillment.

He pulled back from the kiss, his gaze full of desire. He was driven with the need to remove her clothes and gently tumbled her back on the bed while pulling the dress from her body, and carelessly tossing it aside. Next he reached for the waistband of her panties, nearly ripping them from her in the process.

Before she could react to what he'd done, he quickly maneuvered his body on the bed with her and, like a starving man, grabbed her hips and pulled her to his mouth as if the need to taste her was paramount to the preservation of his sanity.

"Thorn!"

He wanted to make this time different from the times before and went about tasting her with an intensity that made er buck under the demand of his mouth, crying out and thrashing about as he absorbed himself in her womanly flavor. And when he felt her body come apart in a climax that sent shudders even through him, he intensified the intimate kiss and sampled each and every shiver that rocked her body.

Moments later, still dazed as fragments of ecstasy raced through her, Tara watched as Thorn stood and removed his briefs. Her breath caught upon seeing his naked body. She blinked, wondering how they would fit together and said a silent prayer that they would.

He reached down and picked up his jeans, then fumbled in the back pocket to retrieve his wallet. He withdrew a condom packet. He was about to tear it open when she stopped him.

"That's not necessary, Thorn."

He glanced up and met her gaze. "It isn't?"

She shook her head. "No."

He stared at her for a long moment before asking. "Why not?"

A long silence stretched between them before she finally gave him an answer. "I'm on birth control. The pill."

He lifted a brow. "But I thought you said that you couldn't take the pill for medical reasons."

Tara shook her head. "No, I asked you what you would do if I couldn't take the pill for medical reasons. I had to know that you cared enough to do the responsible thing."

He nodded. "Is the pill in your system real good?"

She certainly hoped so, otherwise there was a good chance that with all their heat, combustion and raging hormones they would be making a baby tonight. But the thought of him getting her pregnant didn't bother her one bit. "Yes, I've been on it long enough."

Thorn stared at her, thinking just how much he loved her. Because he had expressed a desire not to use a condom, she had unselfishly taken the necessary precautions.

He would show his love and appreciation in the only way he knew—by loving her totally and completely with his heart, body and soul. He eased onto the bed with her, over her, knowing he had to take things slow and be gentle, no matter how driven he was to do otherwise. His need for her was strong, desperate.

He touched the dampness at the juncture of her legs. She was sufficiently wet for him, primed, ripe and ready. But even so, their first joining would be painful for her. There was no way for it not to be.

When he had placed his body over hers, he gazed down at her, saw desire and trust shining in the depths of her eyes and knew he would keep his word, even if it killed him. A part of him wanted her to know just how affected he was with what they were about to do.

"I think I've wanted you, I've wanted *this,* from the first time I saw you that night, Tara," he admitted honestly. "I've dreamed about this moment, fantasized about it and desired it with a vengeance, and I want you to know I won't take what you're about to give me and what we're about to do lightly."

And since he knew that being on the pill wasn't a hundred percent foolproof, he said, "And although you're on the pill, if you get pregnant anyway, I take full responsibility for any child we make together."

Before Tara could say anything, Thorn began placing kisses all over her mouth, and her heart pounded, full of love. Ever since they had started seeing each other, he had made her feel feminine and desired and she was ready for any sensual journey he wanted to take her on.

And then she felt him, the tip of him, touching her womanly folds, and their gazes locked. He bore down slowly as he began easing into her gently, and although it was tight, he felt her body automatically stretch for him, open to receive him.

Sweat beaded Thorn's forehead. Tara was tight and damp. Entering her body sent a ripple of pleasure through him, from the tip of his toes to the top of his head. He held her hips firmly in his hands as he went deeper, feeling the muscles of her body clamp down on him as he slowly eased inside her and felt her opening her legs wider to smooth the progress of his entry.

He saw that quick moment of pain that flashed across her features when he broke through the barrier, overwhelmed by what was taking place. He was her first lover, the first man to venture into her body like this and a part of him was deeply touched by the magnitude of what that meant.

He had never been the first with a woman before, and in the past that fact hadn't mattered. But with Tara it did matter. She didn't know it yet, but she was the woman he planned to marry. The woman who would have his children. The woman who would always be there for him. The woman he planned to grow old with and love until the last breath was exhaled from his body.

Moments later he was deeply embedded inside her as far as it was humanly possible for him to go. It was tight, a snug fit, and the thought that he was joined to her this way sent a shudder racing up his spine. For a long moment he didn't move; he just wanted to savor their joining. Their union. Neither of them spoke, but each recognized this as a very profound and meaningful moment.

"You okay?" he whispered just seconds before dipping his head and kissing her gently on the lips.

She nodded. "Yeah, what about you?"

He smiled. "I'm fine. I wish I could stay locked to you, stay inside you, forever." He removed his hands from her hips clasped their hands together and whispered. "Now, I take things slow."

And he did.

With slow, gentle precision, he began withdrawing then reentering her body, over and over again, thrusting gently firmly, deeply, establishing a rhythm that she immediately followed.

Tara closed her eyes, savoring their lovemaking, wanting Thorn never to stop what he was doing to her, how he was making her feel. Every time he reentered her, the sensation were heightened and shivers of pleasure raced all through her

Overwhelmed, feeling herself losing control, she reached up and brought his mouth to hers when she felt him increase their rhythm in a beat so timeless it intensified the passion between them. Explosive, flashing heat surrounded them, making her dig her fingertips into his shoulders and whisper his name over and over, revelling in the feel of flesh against flesh.

And then Tara felt herself go. Her body shook beneath the force of his firm hips locking her body to his as sensations poured through her.

"Look at me, baby."

She opened her eyes and did as Thorn requested. She met his gaze when she felt her body come apart and watched as his own body stiffened while waves of pleasure washed through him. He increased the pace of their rhythm and whispered, "mine," at the exact moment he threw his head back and spilled inside her, his release flooding her insides.

"Thorn!"

Her body responded yet again as another climax tore into

her, this one more volatile, eruptive and explosive than all others, triggering him into another orgasm as well. He tightened his hold on her as his body devoured her, mated with hers, and loved her.

In Tara's mind and heart this was more than sex. It was the most beautiful and profound joining, and she knew in her heart that for the rest of her life she would love Thorn Westmoreland.

Chapter 11

His woman was asleep.

After they had made love twice, he had cuddled her into his arms and watched as her eyes had drifted closed. And he had been watching her since.

She was lying facing him, her front to his, her face just a breath away from his. She was a silent sleeper, barely making a sound as she inhaled and exhaled.

Damn, she looked and smelled good.

His arousal stirred and the need to have her again sent tremors through his body. This would be the third time, but he couldn't ride her hard the way he had planned. She was sore, and he knew that only a selfish person would put her through a vigorous round of lovemaking after what they'd just shared.

He would go slow and gentle. Reaching out, he slid his hand up and down her body, his caresses lingering on her breasts, the curves of her waist before moving lower to her belly. He pushed aside the sheet that covered her, and, moving his hand even lower, he gently touched her feminine folds, inhaling the sensuous scent, a combination of sex and Tara.

His heartbeat raced, knowing that this part of her, whether she realized it or not, was now his, lock, stock and barrel. He had taken ownership of it. Her body was her body and her body was also *his*. No other man would have the opportunity to sample the treasures that she had entrusted to him.

Feeling the need to join with her once again, he leaned forward and kissed her awake. She slowly opened her eyes and a sultry, tempting smile touched the corners of her lips.

"You want more?" she asked sleepily, coming fully awake.

He smiled. "What gave you that idea?"

She glanced down and saw his aroused body. "That."

A chuckle escaped his lips. "Yeah, *that* is certainly a giveaway." He then reached out and placed her on top, straddling him. From the expression on her face, he knew she was surprised by the move. "This way you control everything," he whispered, explaining.

The hard length of him was standing at attention, which made it easy for her body to move over it and sink down upon it, taking him within her. It felt hot as it penetrated the depths of her.

She smiled. Thorn had been right. This position gave her more sexual freedom and definitely provided him with visual pleasure. Her breasts were right there in front of his eyes…as well as his mouth, and he quickly took full advantage.

He sucked and licked her nipples to his heart's content while she slowly moved back and forth, up and down over him, establishing the rhythm and speed of his thrusting. She looked down and watched him devour her breasts, the sight making her go faster and deeper, stimulating her mind as well as her body in a way she hadn't thought was possible.

And then it happened again, she became absorbed with pleasure so deep and profound she couldn't help but cry out as she increased their rhythm. Her climax triggered his and he moved his lips from her breasts to her mouth, as waves of pleasure drowned them, leaving them swirling in a sensuous aftermath.

"Are you sure you want to go to the victory party?"

Tara glanced up from putting the finishing touches on her makeup. "Of course I want to go. This is a big moment for you and I'm glad to be able to share in it. Besides, how would it look if the honoree didn't make an appearance?"

Thorn chuckled as he buttoned up his shirt. "I'm sure my brothers would come up with an excuse."

Tara exhaled deeply. That's what she was worried about since she was certain his brothers were well aware of what they'd been doing closed up in a hotel room for the past four hours. Still she didn't want anyone to think of their intimate activities as something meaningless and degrading.

Thorn had assured her that he hadn't told them about the deal they'd made and she was grateful for that. It would be bad enough seeing them tonight knowing they knew, or had a pretty good idea of, just what she and Thorn had been doing.

She was sure that most of the time the winner of such a publicized event didn't disappear behind closed doors right after a race. He would usually start partying, which could go well into the next day. Since it was Sunday, a lot of people would pack up to leave after the race, but most stayed over to Monday or well into the following week.

"Ready?"

She glanced over at Thorn. He was completely dressed, and the look he gave her let her know he liked her outfit but preferred her naked in bed with him. She smiled. Leaving the confines of the hotel room was a good idea. Chances were they would be going another couple of rounds tonight.

"I must say, Thorn, you're in a real good mood tonight," Stone said grinning.

Thorn raised a brow as he glanced at his brothers, Stone, Chase and Storm. The four of them had left the party and stood outside smoking congratulatory cigars, compliments of one of his racing sponsors.

"Yeah, Thorn, it seems that four hours shut up behind closed doors with Tara did wonders for your disposition and mood," Chase added, grinning between puffs of his cigar.

"And I appreciate you helping me to win that bet, Thorn. I told these guys that although Tara was your challenge, you could overcome that little obstacle and would have her eating out of your hands and in your bed in no time," Storm added. "Yeah, victory today was rather nice for you in more ways than one, wasn't it, Thorn?"

Tara had decided to come outside and round up the brothers to tell them their parents were on Dare's mobile phone and wanted to congratulate Thorn. She had stopped right before interrupting them, shocked at what she had over-heard. There had been a bet between Thorn and his brothers that he would be able to get her in his bed? Today had meant nothing to him but winning a bet?

Backing up so they wouldn't see her, she felt tears of hu-miliation stinging her eyes. She felt just as humiliated now as she had three years ago when Derrick had embarrassed her in front of a church filled with people. And it hurt worse than before because of the magnitude of love she felt for Thorn. Her love for Derrick had been a young girl's love that had grown from an extended friendship between two families. But her love for Thorn was that of a woman, a woman who, it now seemed, had made a mistake, a big mistake for the second time in her life.

She quickly turned around and ran smack into Dare. He caught her by the arm to stop her from falling. He frowned when he saw the tears that filled her eyes. "Tara, what's wrong? Are you okay?"

She swiped away the tears that she couldn't stop. "No, I'm not okay, Dare, and I don't appreciate your brothers making a bet on me that way. And you can tell Thorn that I hope never to see him again." Without saying anything else she pulled away and went back inside.

After Storm's statement, Thorn's temper exploded and he looked at his brothers for the longest time without saying anything, fighting down the urge to walk across the space of the veranda that separated them and knock the hell out of each one of them.

"I think I need to set the record straight about something. My relationship with Tara had nothing to do with the bet the three of you made," he said through gritted teeth, trying to hold his anger in check and remember the four of them shared the same parents.

"She means more to me than a chance to score after two years." He sighed, not giving a royal damn what he was about to admit to his brothers. The way he felt, he would gladly shout it out to the world if he had to. "I love Tara. I love her with everything that's inside of me, and it's about time the three of you knew that."

Stone's shoulder was propped against the building and he wore a huge grin. "Oh, we know you love her, Thorn. We've known it for a while. Getting you to realize that you loved her was the kicker. The only reason we said what we did a few minutes ago was to get you pissed off enough to admit what Tara means to you."

"And it might be too late," Dare said, walking up to join the group. He wore an angry expression as he faced his brothers. "Your little playacting may have cost Thorn Tara's love."

Thorn frowned. "What the hell are you talking about?"

Dare shook his head, knowing all hell was about to break loose and that somehow he would have to find a way to contain Thorn's fury. "Mom and Dad called and Tara volunteered to come get you guys. Evidently she overheard the first part of the conversation. When I saw her she was crying so hard she couldn't see straight and bumped right into me when I came to find out what was taking all of you so long."

Dare shook his head sadly. "She gave me a message to give you. She told me to tell you that she doesn't want to see you again."

Hearing enough, Thorn spun around, and, without giving his brothers another glance, he quickly went back into the building in search of Tara.

"She left, Thorn," Shelly Westmoreland said, frowning at her brother-in-law. "She was crying and came back inside just long enough to get her purse. She left through that side door. Exactly what did you do to her?"

Thorn couldn't wait to give Shelly an answer. More than likely Tara had returned to the hotel and he planned to be right on her heels. He had a lot of explaining to do and he also intended to tell her just what she meant to him.

When Thorn got to the hotel he saw that Tara had not been there, and he started to worry. One of the members of his work crew indicated he had given Tara a lift from the victory party back to the hotel to get her rental car. When hours passed and she still hadn't come, his worry increased. Even when his brothers showed up to apologize and discovered Tara hadn't returned, he could tell that it made them feel worse, which, as far as he was concerned, served them right.

He had finally gotten them to leave after Dare had placed a call to the sheriff in Daytona, whom he knew personally. After checking things out, the sheriff had informed them that a vehicle fitting the description of the rental car that Tara was driving had been spotted on the interstate heading toward Bunnell.

Thorn paced the confines of the hotel room. He was angry with his brothers but angrier with himself. He should have spilled his heart and soul to her when he'd had the chance. Now she would assume that what she had overheard was true and would believe that he was another man who had humiliated her.

He knew he had to let her know how much he loved her and just how much she meant to him. Over the past two years she had been many things to him: his challenge, his sweetest temptation and his woman.

Now he had to convince her that he loved her and more than anything he wanted her as his wife.

Chapter 12

Tara woke up early the next morning in her old bedroom. She glanced around. Her parents had pretty much kept things the same, and she was glad that when she'd left home two years ago she hadn't packed every stitch she owned, otherwise she would not have had a thing to wear. Luckily for her, her closets and dresser drawers were filled with both inner and outerwear that still fit her.

She knew her parents had been surprised to see her when she had unexpectedly shown up last night asking if she could stay for the next couple of days, just long enough to get a flight back to Atlanta. They hadn't asked her any questions but had welcomed her with open arms and told her she knew she could stay for as long as she liked. She had also contacted the rental car agency to let them know she intended to keep the vehicle a while longer.

She sighed deeply. Her parents had always been super and

she appreciated them for everything they had ever done for her. Her brothers had returned to college and her baby sister had left that day for an out-of-town trip with the school's band for a week. In a way she was glad none of her siblings were there to see her go through heartbreak a second time.

Flipping onto her back she knew she had decisions to make. Maybe it was time for her to leave the Atlanta area. A friend of hers from med school was trying to get her to think about coming to Boston to work. Maybe relocating to Massachusetts was exactly the change she needed.

"I see that young man of yours won the big race yesterday in Daytona, Tara Lynn. It was in the newspapers this morning and the whole town has been talking about it. You must be proud of him."

Tara smiled over the dinner table at her father. As usual, he had closed his office at noon on Monday and had come home for an early dinner. As long as she could remember, her parents had been members of a bowling league and usually headed for the bowling lanes every Monday afternoon.

"Yes, I'm proud of him," she said stiffly. She knew her parents had figured out that Thorn had somehow played a part in her unexpected appearance on their doorstep last night. She sighed, deciding to tell them an abbreviated version of things, just enough for them to know her relationship with Thorn was over.

She was about to open her mouth to speak when the phone rang. Her father got up quickly to answer it in case it was a parent needing his help with a sick child. He still did house calls occasionally.

"Yes, Sheriff, I'm fine, what about you?" Tara heard her father say. She frowned, wondering why the sheriff was calling her father. She then remembered the sheriff and his wife were part of her parents' bowling team. He was probably calling regarding that.

She noticed her father's gaze had moved to her and she raised a brow when moments later she heard him say, "All right. I'll let her know."

After he hung up the phone he rejoined her and her mother at the table. Her mother asked what the sheriff had wanted before Tara got the chance to do so. Frank Matthews leaned back in his chair with his gaze locked on his daughter while answering his wife's question. "It seemed that Deke just issued a special permit."

Her mother's brow rose. "What sort of special permit?"

Before her father could respond, the sound of thunder suddenly filled the house. "My God," Lynn Matthews said, getting up from the table. "That sounds like thunder. I don't recall the weatherman saying anything about rain this evening."

Frank Matthews shook his head. "That's not thunder, Lynn," he said to his wife while keeping his gaze fixed on his daughter. "Deke issued a special permit for a bunch of bikers to parade peacefully through the streets of Bunnell."

Lynn Matthews's features reflected surprise. "Bikers? What on earth for? Bunnell is such a small peaceful town, I can't imagine such a thing happening."

A smile touched the corners of Frank Matthews's lips when he answered. "It appears one of the bikers, the one leading the pack, who also happens to be the winner of yesterday's championship motorcycle race in Daytona, is headed for our house. It seems he's coming for our daughter."

Tara blinked, not sure she had heard her father correctly. "Thorn? He's coming here?"

Her father nodded. "Yes. It seems he and his band of followers are making their way round the corner as we speak."

Tara frowned, wondering why Thorn and the other cyclists would be coming here and why her father thought he was coming for her. Before she could voice that question, the roar of cycles nearly shook the house.

She sighed deeply as she stood up from the table. The reason Thorn had come meant absolutely nothing to her. The bottom line was that she didn't want to see him. "Send him away, Daddy, please. I don't want to see him."

Frank gazed lovingly at his daughter. Her heart had been broken once and he didn't want to see it broken again, but he felt the least Tara should do was to listen to what the young man had to say. He told her as much.

"But there's nothing he can say to change things. I love him but he doesn't love me. It's as simple as that."

Frank sighed. If that was what his daughter believed then it wasn't as simple as she thought. According to the sheriff, Thorn Westmoreland was wearing his heart on his sleeve. Frank knew he had to be firm and make Tara face the fact that she might be wrong in her assumption that Thorn didn't love her.

"All right, Tara, if that's how you feel, but this is something you should handle. If you want him to go away, then it's you who should send him away. Tell him that you don't want to see him anymore. I won't do it for you."

Tara met her father's eyes and nodded. That was fine with her. She would just march outside and tell Thorn what she thought and how she felt. Evidently Dare hadn't delivered her message. "Very well, I'll tell him."

Marching out of the kitchen Tara passed through the living room and snatched open the front door. Stepping outside she stopped dead in her tracks. Motorcycle riders were everywhere. There wasn't just a bunch of them, there were hundreds, and they were still coming around the corner, causing more excitement in Bunnell than she could ever remember.

It seemed the entire town had come out to witness what was going on. And what made matters worse, Thorn and his group had gotten a police escort straight to her parents' home. Blue lights were flashing everywhere. She had never seen anything like it.

But what really caught her attention was the man who sat out in front of the pack, straddling the big bike that had come to a stop in front of her parents' home. She glanced around. In addition to Thorn, his four brothers were on bikes and two of them carried a huge banner extending between their bikes that said Thorn Loves Tara.

Realizing what the banner was proclaiming made tears appear in Tara's eyes. In a public display, Thorn was letting everyone in the entire town of Bunnell—his friends, biking partners, associates, his family, just about anyone who wanted to know—what she meant to him. She had been more than a bet to him.

She watched as Thorn got off the bike and slowly began walking toward her. She inhaled deeply as she watched him, clad in jeans, a T-shirt and biker boots and holding his helmet in his hand, come to a stop in front of her.

He met her gaze and reached out and gently wiped a tear from her eye. "You should know my brothers well enough by now to know they're full of it and you can't take them seriously the majority of the time, Tara. I didn't make a bet with them, but they did make a bet among themselves. They wagered that I wouldn't realize how much I loved you until it was almost too late."

He glanced behind her, saw her parents standing in the doorway and decided to lower his voice to a whisper so they wouldn't hear the next words he had to say. This part was personal and between him and Tara.

"And it was more than just sex between us, Tara. I love you and should have told you yesterday, but the physical loving we shared blew me away, and I didn't get around to telling you how I felt emotionally. But I'm telling you now that I love you with all my heart and with all my soul."

The tone of his voice then went higher as he said, "And want to proclaim my love to you in front of everyone here. And I want them to see that I'm wearing my heart on my sleeve."

He turned slightly and showed her the sleeve of his T-shirt. There was a big heart on it with the words Thorn Loves Tara. He got down on one knee and took her hand into his. "I Thorn Westmoreland, love you, Tara Lynn Matthews. And in front of everyone, I am pledging my love to you and promising to love you for the rest of my life. I promise to love you honor you and protect you. And I'm asking you now, Tara, on bended knee, with my heart on my sleeve, in front of everyone to marry me and become my wife and soul mate. Will you?"

Tears clouded Tara's eyes and the words she longed to say got caught in the thickness of her throat, but somehow she managed to get them out, words that would ultimately join her life with Thorn's. "Yes, Thorn, I'll marry you."

It seemed people everywhere began clapping, shouting and cheering. In the middle of the pack of cyclists, someone released a bunch of helium balloons that went soaring high into the sky. Each one had on it the words Thorn Loves Tara. Tara was touched at the extent Thorn had gone to in broad casting his love for her.

Thorn got back to his feet and it seemed that Dare materialized at his side with a small white box which he handed to Thorn. Thorn opened up the box and took out a sparkling diamond ring. He reached for Tara's left hand and placed the huge diamond on the third finger, then brought her hand to his lips.

"Thorn's lady and soon to be Thorn's wife," he said softly, his eyes still meeting hers as he kissed her hand. He then pulled her into his arms and kissed her lips, ignoring the cheers and applause.

Tara kissed him back, until she heard her father clear his throat several times. She and Thorn finally broke apart and he turned and smiled at her parents, then said, "Mom, Dad, this is Thorn, the man I love."

Two days later, in a hotel room in West Palm Beach, Tara lay in Thorn's arms. She could hear the sound of the ocean, the relaxing resonance of waves hitting against sand. She closed her eyes as she remembered the intensity of the lovemaking she and Thorn had shared earlier. He hadn't been slow and gentle. This time he had been tender, yet he had taken her with a force that had overwhelmed her, pleasuring them both, riding her with the precision and expertise that was strictly his trademark, and thrusting deep then pulling out, repeating the process over and over again until he had her thrashing about as sensation after sensation tore into her.

He had whispered into her ear words of love, words of sex, promises to be delivered both in and out of the bedroom, and when they had reached a climax simultaneously, she knew that, physically as well as emotionally, she was a part of him and would always be a part of him.

"Tara?"

She glanced up. He was awake and was watching her. "Yes?

"I love you."

She smiled. He had told her that over a million times since bringing her back here from her parents' home. "And I love you."

They had decided to marry over the Memorial Day weekend. Thorn had been open with displaying his affection for her in front of everyone, and it seemed the entire town had been there.

Her parents' bowling game had been cancelled, and some of the neighbors had set up grills and a huge barbecue followed, with all the steaks and spareribs a person could eat donated by Grahams' Supermarket in honor of their hometown girl marrying a celebrity.

Tara had been standing talking to Thorn when she'd turned and seen Danielle walking toward her. At that moment any bitterness she had felt for the woman who'd once been her best friend left her. She knew there was no way things could ever be the same between them, but Tara no longer felt the deep anger just thinking about what Danielle and Derrick had done.

She introduced Danielle to Thorn and told her the same thing she had told Derrick a few days earlier. She congratulated them on their upcoming child, wished them the best and told her that she hoped they would always be happy together.

Not wanting to think about Danielle and Derrick any longer, she brought her thoughts back to the present and thought of something else. "Thorn?"

"Yes, sweetheart?"

"I heard Chase say that you have another race in August. Do you plan to go celibate after our wedding until the race?"

Thorn met her gaze. "No, my celibate days are over."

here's no way I can have you around me constantly and not want to make love to you."

"Aren't you worried about the impact that may have on winning the race?"

"No. I always thought racing and building my bikes were the most important things in my life and at a time they were. But now things are different. You are the most important thing in my life, Tara. You are my life. It doesn't matter to me if I never win another race because I have the ultimate prize, my greatest award, accolade and treasure right here in you."

"Oh, Thorn." She leaned up and her mouth met his. She kissed him like a woman in love as emotions swirled through her. She and Thorn would spend the rest of their lives together and would make many beautiful babies together.

Babies? They hadn't discussed babies. She pulled back, breaking off the kiss.

He lifted a brow. "What's wrong?"

"Do you want babies?" she asked, looking at him intently.

He smiled. "Yes, I want babies."

She returned his smile. "Good. How many?"

He chuckled. "As many as you want to give me." And deciding to go ahead and answer the next question he figured he'd be asking, he said, "And it doesn't matter if they are girls or boys. I will love and cherish any child we have together."

He leaned forward and brushed his lips across hers, then, deepening the kiss, became intent on giving her the greatest pleasure he could. His hands stroked her everywhere and he conveyed the heat of his hunger to her, needing to find solace in the warmth of her body again, knowing in his heart that he would always want her, need her and love her.

He broke off the kiss to climb onto her body, he straddled her and then he entered her warmth, going deep, slow and easy, feeling the muscles of her inner body clutch him, hold him and welcome him. When he looked down at her, he saw love shining in her eyes. Love that he returned.

Then, in one quick movement he began riding her, thrusting inside her, nearly pulling out and going back in again, holding her gaze as he did so, lifting her hips to receive him in this very soul-stirring way. He wanted her panting, groaning and screaming. He wanted to kiss her again until her mouth quaked, her body trembled, and every part of her brimmed over with passion—rich and explosive. He wanted to imprint this night in her mind forever.

This lovemaking was more vigorous than any before and together they moved in unison as he lowered his head, seeking her mouth and going after her tongue. And like everything else he wanted, she gave it to him. He openly displayed his hunger for her—his hunger and his love.

And then it happened. Rampant desire raced through him, caught fire and spread like a blaze to her. He continued pumping, thrusting as their bodies strained and flowed with a pounding rhythm toward a release that lingered a breath away. He felt her dig her fingers into his shoulders and broke off the kiss, threw his head back and sucked in a breath he felt could be his last at the exact moment her body clenched him for everything he had.

This time their joining felt like a spiritual connection, the climax that tore into them stronger, deeper and richer than any before. Before either could recover, she climaxed again and he immediately followed her lead, moving faster, riding her the way he had always wanted to, the way he had always dreamed of, straight through the waves and soaring for the stars.

"Thorn!"

He found strength to look down into her face.

His woman.

He met her gaze and he knew. Their life together would
ways be filled with love and passion, and he couldn't think
having it any other way.

Epilogue

Tara no longer hated weddings.

She inhaled deeply as she looked around the church. Memories assailed her as she remembered the last time she had worn a wedding dress here, and now today, in front of some of those same three hundred guests, she had married the man she loved, Thorn Westmoreland.

She, Thorn and the wedding party had hung back to take a multitude of pictures. Everyone else had left for the reception, which was to be held in the ballroom of a beautiful hotel on the beach.

Thorn had left her briefly to go in the back to talk to the minister about something, and she happened to notice the Westmoreland brothers as well as the Westmoreland cousins who'd all been part of the wedding party, standing around talking. As she watched, she saw three of the Westmoreland brothers, Chase, Stone and Storm, exchange money.

She raised a brow wondering if they had made another wager about something. She smiled upon remembering how Stone, Chase and Storm had confessed to her the whole story, then had apologized for causing a rift between her and Thorn.

Adjusting her veil she decided to find out just what kind of a bet the brothers had made and whether the bet had once again involved her and Thorn.

Chase had just explained the bet that he, Stone and Storm had made to his cousins: Jared, Quade, Spencer, Ian, Durango and Reggie Westmoreland. He was grinning broadly, since he had won. "Hey, five hundred dollars isn't bad for a day's work. I told all of you that Thorn wouldn't be able to hold off on marrying Tara until June."

He looked at the money he'd just gotten from Stone and Storm. "And I appreciate you guys letting me take this off your hands. It will come in handy for that state-of-the-art pressure cooker I want to buy for the restaurant."

The next thing he knew, the money was snatched out of his hand. "What the hell!"

He spun around and came face-to-face with his new sister-in-law's glare. He backed up a step. "Oh, hi, Tara," he said innocently. "I thought you and Thorn were somewhere in the back talking to the minister."

Tara continued to glare and crossed her arms over her chest. "Thorn is the one who's talking to the minister. And am I right in assuming the three of you made yet another bet?"

Stone, Chase and Storm looked chagrined, but Stone came to their defense and said, "Yeah, but this bet was made before we promised we wouldn't be betting on you and Thorn again, so it doesn't count."

She nodded. "Well, this is a church and you shouldn't be

passing betting money around in here so I can only do one thing about it."

Chase raised a panicky brow. "What?"

"Donate it to the church. My father is the Sunday school superintendent here and I'm sure this donation will be appreciated." She then smiled sweetly before walking off.

"Tara?"

She turned around and met Chase's brooding eyes. "Yes, Chase?"

He crossed his arms over his chest. "Only you can get away with doing something like that."

She smiled and nodded. "I know." She turned back around and began walking.

"Tara?"

She turned around again and met Storm's worried gaze. "Yes, Storm?"

"You aren't going to tell Thorn about the bet, are you?"

Tara smiled. "No, Storm, I won't say a thing."

She turned back around and started to walk away.

"Tara?"

She slowly turned around for the third time, meeting Stone's amused expression. "Yes, Stone?"

His smile widened. "Welcome to the family."

Tara chuckled. The Westmoreland men were something else. "Thanks, Stone."

She then turned around and ran smack into Corey Westmoreland, Thorn's uncle. A recently retired park ranger from Montana, he had made the trip back home three times in less than two years to attend his niece and his nephews' weddings.

Tara smiled. According to the Westmoreland brothers, their fifty-three-year-old uncle was a confirmed bachelor. That was too bad, Tara thought, since he was such a good-looking man. What a waste. A part of her hoped there was a woman out there somewhere for Uncle Corey.

"My nephews aren't causing problems, are they?" he asked, chuckling. Then he glanced across the room, sending his eleven nephews a scolding glare.

"Nothing I can't handle, but thanks for asking," she grinned, thinking what a nice smile he had and how much his smile reminded her of Thorn's.

"Good, and if I haven't told you already, I think you're just the woman Thorn needs. I know the two of you will always be happy together. If you ever want to get away and see some beautiful country, tell Thorn to bring you to my ranch in Montana for a visit."

"Thanks for the invitation. I'll make sure to do that."

At that moment Thorn and the minister came from the back. She immediately caught her husband's gaze and smiled. "Excuse me, Uncle Corey," she said, and began walking toward Thorn. When she reached him, he pulled her into his arms.

"Ready?" he asked, placing a kiss on her lips.

Tara knew that all the love she had for him was shining in her eyes. "Yes, I'm ready."

She would always be ready for him and made a silent promise to show him later tonight just how ready she was.

* * * * *

**Two Westmoreland novels—
one classic, one new—from**

NEW YORK TIMES **AND** *USA TODAY*
BESTSELLING AUTHOR

BRENDA JACKSON

In DELANEY'S DESERT SHEIKH,
a mix-up forces
Delaney Westmoreland to
share her vacation cabin with
Sheikh Jamal Ari Yassir—with
passionate results!

In SEDUCED BY A STRANGER,
Johari Yassir wants adventure—
but gets passionate seduction
by a stranger in her homeland
instead!

WRAPPED IN PLEASURE
A Westmoreland Novel

*Coming the first week of January 2010
wherever books are sold.*

ARABESQUE®

KPBJ1770110

www.kimanipress.com
www.myspace.com/kimanipress